Praise for *The Medusa Project*
by Cindy Dees

Available in May 2007
from Mills & Boon Intrigue

The Medusa Game

CINDY DEES

MILLS & BOON®

INTRIGUE™

All the characters in this book have no existence outside the
imagination of the author, and have no relation whatsoever to anyone
bearing the same name or names. They are not even distantly inspired
by any individual known or unknown to the au~~~~~d all the
inc~~~~

All ~~~~~whole or
in p~~~~~ment with
Ha~~~~cation or
any~~~~ny form
or b~~~~copying,
reco~~~~therwise,
with~~~~

Thi~~~~y way of
trad~~~~rculated
with~~~~ding or
cove~~~~ similar
cond~~~~sequent
pur~~~~

MILLS & BOON and MILLS & BOON with the Rose Device
are registered trademarks of the publisher.

First published in Great Britain 2007
Harlequin Mills & Boon Limited,
Eton House, 18-24 Paradise Road, Richmond, Surrey TW9 1SR

© Cynthia Dees 2006

ISBN: 978 0 263 85718 4

46-0507

Printed and bound in Spain
by Litografía Rosés S.A., Barcelona

CINDY DEES

started flying aeroplanes while sitting in her dad's lap at the age of three and got a pilot's licence before she got a driver's licence. At fifteen, she dropped out of school and left the horse farm in Michigan where she grew up to attend the University of Michigan.

After earning a degree in Russian and East European Studies, she joined the US Air Force and became the youngest female pilot in its history. She flew supersonic jets, VIP airlift and the C-5 Galaxy, the world's largest aeroplane. She also worked part-time gathering intelligence. During her military career, she travelled to forty countries on five continents, was detained by the KGB and East German secret police, got shot at, flew in the first Gulf War, met her husband and amassed a lifetime's worth of war stories.

Her hobbies include professional Middle Eastern dancing, Japanese gardening and medieval re-enacting. She started writing for a dollar bet with her mother and was thrilled to win that bet with the publication of her first book in 2001. She loves to hear from readers and can be contacted at www. cindydees.com.

Acknowledgements

Thanks to the dedicated and talented figure skaters at the Dr Pepper Star Centre in Euless, Texas, for their endless patience in answering my every question. I promise, someday I'll learn how to tell the difference between a loop and a flip.

Thanks to Sean Beeman for not calling the FBI on me after all my scary questions about chemical warfare.

Thanks to Larry Lynn, Zamboni engineer extraordinaire and a really nice guy.

Thanks to Judy Tavalli for designing figure-skating costumes that inspire little girls to dream big.

Thanks to Darlene Cain and Lily Erickson, for your knowledge, kindness, sportsmanship and personal grace that exemplify the very best of the sport of figure skating.

Special thanks to Mr Scott Crouse, United States Olympic gymnastics coaching legend, for sharing his expertise about the Olympic experience. It's an honour to know you.

Thanks to Elizabeth Cain Lynch and her brother Peter, Australian Olympic pairs skaters at the 1980 Lake Placid Olympics.

And most especially to Peter Cain. Not only are you a phenomenal coach and a fine representative of your sport, you are also a true gentleman. Or as they'd say down under, you're a dinky di cobber!

Chapter 1

The bus the terrorists had demanded was just pulling up in front of the Olympic village apartment building. The casual observer wouldn't see the dozen German army snipers lying in wait around the street, but Isabella Torres was no casual observer. A trained spotter for military snipers, she ranged her gaze across the scene, picking out the vital details.

An Olympic flag hung limp behind a policeman on the roof. No wind—good conditions for the shooters. A shadow moved on the floor inside the front door of the building. One of the terrorists—no doubt moving there in preparation for the transfer of the surviving Israeli hostages to the bus. The bus driver's bulging muscles and lack of visible fear marked him as German Special Forces.

A lull developed in the scene below. Nobody moved. They hardly breathed. These terrorists were scared, nearly paralyzed with fear. No need to hurry them. It was probably smart of the Germans to let the fear ripen into stupidity. Isabella released a long, slow breath of her own.

This whole scenario was making her acutely uncomfortable. Her last name might be Torres, compliments of her Mexican father, but her mother was a Middle Easterner. Iranian born and bred. Half of Isabella's heritage tied her to those masked terrorists. They might be Palestinians, but in the Middle East, there were only two kinds of people in a crisis like this. Israelis and everyone else.

Of course, she'd never thought of herself as Middle Eastern, even if she did speak Arabic and Farsi, had visited her relatives in Tehran on multiple occasions, and had even worn the heavy black robes and veils of a Muslim woman while she was there. Even when she followed Muslim customs out of respect for her family, she considered herself Americano.

A flurry of radio chatter in German announced that the eight Palestinians were approaching the exit with their hostages. *Finally.* After twenty-three hours of stalemate. Since there were more prisoners than guards, the terrorists would no doubt move the hostages as a group, surrounded by captors. And that meant there'd be an excellent opportunity for the snipers to get clear shots and end this thing here and now.

Each sniper had been assigned a single terrorist target. They'd been watching this nightmare unfold through their telescopic gun sights, long enough for the snipers to easily differentiate between the terrorists, even though the Palestinians dressed in identical track suits and wore black ski masks over their faces. It wasn't hard, really. Individual posture, movement and gesture were easy to pick out for a trained sharpshooter.

These would be very short-range shots. No more than a couple hundred meters. Kid's stuff for snipers. They could put a bullet through Lincoln's eye on a penny at that range.

A command was barked across the sniper radio net. The order to prepare to take their respective shots. Abrupt tension permeated the scene. This was it. This crisis would be resolved in the next few seconds.

Two men in black ski masks appeared in the building's doorway. She registered myriad details about them in the blink of an eye. Lean. Tense. Safeties off their AK-47s, fingers on the triggers. Weapons pointed outward at the police. *Dumb.* The guns ought to be pointed inward at the hostages, so that even if the terrorists were shot, their reflexive grasps on the weapons would fire the guns into the tight cluster of Israeli athletes. The German authorities might not call the kill if the Palestinian guns were pointed at the hostages. But arrayed like this—the op was a go.

The rest of the terrorists and all the Israelis shuffled forward in a tight phalanx. For their part, the athletes looked equal parts terrified and defiant. The Palestinians were smart enough to make at least some effort to use the hostages as human shields. But it was no good. The shooters surrounding that bus had their shots. *There.* The entire group of terrorists was exposed. Every one of them was in position for the snipers to take clear shots.

"Fire!" The command rang sharply across the sniper net.

Nothing happened.

Nothing happened!

"Fire, goddammit!" the German shouted into the radio.

Still nothing. Not a single one of the shooters took his shot.

Jack Scatalone, the Delta force colonel responsible for the Medusas' training, held up a remote control and hit the pause button. He stepped in front of the frozen video image of the Israelis being herded into that bus. It shone obscenely across his crisp uniform, which was encrusted with row after row of ribbons for heroism. For successfully resolving this very sort of crisis *without* the complete breakdown of response they'd just witnessed.

Isabella—considered to be the top real-time, visual intelligence analyst in the U.S. Air Force—stared, her eyes opened wide in shock. She glanced at her teammates, the other five women who comprised the Medusas, the highly classified, and first, all-female Special Forces team in the U.S. military. They gaped as well.

Isabella looked back at Jack and demanded, "You mean to tell me the Germans had the shots, were greenlighted to take them—hell, were *ordered* to take them—and they *didn't?*"

Jack's jaw rippled. "Kat? Care to explain?"

The Medusas' sniper, Katrina Kim, a petite woman of Asian descent, leaned forward. In a voice so calm it *had* to be masking fury at what they'd just witnessed, Kat said, "It's called the Munich Massacre Syndrome. The snipers spent so long watching the terrorists that they started to see them as human beings. As people. As scared young men. Not as targets. By the time they were ordered to shoot the terrorists, not a single one of the snipers could bring himself to pull the trigger."

Outrage still vibrated through Isabella's gut. "In all the news coverage I've seen of the '72 Olympics, nobody ever mentioned that the Germans had a chance to take out the terrorists and save those Israeli athletes."

Jack shrugged. "You probably never saw news coverage of Yasir Arafat's order for the assault, either, but he admitted to it freely by the mid-1990s."

Good point. The press was by no means the purveyor of the whole truth and nothing but the truth. She glanced at the picture sprawled across Jack's gut. "Jeez, that was more than a chance to stop it. That was a slam-dunk. The Palestinians handed themselves to the Germans on a silver platter."

"Conclusions?" Jack asked her.

The words, as dry as sawdust in her throat, wanted to stick there, but she forced them out. "The Munich Massacre never should have happened."

Jack nodded grimly. "That's correct. And out of this incident came counterterrorism as a formalized training specialty within the armed forces of most of the world's major armies. It completely changed how snipers were trained and deployed, and the psychological selection criteria for snipers were heavily revised."

Isabella still reeled. *It could have been prevented.* A tragic and vicious attack on a group of athletes who'd gone to Munich to celebrate the unity of mankind in a demonstration of the best of the human spirit. Instead, eleven young men had been murdered in cold blood, plus five terrorists and one policeman had died. Worse, they could've been saved. It had been the ultimate corruption of everything the Olympics stood for.

"Why was this covered up?" she demanded.

Jack shrugged. "I can't speak for the politicians. It would've been pretty ugly for Germany to admit that Jews were slaughtered on their watch again and they could've prevented it—again. The whole idea behind taking the Olympics to Munich in the first place was to demonstrate that World War II was in the past."

Isabella stared at the frozen images looming on the screen over Jack's shoulder like vengeful ghosts. A cold finger of dread rippled down her spine. "And why did you choose today to teach us about this syndrome?"

Jack nodded tersely at her. "Very perceptive, Adder."

Adder was her field handle. All the Medusas had nicknames that matched the names of dangerous snakes.

Jack continued. "I have a job for you ladies." He clicked the remote and the silver screen went blank. "It's at the Winter Olympics next week. And it involves a girl. Her name is Anya Khalid."

It was a soft, gray day. Desultory snow drifted down toward the tarmac, and Isabella huddled in her white, down-filled parka against the chill blowing across the runway. Her ears aching from the scream of its engines, she watched a jet pull up to a gate at the newly renovated Lake Placid, New York International Airport.

Of course, everything about Lake Placid was newly renovated these days. The sleepy little Adirondack town had spent the past five years and close to a billion dollars revamping its historic Olympic facilities for its third Winter Games, which would begin in a few days. The Games were also why a town of three thousand year-round residents boasted this high-tech terminal and jet-length runway.

With a last look around the ramp for possible threats, she nodded at the marshaller with his orange wands and headed for the steel door to the terminal. The ramp supervisor opened it when she knocked and she hurried upstairs into the main arrival area.

A cluster of Olympic officials waited in the baggage claim area to collect incoming athletes, while several loudly dressed resort employees waited to collect tourists coming to watch the games. A group of camera-toting reporters stood off to one side. Oddly, most of them were olive-skinned. Must be a big delegation of athletes coming in on this flight from some warm-climate country.

She had special permission to be in the relatively deserted, ticketed passenger-only area to meet Anya and her coach. The passengers on this flight had already cleared customs in New York City, and they began to exit directly off the plane and stream toward the baggage claim area. Standing by the gate, Isabella scanned each face as it emerged, looking for her new charge.

Anya Khalid.

·Until a few months ago, not a soul outside of a local ice skating rink in Brisbane, Australia had ever heard of her. But now, she was undoubtedly the most well-known—and controversial—member of the international figure skating community. Born in the emirate of Bhoukar, a small principality smack-dab in the center of the Arab world, she'd had the unmitigated gall to flaunt her country's conservative Muslim culture and become a figure skater. Global debate raged over whether or not that constituted freedom of expression or a capital crime punishable by death. Either way, she was a young lady in need of protection from the numerous threats that had come her way and would continue to escalate if she dared to skate at the Olympics.

The emir of Bhoukar, an Oxford-educated religious moderate, supported her and had authorized her to represent Bhoukar. Although she'd been living in Australia for a decade while her father worked there as a petroleum engineer, her citizenship was still Bhoukari. With the exception of a men's downhill skier nearly thirty years ago, she was the only athlete ever to represent the tiny country in a Winter Olympics.

But instead of embracing her, her fellow countrymen, mostly religious conservatives, had reviled her. They accused her of being immodest and anti-Muslim for showing too much flesh and performing such outrageous maneuvers as raising her leg in the air and exposing the bottoms of her feet.

When she'd burst onto the Olympic scene six weeks ago by finishing in the top ten at the last of the qualifying events and earning a spot in the Winter Games, the rhetoric had started flying. And some of it had taken on a dark enough tone that the IOC—the International Olympic Committee—had requested the Olympic Security Group provide extra protection for the nineteen-year-old upon her arrival in Lake Placid. The Medusas had been called in to do the job in the interest of not further offending the Muslim world by putting male bodyguards on the young woman.

Isabella was chosen as the front woman for the team because she spoke fluent Arabic, Anya's native tongue. Of course, the girl probably spoke excellent English, having practically grown up in Australia. Isabella had only seen a handful of photos of Anya. She was a beautiful, slender girl with black hair, doelike brown eyes, and a dancer's carriage. Whether she would arrive today in the full black robe and veil Bhoukari women traditionally wore in public or merely a hijab, the head scarf preferred by more moderate Muslims was anybody's guess.

The Medusas' reports were sketchy, but intelligence indicated the girl came from a fairly conservative family who'd lived a low-key lifestyle in Australia. The girl had more freedom there than she would have had in Bhoukar—enough to take up figure skating—but probably not anywhere near as much freedom as a typical Australian girl. Thankfully, Isabella knew a whole lot more about life in conservative Muslim households than any of her temporary bosses in the Olympic Security Group.

She shouldn't have worried about spotting Anya. As soon as the girl appeared in the jet bridge, a swarm of reporters rushed forward to the glass window behind Isabella and flash-bulbs went off like strobes. The girl recoiled beneath her red silk head scarf. Her coach, a petite, blond Australian named Liz Cartwright, looked alarmed as well.

Isabella stepped forward. "Welcome to Lake Placid, Ms. Khalid, Mrs. Cartwright. My name is Isabella Torres, and I'm here to escort you to the Olympic village."

The Australian stuck out her hand and Isabella shook it briefly. Normally, she wouldn't tie up her hands in such a manner while on the job, but this wasn't a high-threat situation, and she had no authorization to use force anyway. She'd been specifically ordered to lay low and stay out of sight.

Technically, Isabella wasn't Anya's bodyguard. She was merely under orders to keep an eye on the girl and steer her away from serious threats. How had the IOC security chairman, Manfred Schmidt of Germany, put it? "We do not wish for the United States to act like a police state, for that would be contrary to the spirit of these games."

"The exit's this way." Isabella turned and led them to a revolving door. She stepped through first and nobody paid her any heed. But when Anya and her coach passed through the turning glass, the mob of Middle Eastern-looking journalists descended on them.

Isabella's first impulse was to jump in front of the pair. The two women had stopped, recoiling from the cameras and microphones being shoved in their faces. *Orders, schmorders.* Those two needed help. She wasn't about to stand here and let the paparazzi harass her charge.

There were only a dozen photographers, but the mood among them was nasty. Their tones of voice as they shouted over each other to ask questions were distinctly rude. Isabella's internal alarm system sent a low-level warning humming through her gut. That guy snarling in Farsi sounded Iraqi. His rant about Anya outrageously flaunting her religion was worrisome.

She eased forward to inject herself between the guy and Anya. When the Iraqi refused to get out of her way, Isabella put a casual nerve pinch on the guy's arm that made him howl. As he bent over in pain, she sidestepped him and moved forward until she stood right in front of the girl.

She made eye contact with Anya. "How about we get out of here?"

The girl nodded quickly. Somebody shoved Isabella from behind, almost knocking her into Anya. Eyes narrowed threateningly, she turned and said firmly, "Let us through, please."

Nada. If anything, the journalists surged closer. As a lone woman without a proper chaperone, they weren't about to give her the time of day, let alone a shred of respect. Enough was enough. She snapped, "C'mon guys. Make a hole."

A few of them stepped back, but immediately, journalists from the rear of the group stepped into the gap. Fine. She could play their game. She planted a strategic heel on the top of the nearest reporter's foot. He squawked and hopped out of the way. She gave the same treatment to the guy beside him. Will you look at that? A hole magically opened up.

Grabbing the coach's arm with her left hand and Anya's with her right, Isabella said under her breath, "Stick to me like glue." And then she proceeded to glare her way through the remaining journalists.

In a few seconds, she and her charges burst outside. A half-frozen crowd of media types milled around on the sidewalk, trying to keep their equipment dry in the falling snow, and although every camera swung toward the photogenic skater, nobody made a move to rush them. Hallelujah.

She guided the women to a waiting white minivan with blacked out windows and official Olympic license plates. She ushered them into the back seats and climbed in the front passenger seat. "Let's go, Python."

The vehicle, driven by Karen Turner, the Medusas' six-foot tall Marine officer, pulled away from the curb smoothly.

"What about our bags?" the Australian coach asked in alarm.

Isabella answered, "We have some people inside the terminal now who will get them and bring them to your rooms." *And go over them with a fine-toothed comb to make sure everything is as it should be inside them.* Anya stared at her in shock.

"What?" Isabella asked.

"You laid a hand on those men!"

Isabella shrugged. "Technically, I used my foot. And they wouldn't get out of the way. They were being rude." She grinned crookedly and added, "Welcome to the United States. Where women take charge and kick butt."

A slow smile spread across Anya's face. "I think I'm going to like it here."

Anya and her coach were duly installed in their side-by-side rooms in the Olympic village, in the same wing of the giant, hotel-like facility as the delegations from Belgium, Brazil and Canada, among other *A* to *C* countries. The athletes, all three thousand of them plus the coaches, doctors and trainers who made up the delegations, were housed alphabetically in the brand-new building, which was crafted of rustic stone and wood and would be turned into a high-end resort when the Games were over. The village perched on a mountainside overlooking the hamlet of Lake Placid, which was nestled beside Mirror Lake and the frozen tip of Lake Placid.

Security in and around the village was extensive. The small black domes of security cameras perched on every street corner, and in the public access areas of every building. They were manned around the clock by the best counterterrorism specialists America had to offer. Practically every Special Forces operator in the U.S. Armed Forces who wasn't deployed overseas had been pulled in to work the Games. No Munich Massacre repeats for America, thank you very much.

If there was a juicier terrorist target than an Olympic games on American soil with television coverage going out to billions of people all over the planet, Isabella surely couldn't think of it.

She stepped into the charged quiet of the OSG—Olympic Security Group—headquarters in the large administrative building next door to the village. The OSG was the detachment of U.S. military types working alongside the IOC security committee. The OSG ops center looked like mission control at a NASA rocket launch facility. Bank after bank of video monitors lined the walls. Rows of security men sat in front of them, studying them intently, moving the joy sticks on their consoles to swivel the cameras. Computer screens scrolled a steady stream of information to the soldiers manning them. Everyone wore headsets and received constant audio updates. She didn't even want to think about what all this must have cost. Plus, the civilian IOC security team next door had its own control room on an even grander scale.

Behind her a voice barked, "Torres! In here."

She turned to identify the speaker. And scowled. Major Dexter G. Thorpe IV, commander of the OSG. And possibly the biggest jerk in the Western Hemisphere. He'd been ordering the Medusas around and sticking them with menial "girl" jobs ever since they'd arrived in Lake Placid. He'd made it crystal clear that he thought the whole idea of women in the Special Forces was a bad joke. But, he was her boss. For now. She gritted her teeth and marched toward the large conference room where this afternoon's overview briefing was to start in about one minute.

"And bring me a cup of black coffee while you're at it," he called across the Ops Center.

That remark stopped the general buzz cold. Making and serving coffee was a traditional insult to women in uniform, and one that female soldiers had rebelled against en masse decades ago. Every gaze in the room turned on her to see how the newbie Spec Ops chick would react. Was this a test, or just another demonstration of Thorpe's contempt for the idea of women as special operators?

Eyes narrowed, she strolled over to the coffeepot and poured a big, steaming mug of the brew. Close to a hundred men and the five women of the Medusas crowded in the conference room. Thorpe stood by the podium up front, glaring at her expectantly. Gonna make her deliver his coffee in front of everyone, was he?

One foot in front of the other, she walked through the thick silence. Everyone stared at that mug. She set it down gently on the corner of the podium and joined her teammates, who were lounging against the wall near the front.

Thorpe picked up the coffee and took a long, conspicuous sip.

What an asshole. Isabella spoke up loudly enough to be heard across the quiet room. "So, Viper. Wanna guess which one it was?"

The Medusas' commanding officer, Air Force Major Vanessa Blake, replied, "Which one what?"

Isabella paused until Thorpe lifted the mug to his mouth again. "Remember prisoner-of-war school? Whenever the aggressors made us get coffee for them, we either spat in it or picked our noses and stirred snot into it? Wanna guess which one I did?"

Thorpe spewed hot coffee across his notes as the roomful

of special operators burst into loud guffaws. Laughter drifted in from the ops center outside as well, where the audio feed of this briefing was being piped to everyone's headsets. Thorpe threw a look in her direction that promised revenge. She gazed back at him blandly.

Red-faced, Thorpe began the briefing. He ran through several dozen security issues, assigning operators to each. "A press conference will be given this afternoon by the Bhoukari figure skater, Anya Khalid. She's expected to announce her intention to compete in the Olympics."

Somebody snorted from the back. "Wow. Big news. Athlete comes to Lake Placid and says she'll compete."

Isabella rolled her eyes. The guy didn't know the half of it. She'd spent the last few days reading Middle Eastern newspapers and surfing Internet chat rooms that were discussing this unprecedented event. Opinion was sharply divided. As sharply divided as the conservative fundamentalists and the more liberal moderates within the Islamic faith itself. Women's rights were among the thorniest issues facing the Muslim world today. Centuries-old tradition held that an unmarried young woman figure skating in skimpy clothes with suggestive poses—and furthermore, doing it in front of *men*—was nothing short of blasphemy. As in punishable by flogging or even death. Anya declaring that she intended to skate, particularly after she'd been specifically ordered by Bhoukari mullahs—Muslim clerics—not to, was a direct challenge to the leaders of her country's faith. This press conference was a *huge* deal.

"Torres, if you can keep your fingers out of your nose, I want you to cover the Khalid girl at her press conference," Thorpe barked.

"Define cover," she retorted. "Am I her bodyguard or simply her minder?"

"Stay out of the cameras and keep her alive."

An ambiguous answer. It gave her plenty of wiggle room to operate, but no clear authority to do a darned thing. A politically correct answer. And damned annoying. But then, everything about Major Dexter Thorpe was annoying.

The press briefing room was surprisingly full. Isabella glanced around and spotted her five teammates spaced unobtrusively around the edges of the crowd. Several faces from the unpleasant encounter at the airport were here, too.

She looked over her shoulder at Anya, who was sporting a dark suit and a black scarf over her head, its ends thrown back over her shoulders. The girl was stunning in the stark outfit. "Ready?" Isabella murmured.

The girl nodded resolutely.

They stepped into the room, and camera lights burst on in a blinding glare. Anya lurched. *Steady, girl.* Isabella stepped onto the dais and backed into a corner as Anya moved to the podium clutching a sheet of paper.

A man shouted, "Tell us, Anya, are you going to skate in the Olympics?"

The girl took a shaky breath. "I have a short statement to read." She cleared her throat and began, "I would like to thank His Most Serene Highness, the emir of Bhoukar, for allowing me to represent my homeland in these Olympic Games. It is an honor I shall do my utmost to live up to. To that end, I do intend to skate and compete in the ladies' figure skating competition, and I shall do my best—"

The rest of what she had to say was drowned out by the sudden uproar of male voices shouting in outrage. Apparently, not all the people here were reporters. A gray-bearded man sporting an embroidered skull cap stood up near the back of the room and began to shout in Arabic. His bellowed words reverberated throughout the space.

Isabella listened in burgeoning horror while the roars of his supporters grew louder and louder. Finally, the mullah ended his diatribe on a howl of rage and his avid audience turned, surging toward the stage.

Holy shit. With one look at the frenzied mob advancing on her charge, Isabella took a running leap at Anya, knocking the girl clean off her feet and slamming the skater to the floor.

"Help!" she shouted into her microphone.

Please God, let the Medusas get up here in time.

Chapter 2

A female voice barked in Arabic for the men to stop where they were or be subdued by force. *That was Vanessa.* Isabella glanced up and saw five women parked defensively around her. *The Medusas.* Isabella allowed herself a milli-second of relief.

She spoke urgently in Anya's ear. "I'm going to stand up, and then I'm going to help you to your feet. A bunch of women are going to crowd in close and we're going to hustle you out of here. Just go with the flow and let us move you. Okay?"

The skater stared up at her, terrified. No way to tell if the girl understood or not. No time to calm her down, though. That mob was out for blood. The maneuver went off exactly as Isabella had described it. The mostly Middle Eastern men were taken aback by the aggressive posture of the Medusas long enough for the women to whisk Anya into a back hallway, closed off from public access.

Python slammed a door shut behind them, and sudden

quiet enveloped the seven women. "What was that all about?" the Marine asked tersely.

Isabella answered, "That gray-bearded guy said he's a Bhoukari cleric of some kind. He just declared a fatwa on Ms. Khalid."

Karen asked, "And a fatwa is…"

Isabella finished for her. "A formal ruling on a matter of Islamic law. The guy with the beard declared a death sentence on our girl here. Every Muslim is essentially ordered to kill Anya on sight. They'll get in trouble with Allah if they don't."

Karen retorted in disbelief, "And some guy is just allowed to stand up in the back of the room and declare this for the entire billion plus Muslims in the world? No trial, no discussion, just boom, she's to be killed?"

Isabella shrugged. "If he's a cleric of sufficient authority, yes, he can. We'll have to find out who that man was, ASAP."

Anya spoke from behind her. "That was Ahmed al Abhoud. He's the high mufti for all of Bhoukar."

Isabella swore. A mufti was a Muslim scholar who interpreted Islamic law. He would, indeed, have the authority to declare a fatwa. "Anya, do you understand what he just did?"

The girl shrugged. "I haven't lived in Bhoukar since I was a little girl. I grew up in Australia. People there don't listen to crazy old men like him."

Isabella stared. "If you don't mind my asking a personal question, how religious is your family?"

Another shrug. "They're as religious as they have to be when they're back in Bhoukar. But in Brisbane…" The girl paused, searching for words. "We wanted to fit in. My family lives by western rules there."

"How familiar are you with the conservative ways in Bhoukar?"

"I've heard stories. I mean, I know about the five pillars of Islam and all that."

Great. This girl was up to her neck in a religious controversy, and she hardly knew a thing about it.

Karen asked, "How seriously will people take this man and his fatwa?"

Isabella explained carefully, "What that mufti just did is very serious. While the majority of Muslims may not try to act on that order, plenty of them will."

"You mean people Anya's never met are going to try to *kill* her?" Karen exclaimed.

Isabella looked her square in the eye. "That's exactly what I mean."

Manfred Schmidt rolled his eyes. "Ms. Torres, that's the dumbest thing I've ever heard. This is the twenty-first century. These are the Olympic Games. Athletes aren't going to run around trying to kill each other because some guy stood up and told them to."

Isabella huffed in frustration. "The Olympics bring together people from around the world. It's a microcosm of mankind. We've got three thousand athletes and their support staffs here, and several dozen of them are Muslim. Statistically, at least a few of them will feel obliged to act on that fatwa, Olympics or not."

"Preposterous."

"Actually, Captain Torres is right."

Isabella whirled at the sound of the male voice behind her. Major Thorpe had just stepped into the room. Was he actually backing her up? Surely her ears deceived her.

He spoke with quiet certainty. "Anya Khalid is in danger, not only from outside the Olympic village, but potentially from within it."

Schmidt scowled at Thorpe. "And what do you propose to do about it?"

The major scowled back. "I'm going to assign Torres and her pals to pull around-the-clock bodyguard duty on the Khalid girl."

Schmidt drew himself up officiously. "We do not put body-guards on athletes. It goes against everything the Olympics stand for."

Isabella dived into the argument. "So did the Munich Massacre. But it happened anyway. If you don't want blood on your hands, you'd better let us protect this girl." It was a low blow, invoking Munich to the German, but this guy had to understand the threat.

Schmidt glared at the pair of them, and she became aware that Thorpe had moved up beside her, shoulder-to-shoulder with her. It took a few seconds, but Schmidt eventually gave in to the two commandos glaring him down. His belligerent posture wilted. "Okay. *Fine.* But keep her protection completely invisible. And I mean *invisible.* I don't want the media picking up on this. Understood?"

Isabella and Thorpe nodded, and then together watched the security chairman storm out of the briefing room.

She looked over at her temporary boss. She'd never paid attention before, but he was a good-looking guy up close like this. His brown hair had red highlights, and his eyes were a dark gray-green that reminded her of moss on granite. His face ran to the lean side, but his features were classically handsome. "Thanks," she muttered.

He nodded briefly. "What's your handle?"

"Adder."

"Ahh, I get it. Medusas. Snakes. You all go by snake names?"

"Yeah."

"Let me know if you need help with your girl."

"Right." Like she'd *ever* go to him for help.

"My handle's Dex."

Not real original. But she was startled he'd even told it to her at all. Handles were shared among teammates and friends, not with outsiders.

Thorpe turned and strode out of the room. Well. That monosyllabic exchange was the most pleasant the guy'd been since she'd met him. Jerk. Time to go find Anya and the rest of the Medusas, who were babysitting the skater right now.

She was alarmed when nobody answered the door to Anya's room. She pounded on it, and the next door down opened up. Liz Cartwright stuck her head into the hall. "Anya was hungry. Your friends took her down to the food court."

Isabella nodded. "Have you got a minute?"

The coach stepped back, gesturing into her room. Isabella followed. Man, these digs were plush. The hotel chain, which was acting as a corporate sponsor that would buy this facility after the Games, had already decorated the place like a five-star hotel.

"Mrs. Cartwright—"

"Call me Liz. We Aussies don't go for much formality."

"Liz. My colleagues and I realize Anya needs to prepare for her competition, even with twenty-four hour security. I just want to assure you that we'll do our best to cooperate with both of you and stay out of your way as much as possible."

"Thanks. But I think your biggest challenge is going to be getting Anya to cooperate with you."

"What do you mean?"

"Despite growing up in Australia, she has lived a fairly sheltered life. And now she's halfway around the world at one of the most exciting places on the planet. She may not take too kindly to you and your friends hovering over her and limiting her freedom."

Lovely. Just what every bodyguard wanted to hear. That her protectee was a wild child who wasn't going to help her do her job. "Thanks for the heads-up. We'll do our best not to restrict her enjoyment of the Games."

The Australian woman's eyes twinkled. "Good luck."

And on that ominous note, Isabella headed down to the twenty-four hour food court and its global array of cuisine. Food lines stretched the length of a giant ballroom and absolutely every food from all corners of the world was here.

Moving through the serving area and between the tables where the athletes dined, she scanned the space and didn't spot her teammates. Crud.

She moved on to the arcade beyond the dining room. Every conceivable video game was here—free, of course, along with tall stacks of limited edition gifts from all the major sports equipment and clothing vendors. There were two discos, and on the terrace outside, a stage was set up for private concerts by internationally renowned bands. Lights and colors flashed everywhere, giving the place a casino-like glitter.

And then, of course, there were the workout facilities. A health club to end all health clubs stretched away behind glass windows to her right. She could see why Anya was going to be difficult to corral with this wonderland available around the clock. And that didn't even take into account the town of Lake Placid itself, and the nonstop party it would turn into when the Games started.

Over there, across the expanse of video games, she caught a glimpse of Misty Cordell, the tall, blond Medusa from California. Isabella started toward her teammate, but with her highly trained peripheral vision, she caught sight of something odd. Two men were moving across the room at the same time, probably fifty feet apart. That, in and of itself, wouldn't have drawn her attention, but she'd seen the two men trade looks and slight nods. Were there more of these guys? The guy nearest her looked in her general direction. And nodded again! She glanced to her right and immediately spotted the third guy.

They wore nondescript white polo shirts and dark slacks. Could be staff or athletes. And they were definitely converging on the wide ring of Medusas with Anya in its center. Isabella's internal threat-warning system exploded. Now what? She needed to warn her teammates, but Schmidt's orders rang in her head. They were to be invisible.

It didn't look like the men had spotted her. She increased her speed enough to get in front of them. She wasn't worried about her teammates' ability to defend the skater, but that damned invisibility order would be blown to hell if they had to fight off a trio of assailants in a public place. If only the Medusas were wearing their usual throat microphones and earpieces! Schmidt had vetoed use of their full military equipment in the name of their blending in and not appearing threatening to the public. Whatever.

As she closed in on the Medusas, she willed one of them to spot her. Thankfully, Misty did. Isabella flashed her a hand signal for hostiles incoming. Her teammate turned and signaled to the others. Isabella ducked behind a video game, bending down like she'd dropped something. Time to stalk the stalkers.

As the Medusas collected Anya and moved swiftly toward Isabella, the three men scattered. Damn! She didn't want to lose the men! Aleesha Gautier, the team's doctor from Jamaica, peeled off to follow one guy, while Misty followed another one. Vanessa signaled Isabella to take the guy nearest to her, and Isabella signaled back an affirmative—not a tricky hand signal; it was an old-fashioned thumbs-up. They *so* needed their radios!

Her guy darted down a side hallway, and used a magnetic strip card to unlock and dive through a service entrance. Nice try, but she had one of those, too. She dug a master key card out of her pocket and let herself in after the guy. And looked around in dismay. A stainless steel jungle of counters, cooking equipment and chefs stretched in front of her. Dozens of men and women moved around the space, and she hadn't gotten a good enough look at her target to pick him out of this sea of faces. Dang it!

She spied a male figure who might be her guy moving quickly down one of the rows. She took off after him and prayed he was the right one. He ducked out another door on the far side of the room. Isabella followed quickly.

The door led outside. A gust of icy wind showered her with powdered snow. Her arms prickled with goose bumps as she looked both ways. A male silhouette was just ducking around a corner up ahead. She broke into a run, slipping and sliding on the slick layer of snow dusting the sidewalk. The sun shone brilliantly, glaring off the blanket of white until it nearly blinded her. She turned into the alley's relative darkness, and pinpricks of light danced in her eyes.

A dark form barreled at her. Aww, crap. Not the old bowl-over-the-tail stunt. She braced a shoulder to take the blow, but the guy dodged around her at the last second. She leaped out of the alley to give chase when a much bigger, faster form slammed into her. This time, she landed square on her behind, with a guy wearing a dark blue Olympic security jacket sprawled across her lap. She'd seen him before, on the military side of the house, but had never met him.

He swore copiously as he pulled out a radio. "Track the bastard on camera!" Scowling, he climbed to his feet and helped Isabella up. "You all right?" he growled.

"Yeah. I bump heads with rhinoceroses every day."

The guy grinned briefly. "Most women would cry at a crash like that."

He didn't seem to be holding a grudge that they both lost their man. That was decent of him. She shrugged. "I'm not most women. Let's get back to the ops center and see where that guy goes. And don't offer me your coat," she snapped as the guy started to unzip his jacket.

"Sorry. My mama raised me to be a gentleman. Name's Beau Breckenridge."

That rang a bell. "Is your handle Hobo?" she asked. "Delta Four?"

He flashed her a killer smile. "Yup. That's me."

Delta Four was Dex Thorpe's team. Curious, she asked, "What kind of team leader is Major Thorpe?"

Beau didn't hesitate. "He's the best I've ever seen."

Wow. The jerk earned the unswerving loyalty of his men, did he? Hard to picture. She trudged back up the slippery hill to the hotel entrance and stepped inside gratefully. She was an ice cube. Her teeth chattered as she made her way to the ops center.

"Whatchya got?" Beau called as Thorpe motioned the two of them over to a cluster of men around a bank of cameras.

"Lost him. He ducked out of the village before we could close the gates."

How had *that* happened? She glared at the major. "How hard is it to call the guard shacks and tell them to stop traffic?"

"Schmidt has to give the order."

"That's bull—"

Thorpe cut her off. "I'm with you, Torres. With this incident to back me up, I'll argue against the policy again at the IOC staff meeting in the morning."

"While you're at it, get us our radios, will you? It's damned hard to coordinate anything with my teammates if I can't talk to them."

Dex raised a sardonic eyebrow. "Didn't they teach you hand signals in Special Forces school?"

She replied sweetly, "Gee, they only taught us this one." She flipped him her middle finger.

While the guys around her developed a sudden case of the coughs, she asked, "Did Sidewinder and Mamba catch their runners?"

"Nope. Their guys ducked into a men's locker room, and by the time your friends worked up the nerve to go in, the men had slipped out another way."

She gritted her teeth. No way had it been a lack of nerve that caused her teammates not to give chase. There must've been a bunch of athletes in the locker room who would've been freaked out if the Medusas had barged in.

Damn! Round One to the bad guys. Except it wasn't a total loss. At least the Medusas knew three of them had credentials to get into the Olympic village, probably as employees. That list was finite, and the people in this room had access to it. Knowing Thorpe, they'd examine it under a microscope until they found the runners.

Thorpe's jaw flexed. "We got a couple facial shots of them. The computer boys are enhancing the images now. We'll ID these guys before too long. I'll call you when we get something."

Hey, that was an improvement! Thorpe had spoken to her like a human being. Would wonders never cease. With a terse nod in his direction, she turned and headed for Anya's room.

"That old man is going to ruin everything!" Abdul, griped, exasperated. If only he could afford to tell his father about the plan. But he dared not. Ahmed might be inexorably conservative, but he also was totally opposed to…direct action. In a word, to terrorism. "The fatwa has drawn the attention of the security forces right to the figure skating event. It didn't help that you three hotheads took it upon yourselves to tail the Khalid girl. In the future, you will not take such initiatives by yourselves. Understood?"

The three cousins nodded glumly.

He sighed. "We must be careful and execute the plan properly. Our countrymen are depending on us. We must send the message strongly to the Americans to keep their hands off Bhoukar. No more foolish stunts out of you. Do only what I tell you to do."

More extreme elements within the Red Jihad would have cut these overeager boys' heads off and fed their entrails to dogs to teach the other members of the cell to follow orders. But these three were his nephews. He wasn't going to kill family members for being too zealous in their patriotism. He wasn't a fanatic, after all. He was a reasonable man.

One of his nephews shifted his weight from foot to foot and asked nervously, "Have we ruined the plan? Should we scrap it?"

The mere thought made him ill. "After all this planning? After all our hard work and sacrifices? When will there be another chance like these Olympics to strike such a blow against the United States? Oh, no. We proceed as scheduled. Tonight, we grab the woman."

Anya was not a happy camper. Her coach had declared a mandatory nap to help the skater adjust to the time zone change. Isabella watched the girl pace her room, as restless as a caged tiger. In big sister fashion, she said soothingly, "After dinner you can go out and play to your heart's content."

Anya made a face. "After dinner, I've got a flag bearer rehearsal for the opening ceremonies. Since I'm the only athlete from Bhoukar, I have to carry my country's flag."

Great. Like that wouldn't be a total security nightmare! A giant stadium, thousands of people milling around on the infield, and, if she didn't miss her guess, spectator seating open to the public. "Why don't you watch a little TV? I hear it has on-demand programming in twenty languages."

Isabella left Anya fooling with her television remote control. Karen was posted outside the door while Isabella headed for the ops center to set up what security measures she could for tonight's rehearsal.

Thorpe was there when she walked into the bustling control room. He glanced up from a computer terminal and waved her over. "Your girl's caused quite a stir. Look at this."

She leaned over his shoulder gingerly and scanned the deluge of press reaction to Al Abhoud's fatwa from around the world.

"The media is having a field day with that tackle you laid on Anya. You made all the major news networks."

She flinched. "So much for being invisible."

Thorpe shrugged. "Schmidt was smoking dope if he thought you were going to be able to remain invisible for long. Just stay out of the limelight as much as you can. But, first and foremost, do the job. Keep the kid alive."

Isabella nodded. "We'll do our best."

"I got you your radios. I'm assigning you a discrete channel. That way the guys here can contact you directly. Cell phone capacity for the city isn't going to be sufficient once the Games get rolling and Lake Placid fills up." A muscle ticked in his jaw briefly. "But I lost the fight to get more cell towers installed."

"Careful, sir," she replied lightly, "you're almost starting to sound human."

One corner of his mouth turned up, but it hardly qualified as a smile. "For the duration of the Olympics, we've been asked to suspend use of military titles. We wouldn't want to appear like a police state, after all."

She heard the echo of Schmidt's words and grinned. "Perish the thought."

"Just use my handle if you need me. I'll keep your frequency on my list of critical channels."

"How many do you have piped into your ear?" she asked.

"Ten so far."

Yikes. Talk about multitasking. She didn't like to listen to more than four channels at once. Aloud, she said, "We shouldn't be hard to pick out. We'll be the only girls talking to you."

"Right," he growled, abruptly surly.

Didn't like the reminder that he had to work with women, huh? Tough. Abruptly feeling surly herself, she turned to leave. Kat and Vanessa were meeting her at the Olympic stadium in fifteen minutes.

After a dismayed survey of the giant Torch Stadium, they concluded there wasn't a damned thing they could do to protect Anya out here. The security people screening the crowd would be the only real line of defense.

The good news was they knew that anyone who wanted to kill the girl would do so as a political and religious statement. They'd make the attempt while Anya was on the center of the world stage. And tonight's rehearsal wasn't televised. The assassin would wait until the actual opening ceremonies or some other moment with similar media coverage.

Nonetheless, Isabella insisted Anya wear a bulletproof vest under her parka for the walk-through of the parade of nations. It was better than nothing, but not much. Any sniper worth his salt would see the suspicious bulk of her coat, shift his aim to her head and kill her anyway.

The rehearsal went off without a hitch and Anya was safely tucked into bed before 10:00 p.m. She had ice time the next morning at nine, and despite her desire to sample all the fun at her fingertips, she was still a disciplined athlete with the biggest competition of her life only days away. Thank God.

During the first night shift, sitting in the dark watching Anya sleep peacefully, Isabella eyed the girl. Was Anya truly unaware of the turmoil brewing around her, or just totally disinterested in it? She *seemed* like a bright kid.

Isabella sighed. Sometimes she forgot how naive she'd been at nineteen. Even though she was only half-Iranian, it had been her mother's copious relatives who dropped in for coffee and generally meddled in each other's lives. It had been her Iranian aunts who tsked at her mother's decision to raise the girls as Americans, her Iranian grandfather who bellowed over Isabella and her sisters not being raised as Muslims.

Thank goodness her father had stood his ground on that one. He'd insisted his children be free to choose their own faiths. He'd probably expected them to choose between Catholicism and Islam, but for her part, she'd chosen neither. She'd lived trapped between the two worlds with neither church to act as a buffer against the other.

Anya was in the same boat. She lived in a Western society, but she had been raised, at least partially, according to the traditional Bhoukari culture. Her parents were fairly liberal, after all they'd let their daughter figure skate in the first place. But her extended family was from ultraconservative Bhoukar. Did Anya know what she was doing by being here? Surely, it had been explained to her. Maybe when she found herself alone in the middle of this mess, she would learn to handle the conflict between the two halves of her identity.

Just as Isabella had when she'd left home and joined the Air Force. She'd applied for and received an ROTC scholarship to finance her education at an expensive private college. The oldest of four girls, she'd felt guilty about hogging the family budget for higher education. However, she shouldn't have worried. Only her youngest sister attended college, and she'd dropped out as soon as she married the law student who would support her in fine style for the rest of her life.

Leaving home had forced Isabella to choose her identity. And she'd chosen to be neither Mexican nor Iranian, but to be American.

She was the black sheep of the family because of it. Her relatives simply couldn't understand what she gained by being in the military. Her father's family bought into the traditional Mexican-Catholic role for women—staying at home and having kids ad nauseum. Her mother's Iranian relatives didn't have a problem with her having a profession like photo intelligence analyst, but they could *not* wrap their brains around her being a military officer able to give men orders.

She hadn't told any of them about her assignment to the Medùsas. How could she explain her need to escape their restrictive expectations, to be different from her veiled aunts and cousins, her compulsion to push herself to the very limit? She would've suffocated in the safe, cloying confines of the traditional lifestyles her family offered. If other women chose that for themselves, fine. But it would've killed her.

She'd been driven to succeed at her chosen career, to endure pain and misery beyond comprehension in the first days of the Medusas' training when Jack Scatalone had been determined to break them. And truth be told, he'd come damned close to breaking her. The only reason he hadn't was because failure, for her, was unthinkable. She would never go back to the world of her youth.

She wasn't a gifted athlete. She'd gone to an all girls' school where anemic, intramural volleyball was as physical as anyone got. Regular old basic training in the Air Force had been a challenge. But she'd worked on her physical fitness. And when Vanessa Blake had offered Isabella a chance to join the first all-female Special Forces team, she'd worked her butt off to get fit, even before their training began.

She'd made it through on sheer guts and the generosity of her stronger, fitter teammates who'd helped her. A lot. She was still working hard to improve her strength and stamina, but her sense of inferiority was hard to shake. Maybe tomorrow when she got off shift she'd head over to that incredible gym and work out.

Sometimes there was no use in overthinking a problem. Sometimes you just had to go with your gut. She might not have any business being a Medusa, but she belonged in this room at this moment, guarding this girl who was so much like her.

Harlan Holt lay in bed, tossing and turning. His wife, Emma, had crashed hours ago. With the Winter Olympics and the first-ever international competition on the super ice he'd developed only days away, he wasn't so lucky.

He vegged out in front of the murmur of late night talk shows and maybe that was why he didn't hear the four black shapes until they burst through the window. They ran at the bed so fast he barely had time to be shocked, let alone react, before the men were on him.

He yelled, but too late. Two of the men jumped on Emma, slapping a cloth bag over her head as the other two shoved pistols in his face. This couldn't be happening to them! They lived in a modest little bungalow on a sleepy street in a quiet college town. They didn't own anything worth stealing!

Emma kicked and screamed, but the two men who held her by the arms were strong. She couldn't break free. He tried to lunge for her, but hands grabbed him roughly around the neck, choking him viciously. He was thrown on the mattress where he bounced to a stop. He curled up in a ball and covered his head as one of his assailants raised a pistol high in the air as if to smash it down on his skull. The second masked man stopped the arm holding the gun.

This was a nightmare. The sleeping pill he'd swallowed dry a little while ago was making him hallucinate. Emma struggled again and one of the men slugged her through the bag. That was a very real, if muffled, scream. Impotent fury surged in his veins—except he didn't have the faintest idea what to do! He was a scholar. A scientist. He'd never hit anything in his entire life, not even a baseball.

"Leave her alone!" he shouted.

A gloved hand slapped him hard across the face, bloodying the inside of his cheek against his teeth. Pain exploded inside his mouth, and with it, fear. Desperate, he surged toward Emma as her attackers dragged her off the bed. She landed on the floor with a thump and cried out. Something cold and hard jabbed his right temple, bringing him up short. Oh, God. The muzzle of a shotgun. He froze. He couldn't help her if he was dead.

A heavily accented voice snarled, "Dr. Holt. Your wife is going to come with us. You will do exactly as we say. You will not contact any law enforcement official or tell anyone what has happened, or your wife will die. Do you understand?"

They were kidnapping his Emma? What for? Her biology research in recombinant DNA wasn't of any great significance to anyone outside the medical community and her department at Syracuse University. "No! Take me. Leave her alone, for God's sake, I'm begging you!"

Whimpering filled his ears. And then he realized it was *him* making those awful keening noises. He tried to stop. Failed. Hysteria crept over him. His legs shook uncontrollably, and he felt a nearly overwhelming urge to wet himself.

"Listen closely, Dr. Holt. If you wish your wife to live, this is what we require you to do...."

The next morning dawned clear and bright, frigid cold. Last night's snow crunched underfoot and Isabella's breath hung in the air as thick as a cloud. The giant Olympic ice complex loomed before her, seven rinks contained in three connected buildings. The original brick ice rink, now called the Lussi Rink, was built for the 1932 Olympics. The 1980 Olympics saw the construction of more rinks, bringing the total to five. Last year, two more rinks had been finished, one of them the giant Hamilton arena where the figure skating competitions would be held in this third Lake Placid Olympiad. It seated close to thirty thousand spectators.

Isabella, Anya and Liz had to clear five separate security checkpoints before they finally gained entrance to the facility. Isabella was relieved to see that the media's and officials' area was completely separated from the athletes' and coaches' area. To get from one to the other, a person had to leave the rink and go outside around the massive building to a different entrance and another gauntlet of checkpoints.

Isabella watched as Anya put on her skates. Large bunions deformed the ball of each of the young woman's feet. Her ankles were bony, and calluses covered the tops of her toes. "Man, and I thought ballet dancers were hard on their feet."

Anya looked up with a shrug. "My feet aren't too bad. Lots of skaters wreck theirs completely. I haven't had to have any surgeries yet."

Isabella watched as the skater pulled out gel pads and stuck them on various parts of her feet, then laced up the rigid skates as tightly as she could. "Doesn't that cut off your circulation?"

Anya laughed. "You need the ankle support if you're going to land triples on hard ice while skating at twenty miles per hour."

Put that way, Isabella could see the need for skaters to torture their feet.

Anya said eagerly, "I can't wait to try out the new ice. I hear it's amazing."

"New ice?" Isabella echoed. "Isn't ice, well, ice?"

"Not anymore. Some Yankee scientist has invented what everyone's calling super ice. He's added some sort of chemical to it that makes it glide smoother and gives it more spring than regular ice."

"What kind of chemical?"

Anya grinned. "I haven't the slightest. I flunked chemistry."

Isabella waxed serious. "While you're skating this morning, if you hear me shout for you to get down, I want to you dive for the ice and then make your way over to the nearest wall. Wait there for me to come get you."

"They're called boards."

"Excuse me?" Isabella asked.

"The walls around the ice. They're called boards."

"Okay. Get over to the boards. If I yell for you to move out, I want you to skate as fast as you can to the exit. But don't skate in a straight line. Zigzag."

"Zigzag. Got it. And why are you planning to do all this yelling at me?"

"In case someone tries to kill you. I'd come out onto the ice to protect you, but the ISU—International Skating Union—officials won't let me."

"Just as well," Anya replied. "You'd hurt yourself. Street shoes and ice don't mix. If someone in skates ran over your foot, they'd cut off your toes unless you have steel-lined shoes."

"You're kidding."

"Nope. They don't call these blades for nothing. Besides, you'd end up sitting on your bum as soon as you stepped onto the ice. It's slippery, in case you didn't know."

Isabella grinned. "Yeah, I'd heard that. And you're right. I would end up on my rear end. Athletics have never been my strong suit."

Anya looked up in surprise from putting plastic skate

guards over her knife-sharp blades. "Then how did you get into your line of work?"

"I'm just too stubborn to quit."

"You can always train up into better shape. I'll help you if you like."

"You?" Isabella blurted in surprise. "You think you're in better shape than I am?"

Anya shrugged. "People think all it takes to skate is being graceful and having good balance. But skaters are serious athletes. We do aerobic conditioning, weight training, flexibility training, jump classes, dance classes, stroking classes—"

Liz Cartwright called from over by the ice, "Your session's starting, Anya."

Isabella accompanied the girl out of the relative warmth of the dressing area to the frigid rink side. "Dang, it's like a meat locker in here."

"Probably around eight degrees centigrade," Anya replied. "All ice rinks stay about this temperature. It feels great on a summer day in Brisbane."

While Isabella shivered by the boards, Anya warmed up, skimming over the ice effortlessly. Forward and backward crossovers, footwork, spins, easy jumps followed by progressively harder jumps. Idly, Isabella converted the Celsius to Fahrenheit in her head. Forty-six degrees. Brrr. It wasn't bad for a couple minutes, but the cold was starting to soak into her bones. No wonder all the coaches wore fur coats or parkas up to their ears.

Liz called out the occasional instruction in a shorthand slang. Stuff about edges, leans and centering, it all flowed past Isabella. But when a disturbance broke out not far from where she stood, Isabella went on full alert.

Two people were arguing. Stridently. A tall, dark-haired man who looked too sallow and thin to be an athlete was yelling at an attractive, blue-eyed blond woman who looked about thirty. Isabella recognized the woman's face from the hasty briefings she'd received on the major players in the skating community. Lily Gustavson of Sweden was a senior ISU official. Isabella hadn't seen the man before.

She leaned over to Liz and murmured, "Who's the guy?"

"Harlan Holt. The Ice Doctor."

"The what?"

Liz grinned. "The Ice Doctor. He's the guy who invented super ice. This is the first international competition ever to use it. The skaters are wild about it."

"Any idea what he's so upset about?"

"I couldn't say." The Australian turned back to her student and called, "Anya, you're dropping your shoulder as you go into that axel. Try it again."

Isabella headed toward the argument, which, if anything, was growing in intensity.

Holt was saying, "…I'm telling you it's necessary."

Gustavson retorted, "How can that be? The skaters are using it now and they love it. We can't possibly need to replace the ice. It's three days until the first round of qualifying skating!"

"The polymers aren't evenly mixed. Some patches are more slippery than others. It's a safety issue. Somebody's going to get hurt if I don't redo the ice!"

Why did he sound so panicked? Like Anya said, wasn't all ice slippery? These were figure skaters, for goodness' sake. They could deal with slippery ice, couldn't they? Faulty logic aside, there was something alarming in the guy's tone of voice. A note of manic determination. He was dead set on redoing this ice right now. Why? Isabella glanced out at the rink in question. A dozen skaters were flying across the white surface, and not one of them seemed to be having trouble with these supposed patches. Something vibrated way wrong in her gut about this. She eased to the side to better see the guy's face.

The ISU official glared. "You've had six months to get this ice right. This isn't going to bode well for your ice being used in other international competitions."

The man looked pained at that, but he stood his ground.

"It's got to be done. If I get on it right away, you'll have skateable ice by tomorrow evening."

The official shook her head sharply. "I've got practice sessions scheduled all day today. I can't possibly move them on such short notice."

"There are seven rinks. There must be room on one of them for the skaters to practice. You've *got* to let me do this."

The guy almost sounded as if he were begging. Isabella frowned. Definitely something wrong here. She moved away from the pair as the ISU official pulled out her cell phone and started arguing with whoever was on the other end about re-scheduling the afternoon practice sessions. Isabella put her hand in her pocket and keyed the microphone clipped unobtrusively to the neck of her sweater.

"Ops, this is Torres. How do you copy?"

"Loud and clear. Go ahead."

Crud. Dex. He was going to think she was nuts, but here went. "I need a background check run on a guy named Harlan Holt. He's a credentialed official. In charge of the ice at the figure skating venue."

"The Ice Doctor?" Dex asked in surprise. "What's up?"

"I don't know. Call it a gut feeling. Something's funny about the guy. He's insisting on replacing the venue ice. Says it's not safe."

"And this makes you suspicious why?"

She closed her eyes briefly. "I couldn't tell you. It just does."

Dex had keyed the microphone on the other end to say something when a loud cry came from the ice. Isabella looked up sharply, her senses screaming to full alert. She turned just in time to see a large black shape hurtle into Anya. It crashed into her, sending her flying through the air to land with a sickening thud in a heap that skidded across the ice.

Isabella shouted into her microphone, "Subject down!"

Chapter 3

Isabella hit the ice running. As Anya'd predicted, she slipped and slid all over the place like a colt trying to stand up for the first time.

She'd taken her eyes off the girl for barely a second. The other skaters were all moving toward Anya in concern, and coaches were coming out onto the ice as well. Not good. These people knew a serious crash when they saw one, the same way she recognized a deadly threat.

As she stumbled toward Anya like a drunken sailor, she noticed a second figure down on the ice. As she watched, a young man dressed in black sat up, shaking his head. Had the flash that sent Anya flying been a collision? It would make sense. Half a dozen skaters had been whipping around the ice, crisscrossing the rink aggressively.

Isabella dropped to her knees beside Anya, relieved to be off her feet. She shifted into first aid mode. Anya was breathing. *Thank God.* Eyes closed. Isabella lifted one of the girl's lids. White. *Damn.* "Anya?"

It took a few moments and calling her name several times, but finally, the girl's eyes fluttered open. Acute pain swam in their dark depths.

"What hurts, honey?" Isabella asked.

Anya opened her mouth but no sound came out. A look of surprise spread across her features and rapidly turned to panic. Isabella, like all the Medusas, was a trained field medic, and she'd seen this one before.

"I'm an EMT, Anya. You've had the breath knocked out of you. Just relax for a few seconds. I won't let anything bad happen to you."

Anya nodded her understanding.

A tight ring of skaters and coaches completely surrounded Isabella and Anya. For once, she was grateful for a crowd of nosy onlookers. They'd act as human shields for Anya. "Did anyone see what happened?"

Someone commented, "Collisions happen all the time. Two skaters get going backward and neither one sees the other."

Someone else chimed in, "The hazards of practice sessions."

Everyone nodded. And the knot in Isabella's stomach started to unwind a little. It had been an accident. No one had tried to kill her subject.

"Does anything hurt?" Isabella asked as she assessed Anya's condition. No limbs were lying awkwardly and no blood stained the ice.

A nod from Anya was accompanied by a choppy, shallow breath.

"Take lots of short little pants for now. Point at where it hurts."

Her heart plummeted as the girl pointed at her knee. Isabella put her hands gently on the joint. "I'm going to poke at your knee, and then I'm going to move it around a bit." She knew a lot about knee injuries. The most common injury areas for special operators were knees and backs, the weak points of the human body.

Isabella put Anya's knee through a standard field diagnosis routine and sat back on her heels. "The good news is you haven't seriously injured your knee. The bad news is you've strained it and it's going to be sore for a couple of days."

Lily Gustavson looked over at Liz Cartwright. "When does she skate her qualifying round?"

"In five days," the Aussie answered worriedly.

"Did you bring your own doctor with you?"

Liz shook her head. "It was a miracle we even got permission to represent Bhoukar, let alone put together an actual delegation with a team doctor."

The American team's head coach spoke over Anya's head. "We have an orthopedic surgeon on our delegation. If you'd like to have him take a look at Anya, I'll be glad to arrange it."

Isabella said quietly to Liz, "That would be a good idea. Just to be safe."

The surgeon was duly summoned to the rink while a male pairs skater from Russia volunteered to carry Anya off the ice.

Isabella jumped as a voice barked in her ear, "Report!"

Dex. She stepped away from the crowd and murmured, "It was a crash. Another skater ran into Anya and knocked her down. She doesn't appear to be seriously injured."

"Jesus, Torres! You just sent the entire ops center onto high alert because two people bumped into each other?"

She snapped defensively, "It was a little more serious than that. They were both going about thirty miles per hour. It knocked her unconscious."

"Are we clear to stand down?" Dex growled back at her.

She gave one of the required responses to that query. "All clear."

"Get your girl under cover and get your butt back here. Now."

"Yes, sir." Crap. She was about to get chewed up one side and down the other.

Anya waited in a dressing room for the American team doctor. The other Medusas came in a few minutes later. They were walking calmly, but Isabella noticed they were all out of breath. It took a lot to make them pant. They must have sprinted the mile from the ops center. Could this mess get any more humiliating?

"Everything all right?" Vanessa murmured.

"Yeah. False alarm," Isabella answered heavily. "Another skater collided with Anya. She got the wind knocked out of her and sprained her knee. Nothing serious."

Her teammates sagged in relief. Vanessa commented, "The way Dex alerted us, it sounded like a full-out assault was under way."

Great. Not only was Dex going to ream her out, but she was going to catch endless grief about this from everyone she'd panicked in the ops center.

Vanessa put a comforting hand on her shoulder. "Better safe than sorry."

Except Dex sure as hell didn't look like he shared that sentiment when she walked into the ops center an hour later. At least the doctor had agreed that Anya's knee would be fine in a few days. The girl was back in her room with her leg propped up and ice on her knee. Aleesha—a trauma surgeon before she'd joined the Medusas—was babysitting Anya while Karen and Kat pulled guard duty.

Dex looked up from across the ops center and growled at Isabella, "In my office."

Vanessa murmured, "Need me to come along and run interference?"

"Nah. But thanks for the offer. I'll take the ass-chewing alone."

Vanessa looked her in the eye. "You did nothing wrong. Your subject went down and was injured. Next time, you call it the same way you just did, regardless of what Lord Dexter the Fourth has to say."

Isabella smiled at the vote of confidence from her team leader. It took a little of the sting out of what was to come.

"Close the door."

Her heart sank. Oh, this was gonna hurt. But at least he had the decency to do it behind closed doors.

Thorpe sat at his desk with his chair turned to face a computer monitor on the table behind him. "Come watch this," he ordered briskly.

She moved—gingerly—to stand beside him. She had to lean down to see the picture clearly. And she just about fell over as she caught a whiff of the guy's aftershave. It was smooth and sophisticated. Sexy as hell, actually. She blinked and focused on the video.

She saw herself standing at the edge of the figure skating rink, watching somebody off camera move.

"That's the figure skating venue this morning," she said in surprise.

"This is the footage from camera 14. Keep watching."

She leaned down further, placing her hands on the table to support herself. She relaxed her eye muscles as she'd been taught in live image analysis school, allowing the scene to flow past her while she absorbed every detail and nuance. About half the ice surface was visible from this angle. Anya flashed across the screen, gliding backward, her left foot raised behind her, preparatory to performing a jump. Her head was centered on her shoulders, chin up, looking straight ahead—hadn't Liz Cartwright yelled something to her about that? Anya had no way of knowing what was behind her. She was skating blind.

A black shape flashed into view from the other side of the screen.

The skater who'd slammed into Anya. He flew around the corner, knees deeply bent and leaning forward, doing powerful crossovers and picking up speed with every stroke of his blades. He cut diagonally across the ice and, in a fraction of a second, his image and Anya's converged into a tremendous impact that sent both of them flying.

Dex hit the pause button and the image of Anya lying crumpled froze on his screen. "What did you see?" he asked shortly.

Something about that scene bugged her. One of the reasons she was the best image analyst in the business was because she listened to the little niggles in her gut. But what was wrong? If only she knew more about figure skating she'd have a better idea of what she was looking at. She replayed the scene in her head, letting the misplaced elements float to the surface of her awareness. And then it hit her. The male skater had been moving forward the whole time. He'd had plenty of opportunity to avoid Anya. *And he hadn't.*

"Who hit her?" Isabella asked urgently. "Who was that skater?"

Dex leaned back in his chair. "You saw it, too, then."

She looked down at Thorpe. "Oh, yeah. That was intentional."

"The kid's name is Lazlo Petrovich. He's a male singles skater from Chechnya."

Chechnya? As in mostly conservative *Muslim* Chechnya? Dismay slammed into her. She should've researched the athletes expected to be at the games. *Sloppy.*

Thorpe rocked forward and reached past her for a file. Her heart hitched as his arm went around her, missing her by inches. *Stop it already.* She was so not about to develop a crush on this jerk.

"I pulled his background folder from the IOC for you."

The International Olympic Committee's background check would be cursory at best compared to what the FBI could dig up on a person. But it was better than nothing. Isabella reached for the brown folder. And damned if her fingers didn't brush against Thorpe's. Her gaze snapped to his. She looked away hastily. Dammit, that was an immature thing to do! She wasn't going to shy away from her reaction to him like some ditzy teenager. She forced her gaze back to him.

He nodded at the corner of the room. "Sit down over there and read it, and then I want your take."

"You want me to do it now?"

His mouth tightened into a thin line. "Do you always question orders like this? How the hell have you survived on a team?"

The rebuke stung. Vanessa or Lt. Col. Jack Scatalone, who supervised the Medusas' missions, could yank her off the team any time they chose, and neither one had done it yet.

"And about your actions this morning," he added grimly. "If you ever screw up like that again, I'll bounce you out of here so fast your head will spin."

She frowned. "With all due respect, my subject *was* down. I made a legitimate call. I'm sorry if I worried everyone unnecessarily."

Thorpe waved an impatient hand. "I don't give a damn about the false alarm. That was a good call."

Huh? Then what?

He spun to face the computer screen and thumped his finger on the glass. "You took your eye off the subject. When the collision happened, you were talking on the radio and had your eyes closed for several seconds. Don't ever lose focus like that on the job again, you hear? If this Petrovich kid had been trying to kill your girl instead of just ramming into her, she'd be dead right now."

He was right. It was a sobering realization. She absorbed the kicked-in-the-stomach feeling and nodded slowly. "Fair enough. You're right. I did screw up. I won't do it again."

He blinked in surprise. As he continued to stare at her in what for all the world looked like mild shock, she finally snapped, "What?"

"That's it? No explanations?" he asked incredulously.

Did he honestly expect her to try to wiggle out of what she'd done wrong? "What else is there to say? I did lose focus. And you were right to slam me for it." No matter that she'd lost focus because *he'd* been exasperating her half to death. And no matter that without a gun, she couldn't have stopped Petrovich from killing Anya if that had been his intent. "Lesson learned and I'll do better next time."

"Well, I'll be damned," he muttered.

That reaction was what finally pushed her over the edge. "Whether you like it or not, Major Thorpe, the Medusas aren't going away. Not from your Olympic security detail, and not from your armed forces. Get used to us."

He leaned forward, a violently displeased scowl on his face. "Women don't belong in this business. You get in the way of men paying attention to their job."

"Why?" she shot back. "Because they can't get past their Neanderthal urges to protect the little woman, or because they can't control their Neanderthal urges to throw us down and have their way with us?"

His eyes went nearly black, snapping brightly in irritation. "I don't have to explain myself to you, Captain."

"Nor I to you," she retorted coolly. "Your correction is duly noted and I will do my best to act on it. Now if you don't mind, *sir,* I need to read that file and assess the potential threat to my subject."

Eyes narrowed dangerously, he cracked his stiff neck just enough to nod fractionally at her. She picked up the file, and just to get his goat, moved over to the chair in the corner of his office and sat down to read the file. She could've gone outside into the main ops center, but she'd be damned if she'd give him the satisfaction of chasing her out of his office.

She read through Lazlo Petrovich's file quickly. His parents were both well-known Chechnyan freedom fighters who'd been confirmed participants in several terrorist hits on Russian targets before Chechnya gained independence from a fed-up Russian government last year. Lazlo had been sent to the

United States at the age of ten to take up figure skating. He lived with an American sponsor family, and all of his ice time, coaching, equipment and living expenses were funded out of an anonymous bank account that received periodic deposits.

The IOC employee who'd performed the brief background check had been unable to ascertain where the money came from. But Lazlo's parents didn't appear to earn a fraction of the thousands of dollars per year necessary to support the career of an up-and-coming figure skater.

Isabella frowned. Where did his family get so much money, and why did they fork it over for his training? Supposedly, he'd only skated recreationally before coming to America so how did they know he'd turn into a world-class figure skater? Something didn't add up.

Thorpe sat at his desk, making a note in the margin of a typed document. "Have you seen this?" she asked.

A nod.

"Were his parents skaters?"

"My impression is no," Thorpe replied.

"Were they friends of a skater?"

"No record of it."

She frowned. "Then how in the hell did they up and decide to send their only son halfway around the world to take up such an expensive and difficult sport?"

Thorpe leaned back in his chair. "No idea. Talk to me about Chechnyan Muslims."

Isabella blinked. How would he know she had any expertise on that subject? Very few—*very few*—people knew that her mother was Iranian, raised Shiite, same as many of the Chechnyan rebels.

Finally, she answered. "The Chechnyans practice all the major sects of Islam, although extreme conservatives numerically and politically dominate the landscape. But, like the rest of the Islamic world, there's a spectrum of beliefs even within the fundamentalist elements. Over a billion people from nearly every country and culture in the world are Muslims, and not all of them believe the same things."

"What about the Chechnyan rebels?"

She shrugged. "They tend to come from the Shi'a sect, which holds that the straightest route to paradise is to die a martyr for your faith. The belief led to a certain willingness to engage in extreme forms of protest."

"Like suicide bombings?" Thorpe asked.

"Among other self-destructive and violent acts, yes."

"Like risking injury to yourself to take out a figure skater who flaunts the faith?"

Isabella's gaze slid to the image of the two figure skaters lying on the ice that still flickered on the computer screen. "Absolutely."

He leaned forward, reaching for his intercom. "I think a more thorough background investigation of our boy, Lazlo, is in order here."

For once, they agreed on something.

Abdul connected quickly to the Internet. He typed in a long, memorized domain name and waited while it connected to a closed-circuit surveillance camera giving a live feed to the very private Web address.

The Holt woman sat on the floor, her knees hugged to her chest, the black bag still over her head. She had been surprisingly strong and his nose was still tender from where she'd bashed it. A less patient man would have hurt her for striking him. But she'd been panicked, in the middle of being dragged from her bed. Besides, he didn't bear her any ill will. She was a tool. Simply a means to an end. She was how they would force her husband to cooperate.

And so far, it was working like a charm. Abdul's nephew, Hassan, reported that the ice was being melted and replaced in the Hamilton Arena at this very minute. The first, and most difficult, portion of the plan was almost in place.

He would not—could not—stand idly by and let America insert itself into the internal affairs of his homeland. The way he'd heard it, a secret American military force went into Bhoukar last year and crushed the Bhoukari Army of Holy War and then let the emir of Bhoukar take the credit.

Admittedly, the Army of Holy War was an extremist group that attracted mostly bored and disaffected young men with nothing better to do than cause trouble. They'd lacked a clear vision. And maybe the emir should have eliminated them. But it was an insult to Bhoukar's honor to use infidels to clean house.

The woman on the screen before him reached out with her hands, tentatively feeling her way along the wall at her back. When she reached the doorknob, she froze. Pressed her ear to the panel for several long seconds. He'd told his nephews to speak only Arabic around the prisoner, so she wouldn't understand anything she heard on the other side of that door.

She backed away slowly. Went back to her corner and sat down. Waiting. She was probably thinking hard about dying. About facing her God. A God who had failed her. He took no joy from the woman's terror, but it was necessary.

A commotion behind him made him jump, and his youngest son came flying into the bedroom excitedly, shouting, "Daddy! Daddy! Can I use your computer to play Robo Wars against Amir? He says I can't beat him, but I can."

Abdul reached for the keyboard fast, slapping the escape key. The image of the woman before him disappeared. The screen went bright blue.

His son clambered into his lap. "Can I? Can I?"

He asked indulgently, "What's this Robo War game all about?"

"Here, I'll show you. You can help me. Then I'll beat Amir for sure."

He laughed and let his son explain the finer points of blowing up the bad guys before they got you first.

*   *   *

Lazlo stepped into his room, his body and heart sore. He'd been going at nearly top speed when he'd slammed into Anya Khalid. Her elbow had caught him squarely in the gut, not to mention they'd cracked heads. He'd seen stars afterward. Of course, he'd been the lucky one. By knowing he was going to ram into her, he'd been able to protect himself from the worst of it, to lead with his shoulder and let himself relax into the fall.

Up until now, he'd had a good reputation in the skating community. He wasn't vicious or self-centered. Wasn't. Past tense. That had all changed this morning. He'd thrown away his good reputation in a single act of cowardice.

He'd seen the way the other skaters had looked at him after the crash. *They knew.* That lady security guard with Anya hadn't figured it out, but the rest of them had silently condemned him. They'd turned their backs on him and huddled tightly around Anya. No one had even looked at him as he'd limped off the ice.

He dumped his bag and turned on the TV to numb his mind. The flickering glow filled his darkened room, and he jolted violently when a male shape rose from the chair in the corner. *What the hell?* His heart leaped into his throat until he realized who it was. Then he flopped down on the edge of his bed, his knees weak from the scare.

"What do you want, Ilya?" Lazlo asked tiredly. "I did what you wanted."

"Have you knocked her out of the competition?"

"An American doctor had to look at her knee. Her qualifying competition is in five days. If she feels half as lousy as I do, she won't be ready to skate by then."

"Let us hope for your family's sake that you succeeded."

Lazlo's anger flared up, and he rose off the bed. "Listen, you piece of shit. You leave my family out of this. I did what you told me to. There's no need to threaten them, and I'm getting damn sick and tired of you holding them over my head."

He saw a shadow of a shrug. "I don't care what you think. I made you what you are, and I can unmake you just as easily."

Lazlo spluttered, "Like hell—"

Ilya cut him off. "You are a tool. A weapon. And I am the hand who wields you. The sword does not tell its master where to swing."

"I don't give a damn for your platitudes."

Another shrug. "Someday you will. The only question that remains is whether or not it will come too late for your parents and your sisters."

Lazlo watched, his fists clenched in impotent fury, as Ilya moved silently to the door. The dark-haired man paused only long enough to murmur, "We will speak again."

And then he was gone.

Chapter 4

The Olympic Torch Stadium loomed in the night, orchestral music and blue light from the opening ceremonies emanated from it. It took something extraordinary nowadays to make Isabella nervous. This did it. She tugged at her borrowed official sheepskin jacket. She'd been assigned to walk in front of Anya and her coach in the parade of nations, carrying the sign that said Emirate of Bhoukar. Dex had decided only this morning to put her on the field, too late for her to attend the rehearsals. An IOC coordinator had talked her through a diagram of the parade and given her a single, succinct instruction. "Don't screw it up."

No pressure there. Billions of people would be watching her on TVs around the world.

As for Anya, she squirmed in the bulletproof vest Isabella had insisted she wear under her green and gold ski ensemble. "It makes me look fat," Anya complained.

Isabella laughed. "I could inflate your jacket like a beach

ball and you'd still look elegant. You're a stunning representative of your country."

Anya glanced at the flag propped against her side. "I'm scared, 'Bella."

Isabella blinked, rocked by the lilting Arabic pronunciation of the nickname. That was exactly how her grandmother used to say it. She mumbled, "I won't let anything bad happen to you. And if you're scared of messing up in the parade, don't be. All you have to do is follow me and I'll go down in history as the numbskull who wrecked the opening ceremony."

Anya laughed.

"We'll get through this together, eh?"

A trumpet, marking the beginning of the parade of nations, sounded inside the stadium. They waited while the *A* nations marched in, and then an IOC official carrying a radio waved at them.

Isabella murmured into the microphone concealed in the fleece of her collar, "We're entering the tunnel. Do I have a go?"

Dex's voice crackled in her ear. "Roger….are a go." He added dryly as they neared the stadium exit and her reception cleared up, "Don't forget to smile for the cameras."

He just *had* to remind her of all those people who'd be watching. Jerk.

When Isabella and Anya stepped out of the tunnel into the giant stadium, the kaleidoscope of colors was almost blinding. How was she supposed to protect Anya amidst all of this? She felt naked before the scale of the stadium, the sheer numbers of spectators. Please don't let anyone take a shot at Anya. Please don't let…

The plea repeated itself in her head. They reached the oval path around which they'd promenade before taking their place on the infield.

"Right! Go right!" Anya whispered behind her.

Crap. She'd been veering left. She corrected course, the Bhoukar sign above her head dipping. She caught sight of the last athletes from the delegation in front of her, and sped up to draw nearer to them. They'd act as a partial shield against shots from in front of Anya.

Then Isabella became aware of a new sound. Cheering. A wave of voices shouting and whistling as Anya passed in front of the crowd. Isabella strained to hear jeers or catcalls buried within the noise, but all she heard were cries of approval.

Pride in Anya's courage and grit surged in Isabella's breast. The girl might be clueless as to her true significance on the world's political stage, but she was back there walking on a sore and taped up knee. She was carrying the flag of a nation that historically treated women as little more than chattel and certainly had never before let them compete in an Olympics. And she represented the hopes and dreams of young girls all over the world who were still caught behind the veil.

Okay, the commando in charge of keeping Anya alive was *not* going to get all choked up here, dammit. But it was still as cool as hell to be with Anya for this moment.

The rest of the long walk around the stadium passed in a blur until they were guided to their spot on the infield. Decorative inflatable tubes disguised large blowers that sent warm air over the athletes as they waited out the rest of the parade in the night's frigid cold. The Olympic oaths were recited, the Olympic torch lit—which was also incredibly cool to witness in person—the Games declared open, and then the opening ceremonies adjourned. A formless mob of athletes made their way toward the exits, already partying among themselves. Isabella grabbed Anya's arm to ensure the two of them didn't get separated. There was only the slightest chance of any harm coming to Anya, surrounded as she was.

When they got back to the village, Aleesha was on hand to have a look at Anya's knee. She gave the girl two approved anti-inflammatory pills, iced the joint and rewrapped it. Aleesha was packing up her bag to leave when a quiet knock sounded on the door. Not a signal from one of the Medusas or the other security people.

Aleesha dropped her bag and glided fast to stand behind the door. Isabella moved just as quickly. "Who's there?" she called through the panel.

A male voice said hesitantly, "My name is Lazlo Petrovich. I'm a skater."

Isabella's eyebrows shot up. Aleesha's face registered surprise as well. This was the kid who'd slammed into Anya. What did *he* want? Isabella cracked open the door. "Ms. Khalid is resting—"

"Let him in!"

Isabella made a slashing gesture across her neck. She did *not* want the young man who'd intentionally hit Anya in her room!

"I mean it," Anya threatened. "I'm not your prisoner and you can't tell me what to do. I want to see him."

Isabella scowled. Indeed, she didn't have the power to dictate Anya's movements. But how had the girl figured that out? Reluctantly, Isabella stepped back from the door, opening it far enough to admit the Chechnyan skater. After a quick glance into the hall to make sure he was alone, she shut and locked the door behind him and Mamba, who followed—or more like *stalked*—the young man into the room. She stopped behind him in such a way that she could jump forward and break his neck in under a second.

Isabella pushed a chair forward and gestured for the young man to sit. He sat.

"I'm here to apologize for running into you," Lazlo said earnestly. "I feel terrible about it. I wanted to make sure you're okay."

Isabella frowned. His body language was sincere. And his vocal vibrations made him sound like he was telling the truth. But the image of him picking up speed as he rounded that corner and aimed for Anya was still fresh in her mind.

Anya smiled up brilliantly at the kid. Aww, crap. That was

a crush glistening in her eyes. Isabella looked back at Lazlo.
He was good-looking in an intense, artistic way.

Aleesha glanced over at her and murmured, "I've got an
OSG staff meeting. Do you have this under control?"

Isabella nodded and her teammate departed.

She watched carefully as the young people traded basic information, where they lived and trained, who their coaches and
mutual skating acquaintances were, favorite movies, bands
and food. It would have been sweet if she hadn't been hovering
on the balls of her feet waiting for Lazlo to attack Anya.

But as the two continued to talk she relaxed slightly. The
boy honestly seemed to feel bad about Anya's sore knee and
apologized for it approximately every two minutes. Not that
it was her job to listen to their conversation, of course. She
was only eavesdropping so she could listen for a threat to her
charge. She let their conversation pass by her while she kept
an alert eye on Lazlo's movements and body language. Gradually, the two young people began to ignore her. Their conversation waxed more intimate as they talked about their
hopes and fears regarding competing in the Games.

Slowly, something profoundly disturbing dawned on
Isabella. Anya and Lazlo—both products of Muslim cultures—
had fallen into the rhythm of treating her like a traditional
Muslim chaperone. *And so had she.* She couldn't count how
many times she'd watched older, married women sit quietly in
the corners of rooms while young lovers whispered together.
Now she was that silent, watchful grandmother or aunt.

No matter how far she ran from her roots, they always
managed to reach out and ensnare her. She was missing only
the black robes and veils of her Iranian heritage as she guarded
Anya's virtue in the centuries-old fashion. Unbelievable. She
was a highly trained Special Forces operator, but she might
as well be in the parlor above her grandfather's tobacco shop
in Tehran. How in the hell had this happened?

Her mind snapped back to the situation at hand as Lazlo

pushed to his feet with a quiet admonition to Anya to get some rest and let him know if there was anything—anything at all—he could do for her. The two skaters shared a long, sappy look before he turned to go. *Egads. Puppy love all the way.*

Isabella escorted Lazlo to the door and let him out, then turned to Anya. Darned if the girl didn't continue as if Isabella was her auntie chaperone. "What did you think of him? Doesn't he have the most gorgeous eyes? And that smile…"

"Honey," Isabella said gently. "Be careful, okay? You will be here for two weeks, and then you'll both go home and be halfway around the world from each other. Enjoy the moment, but keep your wits about you." How was she supposed to explain to an innocent young girl what it felt like to lose a love? Or to make choices that cost you traditional men who couldn't understand why you'd do something insane like skate at the Olympics or join the Air Force.

Anya huffed. "This is my one chance to do exactly as I please. As much as I love my family, they can be a little…suffocating. You wouldn't understand."

Isabella laughed ruefully. "Trust me, Anya. I do understand. Completely."

"How's that?"

She shrugged off the girl's question. "It doesn't matter. Lazlo was right. Get some rest. You have a couple of big weeks in front of you."

Isabella reached for the light switch, and just before the room plunged into darkness, she caught the dreamy smile on Anya's face. The girl said, "They *are* going to be big weeks, aren't they?"

Crap. If Anya and Lazlo saw themselves as star-crossed lovers torn apart by the big, bad bodyguard, they could make Isabella's job a living hell. *Romeo and Juliet both ended up dead, dammit!* Lazlo had tried to harm Anya. And the girl now fancied herself madly in love with him. Well, wasn't this just shaping up to be a fun Olympics?

* * *

When Isabella reported to the ops center the next morning, one of the men from Dex's team called out from across the room, "Mail for you, Torres."

She fetched the overnight envelope, tore it open and was pleased to see the FBI's preliminary background check on Harlan Holt. She settled into a free chair and browsed through the document. Holt's career as a research chemist was distinguished and thoroughly documented. Not a hint of subversive or extremist leanings showed up in the guy's past. He was as clean as the driven snow.

The guy's wife, Emma, wasn't far behind. The pair had led quiet lives of scientific research and college professorship until Harlan applied a technology used by firefighters to ice-skating. Friction-reducing polymers were added to the water passing through fire hoses to increase its velocity and hence the volume of water that could be delivered to a fire. Holt added similar polymers to water to make the surface of ice smoother and lower in friction. In addition, he'd figured out how to add in chemicals that changed the molecular structure of the ice crystals, aligning them so the ice actually had a small amount of resiliency—or spring—to it. Skaters could glide faster and farther and jump higher. It was no wonder that Holt's invention had rapidly earned the name "super ice."

But even with this information, the background check was a dead end. She'd gotten *such* a strong vibe when he'd argued that the ice must be relaid, but the file said her hunch was wrong.

"Whatchya looking at?" a voice said above her head.

She looked up. Dex. "The Holt file."

"Find anything?"

"Yeah. Absolutely nothing. The guy's too clean to be real if you ask me."

Dex shook his head. "You rely too much on your gut feelings. If the facts say the guy's clean, then he probably is."

"You didn't see the way he insisted on laying a new ice surface. He was panicked. I still think something's wrong with him."

Thorpe exhaled sharply. "Look. The IOC's not amused by the waves you ladies are making. You've got to back off for a while. Lay low." As her brows drew together, he added, "Just until the flap over Anya dies down some."

"They'll get over it," she snapped.

He shrugged. "Part of my job is to keep the peace between the military side of the house and the IOC. This is their show. We're just here to supplement the Olympic Security Group."

"You and I both know that's not true," she retorted. "The most highly trained counter-terrorist teams in the world are sitting in this room, not across the hall at the IOC. We're the experts, here."

"Be that as it may, we're still under orders to make nice. And I need you to back off of Holt. He's the skating world's *wunderkind* right now, and we're not going to make any friends by poking around and destroying his reputation."

"But—"

"No buts. Back off."

She huffed, irritated. She understood his dilemma. Jack Scatalone griped about getting caught in the middle of politics, too. But she didn't have to like it. She closed the Holt folder and stood up. "I'm off duty, now. I'm gonna go catch some *z*'s."

"Sweet dreams," Thorpe murmured as she brushed past him.

Was he being sarcastic? Better to assume that he was because the alternative made her stomach flutter uncomfortably. She stepped outside into the gray morning. Temperatures had warmed up overnight to a balmy fifteen degrees Fahrenheit, and more snow was in the forecast. The folks in charge of the downhill skiing events were hoping for a little fresh snow, but too much would give them problems getting the courses groomed in time. Nothing like having to rely on the vagaries of Mother Nature. It was almost as much fun as juggling the vagaries of politics and a young girl's heart.

It felt good to stretch her legs, to breathe in the cold, bracing air. Without thinking about where she was going, she found herself standing in front of the giant Olympic Ice facility. What the hell. She was off duty. And she smelled a rat in Harlan Holt's perfect past.

Isabella's vinyl pouch of credentials, complete with photograph, fingerprint, bar code and hologram, was examined at the rink entrance. Then she was asked to produce the proper bracelet—a hospital-style plastic affair—that granted her access to this venue. Once inside, she had to produce her color-coded bracelet again, this time for access to the field of play or, in other words, down by the ice itself. It took a third stripe of color in her bracelet to let her into the women's locker rooms, but it so happened she had that access as well. One of the perks of being Olympic security.

As it turned out, she didn't have to go any farther than the end of the ice skating rink to find Harlan Holt, who was giving instructions to a burly, black-haired Zamboni driver. The Zamboni rumbled into gear and took off across the ice, laying down a film of spray that glistened wetly.

She'd had a look at one of the giant, propane-propelled, ice resurfacers the day before. They used a two-part process. In front was a long razor blade that shaved off the surface of the ice. A turning screw behind the blade lifted the shavings into the belly of the machine. Then, at the back of the machine, a row of sprayers laid down a mist of heated water to replace the lost ice. It took between two and three hundred gallons of water to resurface a single skating rink. Today, the Zamboni's blade was lifted well above the ice, and only the sprayer function was in use.

Isabella strolled up to Holt. "How's the new ice coming?" she asked casually.

He looked over at her in subtle alarm. "Uh, fine. It's nearly an inch thick."

"Is that good?" she asked.

The scientist in him overrode his caution. "Super ice needs to be thicker than normal ice to maximize its spring. We'll keep laying on layers of water until the ice is around two inches thick."

"Two inches? That's all?" she asked in surprise. "I guess I thought of ice-skating rinks as being like ponds."

He looked down his long nose at her scornfully. "Not at all. The sheets of ice lie on a sand or concrete base and only have to be thick enough not to break or develop holes."

Keep the guy talking. Loosen him up a little and see where he takes the conversation. Maybe at some point she could shift gears and shock him into an honest answer. "How do they get the lines for hockey games and the logos under the ice, then?"

"After about a quarter inch of ice is laid, they paint the lines, circles, or logos right onto the ice. It's a special lacquer that never actually dries. It's designed not to run after it's encased in ice. Once it's painted on, more ice is laid on top of it."

"Does the Zamboni lay down all of the water for the ice?"

"Good Lord, no. Men walked around the rink all night last night with backpack sprayers, putting down a fine mist of water. It usually takes several days to do that, but a double crew did it in under twenty-four hours."

His shoulders were coming down and his facial muscles were relaxing. Almost ready for her to pull an abrupt change of subject and see what popped out. Just another question or two. "How does the ice freeze?"

"Refrigeration coils run through the concrete base, of course. Those are chilled, and then a fine layer of water is sprayed on that freezes almost immediately. Once it's good and cold, another layer of mist is sprayed on the ice. The initial layer is the hardest to put down. Once a substantial sheet has formed, say, an inch thick, then we can start running over it with an ice resurfacer, like that Zamboni, and spray on more and more thin layers."

This guy was clearly proud of his super ice. That would be the best opening hook. Trying her best to sound impressed, she asked, "Do the additives in your ice make the process harder?"

"On the contrary. The polymers in the water allow it to flow more freely and create an extremely even surface."

Bingo. She swooped in the for the kill. "Then why was it so urgent that you resurface this ice before the skating competition?"

He froze. As still and cold as the ice behind him. She'd bet her next paycheck that was pure, unadulterated terror shining in his feverish eyes. What the hell was going on? Time for another shocking shift. It didn't matter what she asked, she just had to keep him off balance. Randomly she challenged, "Where's your wife today, Dr. Holt? I'd love to meet her. I understand she's a brilliant scientist in her own right."

Way too fast, Holt snapped, "Her work has nothing to do with mine. I'm a chemist and she's a microbiologist. Besides, her work keeps her very busy. Too busy to talk to you, I'm sure."

Didn't want her talking to his wife, did he? Then it had just become imperative that she do exactly that. Funny how the occasional shot in the dark struck home.

She'd gotten enough out of Holt for now. Time to go. But then an angry voice rang out behind her. "What the hell are you doing here?"

Oh shit. Dex.

Chapter 5

Thorpe grabbed her by the arm and dragged her away from the irate scientist. They were outside the building before he snarled, "I told you to stay away from him!"

"Oh, look. There's a coffee shop across the street," she said with artificial brightness. "I could use a cup." Without waiting for his response, she took off, walking briskly. If she could get him into a crowded, public place, maybe he'd be forced to shut up and listen to her before he passed judgment.

Scowling, he caught up to her as she stepped into the coffee bar. He was silent as she ordered. She stepped away from the counter and headed for a booth. He could get his own damn coffee if he wanted some.

She slid into the seat and watched him make his way toward her. The guy moved like a warrior, full of tightly controlled power, as fit as a god, confident in his ability to use his body. She'd never slept with one of the men she now worked with, but she expected they'd be impressive in the sack. That is, if they didn't get so caught up in their own egos that they were totally self-centered.

Dex slid into the booth across from her. "What are you thinking about?"

Her eyes narrowed. "I was coming to the conclusion that you'd be too selfish a lover to be any good in the sack."

He gaped in shock, and then the insult to his prowess sunk in and slammed his eyebrows together. "Don't be so bloody honest the next time I ask."

In her experience, men who didn't feel a need to defend themselves as lovers were the good ones. Hmm. Interesting. He took a sip of his coffee, keeping his hand wrapped securely around the porcelain mug. Guarding it from any impromptu additives from her, was he? A smile tickled the corners of her mouth.

"What were you doing talking to Holt?" he asked tersely.

She matched his tone, but kept her voice low so they wouldn't be overheard. "I was doing my job. I'm supposed to protect Anya by whatever means necessary."

"You were disobeying orders."

"I was protecting you from political fallout by giving you plausible deniability if Holt complains. You can say I acted alone, and I'll take the fall, not you."

"You were protecting me?" His voice vibrated with disbelief. "Bull. You're just out to show me how shit-hot you are."

She paused, considering his accusation. There was a certain truth to it. He did rub her the wrong way, and she'd love to shove the Medusas' effectiveness back in his face. She leaned forward. "You know, I would enjoy rubbing your nose in how good we are. But I'm not about to sacrifice Anya's safety to convert a male chauvinist pig like you."

He leaned back sharply, scowling. "Do you hate all men, or just me?"

She shrugged. "I don't hate you. But neither do I need you interfering with my ability to protect Anya."

"Tell me about the Medusas."

Okay, it was her turn to be startled by the abrupt turn of the conversation. "That's classified. Need to know."

"All the Delta team leaders were briefed on your existence."

No kidding? "We were formed last year as a test project to train women as special operators. The idea was to set up a bunch of women to fail so the issue of women in the Special Forces could be closed once and for all. Problem was, we didn't fail. General Wittenauer tried to disband us anyway, of course. But before he could do that, our trainer went missing—"

"Scatalone from Delta 3, right?" he interjected.

"Right. We volunteered to go get him."

"I heard about that mission. You ran into a few terrorists, didn't you?"

She snorted. "That's an understatement. But more to the point, we succeeded. After that, Wittenauer went to bat for us, and we were funded. We've been training like maniacs and picking up the occasional mission ever since."

"A year's not long in this business."

He was referring to the fact that it typically took several years to completely train a Special Forces soldier. Like him. She shrugged. "You're right. We don't claim to be up to full speed. But we're still useful for some things."

"Like babysitting young Muslim girls in sensitive public situations."

Like single-handedly rescuing fifteen hundred people from a hijacked cruise ship, on their last mission. "We're good for a little more than that," she replied dryly.

"That remains to be seen."

She laughed, not offended. "Let's hope we don't have to show you what we're made of while we're here. I'd just as soon have you continue in ignorance of who and what we really are." Except he was looking at her with intensity, not polite disinterest. It couldn't be the look of a man interested in a woman romantically; it was more like she just confounded the living hell out of him.

Time for an impertinent question of her own. "So how'd you get stuck with a boring handle like Dex? Why not something more…colorful?"

His eyes glinted. "If Dex isn't to your taste, my middle name's Godfrey. You can call me God if you like."

She laughed in spite of herself. Who'd have guessed beneath that dry-as-a-desert exterior lurked a sense of humor?

"I've got to get back to the bunker," he said. "Where are you headed now?"

Her lips twitched. "Don't ask and I won't tell."

He leaned forward. "Let's get something straight while we're having this little heart-to-heart. I don't like your methods, Torres, and I don't like your attitude. I especially don't like the fact that you don't follow orders. In our line of work, mavericks are dangerous, not only to themselves but to their entire team. However," he sighed heavily as if he didn't like what came next, "I was standing behind you when you brought up Holt's wife and he went nuts. I can't believe I'm saying this, but I smell a rat, too. I want you to look into it. But for God's sake, keep your head down."

She blinked, surprised at his reversal on Holt. "You've got it," she replied. "And while we're sharing true confessions, I *will* do my best to cover your six as long as I'm working for you."

A crisp nod, then he stood up, spun on his heel, and walked out of the coffee shop while she checked out the "six" in question. Oh, yes. Buns of steel. Very nice. He exited the shop without looking back and seemed to take some of the light out of the room with him. Slowly, she slid out of the booth and followed. Time to call Emma Holt and find out why her dear husband was being so damned protective.

By the time she reached the street, Dex was long gone. Too bad. It might've been fun to tail him and to see if he spotted her. Speaking of which, she ought to keep a sharp eye out to make sure he didn't do the very same thing to her.

As she headed for the complex of buildings that comprised the administrative heart of the Olympics, she ducked into a random alleyway to make sure he wasn't behind her. She moved quickly into the narrow street's dim depths, and heard footsteps behind her. He *had* followed her! She spun around to face him—and stopped short.

Three silhouetted figures were approaching her, shoulder to shoulder across the alley. And all three of them held out their hands preparatory to attacking.

Her first reaction was disappointment that they weren't Dex. Her second reaction was irritation that she had to deal with this now. Her mindset had definitely changed radically over the past year. Before she'd become a Medusa, she'd have been scared silly at finding herself in a dark alley with three hostiles. But no more.

She squinted, trying to make out more details. Were these simple muggers about to get the shock of their lives, or were these guys more sinister? Trained fighters perhaps? Their stances weren't giving away enough to tell. She'd go into it assuming the worst.

"Can I help you?" she called loudly. Maybe she'd get lucky and draw a passerby's attention.

One of them called her a foul name in Arabic.

Arabic? *Oh, shit.* The threat value of this situation had just gone up. A lot. And she wasn't armed, either. She hit her microphone button and muttered, "I'm being mugged in an alley just south of School Street."

She slid to her left and turned, placing a wall at her back. She needed to keep them in front of her. Much more calmly than she felt, she said, "Gentlemen, I'm required by law to warn you that my hands and feet are considered lethal weapons. If in the course of defending myself, I happen to harm you—badly— the law does allow for that. Do you understand my warning?"

The thugs laughed. She'd take that as a yes.

The trio lunged. She picked out the most aggressive-looking one and spun, unleashing a vicious kick at his knees while she flailed her fists at the second man. The third guy got in a good body blow to her ribs, but she yanked back her arm and clocked him in the nose with her elbow. He staggered, out for the moment. The first one took a swing at her and she dodged the blow, burying her fist in the softness of Number Two's groin. Not a full-force contact, but enough to make him jump away in caution.

"Bitch," the guy snarled.

She raked her fingernails across Number One's face and felt blood on her hand. He cried out. What a baby. He had no idea what real pain was. Number Three dived back into the fray. He and Number Two made a grab for her arms. She twisted violently, letting the movement flow into fists that landed on Number One's face. Her right arm broke free. She lashed out with her right foot, using the guy's grip on her left arm for additional balance. Pain in her toes exploded as her shoe connected hard with somebody's shin.

She heard shouting and realized it was her own voice, screaming in fury. She rode the wave, charging Number Two and head-butting him in the chin. Oww! That felt like she'd just been hit over the head with a hammer. But Number Two staggered back, looking stunned and disoriented. A hard fist connected with the side of her head, knocking her off balance. She fought to keep her feet. She mustn't go down! Once she did, they'd start kicking her and then she'd be in serious trouble. Feet could kill a person. Fast. She found her balance and lashed out again, aiming for knees, groins, and bellies.

A few of the thugs' blows got through her defenses. Something connected with her left cheek, and it felt like her lip was split. But the adrenaline ripping through her ignored all pain and bodily damage. These bastards thought she was weak, vulnerable, because she was a woman. Because she was alone and unchaperoned, they'd taken advantage of her. A lifetime's worth of rage cut loose from somewhere deep within her, and she let it flow outward to the very tips of her fingers.

Somewhere in the flurry of kicks and punches she delivered, her attackers began to think better of this little project. Two of them backed off, and the third threw one last pair of punches— easily blocked—before snarling in Arabic, "Tell the girl to forget skating and get herself behind the veil before this happens to her."

The third guy turned to follow his comrades, who'd already taken off running down the alley. Oh, no. They didn't get to jump her, beat her up, and then get away. She made a running leap and dived for his feet. She grunted as one of his heels rammed into her chest. She hung on for all she was worth as the guy struggled furiously to free himself.

She scrambled to her knees and leaped on top of him, landing on his back with her full body weight. "Not so fast," she panted. "I've got a few questions for you."

"Go to hell," the guy snarled in heavily accented English.

"You're gonna wish you were there by the time I'm done with you, buster." She grabbed his wrist and wrenched it up and back. He fought beneath her, but he couldn't do much with his arm jacked up behind him. She shouted for help at the top of her lungs and footsteps pounded into the alley.

"What the hell have you done now?" Dex asked from above her.

"Well, three guys decided to deliver a message and rough me up a little. Thought I might keep one as a souvenir and see how well he sings," she replied lightly.

Dex put a casual foot on the guy's neck and, surprisingly gently, he helped Isabella to her feet. Assorted aches and pains hinted at the discomfort to come later.

To the guy on the ground, Dex said, in a voice that promised worlds of pain, "You messed with one of my troops, buddy. And that means you messed with me."

"I don't know how good his English is. He used Arabic with me."

She blinked in surprise as Dex repeated his threat in flawless Arabic. To her he said, "OSG's on the way."

She noted that he hadn't brought the IOC security team with him. Yup, this business should stay on the military side of the house. A dark blue minivan pulled up at the mouth of the alley and four men moved out quickly in a standard threat formation. Dex's Delta team.

Even her blood ran cold when Dex stared intently at the now handcuffed man and, "You got a name, son?"

The kid glared defiantly at Dex.

Probably a mistake. She'd been on the receiving end of a trained Delta Force interrogator in her prisoner-of-war training, and the mugger's life was about to be really, really unpleasant.

"You okay, Adder?" Dex asked as the kid was hustled toward the van.

She nodded. "Yeah. I need to wash out a few minor dings and then I'll be fine."

"Gentlemen," Dex called after his men, "squeeze him dry. I want to know everything about this guy and his friends."

The Delta team nodded grimly and dragged their prisoner into the van. She followed the men back toward the street, and without comment, Dex walked beside her.

More cars pulled up, some of them the white vans of the IOC Security team. But his men were already driving away with their prisoner. Dex managed to snag a set of keys and stuff her into a car before Manfred Schmidt himself was barely out of his vehicle. Dex ignored the shouts from his boss, pretending not to hear him as he pulled into traffic.

She asked cautiously, "Isn't this technically fleeing the scene of a crime?"

"You can make a report later if you want. The way I see it, we're still involved in a clean-up operation."

Dex turned into the security staff housing complex. It would become an apartment complex after the Games. She pointed out her building and was surprised when Dex passed it up. He activated the automatic door locks as he got out of the car, effectively trapping her inside or forcing her to set off the car alarm to open her door. Then he stunned her speechless by coming around and opening her door for her.

She stepped out and paused to look up at him. "While I appreciate the chivalry, I'm fully capable of opening my own doors."

"I know you are. So shut up and deal with the chivalry."

Well, okay then! Amused, she followed him in silence to a second-floor apartment. The place was furnished nearly identically to hers, except there was a subtle difference to the atmosphere, an infusion of masculine essence. It smelled like a combination of his sexy cologne, lemon oil—the place was spotless—and grilled steak. Last night's supper, no doubt. The scents blended well.

"I'll be back," he said over his shoulder as he disappeared into the bedroom. He returned carrying the distinctive, bulky backpack of a field medicine kit, better known as a crash kit. You could do everything from splint a leg to deliver a baby out of that bag.

"Hey!" she protested. "I've only got a couple scrapes."

"In the kitchen," he ordered, ignoring her.

She rolled her eyes. *Macho jerk,* she thought without any real heat. She let him swab her facial injuries with disinfectant and managed not to suck in her breath when alcohol hit the wounds. He smeared antibiotic cream onto her cheek then stepped back to survey his work.

"You'll live," he announced.

She had to give him credit. He'd done that as efficiently as she could've. Although, she didn't have a crash kit stowed in her closet. Clearly her preparedness and paranoia still needed work.

Speaking of which, she said aloud, "It would've been nice in that alley if I had been armed. How do I get permission to carry something? I don't necessarily need a gun, although that would be nice. A switchblade or an ankle knife would do."

He sighed. "I've argued and argued that one and I get shot down every time I bring it up. The IOC is totally opposed to the United States using force of any kind to secure the Games."

"That's ridiculous!" she exclaimed. "How are we supposed to keep terrorists from having a field day if we can't fight back?"

He picked up her hand to clean her raw knuckles. "Looks like you did a decent job of fighting back today."

"Colonel Scatalone is hard-core when it comes to unarmed combat. He thinks it's one of the Medusas' greatest assets. People don't expect girls to whup up on them. They underestimate us."

"Did the guys in the alley make that mistake?"

She smiled and her lip stung painfully. She winced and smiled smaller. "They don't know what hit them."

"I've got some lip balm in the other room. Lemme get it."

She followed Dex from the kitchen but stopped in the doorway of his bedroom. The male aura in the room was too overwhelming. She took the little pot of lip balm and backed into the relative safety of the living room.

"I'm going to need a written statement about what happened in the alley. That way I can keep your guy in custody for more than forty-eight hours. Oh, and there's a staff meeting at four o'clock this afternoon. You're on the agenda."

"Me?"

"Yup. I want to cover possible threats to Anya so the guys on the cameras can keep a better eye out for threats to the two of you."

She nodded, suddenly too tired to argue about needing to be watched over. "I'd like to go back to my place and change. Then I'll come in and write your statement."

"I'll walk you home," he said casually.

Enough was enough with the chivalry bit. "Car doors I can stand. But I *don't* need an escort to get me across the parking lot!"

"Fine. Then I'll follow you."

"You like irritating me, don't you?"

"I do," he answered evenly. "Your eyes are pretty when they sparkle like that."

Whoa. Time to get out of Dodge! She headed for the door, pronto. And, dammit, she was brought up short when his hand got to the doorknob. He opened the door with a flourish. She scowled over her shoulder but didn't deign to comment. She sailed down the stairs as regally as her aching ribs would let her and headed for home. Dex could come along or not as he pleased.

He pleased. He strode along beside her all the way to her front door, and stood there watchfully while she unlocked it. Before she pushed it open she announced, "And I don't need you to check inside the closet or under the bed. I can clear my own space, thank you very much."

"Don't forget to do it, then," he replied steadily.

"Thanks for the first aid," she mumbled.

"Any time."

Any time indeed. Why did it make her acutely uncomfortable to know exactly which apartment Dex lived in and what his temporary home smelled like?

Isabella shook off a case of writer's cramp from the hasty report she'd just composed, describing the attack in the alley. She headed into the briefing—without a cup of coffee for the boss—and noticed right away that a new warmth permeated the crowd, like she'd passed some test. The Medusas were in their usual place, leaning against a wall near the front. She joined her teammates.

"How're you feeling?" Vanessa murmured to her.

"A little creaky."

Aleesha chimed in, "I'll bring some of grandmama's goop over to you tonight."

Isabella grimaced. The Jamaican herbal recipe worked great on aches and pains, but it smelled like rotten grass. No, make that rotten grass concealing dead fish.

Dex started the meeting. "For those of you who aren't aware of it, Captain Torres was jumped by three men in an alley this afternoon. She fought them off and apprehended one of them. He's in custody and being questioned now. He appears to be of Middle Eastern descent but is pulling a John Wayne and refusing to speak at the moment."

A voice from the back of the room piped up, "You mean *Torres* beat up that guy? He's a mess!"

Dex replied, "She did that to all three of her attackers before they attempted to flee." Was that actually a note of pride in his voice? Isabella stared in shock. She was only vaguely aware that a hundred male gazes had swung to her, most showing approval, a few registering something more along the lines of disbelief.

"Cripes," Misty muttered. "They're acting like they don't think a girl can make a proper fist, let alone throw a punch."

Vanessa added under her breath, "Welcome to the twenty-first century, boys."

Isabella schooled her expression to neutrality, but a kernel of pleasure warmed her. She'd done it. She'd acted like a real Medusa and kicked butt. Maybe she wasn't as big a fraud as she'd thought.

The briefing broke up after Dex told everyone manning the cameras to keep an eye out for small groups of young Middle Eastern men approaching Anya Khalid.

Isabella snagged a spare desk and called the home phone number listed in Harlan Holt's file. No answer. The wife was probably still at work. She dialed information and was passed to the main switchboard at Syracuse University. Emma Holt's office phone rang a good twenty times, but no one picked up.

Isabella redialed the switchboard and asked for the Biology Department. A secretary answered.

Isabella said, "Hi, I need to speak to Professor Holt. Could you tell me when a good time to catch her would be?"

"Normally, she'd be in her office from two to four on weekdays for office hours."

"Normally?" Isabella queried.

"She's not in today. She hasn't been in for the last several days. She's ill."

"What's wrong with her?" Isabella asked.

Luckily the secretary was the chatty type. "I don't know. Her husband didn't say."

Her husband? Emma Holt hadn't called in herself? "Did he say when she'd be back to work?"

"No. Maybe you should try again next week."

Isabella answered absently, "Thanks. I will."

She hung up and logged onto the computer. Using a good Internet phone book, she looked up the Holt's phone number and was directed to their street address in Syracuse and was even provided with a pop-up map to the Holt residence. She clicked the mouse to display several addresses on the same street, then did a reverse search in the phone book and was rewarded with the names and numbers of the Holt's neighbors. She picked the house next door and dialed the number.

"Mrs. Tannager? I'm sorry to bother you at home, but I'm a friend of Emma Holt's. I'm trying to reach her. I heard from the university that she's ill, and I haven't been able to get in touch with Harlan. The Biology Department gave me your name as an emergency contact."

The woman made a sound of surprise. "She's sick? Why, that's strange. Harlan told me just the other day that Emma had to leave the country on a research trip. I hope she hasn't picked up some horrible disease like one of those African fevers that melt your body. I saw a television show on it just last night. I was telling my husband how terrible it would be to die that way—"

Isabella interrupted gently. "When did you say she left the country?"

"Well, let's see now. I saw Emma four—no, five—days ago checking the mail. Such a pretty thing she is, so slender and graceful. I keep telling her she'd make a fine ballet dancer—"

"Five days? Have you seen her car come in or out of the driveway since then?"

"Why, no. It's parked right where it always is, behind the house. I'm sure Dr. Holt must have driven her to the airport."

"Of course," Isabella agreed. "Have you seen him in the last several days?"

"Oh, no. You know, he's the fellow who invented that new ice everyone's talking about. He's over in Lake Placid making sure it all goes just so. Emma told me he's hoping to sell his formula to the National Hockey League and some big international figure skating group. He's hoping to quit teaching and go into research full-time on the money he makes from the sale."

Isabella made a sound of pleased surprise while her mind raced. Told the office she was sick. Told the neighbors she was out of town. Nobody'd seen the woman in days. Two things were for certain: Emma Holt had disappeared, and her husband had something to do with it. She ended the call and dialed Vanessa. "Aleesha and Karen have babysitting duty until midnight. And I need to make a visit to Harlan Holt's house in the meantime."

Vanessa replied, surprised, "The guy who's doing the ice?"

"Yup. But I can't go alone or His Highness will have my head for taking too big a risk. Because, you know, I'm a weak female who can't look out for myself."

Vanessa chuckled.

"So, Viper, are you up for a field trip?"

Chapter 6

Lazlo glanced around the airport nervously. Ilya should be here, but damned if he could spot the guy. Knowing the bastard, he'd sneak up behind Lazlo and scare the piss out of him just to show that he could. The guy was psycho.

The commuter flight from New York pulled into the gate, and in spite of himself, Lazlo's pulse leaped. He hadn't seen his family in more than two years. Although he'd lived away from them for the past decade, he still missed them fiercely.

Thankfully, seeing their son skate in the Olympics had been sufficient reason for the Chechnyan government to issue visas for this trip. Because of the incriminating knowledge his parents possessed about certain now-legitimate members of the Chechnyan regime, they'd never been granted exit visas before. Of course, these visas also came with three minders— Ilya Gorabchek and two of his associates.

Somehow, some way, Lazlo *would* figure out a way to get his parents and two sisters away from the Chechnyan thugs. For good.

* * *

Harlan Holt cowered behind the steering wheel as a man slipped into the car beside him. One of the guys from his bedroom!

"Drive."

"Where to?" He took his foot off the brake.

"Around."

He pulled into traffic. "You said you'd bring me proof that she's alive."

The man reached into his coat pocket and pulled out a sloppily folded piece of paper. Harlan snatched it, unfolding it and squinting down at the writing. He glanced up and jerked the car back into his own lane. His heart pounded as the passenger snarled something about not getting them both killed.

H.—I'm alive and they're not hurting me. Please do whatever they ask. I love you—E.

That was it? He'd expected more. A description of the living conditions, what she was eating, maybe even a confession of being afraid. Emma might be a scientist, but she was more talkative than evidenced by this terse little note. "What have you done to her?"

"We have done nothing to your wife." The guy added menacingly, "So far."

If it wasn't his beloved Emma they were talking about, Harlan would curl his lip at the guy's melodrama. But, Sweet God in Heaven, they had his wife, and he could only imagine the horrors they were inflicting upon her. Sudden certainty overcame him. "You dictated this note to her, didn't you?"

The man shrugged. "This is not intended to be a communication. It is merely proof that she still lives."

"I want to talk to her. Now."

"No."

Hysteria rose in his chest. Wild thoughts spun in his head

about driving off a mountainside and turning this monster into a bloody pulp. Except then there'd be no one left to save Emma. It was a struggle, but he squashed his violent impulses.

"Did you do as we instructed?"

"Yes," Harlan said through gritted teeth. "The chemical you gave me was mixed into the ice."

"All of it?"

"Yes, all of it. And I had to mess around with the polymers to get it to freeze with that stuff in the mix. What is it, anyway?" The big bags of white powder he'd been given weren't labeled. The substance hadn't given off any distinctive odor or shown any unique qualities that would identify it. It hadn't bothered his skin when he'd touched it, and a tiny taste of it on his tongue hadn't produced any numbing or painful effects. And there'd been a lot of it, several hundred pounds. Thankfully, it had been a fine, talcumlike powder that didn't add any appreciable grit to his glass-smooth ice.

"I will ask the questions. You do as you're told. Turn right here."

He followed the guy's directions for the next several minutes.

"I did what you wanted and put that stuff in the ice. Now give me back my wife."

"All in good time, Doctor."

"When?" A note of hysteria crept back into his voice. "You said you'd set her free when I'd gotten the ice relaid with your chemical in it."

"Until we are finished with our work we also need you to be silent. When we are done, you may have your wife."

"Alive and well," Harlan added forcefully.

"Yes, yes. Alive and well. Stop the car."

Harlan stepped on the brakes so hard the tires squealed, and both men were flung against their seat belts. His passenger swore in some foreign language.

The guy threw open the door and paused long enough to

say, "Keep your cell phone on. We'll contact you that way. In the meantime, disappear."

He stared. "Excuse me?"

"Disappear. Don't talk to or be seen by anyone. We'll know if you contact the authorities. If you do, your precious Emma is history."

Holt stared in dismay at the man's retreating back. The Lake Placid bus station was crowded with tourists heading out for an evening of fun. A small town, Lake Placid's streets couldn't handle thousands of additional vehicles. So, during the Games, spectators were forced to park outside the city limits and use the many white Olympic buses with their stylized, multicolored, five-ring motifs. Only residents and Olympic officials got cars.

The man disappeared into the crowd, just another tourist among the thousands. Except that tourist was up to something terrible. Something he was willing to kill an innocent woman to protect. Harlan fingered the baggie of powder in his pocket. He pulled away from the curb and pointed his car southwest. Toward Syracuse. Or more precisely, toward his lab.

Isabella crouched in a frozen rhododendron bush, last year's leaves pitiful protection against the abundant light. With all the glaringly white snow cover here in Syracuse, it didn't take a lot of moonlight to turn the Holt's backyard into a brightly lit expanse. God, it felt good to wear all her usual gear. Her Glock pistol felt solid against her hip. Who'd have ever guessed she'd grow up to miss having a gun strapped to her side? Not bad for a girl who was supposed to stop her education after high school, find a nice boy, marry into a big family, and be an obedient, silent daughter, wife and mother.

"No movement back here," she whispered into her throat microphone.

"None here," Vanessa reported from the front of the house.

"None over here." Kat's hiding spot was over by the detached garage. "One car inside the garage. Engine block's cold."

Isabella blinked. Kat had gone inside? She hadn't heard sounds of entry or movement, and the wall of the garage was right at her back. But then, as a sniper, getting into and out of places quietly was part of Kat's job.

"Let's converge on the house," Vanessa murmured.

Isabella took one last look around. Given the blue glow emanating from a back window of the bungalow next door, the neighbor, Mrs. Tannager, was watching television. No other neighbors appeared to be awake. Wincing as her feet crunched in the snow, Isabella sprinted across the yard and crouched under the master bedroom window. She glanced down. Stared. And looked again. Pointed a narrow flashlight beam at the ground.

"I've got something," she murmured. "Back bedroom. Come have a look."

Frozen into the mud at her feet were a jumbled set of footprints. Why would those be here in the back of a dormant flower bed in the dead of winter? She squatted down. At least three men had been here. And—holy cow! A barefoot print. It was February in upstate New York! Nobody in their right mind came out here at this time of year *barefoot*. She looked closer. Narrow foot, about the same length as hers.

Two shadows materialized beside her.

"What do you make of these prints? Check out that bare print. It's female."

While her teammates examined the tangle of prints, Isabella shined her flashlight at the side of the house. "Forced entry marks." The paint around the sill was chipped, and the wood hadn't had time to age.

"This bare print's pointed away from the window," Kat breathed. "Whoever made it was headed out the window, not in."

"Emma Holt ran away from home?" Vanessa asked.

"After she broke into her own bedroom through the window?" Isabelle added.

The three women squatted, taking a hard look at the foot-prints. Carefully, they used their hands to dust away snow that obscured the trail as it led away from the house. Vanessa pulled out a camera and took pictures with low light film. They found two more partial bare prints frozen into ice beneath the fresh snowfall from last night.

"She stepped here and the heat of her bare skin melted the snow enough to make these frozen prints." Isabella said. "Why did she leave her house barefoot?"

Kat added, "We could tell more if we got inside and had a look around."

The Medusas were trained in rudimentary crime scene analysis. The other side of that forced window might indeed yield some interesting information. Isabella whispered, "We have no authorization to break in."

Vanessa's grin flashed. "Then I guess we'd better not get caught."

Isabella grinned back. The Medusas never had been very good at playing by the rules. Quickly, she assumed a wide-legged stance under the window. Kat stepped onto her thigh and quickly jimmied the simple window lock—and undoubt-edly didn't leave scratch marks behind like the last intruder. In a matter of seconds, the sash slid up quietly. A quick push against Isabella's leg and Kat disappeared inside. Vanessa climbed up next, and then it was Isabelle's turn to reach up and grab her comrades' hands. They lifted her over the sill until she could lay across it and ease herself inside.

The room was a shambles. Bed sheets and pillows were strewn over the floor.

Kat knelt by an askew area rug. "The way it's laying, I'd say someone was dragged across it from the bed toward the window."

"Could Harlan have fought with his wife, maybe knocked her out, and then dragged her out of here?" Vanessa asked.

Isabella shook her head in the negative. "Emma put her

weight down on those footprints. She was conscious when she made them." She knelt down to examine the bedspread where it lay on the floor. And frowned. "Why hasn't Holt cleaned up this room? Correct me if I'm wrong, but that looks like a layer of dust."

The others knelt down and pointed high-intensity flashlight beams at the fine dusting of beige covering the fabric. Isabella leaned back on her heels.

"So," Vanessa said. "There was some sort of break-in, a big struggle, Emma Holt leaves barefoot via the window and Holt leaves the house and doesn't come back. Where's he been since this happened?"

"He skedaddled to Lake Placid," Isabella answered grimly. "He insisted on tearing up the ice at the figure skating venue like a man possessed."

Kat commented, "Okay, color me confused."

That made two of them.

Isabella barely made it back to the Olympic village by 4:00 a.m. after the long drive back from Syracuse to take over the late shift watching Anya. While Misty, Aleesha and Karen were briefed on what the others had found at the Holt house, Isabella settled in beside the sleeping girl. Kat had volunteered to share the shift so they could take turns power napping. Both of them managed to get an hour of solid rest before Anya's wake-up call at 7:00 a.m. Kat left to fetch breakfast while Isabella stayed with Anya.

The skater got up, showered, dressed, and then proceeded to spend an inordinate amount of time drying and styling her hair and putting on makeup. A suspicion blossomed in Isabella's gut. After all, she had three little sisters. She called out casually through the partially open bathroom door, "Are you expecting to see Lazlo today?"

Anya emerged, looking beyond gorgeous. Her eyes

sparkled and her skin fairly glowed with happiness. "We have practice ice together this morning."

Isabella frowned. "If he rams into you again, I'm going to hurt him. Bad."

Anya laughed. "He won't. It was an accident. He's apologized a hundred times."

Her frown deepened. "I'm not joking, Anya. My job is to be your bodyguard. If he hits you again, I'm going to respond to it as a violent attack, and I'm required to neutralize him using whatever force is necessary."

Anya's smile dimmed. "You don't have to be such a wet blanket."

"Wet blanket's my middle name. It's my job to protect you."

"Yeah, well, I never asked to have bodyguard," the girl said resentfully.

Isabella understood. This girl had finally slipped out of her cage, and she didn't want to land in another more constrictive one. "Sweetie, I don't want to ruin your fun. Lord knows, you've earned it. I just want to keep you safe. You work with me, and I'll do my level best to work with you. Okay?"

Anya nodded.

Isabella said lightly, "That pink lip gloss you had on yesterday was awesome. Why don't you go get some and we'll be on our way. You can eat in the car. We don't want you to miss a minute of your ice time this morning, eh?"

The girl smiled widely and whirled, disappearing into the bathroom.

When they arrived at the ice complex, Isabella and Kat had to all but sit on Anya to get her to wait for a security check before she leaped out of the bulletproof car. Ah, the exuberance of first love. Isabella shook her head as she all but broke into a jog to keep up with the girl as they headed for the skating rink.

Anya threw on her skates, stretched at the speed of light, and hastily declared her knee fine. Thankfully, Anya's coach played bad cop this time and forced the girl to spend several more minutes carefully warming up the sore joint and working out the kinks before she took to the ice.

Isabella spotted Lazlo the second they stepped into the arena. He was the surly guy dressed in black waiting off to one side. The big clock on the hockey scoreboard clicked over to the top of the hour, and a stream of colorfully dressed skaters stepped onto the ice. As a group, they commenced stroking around the rink like speed skaters, getting blood flowing to the heavy thigh muscles endemic to their sport. Anya looked disappointed that Lazlo hadn't waited for her. Poor kid.

As the session progressed, two things became clear. One, Anya's knee was not up to full speed and she was skating in considerable pain. Two, Lazlo was completely ignoring Anya. That was strange. The two of them had all but dripped syrup together night before last. And now he was freezing her out? What was up with that? He could just be a colossal jerk. But that felt too simple. She glanced over at the boy's longtime coach, an American named Peter something. Surely he wouldn't have any strong moral objection to Lazlo seeing Anya.

Several hundred spectators watched the session. Isabella overheard a coach telling a skater that the judges came to the practice sessions to learn the skaters' programs before the competition. Apparently, there were a few hecklers here today, too. Every time Anya did a spiral—lifting one of her legs high in the air and sailing across the ice like a flying bird—shouts came out of the crowd in Arabic, calling her lewd and other unrepeatable insults. How Anya was ignoring the catcalls, Isabella didn't know. Hopefully, her concentration was such that she honestly wasn't hearing any of it.

About halfway through the session, Anya and the other skaters lined up along one side of the rink to take turns running through their programs. Isabella was already moving in that direction, to inject herself between the crowd and her charge, when something flew out of the stands and hit Anya in the back of the head.

As she took off running, everything went into high focus. The object that hit Anya was melon-sized and brown. It didn't drop the girl. Anya flinched, and grabbed the back of her head. The American skater beside Anya had the presence of mind to yank her down below the level of the waist-high boards. A quick glance up at the crowd didn't reveal anyone with an arm extended or trying to flee the scene.

Isabella reached Anya, leaping over the boards and onto the ice. "You all right?" she bit out.

"Yes. It wasn't hard."

Isabella already had her eye on the projectile. It looked like a paper lunch sack was split open with a brown substance visible inside. She approached it cautiously, and scowled when she recognized the contents by the stench rising from the bag. But she didn't let down her guard. It was fully possible for some sort of device to be concealed within what smelled like dog poop.

She keyed her microphone. "Ops, Torres here. Someone just lobbed a paper sack of doggie doo-doo at Anya. Do you want me to treat the bag as a dangerous object and get the bomb squad over here, or do you want me to pick it up and move it?"

Dex snorted in disgust. "Is it ticking?"

"Negative on the ticking poop," she replied dryly.

"Let's get a dog over there to have a look at it."

Isabella retorted, "What, so he can mark it?"

Dex laughed. "No, a bomb dog. Let's not send in a full squad. That would make too much of a fuss. Mamba, are you up on freq?"

Aleesha piped up immediately, "Mamba here. Whatchya need?"

"You're EOD, right?"

"I'm trained in explosive ordinance disposal, not doggie doo-doo."

"Go have a look at that bag. Adder, the guys here say rink four is empty. Send the skaters and coaches over there to finish the practice session. I'll notify the rink security guys not to let the crowd follow the skaters next door."

Isabella felt patently stupid clearing a skating rink for a stink bomb, but there was no help for it. They had to do what they had to do. "Not to further complicate this scenario, but if we're going to treat this as a threat, should we bring in a biohazard team?"

"Oh, for God's sake," Dex muttered. A heavy sigh in her ear. "Yeah, that's a good thought. I'll make the call. Just get everyone out of there before the guys in the space suits come to look at the Fido Surprise. We'll never live it down otherwise."

It was easy enough to clear the skaters from the ice. As soon as they were apprised as to the contents of the bag, they were more than happy to adjourn to another rink. Security guards took care of the spectators, and in a little under ten minutes, the cavernous stadium was empty except for Isabella, Aleesha and the offending bag. The rest of the Medusas were next door, keeping an eye on Anya.

Isabella watched her teammate kneel beside the bag with a handheld X-ray machine, examining the bag without touching it. To lighten Mamba's irritation, Isabella asked gravely, "Can you tell what kind of dog it came from, Doctor?"

"Yeah," Aleesha muttered. "A big one who ate Mexican for supper last night. This stuff reeks." Aleesha sat back. "There's nothing in that bag but crap."

Isabella looked up as two men, each carrying a bulky metal box, arrived. "You fellas the biohazard guys?"

They nodded.

"Did you hear what we've got?"

"Yup. The dog shit of doom. Let's have a look at it."

Isabella watched intently as the two men went to work. It turned out the big boxes were elaborate chemical detection machines. While one guy waved what looked like a vacuum-cleaner hose in the air around the bag, the second guy prepared sterile paper swabs and wiped down the outside of the bag. He placed the specimen in a little drawer in the side of his box.

The first guy announced, "No airborne biohazards were detected. Other than that stench. Sheesh. Wouldn't want to meet the dog who did that."

But then Isabella noticed the second guy frowning at his monitor. "What's up?" she asked.

The guy spoke quietly. "I got a hit."

All of them froze, staring down at the paper bag.

"Talk to me," Isabella said.

He glanced around the huge arena and spoke in a hushed voice that only carried a few feet. "This paper bag has been in contact with a nerve agent. A really freaking nasty one. Military grade. Supersecret. Even its name is classified."

Isabella stared. "You've got to be kidding. Run the test again."

They all waited in tense silence while the guy reswabbed the bag and redid the test. Sure enough, the machine emitted a quiet beep. The two biohazard men traded grim looks.

"It's a trace hit, but it's definitely a hit. Whoever handled this bag has probably recently handled the chemical. Uh, we need to secure this bag. We've got to take it back to the lab and run some more tests."

Isabella nodded in minor shock. A *nerve agent?* Whoever'd lobbed that bag at Anya was obviously part of something much bigger and much more dangerous than merely scaring a girl away from skating in the Olympics.

She keyed her microphone grimly. "Dex? We have a little problem."

Chapter 7

Isabella spent the rest of the day making classified reports to various officials and agencies about the incident at the ice-skating rink. On top of getting a short night's sleep last night, she missed lunch, too. By suppertime, she needed a shower, a decent meal, and a few hours' rest before she went on duty guarding Anya. She'd just stepped out of her shower and thrown on jeans and a sweater when she heard a knock on her apartment door. She called through the closed panel, "Who's there?"

"Dex and dinner."

She opened the door. "Dinner you say?" she asked without bothering to say hello.

"Yeah. I realized I never let you eat lunch today what with all the paperwork I piled on." He added wryly, "And I figured I'd better come bearing a bribe if I expected you to let me in."

"That all depends on how good a bribe it is," she retorted.

"Amazing Japanese takeout from a little place I found a couple weeks ago."

"Sold." She stepped back and waved him in.

He walked inside the tiny space and looked around, inhaling the scent the same way she'd done at his apartment. She took a sniff herself. The roses dying on the kitchen table mixed with laundry soap and her ridiculously expensive coconut oil shampoo and conditioner. At least it didn't smell like dirty socks or rotten fish.

"Mind sitting on the floor?" he asked.

"What's wrong with the table?" Besides the dead rose petals lying all over it.

He shrugged. "It feels funny to sit at a western table when I eat Japanese. Old habits die hard, I guess."

"Have you lived in Japan?" she asked. To her knowledge, no American soldiers were actually stationed there, so he'd have been a civilian when he lived there.

"Let's just say I've spent a fair bit of time in country."

Meaning he'd done Special Forces work there and she shouldn't ask any more questions. *Got it.* She knelt on one side of the coffee table while Dex did the same on the other side. Her mouth watered as he pulled out trapezoidal white cardboard boxes. Out of the bag emerged black, square, ceramic plates and pretty, painted chopsticks.

"Wow. Classy. I usually do paper plates and bamboo chopsticks."

"Only the best for a Thorpe," he quipped lightly.

She gazed speculatively at him. That had sounded suspiciously like bitterness.

But then he distracted her by opening the boxes and letting out clouds of delectable steam as he announced the dishes. "Teriayaki chicken skewers, veggie tempura, garlic shrimp, and Kobe beef."

She looked up at him gravely. "You'd better get all you want to eat now, because once I get started on all this, I'm going to eat everything that's left."

He grinned at her. "Thank God. A woman with a real appetite. I get so sick of women who only eat rabbit food."

"Yeah, but you don't gripe about their supermodel stick figures."

He waved a chicken skewer at her. "Not me. I like my women to have some substance. I don't want to worry about breaking them."

Breaking them? The boy enjoyed vigorous sex, then, did he? Whoa, girlfriend. Brain back on track, here. This was the man she worked for. "You men all say that. And then you take home the skinny blondes." Like elegant Misty. Not dark, round Isabella.

He leaned back, nibbling on a cluster of julienned carrots covered in fried tempura batter. "Actually, I don't generally take women home."

Her eyebrows shot up. Well, wasn't he just Mr. Chatty tonight? "Don't you like girls?" she asked sympathetically. "You must really suffer, cooped up with all those good-looking guys. Does your team know?"

He coughed hard a couple times before he managed to choke out, "Jeez, Isabella. Don't say things like that when a guy's got food in his mouth. I like girls just fine."

Hey, he'd used her first name. A breakthrough! She grinned. "Glad to hear it. May I quote you on that?"

He rolled his eyes. "I didn't say I like working beside them. I'm not supposed to worry all the time about looking out for my teammates. But I would with women in the field."

"You'd get over that soon enough," she commented, waving a chicken skewer at him. "As soon as you realized we're competent at our jobs, you'd relax. But in the meantime," she said lightly, "I really enjoy making guys like you miserable. It makes all the hard work to get into the Special Forces feel so worthwhile."

"Glad I can be a source of motivation for you."

Isabella leaned forward, abruptly serious. "Actually, you are."

He blinked, taken aback. "How's that?"

"Teams like yours give the Medusas a goal. Without your success to emulate, I don't know that I, or any of the Medusas, would've gotten where we are today. Lots of the guys think we want to be better than the men. But that's not true at all."

She took a bite of the succulent Kobe beef and savored the way it practically melted in her mouth. Then she waved her chopsticks at him to emphasize her words. "It's not a battle of the sexes. We're all American soldiers, working together to protect our country. There are times when having women in the field can be a benefit, and we simply want to be those women."

He stared at her in genuine surprise as she continued, "All I've ever wanted was to be good enough not to impede the men we work with, and to be able to do what I have to, when I have to, to get the mission done. And believe me, not impeding you guys is no easy feat. Sometimes I think the male Delta teams are superhuman."

"The way I hear it, you ladies are pretty buff, yourselves."

"Maybe the others," she answered candidly. "I'm the brainiac of the outfit. I'm probably the weakest link, physically."

He helped himself to another chicken skewer. "You can always work out and get stronger. It's pretty hard to get smarter, though."

He had a point. "Speaking of intelligence, my overdeveloped brain is wondering if there's more to this visit than sharing life histories?"

His demeanor changed in an instant. Gone was the relaxed, good-looking guy chowing down tempura, and in his place was a Delta team leader, tough, alert and macho enough to set her teeth on edge. She liked the other guy a lot better.

"We need to talk about what's going on with Anya."

"Not much, other than her crush on Lazlo and an urge to go play. If you mean what's going on around her—that's another story."

"Do you see any pattern to the threats?"

She leaned back against the sofa, thinking hard before she answered. In the back of her mind, she'd been turning over that very question for most of the afternoon. "Clearly, a Muslim fundamentalist group is mad enough about her skating to take action to stop her. To date there've been several small attempts to intimidate her—the guys following her, the collision with the Petrovich kid, and today's incident. What concerns me is that they might actually be efforts to probe the security around her."

"To find weak points?" Dex asked.

She nodded. "And to identify possible points of attack."

"Have they found any?"

"Oh, yeah," she replied grimly. "That ice rink is huge. There's no way I can cover her there without being armed myself and having a couple snipers in the rafters. I think it's by far the likeliest place to stage an attack on her."

"Where will it come from?"

"I don't know. The metal detectors and other security devices on the Hamilton Arena are pretty good. I'm awfully worried by the presence of the nerve agent on that bag, though. Is there any way the IOC could set up a chemical detection station as part of the security apparatus at the rink?"

Dex shook his head regretfully. "Doing that to a large crowd is incredibly time consuming. You have to swab each person down individually and then run the test paper through the machines. Schmidt and his IOC buddies would never go for it. Not unless we had a specific and verified threat to the venue."

"Well, it's verified that traces of a nerve agent were there today."

Dex's eyes went a steely shade of gray. "Schmidt's convinced that the chemical the biohazard guys detected will turn out to have some innocuous commercial usage."

She shook her head. "Does that guy live with his head buried in the sand?"

Dex grinned. "I dunno. But he sure leaves his ass sticking straight up in the air often enough. He said we overreacted to the chemical hit."

"Overreacted? That's nuts! If anything we underreacted."

"Welcome to the world of civilians who don't see things quite the same way we do."

She'd run into this before. Regular people living regular lives didn't always grasp the reality of threats. In her capacity as an intel analyst, she'd been privy to some narrow misses with catastrophe that made her toes curl. But never had she seen such solid evidence ignored so completely.

"What are you going to do?" she asked Dex.

"I've asked the lab boys to verify their findings and tell me everything they can about that bag. If we're lucky, we'll get more evidence to back up the threat."

She shook her head. "And in the meantime?"

"That's why I wanted to talk to you. Alone. Outside the office."

Lazlo slouched in the booth in the back of the noisy pub. At least it was dark back here. He'd chosen this as a place to meet Ilya because it was the sort of bar where hockey fans might hang out to get drunk and rowdy, but not where anyone who watched figure skating would be caught dead.

Ilya was late. But the guy was crazy security conscious. He was probably lurking in a trash can somewhere, making sure no one had followed him. Lazlo shifted in his seat and swore under his breath just as a familiar figure slid into the seat opposite him after all. Damn, he didn't like it when Ilya snuck up on him like that!

"She's skating again," Ilya snarled without preamble.

"Were you there today?" Lazlo asked. He knew damned good and well the guy'd been there. He'd seen Ilya sitting in about the sixth row the second he'd stepped onto the ice. He'd wondered all afternoon if Ilya was behind that bag of dog crap that had chased everyone off the ice. It seemed too sophomoric for this seasoned terrorist, though.

The guy waved off Lazlo's question. "Irrelevant. What is relevant is what you're going to do to make sure this whore doesn't compete."

His gut churned. He'd already hurt Anya's feelings by ignoring her today. Not like he'd had any choice with this maniac watching him. Especially not after the maniac in question had threatened his family the last time they'd talked. "How are my parents? My sisters?"

"Fine. For now."

Oh, brother. Cut the drama already. Must be part of the terrorist handbook—talk in threats. The bastard had whisked them away from the airport before Lazlo'd done much more than hug them. "When can I see them?"

"Tomorrow."

Lazlo sat back, smiling. Tomorrow. After all the years of waiting, of being held hostage and forced to skate as if his life—or rather their lives—depended on it. And it was all about to end. Maybe not tomorrow, but very soon. The biggest hurdle, getting his family onto American soil, had been crossed. He'd dreamed about this ever since he'd been dragged away from his family and carted off to America, under orders to become a champion skater, or else. To hell with being this man's sleeper. Lazlo had been a child when he'd agreed to come to America and establish a long-term cover. Chechnya was a nation now. He'd almost made it. Freedom for him and his family was just around the corner.

Isabella laid down her chopsticks. She knew that calculating look in Dex's eyes. "Spill it. What do you have in mind?"

"First, I have to ask you a difficult question."

That sounded ominous. "Uh, okay."

"I had a look at your personnel file today."

She frowned. Now why did he do that? And why today?

He continued, "And I noticed that you are of mixed heritage. Mexican on your father's side, but Iranian on your mother's. Is that correct?"

"It is," she answered shortly. He'd been looking at her *Top Secret* personnel file?

"What religion were you raised in?"

"You said you had one difficult question to ask me. That's two."

"Neither of those are the difficult one."

Damn. She'd been afraid of that. "How did you get a hold of my classified folder?" For that was the *only* place her mother's nationality was listed.

"I'm chief of the U.S. military security mission to the Olympics. I can have anything I want from the Pentagon right now short of the nuclear launch codes."

"So what's your question?"

"Answer mine first. What religion were you raised in?"

She smiled without humor. "Hell of a choice, isn't it? Catholicism or Islam."

He waited, silent, for her answer.

She sighed. "I was exposed to both and not forced to practice either. Whenever we'd go visit my father's family, my grandmother dragged me to Mass and taught me how to say rosaries and Pater Nosters. But whenever we visited my mother's side of the family, I was expected to pray five times a day in Arabic and the whole nine yards."

Dex frowned. "Do you have a preference for one over the other?"

"How is this relevant to my job?"

"You're caught in the middle of a religious controversy involving a young woman and her interpretation of Islam. You tell me how relevant it is."

"It's not. While I am familiar with its tenets, I am not a practicing Muslim."

"What is your personal opinion as to whether or not Anya should skate?"

"Oh, for God's sake, Dex. I think she ought to be allowed to do whatever she pleases. This is the twenty-first century and figure skating hardly qualifies as obscene behavior."

"So there's no conflict of interest?"

"None," she snapped.

"I just had to ask," he responded mildly.

"Okay, my turn," she fired at him. "Why were you looking in my classified personnel file?"

His gaze slid away for the merest moment but then came back to her. "I wanted to know more about you."

Whoa. Open to several interpretations, there. And a couple of them made her pulse leap. "Why?"

"I can't remember the last time I met a woman who speaks six languages, runs a six-minute mile, can shoot a gun better than most professional snipers and who'll spit in my coffee just to make a point."

She shrugged. "Obviously you don't hang out with the Medusas much. We've blown up buildings just to make a point." She noticed that he hadn't really answered her question, either. Maybe one of those pulse-leaping reasons was closer to the truth than he cared to admit. Double whoa!

"Here's another one for you, Dexter Godfrey Thorpe the Fourth. What kind of family do you come from to end up stuck with a name like that? Do your parents just hate you or are they as rich and stuffy as it sounds like they are?"

"The latter."

"What do they think of your career?" she blurted out, surprised.

"I'm the black sheep of the family for not going into the actuarial business."

She gaped, trying to envision him sitting at a dusty desk all day forecasting how many old, fat men would keel over from heart attacks next year or how many kids would get drunk and drive off bridges. She couldn't do it. She hadn't seen the guy in combat, but she didn't need to. The leashed energy of a special operator oozed from him. He'd be a force to reckon with in the field. Heck, he was a force to reckon with now, sitting on her floor mopping up the remnants of a take-out dinner.

"I know the feeling," she said. "Neither side of my family is too keen on my Air Force career. If they found out about this new gig in the Medusas, they'd croak."

"Are you ladies allowed to reveal it to your immediate families?" he asked.

It was common practice that special operators didn't tell their loved ones what they actually did. "We were given permission in very broad terms to tell our families we'd taken jobs on a traveling team that assesses problem spots in the world."

He laughed. "That's one way of describing what we do."

Isabella managed not to stare. For the first time, he'd talked in the same breath about the Medusas and his Delta team doing the same work. It was a major breakthrough for the guy.

"Speaking of which," he said seriously. "I'm going to talk strictly off the record here, and I'll deny having said it until my dying breath."

Finally. He was going to get to the point of why he'd shown up on her doorstep bearing food. "Okay. Lay it on me."

"There's something bad going on. And whatever it is, it's building around Anya. And my gut says it involves religious fanatics and that nerve gas."

"Hark! The man finally admits that he listens to intuition!"

Dex scowled. "I never said I don't listen to it at all. I just think you depend on yours too much."

"Until my gut steers me wrong, I'm inclined to keep right on listening to it."

"Well, let's hope it doesn't steer you to your death, and Anya along with you."

She exhaled a little harder than necessary. "It's not like I rely solely on crystal balls and Ouija boards. I do back up my intuitions with hard facts."

"What are the hard facts telling you right now?"

She frowned. "Darned if I know. We've got this radical Islamic cleric in town issuing fatwas. Then there's Holt. He's acting completely weird and his wife is missing."

"His wife is missing?" Dex squawked. "How the hell did I miss that?"

Wincing, she answered, "Well, we would have had to tell you about it for you to have actually missed it."

"Start talking, Torres."

She hated when he used her last name like that. It always meant she was in trouble. "We paid a little extracurricular visit to Syracuse last night. I tried all day yesterday to track down his wife and I kept getting different stories. Holt told her employer she was sick. He told the neighbor she was out of town. But when we had a look around his house—"

"His *house?*"

"Well, yeah. We found signs of a forced entry and barefoot female footsteps frozen into the snow leading away from a bedroom window, along with several sets of male prints."

"Jesus H. Christ! And why did you neglect to share all this with me?"

"Because we knew you'd have a cow and we couldn't figure out what it all means. We have no jurisdiction to file a missing persons report on her—we don't, in fact, know that she's missing."

He scowled. "Okay, so there's something weird going on with Harlan Holt and his wife. Anything else?"

"Well, there's that kid, Lazlo Petrovich. He was acting really strange this morning."

"How so?"

"First, he intentionally ran into Anya and hurt her. Then, he stopped by her room to apologize profusely, apparently sincerely, for slamming into her. The two of them were completely gaga over each other, and I'd have bet my life that it was a legit crush. But before the brown bag incident today, for no apparent reason, he gave her the coldest shoulder this side of the North Pole. Something's going on with that kid. His mood changes are too abrupt and too inexplicable."

"Maybe he's bipolar?"

She shook her head in the negative. "I smell a rat. I just can't see it, yet."

"So we're looking at a minimum of three threads that need to be followed to their logical conclusion." He leaned forward, tension pouring off of him. "Tell me something. How would you and your teammates feel about doing a little behind-the-scenes pulling on the ends of these threads?"

No wonder he'd quizzed her on her beliefs! He didn't want her to turn out to be a religious fanatic herself if he was about to sic her on one. Aloud she asked, "What did you have in mind?"

"Going fully operational to track down what's going on. Under Delta rules."

Which meant there would be no rules at all. Anything went in the course of a Delta mission. "Have you talked to General Wittenauer at JSOC or our control officer, Jack Scatalone, about this?"

"Nope. It has to be completely off the books. Just between me and you ladies."

"We'd have no sanction to operate. And we'd be on U.S. soil. That would really limit what we can do." In the U.S., soldiers were not allowed to use deadly force without all kinds of special permissions from everyone and his brother. In a democratic country, it was *strictly* forbidden for the military ever to turn on its citizens.

Dex nodded. "You're right. But I can't spare anyone else to do it. The Medusas were only brought in to deal with Anya, so you're not committed to lots of other security tasks. I need you to go into stealth mode. Stake out everyone who is suspicious and get a lead on what the hell's about to happen. We've got to stop it. It's going to be big-time bad. I can feel it."

And now that he mentioned it, so could she. A sense of impending doom had been building around Anya for the last couple of days, like the girl was sitting in the middle of a giant bull's-eye.

"Want me to talk to the other Medusas?"

"Regardless of what they say, I'd like you to do this for me. Make that, I need you to do this for me. This op is chock-full of big-time fundamentalists. Nobody among them will expect a woman to go after them. At the end of the day, you may be the most effective resource I can bring to bear on the problem."

She looked him square in the eye. "And that's precisely why the Medusas exist."

He looked at her for a long time. Nodded slowly. "I get it now." A pause. "So. Will you help me?"

Chapter 8

Isabella dialed the phone number and waited impatiently for the call to go through.

A voice said in her ear, "Detective Hoffman."

The Lake Placid police officer sounded harried. Not that she blamed him. His sleepy little town had become an international metropolis overnight, and no amount of preparation could match the reality of partygoers from every corner of the globe descending on your turf all at once. "Isabella Torres here from the Olympic Security Group. I'm trying to track down a man named Ahmed al Abhoud. He's visiting from the emirate of Bhoukar. I was hoping you might be able to help us find out where he's staying. We've already checked the major hotels' guest lists and he's not registered."

"There are no home owners in the area from Bhoukar that he'd likely be staying with, if that's what you're asking. He could be leasing a private home, though. A number of the locals have rented out their houses for the duration of the

Games. There are also a couple of high-end resorts in the area that don't release their guest lists—too many celebrities protecting their privacy. How urgent is it that you find this guy?"

"I'm afraid it's a matter of national security." She felt bad invoking those words. It forced the detective to help her, whether he had time for it or not, and whether he wanted to or not.

He sighed. "All right. I've got a sergeant named Mario Picconi who's on desk duty with a busted leg. I'll have him make some calls."

"Thanks, Detective. I'm sorry to bother you with this. But it really is urgent."

"No sweat. I hope we can help out."

Isabella disconnected her cell phone and looked up at her expectant teammates. "They're going to look into it and get back to us."

Vanessa glanced at the fading light seeping in around the closed curtains of the living room window. "It's almost dark. We can get going soon."

Karen asked, "Are we gonna sneak out of here or do we get to walk to the van like normal people?"

Vanessa frowned. "I think we'd better sneak. Too many of Schmidt's people are staying in this complex. If someone spotted us, questions would get asked."

Vanessa was right, but what a pain in the butt. Isabella sighed. She stuffed her gear into a white laundry bag and checked the hidden microphone connections under her sweater while the other Medusas, minus Misty who was on guard duty, disguised their gear, too. The plan was for Isabella to approach Lazlo this evening and talk about Anya. It was purely a fishing expedition to try to get a read on the young man. The other Medusas would hide nearby, listening via the wire taped to her stomach.

Time to go. It felt much later than 7:00 p.m. The only ambient light in the sky was the downtown glow of Lake Placid and the Olympic complex. Other than that, the night sky was the pure black of isolated, upstate New York.

Isabella's wire and transmitter set off the metal detectors as she entered the Olympic village, but she stepped aside and had a quiet conversation with the guards manning the checkpoint. After checking her credentials, verifying her identity, and listening to a quick, but vague, explanation from her that the wire was official business, the men let her through. Vanessa, Karen and Aleesha would stay in the van with the monitoring equipment.

She strolled into the village, which was teeming with people. Athletes—uniformly young and beautiful in their fitness—roamed all over the place, and the atmosphere was joyous, almost carnival-like. A dozen languages floated around her, and the colors of many nations were bright everywhere she looked. It was hard to believe that within this exuberant show of global unity lurked a possibly lethal threat.

It was dinnertime. She headed for the buffet lines and eating area. It would be handy to bump into Lazlo in a public place like this. It would look less like she'd sought him out and more like a chance meeting. No such luck. Maybe in the arcade. He'd mentioned to Anya that he was enjoying the free video games.

Isabella wandered up and down the rows of games for several minutes. Bingo! She caught sight of the lean, dark-haired skater sitting in a car racing game. She strolled up to him just as he was finishing a race. "How's it going?" she asked casually.

He glanced eagerly over her shoulder. Looking for Anya was he? What in the bloody hell was with this on again, off again interest in the girl? His face fell as he realized Anya was not with her keeper. Isabella said dryly, "Sorry. She's got her qualifying round of skating tomorrow and packed in early tonight."

"Is she upset over this morning?" Lazlo asked.

"Yes, she is. She couldn't figure out why you wouldn't talk to her."

"Well, I, uh, didn't want to distract her at her last practice."

He was a lousy liar. Aloud she replied, "For future reference, you distracted her more by ignoring her than you would've had you at least said good morning and wished her luck."

He frowned. Danged if he didn't look upset that he'd hurt Anya's feelings. Okay, so if he really did like the girl, why the cold shoulder this morning? "Are you embarrassed to be seen with her in public?"

"No!" he exclaimed.

"You don't have to worry about your safety when you're with her, you know. My colleagues and I are charged not only with Anya's safety, but the safety of all the athletes here. We'd take care of you, too."

"That's not it—" he started. But then he stopped tantalizingly.

"Is everything okay?" Isabella asked quietly. "Is there anything I can do to help?"

"No, I'm fine," he blurted angrily. "Just leave—" He broke off again.

He'd been about to tell her to leave him alone. She'd probably pushed him hard enough. Any more and he'd get suspicious. But then one last brainstorm hit her. "Is there a message you'd like me to pass on to Anya?"

The kid's face lit up like the Olympic flame. "Would you do that for me?"

She shrugged. "Sure."

"Tell her I—" Another abrupt halt. "Wish her good luck for me. Tell her I'll be watching and cheering for her."

Isabella nodded. "I will."

"And—" a hesitant pause "—if she has any message for me, I'd…like that."

Isabella held back a smile. God, she was good. She'd just been appointed official messenger for the two of them. That should prove very informative. "Well, I'll let you get back to your race."

Lazlo glanced at his watch and a moment's apprehension crossed his face. "I've got to go out in a few minutes anyway."

She nodded and drifted away.

"Nicely done," Vanessa murmured in her ear.

"He's really tense about wherever he's going. How about

we follow him? I'll pick him up from here and tail him until we can all hook up."

"Done."

She loitered among the video games until Lazlo left, then she tailed the skater most of the way back to his room. She stopped just shy of the hall he was staying in. How to look like she had a good reason for standing here? She caught sight of a familiar male form heading her way. Beau Breckenridge. The man she'd bumped into the day she'd chased that guy out of the Olympic village.

"Beau? How've you been?" she said in a pleased speaking voice. Under her breath she muttered, "You busy?"

"I've got a couple minutes. Why?" he asked in a matching tone.

"Give me a cover. I'm watching someone who just went into a room."

"Watching as in tailing? What's up?"

She smiled up at the big man. "Dunno. That's what I'm trying to find out."

"You working on anything solid?" he asked, smiling back like they were talking about the weather.

"Can't answer that one." Which was Special Forces speak for, "It's classified and I can't say any more so quit poking around."

"Got it. Did you hear they're forecasting a big blizzard in a couple days?"

That arrested her attention. "Really?"

"Yup. Two feet or more of snow up in the mountains. The weathermen can't decide how much the city's going to get. Somewhere between six and thirty inches."

"Yikes. That's a wide spread." A big snowstorm right now could seriously impair the Medusas' operations.

"My target just left his room," she murmured.

"Do you need me to block you from his view?"

"Nah. He knows I'm security. I just needed an excuse to be standing here."

Beau grinned down at her and drawled, "Happy to oblige, ma'am."

She glanced up at him. "Where are you from anyway?"

"Mobile, Alabama."

Lazlo was almost even with them. "Can't get much more Southern than that," she remarked. She made eye contact with Lazlo as he moved past, nodding at the skater in a friendly fashion. He nodded back and then moved on.

"So, is the accent working on you?"

Isabella's attention snapped back to her companion. "I beg your pardon?"

"Didn't you know a Southern drawl is irresistible to women?"

She laughed aloud. "Sorry. I didn't get that memo. I'll remember to throw myself at you the next time I see you."

His eyes gleamed. "I'll hold you to that."

She rolled her eyes. Thankfully, Lazlo had just disappeared into the main lobby. "Gotta go, Beau. Thanks for the help."

"Any time, Adder."

He'd used her handle. A tacit sign of acceptance in the Special Forces community. Nice to know they weren't all chauvinist jerks. She flashed a quick smile at him as she turned to follow Lazlo, who was moving quickly, not looking around. She muttered into her collar, "The south exit onto Olympic Boulevard. Moving fast on foot. Black warm-up pants, black leather jacket. No hat."

She sped up as Lazlo exited the building. The night's cold made her suck in her breath as she stepped outside and glanced both ways. There he was. "Moving east on foot, north side of the street."

The other Medusas would trail behind her in the van until she called them. It would be easier to follow him on foot as long as he was walking.

"Looks to be heading for the bus stop. Stay back. I'll call if he boards a bus."

She loitered well behind Lazlo. The crowds were heavy. It

was party time in Ringtown—as Lake Placid had been nick-named by the media in honor of the five Olympic rings.

A white bus had just pulled up and he was heading straight for it. Probably shouldn't try to board it with him. If she showed up behind Lazlo three times in under an hour, even the rankest of amateurs would get suspicious. She opted to hurry down the sidewalk and catch a glimpse of the bus's destination on the electronic board mounted in its rear window. Main Street/Olympic Village.

"Come and get me, girls," she radioed.

Within a matter of seconds, the navy minivan pulled up beside her. "There you are!" Karen called out through the window. "Get in. It's freezing out there!"

Isabella jumped in the van. "Man it's cold tonight! I'm glad I didn't have to walk the whole way…." The door closed behind her and she cut off the inane chatter. "It's that bus just pulling out of the station."

Vanessa pulled out her cell phone. "Hey. I need to know how many stops the Number 4 bus makes and where." There was an impressively brief pause and then she said briskly, "Got it. Thanks."

She turned to the others. "Four stops, all along Main Street, then it loops back to the Olympic village."

Piece of cake. Karen maneuvered the van until it was right behind the bus. They waited through the first two stops and there was no sign of Lazlo getting off the bus. At the third stop, he was the first guy out. Vanessa left the van to take over the close quarters surveillance as Lazlo entered a cafeteria-style restaurant. To their knowledge, Lazlo had never seen Vanessa up close and he wouldn't recognize her now.

Karen snagged an official parking spot because of their Olympic Committee license plates, and they sat in the vehicle listening to Vanessa's murmured reports.

"He's in a booth by himself. Can't sit still. Is he always this antsy?"

"Negative," Isabella replied. He'd never been fidgety around Anya.

"He's checking his watch about once a minute."

Isabella glanced at her own watch—7:26. She'd bet he was supposed to meet someone at 7:30. Except the half hour came and went, and nobody showed up. At 7:40, Vanessa reported that he was mopping sweat from his forehead.

At 7:45, Vanessa said, "If I didn't know better, I'd say he's on the verge of having a panic attack." And then on the heels of that, "His cell phone is ringing." Seconds later, "He's on the move. Fast. Get the car started."

Lazlo stayed on foot, as did Vanessa. Karen expertly moved the van, parking twice when traffic forced her to move well ahead of Vanessa's position. Lazlo moved along the crowded sidewalks of the downtown area toward the large city square, which held several thousand people in front of a stage.

"Crud. He's stopping in the square. I'm gonna need backup out here."

Isabella and Aleesha piled out while Karen parked the minivan. With their radios, it wasn't necessary for them to stay in visual contact. The square was a riot of color and movement—of fun. The crowd was so innocent. So unaware of what was going on its very midst. Isabella searched for her target, and felt like a total outsider to the festivities. How her life had changed in a year.

No luck spotting Lazlo. "Where is he, Viper?"

"In front of the movie theater," Vanessa answered. "About fifty feet due east of it."

There. Off to the west side of the square. "Got him."

Lazlo was looking around. Definitely meeting someone here. Why the double rendezvous? What could a figure skater be embroiled in that required such secretive—and professional—tactics?

She could swear she felt the intensity of the night's cold deepening. A bitter wind was blowing in off Lake Placid from the north, and it went straight to her bones. All of a sudden, a man appeared. He was speaking to Lazlo. The guy had materialized out of the crowd, just like a trained special operator would have. Lazlo's shoulders went up around his ears as the man leaned close and said something. Oh, yeah, this was the meet. The man looked to be in his mid-forties. Dark hair and eyes. Bushy mustache that hid his upper lip. Husky in a street brawler sort of way. Not the sort of person she'd envision befriending an Olympic athlete. But clearly they had something to talk about.

Strike that. They had somewhere to go together. The two men moved off side by side at a brisk pace. Crap! Headed straight at her! She turned away fast and ducked her face nose-deep into the folds of her sweater, then grabbed her dark ponytail and stuffed it up under her knit ski hat for good measure. She needed to shift over to the other side of the street and switch places with Vanessa. Viper could afford to be seen by these two men, but Isabella could not.

"I'll take the north sidewalk," she muttered.

Vanessa muttered back, "Roger, I've got the south."

They'd practiced team surveillance so many times they fell into its intricate patterns almost without thinking. She showed no reaction when the two men cut across the street and continued walking directly in front of her. Their backs retreated out of the brightly lit square. Even if they looked back now, all they'd see would be her dark silhouette. Whew. That had been close. She let the two men pull ahead of her a little farther just to be safe. Vanessa was ahead to the right, almost parallel to the pair.

The men walked well away from the beaten tourist track and into what had to be the rough side of this hamlet. The area was all of a block long. Lazlo and his longshoreman look-alike buddy ducked into a dark pub. Isabella skidded to a stop beside the front door, while Karen disappeared down the alley beside the bar to cover any back exit.

A couple minutes passed.

Karen murmured, "No movement here. I think our boys are inside for a while."

Vanessa ordered, "Python, stay out back until we go in and get visual on them."

Karen acknowledged the instruction.

Isabella started as Vanessa materialized right beside her elbow. "Go inside with me. You know this kid's body language a lot better than I do."

Isabella nodded and walked inside.

It was a rough joint, its act marginally cleaned up for the Olympics. A grimy Olympic flag was draped behind the bar, but that was this place's only concession to the Games. It was crowded. She moved into the room, keeping a solid wall of bodies between her and her quarry.

She bellied up to the bar and did her best to give off man-hater vibes. She didn't need to get caught up in fending off passes from drunks while she was trying to work. A middle-aged woman slid out of a booth and smothered Lazlo in a bear hug any mother grizzly would be proud of. Two more women and a gray-haired man sat in the booth along with Lazlo's burly contact.

Vanessa's voice vibrated quietly in her ear. "Get pictures."

"Move that group of guys in hockey jerseys away so I've got a clear shot," Isabella replied.

Vanessa groused, "Where's Misty when you need her? Lemme see what I can do." Isabella watched, amused, as her boss sashayed up to the group of men and engaged them in flirtatious banter. Viper took a step back. Another. And like good little lemmings, the drunks followed.

"Way to go, you vixen," she teased her boss.

Kat chimed in. "Nice butt wiggle. Didn't know you had it in you."

Vanessa, who was still talking to the drunks, couldn't respond, but she did scowl.

Grinning, Isabella pulled out a digital camera and held it chest high beneath a plastic covered menu. Looking down into the nifty—and sneaky—top-mounted viewfinder, she lined up and shot several pictures of Lazlo and the group with him. She looked up as two more tough-looking men joined the guy who'd met Lazlo in the square. They exchanged brief nods. They knew each other then. She got pictures of them, too.

"Want me to get a picture of you with your boyfriends to send to Jack?" she asked Vanessa.

Kat and Karen clicked their mikes to indicate their amusement.

"Say cheese," Isabella crooned.

Vanessa broke away from the drunks. "You better not have taken a picture of me with those goons."

"Too late," Isabella said breezily. "Jack's gonna love it."

Vanessa laughed. "Go ahead. Send it. It'd be good for him."

Isabella eased further down the bar toward the party comprised of three women, four men and Lazlo. A waitress plunked down beers in front of the last two men and spoke to the others as if she was taking a drink order. They planned to sit and talk, then.

"We need to hear them," Isabella mumbled.

"Say what?" a guy beside her yelled in her ear over the racket.

"I said I need a beer," she yelled back. She moved away from the guy lest he try to engage her in any more brilliant repartee. She had to get closer to that table! She glided to the far end of the bar, nearest the booth, her back to the rendezvous. Not a word of what they were saying reached her. Drat. She sipped her way through a soda, and then the booth beside Lazlo and company's was opening up. Hallelujah!

"I need a couple warm bodies back here, ASAP," she muttered.

She moved to the table fast lest someone else claim it, and she slid into the sticky vinyl seat. To the waitress who was still cleaning up, she said, "I'd like three sodas, and I'll tip you like my friends and I are drinking."

The woman smiled and left with an armload of bottles from the previous patrons.

Vanessa slid into the booth moments later. "Can you hear them from here?"

Isabella shrugged. "Haven't tried yet."

Vanessa leaned back against the tall wooden chair back for a few seconds, then murmured, "Sounds like Russian. Too bad Misty's not here. Any ideas?"

Misty was the only member of the Medusas who spoke Russian. Isabella suggested, "If one of us goes back to the van and parks it nearby, we could use a throat mike to pick up the conversation and transmit it to the tape recorder in the van."

"How're we gonna get the mike close enough to pick up their voices with all this background noise?"

Isabella glanced around then leaned over sideways to peer under the table. "These seats don't go all the way to the floor in the middle. I can crawl under the gap and attach the wire to the underside of their table."

Vanessa blinked. "That's insane."

Isabella grinned. "And that's why you're going to let me try it, aren't you?"

Vanessa frowned. "What will you need to pull it off?"

"A broom handle and some tape."

Aleesha, who'd just joined them, piped up. "I've got some duct tape."

Kat added, "Ten to one there's a mop in the bathroom for cleaning up after the drunks who miss the toilet."

Vanessa nodded slowly. "Okay, let's give it a try."

Isabella tucked her chin on her right shoulder as she moved quickly past Lazlo's table. The bathroom was dark and disgusting. Her feet peeled nastily off the floor with every step as she had a look inside the stalls for a mop. Nada. There wasn't one by the sink, either. But then she spotted a door behind the entrance. She tugged at the storage closet door. Locked. Damn! She pulled out her lock picks—a simple straight pick would do—crouched in front of the lock, and popped it in a matter of seconds.

Someone banged into her with the bathroom door, knocking her over on her butt. She stared up blearily at the offender and slurred, "Wha' choo do tha' for?"

The woman, a peroxide blonde on the backside of fifty, sneered at her and called her a filthy name. Isabella crawled around on her knees, trying unsuccessfully to hoist herself to her feet until the woman reemerged from a stall, gave her hands a cursory rinse and departed. Isabella stood up and opened the closet door and found a mop and bucket smack-dab in front. She propped the mop handle against the counter at an angle. A couple powerful stomps on the middle of the broom and the wooden handle splintered and broke in half. The piece without the gnarly grey mop strings was about two feet long. She'd been hoping for a longer piece, but this would have to do. Gritting her teeth, she ripped off the radio transmitter still taped to her stomach and attached it to the mop handle.

While Vanessa provided physical cover between her and the rest of the room, Isabella ducked down under the table as if she'd dropped something. After a moment, she slid all the way under, still as if she were searching for something she'd dropped.

Vanessa murmured over her earpiece, "All clear. No one's looking at you."

Isabella flattened herself on the floor. Aww, jeez! And she thought the bathroom floor had been bad. This linoleum hadn't seen the business end of a mop in months. It was greasy, sticky and littered with peanut halves, pretzel crumbs, and a brown film of gunk she didn't want to know the chemical composition of.

The seats in the booths had about a twelve-inch gap

between their bottoms and the floor. Moving carefully, she was able to angle her right shoulder under the seat. Her head was next. Oh, God. It felt like any second Vanessa would shift her weight and crush Isabella's skull. *Breathe, girlfriend.*

Her torso squeezed under next, but it was a really tight fit. And then her head was under the next chair. A jumble of feet, male and female were in front of her at eye level. And in the middle, the lone, metal pole that supported the table above.

"Crap. Incoming," Vanessa muttered.

Isabella froze. Now what?

Kat murmured, "I've got it covered." Off mike, Isabella heard her teammate coo at someone in a really convincing Japanese accent, "Ooh, you American boys so big and strong! Come buy me drink and tell me about yourselves. I just love American men!"

"Clear," Vanessa breathed.

Karen commented, "I didn't know Kat had it in her. She's never been one to go for guys much."

"Touchy subject with her," Vanessa replied. "Bad history with men."

Meanwhile, Isabella eased her right arm forward, the mop handle clutched in her fist and the radio taped to the other end. She extended it toward the underside of the table, near where the pole met the tabletop. She was maybe two inches from touching the exposed sticky side of the tape to the table when somebody shifted. And bumped her arm hard, knocking the broom handle into someone else's knee.

Oh, crap. *Busted.*

Chapter 9

She jabbed the pole up fast and hard, and then jerked her arm back. A foot landed on the mop handle. Trapped it in place. Not good!

A male figure above maneuvered to the side, leaning down to have a look under the table. She shoved backward with her hands against the floor, pushing her head under the seat. A hand—felt like Vanessa—grabbed her waistband from behind and gave a good tug that was the little bit that saved her. Inches from her nose, a stubby-fingered hand with dirty fingernails grabbed the mop handle. Please God, let the radio not still be attached to it! She couldn't see from this angle. No time to stick around and find out. She wiggled backward as fast as she could with Karen's help, shimmying out from under the seats and onto her knees beneath the Medusas' table.

"Can I come out?"

"Wait a sec," Vanessa muttered.

Isabella closed her eyes. Her heart was in danger of

pounding right out of her chest. Damn, that had been close! She heard an outburst of Russian from Lazlo's booth. It sounded annoyed, but not furious. Maybe the radio had come off the end of the mop handle after all.

"Come on up," Vanessa said.

Awkwardly, Isabella slid back up into the seat. Her clothes were knocked askew and she was filthy. She set herself to rights as best she could. "Any audio feed, Python?"

Karen had left to turn on the van's receiver and move the vehicle closer to ensure reception. "I'll check it in a minute. I'm parallel parking right now. God, I hate driving mommobiles. These minivans are too big for me."

Never mind that the Marine could zip all over the combat training range in an armored personnel carrier and think nothing of it! Isabella snorted. "Get married and have a couple kids. You'll be a pro at it in no time."

Karen laughed. "Kids I can handle. A man—I don't know."

Isabella waited in an agony of suspense for the next minute. At least no one from the next table confronted them about any microphones under the table.

"Coming through loud and clear," Karen reported. "At least I think so. Whatever language they're speaking sounds like grizzly bears gargling to me."

Thank God.

Vanessa asked, "Wanna stick around and watch some more or depart the fix?"

After one insanely dangerous stunt tonight, Isabella was all about discretion over valor. "My fight-or-flight reflex is telling me to run like hell, so you'd better make the call. My knees are still banging together."

Vanessa smiled knowingly. They'd all experienced after-the-fright adrenaline surges. "Lemme know when you've got your legs back, Adder."

Isabella nodded. After a few minutes, her pulse returned to a semblance of normal and her brain began to function at full speed again. Which turned out to be fortuitous, because Lazlo and company paid their bill and got up to leave. Vanessa, Kat and Aleesha followed suit and waited just inside the door while Karen reported from the van, "They're getting into a pair of vehicles. You're clear to come on out."

The three women moved outside quickly and got into the van.

Karen looked at Isabella who was riding shotgun. "Which car do we follow?"

Isabella studied the two cars through a pair of binoculars she pulled out of the center console storage compartment. "The second car."

Vanessa asked from the back, "Why?"

"The first car, with Lazlo in it, will probably go back to the Olympic village and then on to its final destination. The second car has the women and the gray-haired man in it. I'm interested to see where they go."

Aleesha announced from the far back near the recording equipment, "I've burned a CD of the conversation we caught on tape in the bar. It sounds great. Misty shouldn't have any trouble translating it."

Karen spoke up. "I'm gonna have to back off, here. They're turning onto a pretty isolated road."

Isabella watched as they passed the street the sedan had just turned onto. It looked like little more than a country lane. Karen turned around in a driveway. She turned off the headlights and headed up the marginally plowed side street their quarry had turned onto. They eased forward slowly in the dark, looking out both sides of the van for any sign of the car.

Open curtains gave them glimpses into cozy homes. Large-screen TVs glowed, and average Americans lived their lives behind the windows. Isabella frowned. What in the world were she and her teammates doing, sneaking around in the midst of such normalcy? It offended her sense of order in the universe. Third-world countries embroiled in political upheaval and drug wars were their hunting ground. Not here. Not *home*.

A few minutes later, Isabella called out, "There it is. Parked in front of a house up that hill. The house is a couple hundred feet from the road."

Vanessa said, "Let's park up the street and come back on foot. I want to have a look around and see what we can learn about this bunch."

They parked in a cul-de-sac as if they might be visiting one of the three houses facing it. They grabbed their backpacks of surveillance gear and headed out, cutting through a vacant lot, and wading through thigh-deep snow. They climbed a ridge that ran behind the neighborhood, and it was a miracle none of them broke their necks on the icy rocks. From there, they headed toward their target, relatively unimpeded.

A few minutes later, they lay on their stomachs, looking down at the house. Lights were on in the kitchen, and the older woman could be seen moving around. Looked like she was cooking supper for a large crowd.

"Let's put some eyes and ears on them and see what we get," Vanessa murmured.

Isabella pulled out a portable parabolic microphone and unfolded its sensitive dish. She put the clamshell headphones over her ears and pointed the mike at the house. "I've got two female voices. Did you leave the recorder running in the van, Python?"

"Affirmative," Karen replied.

Isabella pushed the button to start transmitting the signal to the van's receiver while Aleesha pulled out a paparazzi-sized telephoto lens and screwed it onto a camera.

Vanessa murmured, "That got the high res film in it?"

"Yeah, mon," Aleesha answered. "Me baby heah' see de fleas on de dog."

The team chuckled. Vanessa replied dryly, "All I need are their faces."

Aleesha pointed the camera down the hill and muttered

from behind the nearly two-foot long lens, "You'll be able to see their whiskers with this puppy."

Vanessa nodded. "Just get the shots."

"Roger, girly-o."

Aleesha's Rasta rap meant she was either under severe stress or having a ball. Must be the latter. As for Isabella, she was getting cold. Even in arctic gear, a person could only lie on the frozen ground for so long before the cold made a Popsicle of her.

Something cracked behind them, and she whipped her head around to look for the source of the noise. No heat signatures leaped out at her in bright relief through her night-vision goggles.

"Movement on the road," Karen murmured.

Isabella looked back at the driveway. Bingo. The second car. The three burly men from the earlier meeting piled out. She gaped as two of them peeled off and proceeded to head out into the woods around the house! For all the world, it looked like they were walking a perimeter security patrol. Who *were* these guys?

Vanessa signaled sharply for everyone to get down. Isabella plastered herself against the rocks and peered down at the twin blobs of bright white as they made their way through the woods. One of them turned, and she caught a momentary glimpse of a tubular black void in one of the man's hands. *Weapon.*

She signaled that at least one of the men was armed. Her teammates nodded grimly. No doubt wondering the same thing she was. *Why were armed men patrolling this quiet little corner of nowhere?*

Vanessa gave the signal for the Medusas to spread out. Very slowly, moving by inches, the four women eased apart, sliding across the summit. Vanessa signaled Isabella and Karen to move down into the woods behind the two men, far enough back not to risk engaging them. The men separated. Python would follow the man closest to her, while Isabella tracked the other guy.

The snow was deep and heavy. Hard to move in quietly. Step by careful step, Isabella waded forward. Her legs burned from the effort of keeping her balance and moving in such exaggerated slow motion. But she dared not let the discomfort distract her. The guy in front of her looked like the sort who'd shoot first and ask questions later.

It took the men about fifteen minutes to complete a circuit of the woods. One of them started up the rocky slope toward Vanessa's last position.

"Incoming," Isabella breathed in warning.

"We're on it," Vanessa murmured.

Meanwhile, Isabella's guy turned abruptly, veering into a crevasse between two huge boulders. There wasn't squat for cover over there. She crouched in some dead scrub and waited to see if the guy would come back out this way or if there was an exit from the other end.

Karen whispered, "I've got visual on your guy, Adder. Just exited the crevasse."

Isabella eased forward on her belly, eating a faceful of snow as she low-crawled forward on her elbows. God, that hurt. She never had built up quite enough upper body strength for this maneuver. At least the snow wasn't deep in here. Only a foot or so of it. She stopped short as a wire appeared in front of her nose. That was a trip wire!

Isabella traced it carefully with her fingertips to a small pile of sharp stones off to one side of the passage. She grasped the end of the wire between her fingertips to make sure she didn't move it, and with the other hand, one by one lifted away the stones.

They'd hidden a small explosive charge. It was just enough to send the pile of rocks flying at whoever tripped the wire. There was no doubt the trap was aimed at humans, as opposed to the local bunnies, because the wire was set about fifteen inches off the ground—too high to catch any rodents moving through here.

She whispered into her mike, "Trip wire."

Doubly cautious now, she crawled to the end of the crevasse, crouching low to peer around the end of it. Her target was moving back toward the house. Karen's guy was converging on the back door as well. Must be suppertime. The two men went inside. She and Karen made their way back up the slope, watching for more wires or other joyful surprises.

Finally, panting hard, she plopped down on her stomach beside Aleesha. "See anything good in the house?"

"Well, subjugation of women is alive and well in Chechnya. The men are sitting at the table eating and the women are serving them." Aleesha lapsed into her island accent. "Any mon ask my grandmama do dat for dem, she put a voodoo curse on dem, make-a de pee-pee fall off, mmm hmm, bye-bye wonker."

Isabella suppressed a laugh. Unfortunately, she remembered well watching women wait on men hand and foot in her mother's family. She'd been told that not everyone in Iran lived that way, but it had always left a sour taste in her mouth.

They waited in the dark and cold for another hour while the men finished eating, and the women ate a hasty meal then cleaned up the kitchen. Gradually, the lights in the house went out. There were no more forays by the thug types out into the winter night.

Vanessa called a halt to the surveillance a little after 11:00 p.m., which was just as well. Karen and Isabella were due to relieve Misty at midnight. They drove back to town, and Isabella went straight to the ops center. For once, Dex wasn't there when she walked in. Beau Breckenridge was, though.

"Hey, Hobo. Thanks for the help earlier."

He grinned. "Always a pleasure to help out a pretty lady."

Darned if she didn't feel herself blushing a little. It wasn't like she was attracted to the guy, but it was weird to have such a hunk making nice with her. For the last year plus, she'd spent her life covered in mud and running around in combat boots. She'd almost forgotten what it was like to have someone look at her like she might be a moderately attractive woman.

She allowed herself to smile back at Beau. "I've got some high-res film I need developed ASAP, and then we'll need IDs on everyone in the pictures. We know one of the subjects. The young, lean kid is a Chechnyan figure skater named Lazlo Petrovich."

Beau reached out for the film, but another tanned, hard hand reached around from behind her to grab it. Isabella didn't even have to look over her shoulder to know who it was. Dex.

"I'll take care of it," he growled.

What was he so grouchy about?

She turned around, frowning, and stopped cold, staring straight at his chest. His naked, sweaty chest. His naked, sweaty chest covered in slabs of muscle and just enough dark, curly hair to make her palms itch to feel it. *Hel-lo.*

"I, uh, have a, um, CD, too. We recorded it," she added stupidly.

"What's on it?" Dex asked, still irritable.

Oh, God. His pecs just flexed. *Do that again!*

"Uh," she mumbled, "we recorded a conversation in, um, a bar. It's probably in Russian and, um, Misty speaks that. We'll translate it."

"Aren't you supposed to go on guard duty about now?" he snapped.

She mentally shook herself. "Yeah."

"I'm headed over that way," he said.

Okay. And? She turned to walk out and realized his comment had been intended to explain that he was going to walk with her to the village via the underground tunnel connecting the two facilities. The tunnel was well lit, but on the cool side for a guy without a shirt who was covered with a fine sheen of sweat. Although why she should notice it was a fine sheen, she had no idea. Couldn't be good.

"Where are you headed?" she managed to ask in a semblance of a normal voice.

"Back to the gym to finish my workout."

"You work out at this time of night?" she asked.

"Only time I've got off."

She sighed. "I ought to do the same." Her shoulders were suspiciously achy after all that low crawling earlier.

"Meet me at the gym tomorrow at eleven. I'll work out with you."

Her gaze snapped to his in surprise. She stammered, "I wouldn't even want to try to keep up with you. I've seen you guys work out."

He laughed. "Some of the kids in this gym are putting me in my place."

She'd bet it wasn't many of them even if they were Olympic athletes. He peeled off as they passed by the health club. She managed not to stare at him as he went over to the nearest weight machine, knelt and began pulling down a crazy number of slabs of iron. She wasn't watching him, dammit!

Thankfully, her feet kept moving of their own volition and carried her out of visual range of all that lovely brawn. She'd caught her breath by the time she reached Anya's room, but it was most of the night before the image finally faded enough for her to breathe normally again.

Morning came at about the same time her eyes began to feel like sand had been poured into them. God. Two nights in a row of practically no sleep. She'd played sleep deprivation games in training and knew she could, in fact, go quite a bit longer without rest if she had to, but that didn't make it feel any better.

Anya boinged out of bed early, tense, almost feverishly so. Game day jitters. Today was her qualifying skate. All of the female figure skaters would perform their long programs, and only thirty with the highest scores would progress to the next round of competition. For the top skaters in the world, today was a formality. But for an unknown like Anya, it was a critical do-or-die moment.

Isabella did her best to stay out of the way as Anya and her coach ate breakfast and began the mental psych up for this afternoon's skate. The two women talked through Anya's program, reviewing every detail. It was shocking how involved a single, four-and-a-half minute long routine could be. It was planned, literally, down to the exact number of foot strokes.

At about midmorning, Anya and her coach went for a walk for a change of scenery and a mental break. Karen stayed ahead of them and Isabella trailed close behind. After a light lunch, Anya headed back to her room for a nap while her coach ran a few errands.

Isabella and Karen cleared the room, then stepped outside, preparing to hand over guard duty to Misty and Kat.

A scream erupted from inside Anya's room. It was followed by an anguished wail. Isabella charged inside, ready to kill. They were through the door before Isabella registered that it had been locked and they'd busted right through the doorjamb. Anya stood in the middle of her room, keening, handfuls of rags grasped in her hands.

"What's wrong?" Isabella asked her sharply.

"My costumes!"

Isabella frowned. "What about them?"

"They're ruined!" Anya cried.

Isabella's gaze went back to the brightly colored rags. Those were her costumes? They were shredded to ribbons.

She noticed a small crowd had gathered in the hall. "Show's over, folks." She closed the door in the onlookers' faces. It only half-latched, but it was enough to keep the gawkers at bay.

She turned to deal with the disaster. "Are any of them salvageable?" she asked Karen, who was examining the dresses. Her teammate was having trouble even finding a recognizable top so she could hold them up. Karen shook her head in the negative.

"When's the last time you saw them intact?" Isabella asked the skater.

She repeated her question before Anya gasped out between what had turned into wracking sobs, "Th-th-this morning."

When they were out taking their walk and eating, then. Housekeeping had come in during that time to clean the room and straighten the bed. And someone had come in to wreak a little havoc, too, apparently. She keyed her throat mike. "Ops, Adder."

"Go ahead, dahlin'," Beau drawled.

"Someone got into the subject's room and destroyed all of her costumes. Probably within the last thirty to forty minutes. Subject is safe."

"Gee whiz. That sucks. Doesn't she skate in a few hours?"

"Yeah."

"What's she gonna wear?" Beau asked.

Isabella sighed heavily. "No idea. We'll cross that bridge later. Can you locate her coach, an Aussie named Liz Cartwright, and get her here ASAP?"

"You betchya, sweet pea."

Never in her wildest dreams would she have guessed any man could call her sweet pea and not completely piss her off, but the guy was harmless.

Roughly ten minutes later, Liz Cartwright burst into the room. She took one look at Anya's ruined costumes and her eyes snapped like lightning. She might be a tiny thing, but she clearly had a she-bear's king-size temper. She gathered Anya in a motherly hug and let the girl cry on her shoulder.

Eventually, she murmured over Anya's head to Isabella, "I need you to call the ISU. Tell them what's happened. Ask for permission to skate in training wear or something."

Isabella nodded and called Beau. "Hey, Hobo, it's me. I need a phone number. Woman's name is Lily Gustavson. She's an ISU official."

"I S who?"

She smiled. "ISU. International Skating Union. The governing body for the women's figure skating competition."

Beau was still tracking down a phone number for Ms. Gustavson, who happened to be the only ISU official whose name Isabella knew off the top of her head, when a knock sounded on the door.

Phone still plastered to her ear, Isabella cracked it open. Blinked. Opened the door all the way. No less than twenty young women stood there, all carrying garment bags.

"Uh, Beau," Isabella said into the phone, "never mind. If I need that number, I'll call you back." To the young women she said, "May I help you?"

"Well," said one of them, "actually, we were wondering if *we* could help *you.* We heard what happened. So we brought our extra costumes to see if one of them might fit Anya. My name's Ashley Caldwell. I'm American."

As if Isabella couldn't figure that one out by the girl's Texas twang. "Come on in, ladies." She stepped back from the door.

Anya looked up, red-eyed, as nearly two dozen of her competitors piled into the room and proceeded to unzip their bags and spill out a riot of silk organza and crystals all over the king-size bed. Giggles erupted before long and the party was on. The girls laughed and chattered, trading their opinions on everything from the latest rock music to which of the male skaters was the cutest.

Before long, Anya was smiling tentatively. Half a dozen costumes into the impromptu gathering, she was laughing along with the others. It turned out the girls came from all over the world: Karis Neidermeier of Germany, who was one of the favorites to win; Kimberly and Stephanie Takamura, sisters from Indonesia; Shyamali Fernandes from Argentina; Alyssa Walcheka of Russia; Sara Dormonkova of Ukraine; Alexandria Marweshandra of India.

And every last one of them offered up gorgeous costumes worth thousands of dollars to an unknown skater from a tiny country who had no realistic chance to win this competition. Isabella was touched enough that she finally asked, "Why are all of you doing this?"

Darlene Cameron, a Canadian, answered for all of them. "Because she'd do the same for us. Skaters get a bad rap for being cutthroat and unfriendly, but it's not true. Sure, there's the occasional nasty skater. But all of us have worked so hard to get here, we can't help but respect each other."

Karis Neidermeier piped up in her precise English. "Each of us competes against a numerical standard. All I can do is skate my best and post the highest score I can. We only compete against each other to the extent that I hope my best is better than someone else's best on a given day."

"And anyway, judges are sometimes right and sometimes not," one of the Takamura sisters added. "Not always does best skater win. You do your best and not worry about results."

Alyssa, the Russian skater laughed. "I admit I sometime wish for other skater bad day have. But nothing I do make them do better or worse score. So it is nothing if I hope for them to fall or skate clean."

All the girls laughed. Isabella got the gist of what the girl was trying to say. It didn't matter whether the skaters rooted for or against each other, because it was up to each skater to do her best or not do her best. Therefore, the skaters didn't bear each other any direct animosity. They concentrated instead on skating well themselves and not worrying about the others. A pretty healthy attitude overall.

Anya stepped out of her bathroom in a stunning yellow silk costume that faded into fire-engine red at the bottom of the skirt. It had plunging V's of flesh-colored tricot, front and back, that went practically to her waist. It was slathered in faceted crystals and burned like fire against Anya's skin. All the girls oohed and ahhed.

"That's the one!" they exclaimed.

Isabella sighed, and spoke up from her perch by the door

where she was keeping an eye on the maintenance man fixing the door frame. "I hate to be a wet blanket, Anya, but that's a pretty…suggestive…costume."

Anya rolled her eyes. "It's got fabric up to my neck. Nothing shows!"

"Honey, on television, it'll look like you're half-naked. There's already an uproar over the fact that you're skating at all. I really don't think you should fan the flames by wearing something that racy."

The room went silent. With a defiant edge to it. Crud. The other girls had no idea what was really at stake here. Isabella tried again. "People want to kill you. There's no reason to egg them on by waving a big red-and-yellow flag at them."

Anya scowled. "I understand you're trying to look out for me. But I am *not* here to make a political or religious statement. I'm here to skate in the Olympics. Period. And I'll wear whatever I want. This costume is gorgeous, and if Karis wouldn't mind my borrowing it, I want to wear it. It makes me feel pretty."

Several of the girls jumped in. "It makes you look pretty, too…. Those colors are awesome with your coloring…. I say go for it…."

Isabella closed her eyes in a combination of frustration and dismay. "Anya. My job is to keep you alive. If you do this, you're going to enrage people who are already gunning for you. Literally. I can't let you do this."

Anya spoke firmly. "'Bella, you *must* let me do this. On behalf of all the women who are still trapped behind the veil."

Aww, hell. Did Anya *have* to nail her Achilles' heel like that? A sinking feeling settled in the pit of her stomach as she realized she *was* going to let the girl skate in the gorgeous costume. And just as surely, they both were going to regret it.

Chapter 10

Isabella escorted Anya and her coach into the covered tunnel that took the skaters practically all the way to the ice, protecting them from the spectators. But nothing could protect Anya once she stepped onto the rink. Thirty thousand people would be within striking range, and the girl would have nothing but a thin layer of silk between herself and all of them.

Anya was parked in a mirrored, heated waiting room, hanging on to a ballet bar with her foot over her head, stretching, when Isabella's cell phone rang.

"Go ahead," she murmured.

"Hey, baby. It's Hobo."

Baby? This was an open frequency, able to be monitored by anyone in the Ops center. She replied briskly, "What do you need?"

"I've got a pile of news for ya."

She stuck a finger in her free ear and turned away from the speaker blaring music into the room. "Lay it on me."

"Well, you remember that fella you and me were both chasing the day we first bumped into each other? When we got all tangled up and—"

She cut him off. "I remember. What of it?"

Breckenridge laughed. "You're just playing hard to get, aren't you?"

Hard to get? God help her if Dex was monitoring this call. "Did you have some news for me or not, Rhett?"

"As in Butler?" He laughed heartily in her ear. "Why, thank you kindly for that. Let's see. First, the FBI got a fingerprint match on that guy you whupped up on in the alley. He's a Bhoukari kid named Reda Aziz. We don't know much about him, but we're trying to find out more from his government."

"Ask if he's a disciple of Ahmed al Abhoud's."

"Wilco, baby."

Her voice silky with the promise of violence, she said, "Beau, quit calling me baby."

"All right…dahlin'."

Incorrigible. "Anything else?"

"The FBI also ID'd some of Lazlo Petrovich's friends from last night. Turns out they're the skater's father, mother and two sisters. One of the other three guys is a dude called Ilya Gorabchek. Chechnyan terrorist with a rap sheet a mile long. The Russians have already asked the Justice Department for permission to nab him, but they got turned down. It's the Olympics, after all. So now they're trying to work some quickie extradition deal for the Americans to arrest him and ship him back to the motherland."

"What about the other two thugs?" she asked.

"Still working on it. FBI's guessing they'll turn out to be associates of Gorabchek's."

She frowned. Associates? As in, say, members of the same terrorist cell? That didn't sound good. "Any other news?"

"Some guy named Picante or something called. Said to tell you no luck on the search yet. Should I be jealous of this guy, baby?" Fumbling noises came from the other end of the phone as if Beau had just jerked the receiver well away from his ear.

She gritted her teeth. "The name is Piccone. Lake Placid police. He's looking for Al Abhoud for me. And if you call me baby again, I'm going to have to hurt you."

A new male voice replied dryly, "Sounds like fun, but I'll pass. And trust me, I'll never call you baby."

Aww, jeez. Dex.

"Hello, Dex," she mumbled in chagrin.

"Adder."

"Anything I can do for you, sir?"

"How's it going over there?"

"So far so good. But I haven't put her on the ice yet."

"I've sent every warm body I can spare to the arena to mingle with the crowd and keep an eye out."

"Thanks. And we'll need the help. Wait till you get a load of her costume."

"What did she do?" Dex asked in alarm.

"Watch her on television. You can't miss it."

He swore under his breath. "We didn't need any more complications."

"Tell me about it. I tried to talk her out of it." Her conscience twinged. She could've tried harder. But a secret part of her wanted Anya to wear that daring costume, wanted her to make the bold statement it represented.

"Yell if you need anything."

"Yes, sir."

"Quit sirring me. You're making me feel like an old man."

She retorted, "Hey, at least I'm not calling you 'baby.'"

"You need me to kick Hobo's ass for you?"

So, he *had* been listening in on the frequency. "Thanks, but I'll kick his butt myself if it comes to that."

"I'm serious. Do you need me to back him off?"

"I'm serious, too. I'll take care of it myself."

"But—"

She cut him off. "If one of your men were having a problem with another guy calling him names he didn't like, would you intervene?"

"Hell, no. I'd tell him to either get over it or do something about it."

"There you have it," she said firmly.

He exhaled hard. Sounded frustrated.

"You gotta let go of this need to protect the girls, Dex. I'm telling you. I can take care of myself."

He retorted, albeit very quietly, "Just because you can doesn't mean you should always have to."

"It does until we've earned the respect of everyone in the Special Ops community."

Another sigh. "That's going to take a while."

She shrugged, even though Dex couldn't see it at the other end of the line. "Then I guess I'll be fighting my own battles for a while to come."

Dex must not have known what to say in response for there was heavy silence at the other end of the line.

"Gotta go," she announced. "It's time for Anya's warm-up."

"Be safe."

"Always."

She pocketed the phone and escorted Anya into the tunnel. Someone came rushing at them from behind, and Isabella whirled, her hands up at the defensive. Lily Gustavson. The ISU official. The woman shoved something at Anya, and Isabella intercepted it reflexively. She looked down. The black fleece wad resolved itself into a jacket and a cap with a jaunty, multicolored pom-pom.

"What's this?" Isabella asked.

"We heard about what happened earlier. We're concerned about the safety of all the skaters, so the ISU is providing matching warm-up jackets and hats for all the female skaters. All the other girls have agreed to wear them during the warm-up so that Anya will be difficult to distinguish."

Isabella looked around. Sure enough, the other skaters crowding into the tunnel, talking to the their coaches, taking off their skate guards and jumping up and down were all wearing identical jackets. She handed the garment to Anya, who was already taking off her red sweater.

Anya put on the jacket and looked at the ISU official. "Thanks," she whispered.

Isabella started. Anya looked close to tears. It was the first chink she'd seen in the girl's otherwise bubbly armor. "That was very kind of you," Isabella added.

The blond woman smiled. "Good luck, Anya. The hearts of millions of women around the world go with you."

Anya's eyes widened. *Never thought of it like that, huh?* Abruptly the girl looked nervous. Aww, hell. Isabella knew from her own training that sometimes it was a bad thing to think too much about what you were doing. Sometimes you just had to put the danger and the difficulty of a task out of your mind and go for it.

She put a hand on Anya's shoulder. "Just focus on your skating. There'll be plenty of time to worry about all the rest of it later."

Liz piped up, "What's the first thing you have to think about?"

"Take my time on the opening arms, then push off strongly. Long glide…"

Isabella smiled as the girl fell easily into the litany of her program. She was ready.

A male ISU official called from the gate at the edge of the ice, "Group three, onto the ice please. You will have six minutes to warm up. Our first skater will be Kimberly Takamura. She may stay on the ice at the end of the warm-up period."

As a group, the young ladies stepped up to the gate and onto the ice.

And Anya was gone. Out of Isabella's hands and into the fingers of fate.

In the past week, she'd started to feel almost like a big sister to Anya. And all she could do now was stand by and watch. She moved up to the rail beside Liz.

"How do you stand here and watch so calmly?" Isabella murmured to her.

Liz laughed. "I'm a mess. But I can't let my skater see that. Besides, she's either ready or she's not. No coaching I do now will make a difference. My only job at this point is to get her into the right frame of mind. The rest is up to her."

Isabella glanced around the big arena. If other OSG types were roaming around, they were being subtle about it. She looked back to the ice. The matching black jackets and hats were working. All the skaters looked the same. The only reason she could pick out Anya was because she was so familiar with the girl's build and movements. Still, it was the longest six minutes Isabella had ever experienced.

A bright light exploded to their left, and Isabella coiled to launch herself at Anya before she registered the source of the flash. A team of television broadcasters had just gone back on the air and were talking into the cameras directly beneath the row of bright lights. Oh, good Lord. Now she was jumping at stage lights.

She walked beside her charge back to the waiting area but stayed outside, out of the way, Anya parked in a corner, plastered a headset on her ears and, eyes closed, walked through her routine until Liz touched her arm to indicate it was time to go.

For once, Anya was silent as she walked down the long tunnel. Her jaw was set, the look in her eye determined. It was the first time Isabella had seen this side of her. But then, she supposed nobody made it to the Olympics without being a hell of a competitor.

Anya took off her jacket, and Isabella couldn't help but wince. The costume was stunning…but man, oh man, was it going to tick off Al Abhoud and his ilk. Anya gazed straight at her, almost daring her to say something.

"You look beautiful." Isabella smiled. "Go get 'em."

Anya smiled back and nodded.

Perhaps she'd underestimated the girl. Maybe Anya did, indeed, understand exactly what she was doing. If Anya Khalid wanted to make a statement to the world about the talent and guts of Muslim girls, who was Isabella—a woman of Muslim background herself, who'd broken every rule in the book as to the proper role of women in society—to tell the girl not to?

Harlan Holt sat on the end of the bed, staring nervously at the television. Was this it? Was this the moment for whatever evil those men had planned? He prayed it wasn't. But in a selfish corner of his mind, he prayed it was. The sooner this whole thing was over, the sooner Emma would be returned to him.

What in the hell were those monsters up to?

His preliminary lab tests showed the perplexing white powder to be a man-made substance. What he wouldn't give to be able to talk it over with Emma. From her work with recombinant DNA, she knew a great deal about manipulating chemicals and molecular structures.

The chemical had a complex structure. Under magnification, it looked like a thistle flower with a bulbous structure at one end and a cluster of rods with strange little hooks on the ends at the other. They almost looked designed to latch onto another molecule. But what?

The television announcer's voice caught his attention. That Bhoukari girl was the next skater.

Harlan didn't know for sure that the men who'd snatched Emma were Middle Eastern but they'd looked and sounded Arabic. He also didn't know if their attack might be aimed at the Khalid girl, but it made sense. She was supposedly stirring up controversy in the Muslim world. And clearly the kidnappers wanted to do something to someone who was a figure skater. Why else would they have forced him to mix that powder into the ice?

His heart raced as the commercial break ended and the skating coverage came back on the screen.

Please let nothing happen...please just get it over with....

The previous skater, Sara Dormonkova of the Ukraine stepped off the ice and made her way to the kiss-and-cry area—where the skaters awaited and received their scores on camera before the eyes of the world.

Liz gave Anya one last set of instructions. "Breathe. Focus. You know what to do, just go out and do it." The girl nodded and stepped onto the ice. A murmur went up from the crowd. It sounded mostly like approval for the gorgeous picture she made, but there was a note of consternation in the sound as well. The implications of her daring costume were not lost on anyone.

"Holy shit."

Isabella jumped at the outburst in her earpiece. Well, she knew Dex had the TV on, at any rate.

"Why didn't she just skate naked and really make the point?" he growled.

"The costume is beautiful and she's radiant in it."

"Yeah, and the bloodstains when she's shot full of holes will match it perfectly. What the hell were you thinking, letting her wear that?"

"I was thinking that there's nothing wrong with her wearing whatever she wants. That's the sort of costume all the skaters wear." Isabella's indignation picked up a head of steam. "If she's going to be put to death for lifting her leg in the air or showing the bottoms of her feet, who the hell cares if she wears a dress like that? She's going to piss off those stiff-necked graybeards anyway, so why not go for the gusto?"

"I thought you told me there'd be no conflict of interest. You sound awfully worked up about this." Dex's voice was quiet. Serious. And that made it sting all the more. He was right, dammit. She *was* personally involved in this girl's political statement. How could she not be?

Her gut churning, Isabella waited out the announcement of the Ukrainian skater's scores. Then it was Anya's turn.

Like some sort of magical swan, her arms outstretched as if to embrace everyone in the arena, Anya glided to the middle of the ice and onto the world stage. And damned if she didn't *own* it in that moment.

Pride swelled in Isabella's breast. Even if Anya's program crashed and burned, she'd done it. She'd stepped out in front of the entire world and dared it to look at her. Without a veil. And she was strong and beautiful and free.

Anya's music began, a smoky, mysterious melody from Bhoukar. Her arms moved bonelessly, like a swallow's wings dipping and swaying in flight. A drum began, and Anya pushed off into motion. A strong glide, held for three seconds like she was supposed to. Good girl. Isabella caught herself counting out crossovers as Anya picked up speed…four…five…six… and now the backward glide and deep edge into the triple lutz. The music crescendoed just as Anya leaped into the air, as light and powerful as the swan she resembled. She landed softly on a deeply bent knee, with a good, long, running edge out of the jump. *Yes!*

Isabella actually clenched her fists as the program unfolded, practically skating with the girl as Anya sailed around the ice. Isabella sucked in her breath as Anya bobbled her triple salchow, but managed to right herself and save the jump without touching a hand down to the ice. The music picked up speed, full orchestration kicked in, and Isabella felt almost as if she'd been lifted off her feet and was flying around the arena as Anya picked up momentum and got stronger and stronger as the program progressed.

The audience clapped and cheered, urging her on as they, too, were sucked into the soaring beauty of Anya's skating. There was a freedom—a joy—to it that was infectious. Everyone was on the ice with her, sharing the power of the moment.

And then the last jump—a flawless triple flip. Isabella

recited the end of the program in her head as Anya performed it...*flying camel into a sit spin, count the revolutions, push up strong to vertical, and pull in hard with the arms into the scratch spin...* Anya twirled like a dervish, the brilliantly colored costume flashing like a column of flame. A jab with a toe pick into the ice to stop the revolutions, and Anya flung her arms up into the air in a final, triumphant pose.

It was over.

The crowd went wild. They knew they'd witnessed a historic event. A glorious moment of human transcendence. Isabella looked around and saw tears on many cheeks, male and female. Surprised, she touched her own cheeks and found them wet.

Focus. She was here to do a job. She mustn't let herself get distracted. The applause continued and apprehension built in her gut. Anya had been out there a long time, standing still in the middle of the rink after her program. She needed to get moving. Now. But the ovation went on, and Anya continued to wave and throw kisses to the crowd.

Get off the ice! Isabella shouted silently.

Anya curtsied to the sides and ends of the arena. Waved to the screaming crowd some more. Skated over to where someone had thrown a large teddy bear onto the ice. Flowers rained down. Hundreds of them, wrapped in plastic sleeves to keep petals and leaves from falling onto the ice and making it dangerous for the next skater. Anya bent to scoop up a dozen of them.

Come on!

An army of little girls in white dresses skated out to do pickup patrol, and still Anya wasn't off the ice. The crowd continued to scream, and Anya continued to smile and wave.

Finally, *finally,* Anya turned to skate for the exit. It was all Isabella could do not to jump onto the ice and wrap her arms around her charge. But, after an eternity, Anya finally stepped off the ice. Liz herded her over to the kiss-and-cry area. A tall wall behind the upholstered bench shielded it from the spectators, and a phalanx of television cameras acted like metal armor across the front. Anya and Liz sat down, and Isabella's knees went weak. Anya was back under cover. *Safe.*

Anya's scores were posted and the crowd roared its approval. Fifth place with only seven more skaters to go. She could finish no lower than twelfth. She'd made it into the next round. Isabella didn't know whether to pump her fist and shout for joy or swear. She was going to have to endure that agony of helplessness again and put Anya back on the ice at least one more time, standing by on the sidelines, praying that it wasn't the girl's day to die.

"Congratulations," Dex murmured in her ear. "She made the next round."

Isabella scowled. "Whoopee."

Dex chuckled. "Sucks turning 'em loose, doesn't it?"

Clearly, he'd pulled bodyguard duty before. "You said it," she replied.

"Look at it this way. You've got four more days before the short program to draw out the bad guys and figure out what's going on around her. Take your girl home and celebrate with her. She deserves it. Gutsy kid."

"Thanks. I'll tell her you said that."

When Isabella relayed his message, Anya was so delirious with excitement it was hard to tell if a word of it registered. In the midst of all the celebration, a woman came into the changing room carrying a large bag. Isabella leaped between her and Anya.

"And you might be?" Isabella asked politely.

"Judy Levinson. The seamstress."

"What seamstress?"

The blond woman in her forties smiled. "The emergency seamstress. Every large international skating competition has a seamstress on call to mend last minutes rips, broken zippers, replace lost crystals. You name it. I even carry spare boot laces."

Isabella replied, "How are you at full costumes on no notice?"

Judy smiled. "It takes me overnight, but no problem. That's why I'm here. I understand Ms. Khalid needs a couple of costumes right away."

Anya stepped around Isabella, her eyes big. "You can do a whole costume overnight? With crystals and everything? It takes my mom months to make one of my competition costumes."

The woman unzipped her garment bag. "Well, I cheat a little. These costumes are already partially made. I just fit them and finish the seams. Most of the decorations are already complete. I glue on a few crystals at the seams, and voila! I'm done. Let's see if we've got something in here that might work for you."

Anya oohed and ahhed over the array of costumes.

Judy said, "Tell me about your short program."

"I skate to an interlude from *Swan Lake*. It's light and airy, but it's not the dying swan bit. I don't want any feathers or tutus," Anya declared.

Judy laughed. "I may have just the thing. It's an ice-dancing costume, but given the circumstances, it might be perfect."

"Won't the skirt be too long?" Anya asked in alarm.

"There are always scissors, dear."

The costume was, indeed, spectacular. It was all white, and more to the point, it had long sleeves and a high turtleneck collar. Narrow flowing strips of flesh-colored cloth were inset along the entire length of the white tricot bodice. Long, sinuous rows of clear crystals falling from the shoulder looked like water flowing over Anya's body. The skirt was made up of many narrow strips of white silk so fine it was almost sheer. Even when Anya walked over to the mirror, the strips moved like a breeze caressing the girl's legs. Although the costume covered a great deal more skin than the yellow-and-red one had, the overall effect was, if possible, even sexier. Anya's slender curves were perfectly highlighted, and her skin glowed golden against the stark white. *Kowabunga.*

Anya's face lit up when she looked at her reflection. "It's perfect," she breathed.

Judy cautioned, "When you skate, that skirt is going to plaster itself against your legs and outline them very clearly. It won't leave anything to the imagination." The woman sent a significant glance in Isabella's direction.

Anya nodded. "That's fine. I'm supposed to be a swan flying anyway."

The seamstress peeled the costume off the girl gently. "You'll look like a fairy princess. And this will be ready tomorrow."

Anya stepped into the dressing room to change into street clothes, and Isabella remarked quietly to the seamstress, "She doesn't compete in the short program for four more days, so it's okay if you sleep tonight. And a word of advice. Keep that costume locked up at all times, and don't tell anyone which costume you're preparing for her."

The seamstress absorbed all that then nodded. "How about if I work on a decoy costume?"

"That might be an excellent idea."

Anya stepped out, dressed in a black turtleneck and a black velvet warm-up suit. She packed her skates, and Liz pulled the rolling gear bag as they left the locker room. Isabella would've offered to help, except she needed to keep her hands free to respond to any threat that might arise. Bodyguard she was, packhorse she was not. Next on the agenda: run the press gauntlet and then get the heck out of Dodge.

They entered the press briefing area, a large room split down the middle by a waist-high railing—athletes on one side and journalists on the other. The space in front of Anya was instantly mobbed with reporters shouting for her attention. Thankfully, the vast majority hailed from everywhere but the Middle East, and very few of them asked any questions of substance. Anya was her usual perky, cheerful, nineteen-year-old self, and smiled her way through it all, basking innocently in the spotlight.

Isabella hovered just off camera, her gaze roving across the crowd. She wasn't worried about this bunch. They had to go through nearly as much security rigamarole as the athletes did to get into this special press pit. Nonetheless, she kept a sharp eye on the men and women hanging over the rail, shoving microphones at her charge.

After about a half hour, Isabella leaned over to Liz and muttered, "Time to call it. They're starting to repeat their questions, and that's enough exposure for one night. My nerves can't take any more of this."

Liz grinned and fetched their instant star. They left the press area and headed for the back of the complex where the garage directly under the stadium allowed for protected loading and unloading.

Karen had an SUV waiting for them. It was one of the armored vehicles used for VIP transport. It had blacked out, bulletproof windows, full body armor, and license plates that wouldn't draw attention, as opposed to the Olympic plates on official vehicles.

The ride back to the Olympic village was uneventful. They waited patiently at the vehicle checkpoint while guards ran mirrors under their car and popped the hood for a look at the engine block. Then they were waved through.

Anya bounced into her room and flopped on the bed. "I did it!" she crowed. "I nailed my program!"

She'd done a whole lot more than that, but there would be time later to reflect on it. A lifetime. Isabella asked casually, "So, are you hungry? I noticed you didn't eat much this morning, and it's almost suppertime."

"I'm starving!"

Typical teenager. Isabella grinned. "What's your pleasure?"

"I want to celebrate," Anya announced.

"Pizza? Hot-fudge sundae? Banana split, maybe?"

Anya laughed. "I still have to skate in four days. I can't go too crazy. But I know what I want."

"Name it."

"I want New York pizzeria-style pizza." A pause. "In New York."

"You are in New York," Isabella answered cautiously.

"No, I mean outside of the Olympic village. I want to go downtown."

"Now, Anya—"

"Don't you 'Now, Anya' me! I've been cooped up inside this hotel for a week and I haven't been out once. Tonight I want to party! I'm an adult, you know. You can't treat me like a child."

"Then act like an adult and don't do something foolish and dangerous."

"Sorry. My mind's made up. I'm going out. Are you coming with me or not?"

Isabella knew a losing battle when she saw one. "I'll make you a deal," she said desperately. "You can go downtown, but you've got to let me call in some backup. I can't protect you out there alone."

"You've got a deal, mate! Put the shrimp on the barby, boys!" she sang as she disappeared into her bathroom to put on party clothes.

Oh, Lord. And Dex thought the bold costume was stupid. Wait until he got a load of this. She cringed to even think about how the gang back at the ops center was going to react to this radio call.

"Ops, this is Adder. I've got a strange request. I, uh, need a couple men. To go out on a date."

Chapter 11

Isabella opened the door to Anya's room and stared in shock. Dex and Beau wore slacks and sweaters, both cleanly shaven and for all the world looking like they were going out on dates.

Oh, God. Not Don Juan and the Grinch. Not both of them at the same time. "Where are the Medusas?" Maybe her teammates would bail her out.

"Captain Cordell is in the ops center working on the translation of last night's tapes of Lazlo and friends, and the rest of your team is staking out that bunch again, trying to get more conversation on tape," Dex replied.

"I gather, then, the first tapes are proving interesting?"

"You could say that. Ever heard of a group called the Red Jihad?"

"No. But with a name like that, they don't sound like cookie salesmen."

"Good guess. I'll fill you in later. Until then, you're stuck with me and Hobo."

Great.

Anya cooed not too quietly from the other side of the room, "Way to go, 'Bella! Where'd you scare up two such cute guys?"

Cute? Nah. Hot, for sure. Drop-dead gorgeous, maybe. But neither man was *cute*. They were too mature, too self-possessed, too…lethal…to qualify as cute. Isabella raised an eyebrow at the pair. "Are you two sure you can handle nineteen and perky?"

Beau grinned like the Cheshire cat. "Are you kidding? She's not jailbait *and* she's perky? Sign me up."

Isabella's eyes narrowed. "Lay a hand on her and I'll rip it off. *Kapische?*"

"Aw, 'Bella! Don't be such a party pooper," Anya complained.

Beau winked at Isabella. "Don't go reminding me why I'm all hot and bothered by you, now, sugar. I love it when you talk tough."

Isabella laughed at his silliness and was doubly amused when she caught a glimpse of Dex's jaw rippling in irritation. She turned to her charge, enunciating each word clearly. "Anya, honey, for the record, you've never met any men like these two. Take it from me. They're way out of your league," and as the girl opened her mouth to protest, she added, "And you're way out of theirs. Flirt all you want with them, but don't expect anything in return."

Isabella turned back to the men, and Dex drilled her with an offended look. "Why's she out of our league?"

"Despite spending most of her life in Australia, she has grown up in a Muslim household. Back home, she'll have a big family full of angry brothers, cousins and uncles. You wanna mess with her, you better be prepared to marry her. Are either of you looking for a wife?"

Dex's gaze faltered. Yeah, that's what she thought. It was okay to fool around with perky nineteen-year-olds, but heaven forbid that wedding bells were part of the equation. At least everyone was clear on tonight's rules of engagement.

But then he commented under his breath, "Do the same rules apply to you?"

Whoa. That sounded like more than professional interest. "Who wants to know?"

His gaze narrowed. More irritation. The boy couldn't figure out whether to be civil or irascible tonight. Sheesh, and they said women were moody!

Anya grabbed her coat. "Let's go!"

Isabella had to admit the girl's enthusiasm was contagious. Anya chirped about everything she saw, and all but pressed her nose against the car window as they made their way out of the Olympic complex. They drove downtown and even managed to snag a parking spot reasonably close to Main Street. They got out and the two men fell in on either side of Anya, relegating Isabella to advance lookout position. Isabella moved ahead and took point, keeping her gaze moving at all times, on the watch for any possible threats.

Main Street had an almost alpine feel to it, with quaint storefronts pouring bright, cheerful light into the evening and snow-covered mountains looming in the distance. The occasional car crawled down Main Street, but mostly the road belonged to the pedestrians. Music poured out of Olympic Square two blocks away, and even here, people danced to the beat. Anya was no exception. Beau jumped right in with her, grabbing her by the waist and swinging her around.

Isabella frowned, but Dex muttered, "Better him than a total stranger."

Good point.

Dex and Isabella trailed behind Beau and Anya. She didn't know about Dex, but she felt like a serious fifth wheel. It was incredibly awkward walking along beside him, trying to blend in with the partiers, all the while keeping a sharp eye out for hostiles. Only inches separated their shoulders, but a Grand Canyon-sized chasm yawned between them.

Anya and Beau led the strange little parade to a gourmet pizza joint where Dex had a quiet word with the maître d'. A table was forthcoming immediately.

As they wound through the crowded restaurant, Isabella leaned close and asked, "How'd you do that?"

He scowled. "I called ahead and made a reservation."

She rolled her eyes at him. "Boy Scout," she accused.

"Hardly," he muttered.

They got a booth in the corner, no doubt also arranged by Dex. Ideal for security purposes. For some reason, the fact that Dex had arranged all this bugged the hell out of her. Sure, it was professional and she ought to be impressed with his thoroughness, but they were out on the town. Couldn't he ever see past the job and look at her?

Stop the presses. Rewind. Delete. She was not interested in Dexter Thorpe. He was arrogant, opinionated, chauvinistic and a general pain in the butt. Okay, so he was attractive as the devil. But she was no fool. She had no intention of even hinting at interest in this man, her boss. End of story. But…it might be fun to mess with his head a little bit…and she knew just how to do it.

"Hey, Beau," she purred. "After the Olympics are over and everyone goes home, where are you going to be stationed?"

"I go into training status for a few months down at the schoolhouse."

That would be Fort Bragg, home of the Delta detachment. "Outstanding! The Medusas are in training until the end of the year."

Did Beau cast a glance at Dex? What was up with that? Beau smiled brilliantly at her. "Sounds like a date."

"Hey," Anya protested. "I want to flirt, too."

Beau laughed and leaned back in the booth, stretching his prodigiously muscular arms across the back of the vinyl booth behind both women. "Yup, yup. This is one tough assignment," he sighed, "a beautiful young lady on each arm."

It was a little closer quarters than Isabella was comfortable with, but she wasn't about to move away. Especially not with the cold look Dex was throwing at his man. Anya, however, had no compunction about draping herself all over Beau.

Despite Isabella's earlier threat, she didn't have the slightest worry that Beau would go too far with Anya. He might flirt like crazy, but he was a complete gentleman. He'd make Anya feel like a million bucks and then send her home, virtue safely intact.

"So, Dex," Isabella asked lightly. "Where are you off to after all this fun?"

"To train his sorry ass," Dex grunted.

Isabella leaned close to Beau. "You better share the girls or he's going to make your life miserable when you get back inside the fence." The fence was the heavily guarded compound inside which the Deltas did most of their training. It had been one of the triumphs of the Medusas to be among the first women ever allowed inside that fence to train.

Beau shrugged. "He lives like a monk, anyway. Never goes for the girls."

"Girls being the operative word," Dex retorted. "I prefer mine grown-up."

Didn't like having his appeal with the ladies questioned, did he? Isabella pushed the button he'd just revealed. "Well, I can't say as I'm surprised to hear he doesn't get much action with the ladies," she said.

On cue, Dex straightened indignantly. "And why's that?"

"Oh, no reason," she said vaguely. In her experience, men always hated nebulous answers that relied solely on female intuition.

He scowled and ordered two extra large pizzas with the works when the unlucky waiter showed up at their table. Anya entertained herself by checking out the single men in the restaurant and guessing at their nationalities. Meanwhile, Beau kept up a steady stream of chatter, mostly moaning about Anya's fickle, wandering attention.

At one point, Beau turned to Isabella and said, "Well, at least I can count on you to be loyal."

She cocked a skeptical eyebrow. "Don't be so sure of me, Breckenridge. I'm not yours, yet."

Dex jolted beside her. She glanced at him out of the corner of her highly developed peripheral vision. Damned if he didn't look startled, annoyed even, by her comment. What was going *on* with him? If she didn't know better, she'd say he was acting possessive. But Lord knew, he didn't have any personal interest in her. She glanced over at Beau speculatively. Unless Beau knew Dex better than she did. Why else would the guy flirt like a maniac with her in front of his boss? *Beau was trying to goad Dex.* Was he trying to push Dex at her? *Romantically?* Surely not.

She looked back and forth between Beau and Dex, and the Southerner grinned unrepentantly over Anya's head. Oh, yeah. She'd pegged it dead on. Now what was she supposed to do about it?

The pizzas were delivered to the table, and Anya dug in enthusiastically.

Ever since survival school, where she'd indulged in such delicacies as grasshoppers and earthworms, her perception of edible food had altered radically. The sloppy, loaded pizza looked eminently fit for human consumption right now, but she was working. She took a piece and put it on her plate, but didn't touch it as she kept an eye out for any patrons who might make a threatening move.

A hand touched her thigh under the table and she leaped in surprise. Dex. She looked over at him.

"Eat," he murmured. "I'll take a turn at the watch."

"Thanks." She ate a couple quick pieces of pizza. It really was delicious. The festive atmosphere, Anya's infectious laugh, and the escape, even if just for a moment, from responsibility for Anya's life unwound the tension across the back of her neck for the first time since she'd seen Anya get off that plane. She was more aware of the stress by its absence than she had been by its presence.

"You ought to smile more often," Dex remarked.

She blinked, startled. "Why?"

"You're pretty when you smile."

She retorted. "Yup, and I'm a troll when I don't. Remind me to frown whenever I'm around you guys."

"You're hardly a troll. Hell, I have trouble keeping my men's attention when you walk in during briefings."

She snorted. "With Misty, I'd believe that. But not me."

He glared. "Look at yourself in the mirror sometime."

She rolled her eyes.

Beau chimed in. "He's right, Isabella. Not all of us guys go for untouchable, ice queen blondes. Consensus at the ops center is that you're the babe of the bunch. That's why I'm going to land you for myself one of these days."

She stared in shock and Anya laughed uproariously at the expression on her face.

"Incoming," Dex murmured.

She went from zero to full battle alert in about two milliseconds. She'd never been so grateful for a potential deadly threat in her life. Her gaze roamed the room quickly, and she spotted three young men just walking in. They looked to be of Eastern European or Middle Eastern descent. As much as she'd like not to react with suspicion to all groups of young men with that particular combination of coloring and features, she had no choice. Like it or not, they matched the M.O. of the men in her last two encounters with whoever was trying to harm Anya.

She felt like a fraud, sitting here, sharing the same heritage and yet eyeing those young men like they were probably terrorists. But such were the times she lived in.

"Let's go," Anya announced suddenly. "I want to go to the block party."

Great. Every night at 9:00 p.m. Main Street closed at both

ends to vehicular traffic, and the live rock concert from Olympic Square was broadcast on large-screen TV's up and down the entire street. It turned into a huge party. The good news was that no one knew Anya would be there and so no one would be looking for her. The bad news was thousands of people crowded the street, and the odds of someone spotting her and taking advantage of the opportunity to harm her went up exponentially in a crowd that size.

Dex looked over at her, one eyebrow raised, as if to say, "Your call."

To Anya, Isabella commented, "You really want to find out just how good we are as bodyguards, don't you?"

The girl shrugged. "I'm sorry. But given the choice of living my whole life like a monk or enjoying it and taking a risk, I opt for the latter. Surely you can understand that, can't you, 'Bella?"

She winced. Okay, Anya could quit poking that particular Achilles' heel any time now. "Yeah, I understand," she answered reluctantly.

"Explain it to me, then, because I don't," Dex growled. "Why are you going to let your subject expose herself to danger?"

"How much more danger will she be in lost somewhere in the middle of a crowd than she is standing all alone in the middle of a figure skating rink with thirty thousand spectators?"

"The spectators are security screened."

Isabella waved off the argument. "You and I both know plenty of ways to get around that sort of screening. And so do bad guys if they're halfway serious."

"So you're going to let her do this?"

Isabella smiled, but with an edge to it. "With you two super-heroes here to look after her, why not? You're invincible, right?"

Dex scowled. "I've been around long enough not to be goaded into doing something stupid."

"Aw, c'mon," Anya cajoled. "It'll be fun. You're too serious, Dex. Loosen up a bit." She added slyly, "I'd hate to have to call the IOC and complain about my bodyguards being stick-in-the-muds."

He sighed. "Don't blackmail me, little girl. I'd chew you up and spit you out."

Anya pulled back. She was just experienced enough with men to realize she'd just played with fire and been lucky not to get burned. Isabella grinned as Anya mumbled under her breath, "What a grouch."

Isabella muttered back, "Welcome to my life. He's my boss."

Anya rolled her eyes. "No wonder you're so tense all the time. I feel your pain."

Dex's scowl made Isabella laugh. And it felt really good to find a reason to laugh at Dexter Thorpe. It made him more human somehow. He threw her a look that promised revenge, tossed down the money to cover the pizza and a tip, and the four of them made their way out of the pizzeria.

The block party was loud, crowded, and rife with happy drunks. Anya waded right into the mass of dancing humanity, and to keep up with her, Isabella found herself plastered against Dex in short order. She glanced up at him, chagrined, and he grimaced down at her.

Hey. She wasn't that disgusting! A little annoyed, she waited until the next time the crowd jostled her into him and then she turned slightly so the front of her body came into contact with him. Intense awareness shot through her, an electric jolt that made her shiver all over. *Hunk alert.* He was as hard and over-poweringly masculine as she would have expected.

He got a surprised look on his face. "Wow. You're…more fit…than any woman I've ever—" And then it must have dawned on him where he was taking the conversation.

What the hell did that mean? More fit. That she was hard? Unfeminine? Or did it mean he was impressed with her strength and conditioning? If he thought she was buff, he ought to check out Misty, a triathlete, or Vanessa, who worked out constantly.

After about an hour of being bumped around like socks in a washing machine, Anya'd had enough. Besides, it was ten o'clock, her bedtime. She had to skate in the morning. They made their way back to the SUV and drove back to the Olympic village.

Isabella commented, "I can take her from here, boys."

Dex retorted, "My mother would tan my hide if I didn't walk a girl to her door after a date. And I fear her a whole lot more than I could ever fear you."

"We weren't on a date!"

"Nonetheless, I'm walking you to the door."

Rather than argue further and turn it into a big deal, she acquiesced. A date? With Dex? Never.

Anya was safely tucked in her room when Dex's cell phone rang. A few seconds later, Isabella's rang as well. The two of them stepped outside to get the calls and Beau stayed inside with Anya.

"Go ahead," Isabella said into the receiver.

"Ops here. We got a report that Harlan Holt's lab was just entered. Night security guard for the building says Holt's access card opened the lock. It appears your guy's turned up in Syracuse."

"Thanks," she replied. "Have you paged the other Medusas?"

"Not yet."

Dex covered his receiver and spoke to her. "Tell the Medusas to meet you at the ops center ASAP."

She relayed the instructions to the ops controller, who said he'd call her teammates right away and pass the message.

Dex opened the door and stuck his head inside. "Hobo, you've got guard duty for the next few hours. And no hanky-panky."

Beau's crisp acknowledgment of the order drifted out into the hall.

Dex turned to her. "Let's go."

Chapter 12

"My gear's at my place," Isabella said as Dex pulled away from the curb. He nodded tersely and directed the SUV to their apartment complex. A quick run inside, and she came out with her heavy pack slung over one shoulder and her utility belt slung over the other. Then they were off to the ops center.

"So what does a girl have to do in this town to requisition a helicopter?" she asked.

Dex glanced over at her, eyebrows raised. "You want a helicopter?"

"How else will we get to Syracuse in time to snag our guy and have a chat?"

"Drive over, pick up his trail and track him down the old-fashioned way."

She shook her head decisively in the negative. "It takes hours to drive all the way across the state. We'll lose too much time. He's the key to something major."

"What am I going to tell Manfred Schmidt about why you need a helicopter?"

Ouch. Good point. She thought for a few seconds. "How about telling him there's a problem with the ice in the venue and Dr. Holt is needed at the rink ASAP?"

"So you want me to lie to cover for you?"

She answered slowly, "No, I don't want you to lie. But you're the one who asked the Medusas to make Holt a priority. It's a question of what's more important. Finding Holt and figuring out what he's up to, or chancing a political wrangle with Schmidt and Holt getting away." She shrugged. "You've been in the field longer than I have. You probably know better than I do when the ends justify the means." He was a team leader after all. He was charged with responsibility for the moral choices his men made.

His only answer to her challenge was to say mildly, "In case you haven't noticed, it's after eleven o'clock at night. How am I supposed to convince Schmidt that Holt is needed at this hour?"

She grinned. "The second round of ice dancing qualifications are tomorrow. The ice has to be ready for it."

Dex nodded thoughtfully. "He might buy that."

He wanted to help. He sounded willing to feed the line to Schmidt. He'd shifted his thinking from if the Medusas should get their helicopter to how they should get it. Furthermore, he was greenlighting the Medusas to run an op for which he was taking full responsibility. It was a tacit admission that he thought the all-female team could do the job.

She said helpfully, "If you requisition the helicopter tonight, we can explain it to Schmidt after the fact tomorrow."

He grinned. "The old, 'it's easier to ask for forgiveness than permission' ploy?"

She grinned back. "You do what you've got to do to get the mission done."

Dex's eyes glinted with humor. "Spoken like a true S.F. operator."

He parked the vehicle and they walked quickly into the ops center. He opened the door for her, and since he'd let her carry her pack by herself, she stepped through the door without complaint. As usual, the dim space was filled with operators studying the brightly lit television screens ringing the room.

"So. Are you gonna give us the helicopter?"

He strode beside her toward the briefing room where they could see the other Medusas waiting. "Yes, you can have your helicopter. I can't give you the emergency bird with the crew on short standby, though. I've got to keep that 'copter in the local area for med-evac airlift and local crisis response. You can have the backup Huey. It'll carry all of you. It may take me a while to scrounge up a pilot, though."

Isabella said, "I think I can help with that." They stepped into the briefing room. "Hey, Misty. Do you have a current rating on a Huey?"

"Yup."

Isabella turned to Dex. "Pilot problem solved."

He cocked his head in surprise. "Okay then. It's parked on the roof. I'll fill out the paperwork and you can sign it when you return. So, get out of here, already."

The six Medusas shouldered their packs and moved out. They rode an elevator to the roof and tossed their gear into the helicopter while Misty climbed in and started running the check-lists to wake up the Huey's many systems. Karen, who'd worked in a helo maintenance squadron a few years back, ran around outside pulling engine intake and pitot tube covers. By the time she was done, Misty was on the radios, filing a quick flight plan.

The engines roared to life and the rotor started a slow spin overhead, picking up speed rapidly, until it was only a blur. Isabella put on the pair of headphones that lay in her seat and strapped in as Misty asked for takeoff clearance.

The reply was immediate. "Huey 3152, you are cleared for departure. Climb and maintain three thousand feet, heading two-four-zero. Contact Boston Center on frequency…"

The bird lifted off the roof and climbed straight up in the air. Isabella was no expert, but Misty's flying felt smooth and sure. She remembered overhearing a couple pilots in the Pope Air Force Base Officer's Club a few months back saying that Misty supposedly had the best hands in the entire Air Force. Afterward, she'd teased her pilot teammate about just what it was she'd handled to get that reputation.

The lights of Lake Placid receded behind them, and the night went pitch-black. The steady *thwock* of the rotor blades was relaxing, and despite the confrontation with Holt to come, she could have dozed off pretty easily.

But then Vanessa said, "Adder, what do you know about the Red Jihad?"

"Dex mentioned them. Red usually stands for blood in Islamic symbolism, and Jihad means 'holy war.'"

"Misty finished translating the tapes we made last night. There are two separate references to this Red Jihad. It appears that your hunch was correct. Something is cooking, and young Lazlo is in the thick of it."

Isabella thought back to the last intel analysis she'd read on Chechnya maybe a month ago. "When the Russians pulled out for good last year, literally hundreds of rebel groups came out of hiding under the amnesty the new government granted. The big question now is whether or not all those rebels will reintegrate peacefully into society, or whether they'll find some new cause to latch on to and continue the violence they've lived by for the last several decades." She added, "Was there anything else interesting on the tapes?"

Vanessa answered, "It seems that Lazlo's parents were in some sort of Chechnyan rebel cell with this Gorabchek guy a number of years ago. Right about the same time Lazlo came to the United States to train as a figure skater."

"Maybe that's why his family sent him over here. To escape getting caught up in all the violence of the freedom fighters during that time."

Vanessa grunted. "One man's freedom fighter is another man's terrorist."

"Speaking of terrorists," Isabella said, "what do we know about Holt?"

"Just that his access card unlocked his lab—" she glanced at her watch "—about an hour ago. There are no windows so the campus police can't verify that it's him. I advised the night security guard not to approach Holt or make him suspicious, so we're not a hundred percent sure we've got our man."

"Can the building be locked down so he can't get out?" Isabella asked.

Vanessa nodded. "Already done. And given the suspicious circumstances under which his wife disappeared, I think we have to assume he's armed and potentially violent."

Isabella nodded. "How much longer, Sidewinder?"

"About forty minutes," Misty replied. "I've gotten permission to land at the Syracuse University Hospital helipad. The campus police will meet us there with vehicles."

"Let's hope they don't plan to help us storm Holt's lab."

The other women groaned. While local police were competent at what they did, they didn't have the training the Medusas did for clearing rooms full of hostiles. They had spent months in the schoolhouse at Fort Bragg storming rooms over and over again, until they could burst in, eliminate a dozen or more bad guys and never harm a hair on a hostage's head. Isabella had a tough callus at the base of her shooting hand from the thousands of rounds they'd fired in the course of their counterterrorism training.

Aleesha looked across the bird at Vanessa. "How're those new pills working?"

"I'm holding up."

Isabella threw a sympathetic look at her boss. Vanessa was plagued with airsickness, and Aleesha was constantly experimenting with new antinausea drugs to find a magic bullet for Vanessa. The latest batch of medications was the best so far, not to mention that Vanessa was getting lots of experience on flights like this one and seemed to be desensitizing her system to the motion.

Silence fell over the dark interior of the bird. Each of them prepared for missions in their own way. Karen cranked up heavy metal on her MP-3 player. Kat went into some sort of meditative trance that she wouldn't talk about. Vanessa tried to sleep in order not to barf and Aleesha traditionally fussed over Vanessa like a mother hen. Isabella usually spent the whole time fighting off an urge to think about all the things that could go wrong. It was psychologically counterproductive and put her in entirely the wrong frame of mind. Tonight, she did her damnedest to visualize the forthcoming op going perfectly. Holt would be in his lab. They'd nail him red-handed with evidence about his wife's disappearance. He'd confess what he was up to regarding the Olympics, and the Medusas would come out of it smelling like roses.

Okay, not realistic, but there was no harm in hoping, was there?

Abdul sat at the kitchen table with only the stove's light on. He sipped occasionally at a cup of cold Turkish coffee. It was late, but he couldn't sleep. His nephews were out tonight, trying yet again to find the elusive Ice Doctor, who'd disappeared completely a few days ago. Abdul had told Holt to disappear, but not to be completely incommunicado. His cell phone signal had gone out of service, and they'd been unable to contact him for close to twenty-four hours now. That was worrisome. Holt was flighty. Unpredictable. No telling what the scientist was up to.

Abdul had sent his nephews to Syracuse, to have a look around Holt's home and see if they could find any clues as to where the good doctor had gone.

"Son, you cannot sleep?"

He looked up and smiled as his father shuffled into the room. Abdul replied in Arabic, "And what keeps you up so late?"

His father sat down at the table. "Indigestion. But you—you are troubled. What rests so heavily upon your mind like the gas upon my stomach?"

Abdul sighed. He loved this man, revered his wisdom. But in spite of his robust appearance, the man was frail, his heart enlarged and weak. He was determined to shield his father from the stress of this mission. "Talk to me about paradise, father. Remind me why we struggle so on this Earth."

His father nodded sagely and began to recite the soothing poetry of the Qur'an, passages about the paradise that awaits the faithful, the special glory waiting for those willing to sacrifice anything, even their very lives, to defend the faith. The beauty and power of the words flowed over him, soothing his troubled heart and renewing his certainty of the rightness of his path. The passage ended, and he grasped his father's hand.

"Thank you, Father. Your words are a gift."

"They are not my words." He pointed a gnarled finger up toward the ceiling.

Abdul nodded. "I needed the reminder to stay the course."

His father replied, "It is easy to doubt. It is difficult indeed to carry on in spite of doubt. If your cause be right, then do not question it, but carry on toward the final glory."

"Amen," Abdul murmured. Oh yes. His cause was right. His duty was clear. The moment of doubt past, he stood up and went back to bed.

The Syracuse University police were surprisingly helpful. They'd brought a couple men to keep an eye on the five million dollar Huey while the Medusas went after Holt. They'd brought two cars for the Medusas to use, walkie-talkies set to the campus police frequencies, maps of the campus with clear directions to Holt's lab, and they even had a schematic of the Chemistry Building.

Then the reason for their preparation became crystal clear.

A tall, powerful man in a campus police uniform stepped forward and held his hand out to Vanessa. "I'm Roscoe Tanner. Army Rangers till last year. What else do you need?"

Vanessa replied, as they stepped into an elevator, "I think you've covered it all. We'd like to go in on our own. If your men could cover the exterior of the building, that would be helpful."

Tanner nodded. "I already popped the boys' bubble and told them they wouldn't get to play SWAT team with you. I figured you wouldn't want amateurs in the way."

Vanessa smiled warmly. "If you trained them, I highly doubt they're amateurs, Mr. Tanner."

The mutual admiration society adjourned as the elevator doors opened and the women stepped into a loading dock at the back of the hospital. As promised, two unmarked cars awaited them. The Medusas piled in and took off across campus.

Isabella picked up the walkie-talkie Tanner had given them and transmitted, "What's the status of Holt and his lab? Is he still there?"

A nervous male voice replied, "He hasn't carded out yet, and last time I walked down the hall, about ten minutes ago, there was still a light coming from under the door."

"Thanks," she replied. "Don't do any more walk-bys for now. We'll be there in under five minutes. Have any security types not covering the exit meet us in the front lobby."

"Yes, ma'am," the guy responded.

Isabella smiled. He sounded about fourteen years old and scared to death. She'd been in situations so much more dangerous than this that she was hardly nervous, let alone scared.

They pulled up in front of a brick building. Three security guards huddled just inside the front door. The Medusas threw on their flak vests and utility belts, did a quick radio check with their throat mikes and slung their MP-5s into ready positions at their hips. The campus cops' eyes went wide at the sight of the women racing inside.

"Stay here," Vanessa ordered the men quietly. "Don't come up until one of us radios you with an all clear. This could take a while. We don't always move fast."

The men nodded. Tanner came inside. "I've set up a perimeter around the building. He won't get past us. Oh, and I almost forgot. Here's a master key card for the lab door."

Vanessa took the plastic card, thanked Tanner quickly, and then hand signaled the Medusas to move out. Karen took point, and they moved fast and silent into a stairwell and up to the third floor. A quick check of the hall with a periscope, and then the team was on the move again. In spite of Vanessa's warning to the men below, the Medusas were moving quickly. They raced down the hallway to the heavy steel door of Holt's lab. Vanessa signaled for a standard entry, and they each signaled back, repeating the formation hand sign back to her. When submachine guns might end up laying down a curtain of lead, it was vitally important that everyone be on the same page.

They got into position. They'd enter two at a time, each woman peeling off in a different direction until they'd fanned out and had a field of fire on every corner of the room. Adrenaline ripped through Isabella, making the light around her seem brighter, the sounds louder, her body lighter. *Calm. Focus. You know what to do, now you just have to do it.* For a millisecond, it occurred to her that these were the same words Liz Cartwright had told Anya before she went out to skate. Each in their own way, they were warriors for the same cause— the right of women to do anything they could dream of doing.

Vanessa ran the key card through the scanning slot. A green diode lit and a beep announced that the lock had opened. Misty yanked open the door and Kat and Aleesha burst into the brightly lit room. Isabella and Vanessa went next, and Misty and Karen brought up the rear. Isabella jumped fast to her right, plastering her back against the wall, her weapon in a firing position, and scanned the space for hostile targets. Long, stainless steel counters filled the room. They were cluttered with glass beakers, Bunsen burners and a wide array of electronic equipment. Tall cabinets lined the walls. And there wasn't any sign of Harlan Holt.

Cautiously, they cleared the space, checking under the counters, tearing open cabinet doors and examining every hiding place where a human being could possibly fit. Nada.

Vanessa snapped at Isabella, "Give me that walkie-talkie."

She handed the radio over to her boss.

"Tanner, get up here."

The ex-soldier raced into the room moments later.

Vanessa bit out, "He's not here. Do I have your permission to perform an invasive search of the room?"

Tanner frowned. "Of course. I'm sure he was here. I checked the computer logs myself, and his card definitely unlocked that door two hours ago."

Isabella moved across the room, scanning the rows of equipment, putting her hand on each of the electronic boxes. She stopped in front of a beaker in a metal ring stand. It was partially full of liquid. She reached out to feel the machine beside it. "Hey, Viper. This box is warm."

She felt the glass vial beside the mass spectrometer, and it was faintly warm as well. "Here's the solution he was measuring."

Vanessa hurried over to her. "Let's take samples of everything in this area for the boys back in Lake Placid."

Isabella nodded and took the evidence-gathering kit Aleesha handed to her. The two women pulled on surgical gloves and began the painstaking process of photographing, swabbing and bagging samples of everything in this section of the lab. A fine film of white powder covered the counter around the beaker. What were the odds? Could it be that Holt made the nerve gas agent that had shown up on that paper bag at the ice skating rink? The guy was a chemist, after all.

Maybe the wife had found out what he was up to and he'd eliminated her. That, too, made a certain sick kind of sense.

She continued swabbing other surfaces and listening to Vanessa and Tanner's tense conversation.

"…so where did he go? Your men said they'd locked the building down and he couldn't get out."

"We'll pull the video of the exits, but I'd lay odds he didn't just walk out of here. I trained these guys myself and they're conscientious."

A few minutes later, the police radio crackled with a report that they had isolated video of Holt entering the building, but could find none of him leaving.

Vanessa turned to the other Medusas. "Cobra, you finish collecting samples. The rest of you, we've got a building to clear."

Isabella groaned mentally. This was a big building. Tanner had a team of guys trained to do basic room searches, and he took them and headed for the top floor. He'd work his way down while the Medusas worked their way up from the ground floor.

An hour later, they met in the middle. No sign of the missing professor.

Vanessa said, "Okay, Tanner. Talk to me about alternative exits."

"There's a tunnel to the lab building next door, but it's sealed off with a honking steel hatch. This building is also steam heated and has tunnels that hook it to the campus's main steam power plant. But those tunnels are locked up as well. That's it."

Vanessa said, "You check the tunnel to the lab, we'll take the steam tunnels."

Tanner led them to the heating system, and then headed for the other end of the cavernous basement with his team.

Aleesha took one look at the steel door and muttered, "Uh, Viper?"

"Yes?"

"This thing has been jimmied. Recently." To illustrate her

point, Aleesha unhooked the broken padlock from the door, dangling it from her index finger.

Vanessa radioed her find to Tanner, and in seconds, pounding footsteps approached them from behind. Karen and Misty pushed open the heavy door. A yawning pit of black stretched before them. The Medusas pulled out high intensity flashlights and shined them down the tunnel. The walls were damp and shiny, and honest to God, something skittered away in the dark. It was the stuff of B-grade horror movies.

"Where does this go?" Vanessa asked.

Tanner grunted. "It's a network under the campus. Connects all the major buildings. We can search it, but if he got out through here, he could be anywhere by now. He could've come up into any building on campus and just walked outside."

Damn. They'd missed him.

Vanessa peered into the dark, weighing the value of searching the tunnels. "Would you be willing to search the tunnels with your men while we pursue a different approach up above?"

Tanner nodded. "We can do that. We know our way around down here better than you ladies would. Every now and then students break in to these tunnels to play around. We end up having to chase them out."

Vanessa nodded tersely. "Let us know what you find. We're heading for Holt's house."

The women retraced their steps upstairs and outside. They piled into their cars and headed to Holt's darkened bungalow, which was only a few blocks from the main campus.

The neighborhood was asleep, dark and quiet. They practically walked down the sidewalk to the Holt house. Isabella, Vanessa, and Aleesha took the back, while Karen, Kat and Misty approached the front porch and windows. They would position themselves near the corners of the house to cover anyone trying to sneak away. The women around back would enter the house and apprehend Holt or force him to the front of the house if he was hiding inside.

Emma Holt's car was still parked in the garage. It looked pretty much as it had before, but something wasn't quite right. Isabella reached back into her photographic memory to find the inconsistency. Nothing clicked. She headed for her assigned position. Vanessa would go in the bedroom window. Isabella would take the window to the left of the back door that led into a laundry room. Aleesha would go in through the back door.

It was an easy matter to jimmy the simple rotating window lock. She flashed a thumbs-up at her teammates and got one back from Vanessa.

And while they were waiting for Aleesha to open the door with her lock picks, it hit her. The license plate on Emma Holt's car was different than the last time she'd seen it. Holt must have switched out his plates for hers. Trying to throw off the police, was he? The guy just kept looking guiltier and guiltier.

Lazlo dialed the phone number his father had slipped to him in the bar. There had been a time along with the phone number—0100. At least he hoped that's what the digits were. If it was a time, it was done in the European fashion and not the American style. If he was wrong, he was about to wake up the whole house and piss off Ilya. He could always pretend to be a wrong number.

The phone was answered right away. "Hello?" his father's voice murmured.

"Papa?"

"Son. How are you doing?"

"Good. I made it to the short program round on the competition. I'm in eighth place."

"Your mother will be thrilled."

An awkward silence fell. They both spoke at once and then went silent again. Finally Lazlo said, "Papa, there's something I have to tell you. I don't want to be a terrorist. I know you sent me to America to establish a cover so I could help you, but I can't do it. I have no training. I'm…I'm not even Chechnyan. I'm…American! This is my home now—"

His father interrupted gently. "It's all right. Those days are over. We have our independent homeland. I just hope you're not angry at us for sending you here when it turned out to be for nothing. I never did like the idea of using you as a sleeper terrorist in the U.S. Thank God Russia finally relented and we didn't have to take extreme measures to involve the Americans in our cause."

"It wasn't for nothing," Lazlo said quickly. "I got an education. And I became a world-class skater. Look. I want you and Mama and Ileena and Hekmat to come to America. Permanently. This is so much better a place to live. The hospitals are good, women can go to college, they have five hundred television channels—"

"I've got to go. I hear something."

He called out, "Think about it, Papa—" and then the phone went dead.

Aleesha nodded her readiness. Wow. Under a minute for a knob lock and a dead bolt. She was getting really good at breaking and entering. As the team's surgeon and owner of the most sensitive and nimble fingers of them all, she'd been designated the Medusas' trap and lock expert. She'd taken the job to heart. She sat around all the time with padlocks and the like, picking them for fun.

Vanessa breathed across the Medusas' operating channel, "Go." Not only did it signal Isabella and Aleesha to go in, but it gave a heads-up to the women out front to be extra sharp.

Isabella pushed open the window, chinned herself up to the sill and flopped through the opening onto the washing machine. The metal flexed and gave a loud pop. She flinched and rolled off it, crouching low. Cat smell. Not bad, but noticeable. She looked around. Yup. Litter box in the corner.

She opened the cupboards fast. Nobody hiding in them. A quick look in the narrow broom closet—clear—and she spun out into the kitchen. Aleesha gave her an all-clear signal.

Together they advanced into the dining room. Still nothing. Aleesha headed for the living room, and Isabella turned down the hall toward the bathroom and two bedrooms. A flash of movement startled her. Someone had just disappeared into the spare bedroom.

She ran forward on the balls of her feet and stopped beside the door, listening hard. Nothing. No sounds of movement, not even sounds of breathing. Deep silence enveloped the house. She spun into the room low and fast, her weapon in front of her. A desk piled high with papers stood against one wall, a daybed was on the second wall, also piled high with books, folders and a haphazard stack of towels. A closet took up most of the third wall. The wall to her left was bare.

Using her foot, Isabella shoved open the closet door. No movement. She squatted down and used a flashlight to look along the floor behind the crowded hanging clothes. No feet. Nonetheless, she pushed the outdated clothes aside and peered down the back wall. Definitely nobody in here.

A movement by the window brought her flying out of the closet, slamming the hallway door shut before the target could get out of the room. She spun to face the threat. No one was there. She frowned. She'd definitely seen something move!

Then a cat jumped down off the desk and rubbed against her ankle, mewing.

"Hey, kitty," she murmured. "Where's your daddy?"

Vanessa's voice came over the radio. "Report, Adder."

Isabella grinned. "I used my ruthless combat techniques and found the cat."

"Lovely. The master bedroom is clear. Mamba?"

"All clear out here. Nobody's home. Except the cat, of course."

Isabella opened the door and the cat trotted out into the hallway and headed for the kitchen. She followed his vertical tail and frowned as he headed for a full bowl of dry cat food.

The water dish beside it was full, too. Over her radio, she transmitted, "Who's feeding the cat?"

Vanessa replied, "Call the neighbors in the morning. See if anyone's doing it."

Isabella looked down. "It's a big bowl of food. I'd guess it's enough for a couple weeks. Is the toilet seat up?"

Vanessa replied, "Affirmative."

"I bet Holt was here tonight. Probably fed the cat. He must have changed the litter box, too, because the laundry room would reek if the cat had been alone for nearly a week, and I wasn't overpowered by the cat smell."

Vanessa said, "Mamba, bring your evidence kit in here. I found something."

Isabella and Aleesha joined their boss, who shined her flashlight on the floorboards in the corner of the bedroom. Isabella stared for a moment, and then picked out what Vanessa had. Several tiny drops of darker brown on the light brown wood. In a splatter pattern.

"Blood," Isabella breathed.

Aleesha pulled out a digital camera and took several pictures before carefully collecting the droplets. Isabella and the others spent the next half hour crawling around on their hands and knees, fine-tooth combing the room for evidence. If they were lucky, some of the couple dozen drops of blood would belong to whoever had attacked or kidnapped Emma Holt.

They went through Holt's computer files, the stacks of papers on his desk—ungraded lab reports from several classes of students, scientific journals and household bills, none of which sent up any red flags.

Then Karen startled them all by announcing in a whisper, "We've got company. Two targets. Moving in stealthily."

"Police?" Vanessa asked.

"Not from the looks of them."

Vanessa ordered, "Everyone out the back. Move!"

Just because they were racing pell-mell for the door didn't

mean they were loud or disorganized. Oh, no. Jack had trained them well. Kat stayed inside to throw the dead bolt and then slipped out through the laundry room window. A tug on the string she'd rigged, and she relocked the window as well. Another sharp tug to release the slip knot and they were clear. Vanessa hand-signaled the women to spread out and move around to the front of the house to surround the targets.

The Medusas moved silent and slow, easing into position around what looked like two young men. One of the youths tried to climb on a rose trellis to reach a side window, but the flimsy wood collapsed with a loud clatter. A light went on next door. The young men ducked behind the Holt house, with the Medusas shadowing them every step of the way. If the women were to stand up and say, "Boo" to the intruders, Isabella was confident the men would wet themselves, so close did the Medusas get to them.

A police siren wailed in the distance and got louder rapidly. Ah, fudge. Nosy Mrs. Tannager must have called the police. The youths took off running, and Vanessa waved the Medusas off. They, too, faded into the night. As soon as the team was clear of the Holt house, they ran to their cars and pulled away. They missed the police by mere seconds. But it was enough. They'd gotten away.

Tired and disappointed, Isabella sat in the backseat while they drove back to Syracuse University and the helicopter. She slept the whole flight back to Lake Placid and was groggy when the bird landed. They stumbled into the ops center at nearly six o'clock in the morning.

Why wasn't she surprised to see Dex there, waiting for them. A light brown shadow roughed his jaw. "Well?" he said.

"We missed him," Isabella reported. "And we scared the hell out of his cat."

Dex's right eyebrow shot up but he made no comment.

Vanessa said, "We've got a pile of forensic evidence that will need to be looked at ASAP. This bag contains samples from his lab and probably ought to go to our biohazard buddies. This bag appears to be blood from Holt's bedroom. It'll need DNA analysis."

"Blood?" He cursed under his breath. "I'll get the paperwork going." To one of the men nearby, he said, "I'll need you to run these samples over to Albany."

Dex turned back to the Medusas. "Go get some sleep. You all look like hell. You can sign the requisition for the helicopter later. I'll hold off Schmidt until then."

Isabella sighed in relief. The last thing she needed right now was to wade through a bunch of bureaucratic crap. "Anya has practice ice at noon. I'll go over there and pick up the watch at eleven o'clock if one of your guys can cover her until then. That'll give me a few hours for a nap."

Dex nodded. "My team's on it."

She smiled her gratitude. With an experienced Delta team guarding Anya, Isabella wouldn't worry about the girl's safety. Wearily, she headed for her apartment. The early morning traffic was surprisingly heavy. Mostly tourists making their way to the venues for the day's events. Because of security, parking and entrance into venues was a time-consuming process. Spectators were told to arrive two hours prior to an event. Finally, she turned into the apartment complex. She parked her car—a shoebox on wheels provided by the OSG—grabbed her pack, and headed for home.

She unlocked the door and let herself in just as dawn broke outside. Lord, she was tired. Her cell phone rang, and she dug it out of her jacket pocket, praying it was one of her team members calling to wish her sweet dreams. "Hello?" she said.

"This is Dex. Anya's missing."

Chapter 13

A cattle prod couldn't have jolted her more forcefully to full consciousness. *"Missing?"* she exclaimed. "How the hell did that happen?"

"You'd better come down here," Dex said grimly.

Isabella was enough of a professional not to storm into the ops center demanding to know what idiot took his eyes off Anya long enough for her to disappear. But it was damned hard to control the impulse. Minutes after she arrived, Dex called for a meeting. He wasted no time in getting down to business.

"Here's what happened," he said without prologue. "Sleepy was standing watch in Anya's room."

She recalled hearing the guy'd gotten his handle by being able to stay awake and alert for seventy-two hours at a time. He had some weird metabolic condition that allowed him to need practically no sleep at all.

Dex glanced at his notes. "She woke up at approximately 6:00 a.m., went into the bathroom, and got dressed. She came out and stated her intention to work out in the gym and then get some breakfast."

Anya never got up early to work out. She had to be dragged out of bed every morning and was prone to rolling over and going back to sleep if a person wasn't persistent with her.

"Anticipating being in public with her for a couple hours," Dex continued, "Sleepy told the subject he'd like to use the restroom."

Eating, sleeping, and taking care of bodily functions were the bane of bodyguards. You had to squeeze in life's necessities when and where you could.

"When Sleepy stepped out of the bathroom, Anya was gone."

"How long were you in there?" Isabella asked the soldier.

He looked acutely uncomfortable, but answered forthrightly, "About three minutes. I heard nothing. Nobody forced entry or made any appreciable noise."

Anya took off! Ran away, the little twerp!

Dex picked up the narrative. "Sleepy stepped into the hallway and saw no sign of her. He radioed ops and then headed for the athletes' gym. When she wasn't there, he headed for the cafeteria. We alerted all the camera operators to look for her, but nobody spotted her. That's when I called you, Adder."

So Anya had had eight, maybe ten minutes to get a head start before any serious search began. Plenty of time to be out of the village and on the streets of Lake Placid.

"While everyone was coming over here, I notified the IOC security team…"

Ouch. That had to have been an unpleasant call for him to make.

"…and I called the Lake Placid Police and state police. Given that there's no sign of foul play and we believe she simply walked out of her room, the FBI won't get involved until she's been missing for twenty-four hours. The question is, where did she go? What are your thoughts on this, Adder?"

Everyone turned to look at her. Fortunately, in her prior job as an intel analyst, she'd experienced life-and-death decisions hanging on her judgments. She took a deep breath. Thought about her next words carefully, and then said, "I don't think the question is where. I think it's with whom."

"And your guess at who she's with?" Dex asked grimly.

Yup, he was thinking the same thing she was. She voiced their mutual thought aloud. " My best guess is that she's with Lazlo Petrovich."

Groans went up from just about everyone. If Isabella was right, Anya had walked into the arms of an active terrorist cell with connections to the most conservative and extreme Muslim movements in the world. Great. Just great.

Dex nodded. "I agree with you. Next question. Where would he take her?"

Isabella reasoned aloud. "First of all, for those of you who aren't aware of it, Lazlo and Anya have crushes on each other. Big ones. They see themselves as star-crossed lovers who fate and us big, bad adults with political agendas are keeping apart."

Rolled eyes all around.

"Yeah, it's sappy, I know. But it's a powerful motivator. I don't think Lazlo tricked her into going with him so his family and friends could harm her. My assessment is that this is an innocent case of running off and playing hooky. But, we can't proceed only on that assumption. I think we have to assume the worst and hope for the best."

Dex studied her intently. "Keep talking."

She frowned. "Surely they know I'll freak out, with the rest of you right behind me. They know that we'll go looking for them and that we'll turn Lake Placid upside down in the search. Seems to me they'll either go somewhere very private or they'll go somewhere else. Anya did express a desire to 'see New York.' It's not impossible that they will leave the local area altogether."

Dex frowned. "Does Lazlo have a car?"

"No," Vanessa said, "but his thug buddies, Gorabchek and company, do. Lazlo might borrow wheels from them."

Dex said, "We need to get people over to the Petrovich house and see if Anya's there. If not, is there a car missing? Viper, will a couple of your troops take care of it? You're more familiar with the layout of that place than the rest of us."

Vanessa nodded briskly. "Done."

Dex continued, "Hobo, call the car rental agencies in the area and see if Lazlo or Anya have rented a vehicle. Sleepy, Bungee and Jabba, I need you to canvas the other modes of transportation that leave town. Meanwhile, let's get someone over to the village to verify that Lazlo's gone."

As everyone stood up to get going on their assigned tasks, Isabella heard him mutter under his breath, "Christ, what a mess." She shared his sentiment entirely.

As the others cleared the room, she stayed behind to speak to Dex. He looked up from his notes, his eyes hard.

Quietly, she said, "I know you don't put any stock in gut intuitions, but I'm convinced I've pegged it. I just have a feeling that she's taken off with Lazlo."

"What does your gut have to say about when she'll be back?"

She shrugged. "I don't know. I'd like to think she's responsible enough to make it back for her practice session at noon, but I doubt that's going to happen. I think she's gone for the day. Assuming she doesn't get herself killed, either through her own folly or my wringing her neck when I catch up with her, she'll come back on her own. She has made it clear that it's important to her to skate in the next round. I can't imagine her blowing that off. The ladies' short program is in three days. Worst case, I expect her back for that."

He shook his head. "Three days is a long time for a lamb like her to survive among the wolves. We need to find her before then."

Isabella nodded grimly and turned to leave.

She was surprised when he said to her back, "Let me

know if your gut sends you any more intuitions about where she has gone."

She stopped. Turned around. Nodded slowly. "Since you asked, it seems as if there are two obvious places she'd go if she has left the local area. New York City or Niagara Falls. It's a long drive to the Falls, though, and I don't see her being comfortable doing an overnight trip with young Lazlo. She has a crush on him, but she doesn't want to see her family kill him or force the two of them into a hasty marriage."

Dex blinked. "Her family would *kill* him?"

Isabella smiled without humor. "Welcome to life in a traditional Muslim family. If this boy has besmirched the honor of their daughter, they'd absolutely consider it their right to kill him."

He looked at her closely. "And were you raised in that kind of conservative home?"

It was her turn to blink. And why did *he* want to know? "My dad acted as a moderating influence over my mother's extended family." Then she added flippantly, "Never fear. I'm not usually lethal to date. I won't kill Beau unless he deserves it."

That dropped Dex's jaw. Hark! Was that a blush climbing the man's cheeks?

She waxed serious again. "We have to find Anya before something bad happens."

Dex matched her seriousness. "I know you really like this girl. But stay objective, Adder. Keep your head on straight and keep thinking. You know Anya better than any of us. I need your input if we're going to find her."

Wow. He'd actually complimented her. "Understood. And thanks."

"You're welcome."

Stunned, she headed out into the ops center to find her teammates. To them she said, "You'll never believe it. His Highness just said he needs my input. The inmates in Hell must be having a snowball fight right about now."

Aleesha lapsed into her heavy Jamaican accent. "Aw, girlie, dat mon, he gots it bad for thee."

Isabella gaped. "Get out. He does not."

Misty laughed. "Open your eyes. He's crazy about you. That's why he's so hard on you."

Isabella retorted, "Isn't he a little old for yanking my braids and throwing spit wads to show he likes me?"

There was no time for a response as Vanessa divvied up assignments. Vanessa opted to take Karen, Kat and Misty with her to check out the Petrovich house. When she announced that choice, Isabella protested. "C'mon, Viper. This is my girl who's missing. Let me do something to help find her."

Vanessa was firm. "You may be needed here to answer questions about Anya. You also haven't had any sleep in two days, and I need you to get some rest. You're running on empty."

As the other Medusas left, Dex walked up to her, watching Vanessa's retreating back. "I see Scat taught her about taking care of her team," he said approvingly. "You are too tired to be out crawling around doing surveillance right now."

She ignored his comment on her state of fatigue and replied, "We all look out for each other. The hard part is listening to the others when I know they're right. What can I do around here to help? I'll go crazy with nothing to do."

At least he had the common sense not to try to convince her to go home and sleep. No way could she sleep right now. "You can look at the surveillance tapes. Figure out how she got out of the building without anyone noticing. Maybe get a description of her clothes."

She nodded. Dex pointed out a free console, showed her how to input the camera imagery she wanted to review, and how to rewind and fast forward the digital video. It was a reasonably similar setup to the one she'd used at the Pentagon to review footage taken from unmanned aerial reconnaissance airplanes.

It didn't take her long to spot Anya. But then, she had the advantage of knowing the girl like her own sister.

"I've got her," she called out.

Dex leaned over her shoulder. Isabella pointed at the screen. "That's her in the black leather bomber jacket and hat."

"She used a disguise?"

Isabella nodded. "Yup, and I've seen that coat before. It's Lazlo's."

"Where's he?" Dex asked, scanning the screen.

"No sign of him. He probably went out ahead to pick up a car, maybe meet her out front. Do we have video of the street?"

He nodded. "We'll have to patch in to the IOC security cameras." He reached past her to type in a set of commands. Their shoulders brushed, and he did nothing to pull away from the contact. But then, neither did she.

"There you go," Dex said.

Was she imagining it, or did his voice sound a little tight? Sort of like her throat right now. "Thanks," she mumbled.

She started scanning images of the streetside curb of the Olympic village in the early morning light. She picked up Anya leaving the building, but the girl disappeared down the street too far for the camera's resolution to make out. If Anya and Lazlo had a rendezvous, it happened out of camera range. Damn! Dead end. She'd been so hoping to get a description of a car. Then the police could swing into action and find the teens fast. She sat back, glaring at the screen in front of her.

"Go home."

She turned her glare on Dex.

He said gently, "I'm not telling you to sleep. I'm telling you to get a hot meal in you and rest. Take it from an old field operator. I know what I'm talking about. You need to disengage from this for a little while."

She sighed. He did have a lot more operational experience than she did. And as much as she might protest, he did know what he was talking about when it came to pushing the human body to its limits.

"Okay, fine," she grumbled. "I'm out of here. But you call

me the second you hear anything. None of this I just thought I'd let you sleep a little longer crap."

He threw her a sharp, sarcastic salute. "Yes, ma'am. Now get out of here."

She threw him an equally snappy salute, with the middle finger of her right hand extended and the others curled down in a fist. He laughed at the bird she'd flipped him.

As she'd predicted, Anya's practice time came and went with no sign of the girl. Her coach alternated between panic and fury. Liz agreed with Isabella's guess that Anya was with Lazlo, who had indeed disappeared as well. Surveillance of the house where Lazlo's family was staying yielded no sign of the missing teens nor any conversation regarding their whereabouts. The Medusas stayed parked in the woods behind the home to keep an eye on it.

None of the other investigations turned up any leads, either. The police, both local and state, were keeping an eye out for the teens, but that was all anyone could do for now. They were blind and helpless until a development changed the situation.

Isabella wandered the Olympic village until the buildings closed in on her and her eyeballs pounded with a headache. She was tired. But there was no way she could sleep as long as Anya was possibly in danger. Isabella left the village and took to the streets, examining every face in the crowd, hoping against hope that she'd spot Anya.

Her cell phone rang as the sun slid low in the winter sky, and she yanked it out of her pocket hopefully. *Please, God, let it be news.* "Hello?"

"No news yet," Dex said quickly, quelling her anticipation. "Where are you?"

"Why do you ask?"

"I'm standing at your front door, and you're not resting like I told you to."

Busted. "Uh, I couldn't sit still. I decided to go for a walk."

"Come on back. I know what the situation calls for," he said.

Suspiciously she asked, "Oh yeah? What?"

"Just trust me for once. I've been in this business a long time."

She sighed. "I'll be there in ten minutes."

"I'll be waiting."

He was sitting on the steps leading up to her floor when she rounded the corner of her building. He didn't say much as she unlocked the door and went inside. But as soon as the door closed behind him, he said, "Put on some workout clothes."

She frowned, but actually, the idea of working up a good mindless sweat sounded appealing. About two minutes later, she emerged from the bedroom in red Lycra shorts and a matching tie-dye tank top. She pulled on gray sweatpants and her white, Olympic parka.

"Let's go," he said. He was silent in the car, maybe to allow her to study the pedestrians on the sidewalks, maybe because he didn't have anything to say. Aleesha and Misty were smoking dope if they thought he was interested in her. Here they were, all alone and he said not a word. He parked in front of the Olympic village, and they signed in to the incredible workout facility.

"What's your poison of preference?" he asked as they gazed around at every conceivable piece of workout equipment known to man.

She grinned. "If I'm into pain, I go for a stair climber. If I'm into sweat, I head for the treadmill. After I'm good and warmed up, then I head for the weights."

"Let's go for sweat. Stair climbers make me feel like a Hollywood housewife." He headed over to a treadmill and stepped onto the big machine.

She stepped onto the treadmill beside his and took off at an easy jog. As her muscles warmed up, the tension across the back of her neck began to ease. For once, it felt really good to be doing this. She speeded up the machine to a brisk run. Within a few minutes she'd broken a sweat and pushed herself to a six-and-a-half-minute mile pace. The Medusas liked to do six-minute miles on their group runs, but it was always just a little faster than she was comfortable going. Except today, the slower pace felt sluggish to her. Experimentally, she pushed up the speed to a six-minute mile. Hey, it wasn't bad!

She stretched out her stride, let her arms swing naturally, and found an easy rhythm she could sustain all day. Hmm. Was her trouble running with her teammates all in her head? Was she tensing up in the group runs because she thought she was slower than the others? She inched up the speed a little bit more. Okay, she was working hard at this 5:45 pace, but her breathing was holding up and she still felt strong.

She noticed Dex glancing over at her control panel. He was probably doing four-minute miles beside her, but she didn't care. She was running as fast as the other Medusas usually did and was holding her own very nicely, thank you very much.

She did six miles at the killer pace, and then she slowed the machine down to a baby jog to let her heart recover gradually. Dex's machine wound down beside hers.

He said, "I admit it. I'm impressed. That was a good run you just put in."

She replied, "Where we suffer in comparison to the men is when you add weight to our backs. We can run long distances loaded down, but we lose a lot of speed."

"Is it strength or aerobic capacity that gets you?" he asked curiously.

"We don't have the extra lung capacity to take sixty or seventy extra pounds and still run fast. The trick is, we know that. So, we profile our missions around it. We're inserted closer to the target and we egress away from the op closer in so we don't have to hump gear twenty or thirty miles fast to get to our extraction point."

"What other adjustments do you make to ops to compensate for being women?"

She didn't take the question as an insult. He sounded genuinely interested. "We have to watch the lifting and climbing requirements. Obviously, women don't have near the upper body strength in ratio to our weight that men do. We can all do pull-ups and climb ropes and lift and carry an adult male, but we try not to make doing a lot of that central to mission success."

"What are your special strengths? For surely you must have some or General Wittenauer would never have brought the Medusas on board."

She grinned. "He was a bit of a tough nut to crack. Our greatest strength is that we're invisible. Nobody out there expects women operatives, so they don't look for us. We can stroll in right under someone's nose and they never peg us for who we are. A whole lot of the trouble spots in the world today marginalize their female populations—maybe that's why they're in trouble. We can enlist the aid of all those unhappy women in a way that a male team can't."

"And then there's sex," he remarked.

"I beg your pardon?"

"You can sleep with people to get what you need."

She gazed coldly at him. "Before I hurt you very badly for saying that, were you making that comment purely in an operational context?"

He looked startled. "Sorry. I didn't mean it like that. Honest. I was talking about it in the context of missions."

She unclenched her jaw as he further explained, "It's just that I've thought about it on some of my missions when we're trying to run an infiltration. It would be so much easier to be a woman and sashay into some bar or restaurant and proposition the bad guy straight up. It would save so damned much time over having to prove ourselves and win the trust of a group before they'll let us in."

She shrugged. "To date, we haven't run any ops where it would've helped. And I have to say I seriously hope we never do. I can't imagine Vanessa accepting any op that forced one of us to sleep our way into position."

"That sort of thing would be volunteer only."

Her eyebrows shot up. "You say that like you've seen a mission or two where the operators did sleep their way in."

"It's been known to happen," he said cryptically.

Gaping at his back, she followed him over to the gigantic array of free weights.

"Spot me and I'll spot you," he offered.

She nodded, still stunned over that little revelation. She stood behind his head as he lay down on a weight bench and commenced pressing nearly twice her body weight. When it was her turn, he made suggestions to correct her technique, which made managing the weight easier and allowed her to add ten pounds to her second set of lifts.

She felt like a noodle from head to foot when they finally left the gym and headed back to her place. Dex looked energized, relaxed and refreshed, the jerk. He'd probably get better-looking with age, too!

"Go take a shower," he ordered.

She disappeared into her bedroom, perplexed over all this one-on-one treatment. But hey. If he wanted to babysit her for grins and giggles, who was she to stop him?

It took until she was almost done with her shower before the little voice in the back of her head kicked in. Okay, so she was flattered that he was spending time with her. She hoped it meant that maybe Aleesha and Misty were right after all. And dammit, she was attracted to him. Had a full-blown crush on the guy, for God's sake. She was no better off than Anya. Well, maybe she was. She wasn't a dead woman when she finally got her sassy little butt back home!

She got out of the shower, towel dried her dark hair and brushed it back into a ponytail that promptly commenced dripping between her shoulder blades. With Dex in her living room, she wasn't going to take time to blow dry it.

She stepped out of the bedroom. Correction. Dex was in her kitchen.

"What are you doing in here?" she exclaimed as she wedged herself into the tiny space beside him.

"Cooking dinner. I went back to my place and grabbed a few things."

"A man of many talents, are we?" she asked, peering into a pot of pasta boiling in some sort of broth.

"Move over. I have to add the vegetables."

She complied while he dropped in colorful red and yellow peppers, asparagus tips, zuchinni and yellow squash. Then he tossed in a handful of something else about the size of corn, but light brown. She asked incredulously, "Are those *pine nuts?*"

He glared over at her. "And what's wrong with those? They add a crunchy texture and nutty flavor."

She shook her head, grinning widely. "Now I've heard it all. The trained killer enjoys crunchy texture and nutty flavor."

His gaze narrowed and he said menacingly, "You're a trained killer, too, and you'll like them as much as I do."

She did, indeed, enjoy the pine nuts. She enjoyed the whole meal, in fact. He'd even gotten the vinegar-and-oil mixture just right on the salad, a feat she'd never been consistently successful at.

They'd pushed back their plates and laid down their napkins when she finally decided she couldn't stand it anymore. "So what's up? Why all this personal attention?"

"You are direct, aren't you?"

"Another trait of the trained killer that we both share in common." She threw him a challenging look that dared him to match her directness.

"I'm interested in you. I want to know what makes you tick. I've never met another woman like you."

Okay, then. So he could be as direct as she could. "There are only five more women anywhere like me that I'm aware of."

He planted his elbows on the table and studied her. "Why this job?"

"Initially, I'd have said it was because I'm no good at

turning down a dare. When Vanessa offered it to me, I couldn't resist the challenge."

"And now?"

Damn, he was perceptive. He'd picked up on her reference to deeper motives. She mulled over how to put it into words. He waited, silent. Finally she replied, "I grew up in a world where women were expected to do a little school until they met a guy, got married, had kids, and faded into the background. Eventually, my sons would grow up and I'd be able to henpeck them and boss their wives around. And then I'd die, a grouchy, stooped old woman."

Still he was silent.

She picked up steam as she became more certain of what it was she was trying to say. "I wanted more. But not only did I want more, I wanted to reject all of that. I wanted to blast it to smithereens. Joining the Air Force was a great start. But joining the Medusas—that was the ultimate 'screw you' to my upbringing."

Man, it felt good to have finally let that idea out of the subconscious recesses of her mind.

He nodded slowly. "And that's why you're so close to Anya. You see her doing the same thing—giving a big, fat 'screw you' to her fundamentalist roots."

"Exactly."

"Do you like being a Medusa?"

The question startled her, but she smiled with genuine warmth. "I love it. I love my teammates like sisters. I'd die for them and they'd do the same for me. Surely you know that feeling."

His intense gaze relaxed for a moment. "I wouldn't use exactly those words to describe it, but yeah, I know the feeling."

A moment of silence fell between them. They shared a mutual knowledge of a world few other people understood.

"Does your family know?" she asked.

"My parents know in a vague way that I'm in the Special

Forces. But they have no real understanding of what being a Delta means, and they have no idea what the job entails. My brother desperately hopes I'll die so he can inherit the family business—and the family fortune—all for himself."

"Do I detect some bitterness?" she asked.

He shrugged. "I'm like you. I grew out of wanting to break Randall's neck a long time ago. I don't live for the dollar signs in my bank account like he does."

"Is your family really that rich and stuffy?"

"Yes to both," he answered in disgust.

She threw his own question back at him. "So why this job?"

"I didn't want to be useless. I wanted to do something worthwhile with my life."

"Have you found it?"

"Yup. Being a Delta team leader is the most amazing thing I've ever done or hope to do."

"Any regrets?" she asked.

He thought about that one for a long time, and she reciprocated with patient silence. He remarked unexpectedly, "For a woman, you can go a long time without talking."

She blinked. "For a man, you can say some really dumb things."

He snorted with laughter. "Touché. I meant it as a compliment, but I take it back."

"Good call. You may have just saved your manhood some irreparable damage."

His eyes glinted. "You could try to hurt me, but you wouldn't succeed."

She shrugged. "I'm sneaky. Don't be so sure. Besides, Jack Scatalone taught us everything we know about unarmed combat."

Dex laughed. "Okay, so maybe you could take a chunk out of my hide. That guy is a beast in a fight."

She rolled her eyes. "Tell me about it. I had to spar with him for six months."

Dex threw her a sympathetic look.

"Okay, so you've dodged my question long enough, Dex. Now answer it. Do you have any regrets about this job?"

He sighed. Waxed serious. "Yeah. It consumes your whole life. There's no time for anything else."

"Anything? Or anyone?"

His gaze snapped to hers, pinning her in her seat with its intensity. "Both." He added in grim warning, "You won't have time for anything or anyone else, either."

She answered lightly, "I'm a firm believer in making time for the things that are really important to me. It boils down to a matter of priorities. If you want a personal life, you have to decide to make it happen and then just do it. In my experience, nothing worth having is ever easy to get."

"No, it isn't, is it?" His gaze burned even brighter as he stared directly into her eyes. "So. Are you telling me you want a relationship?"

Chapter 14

Harlan Holt paced the cheap motel room, distraught. He couldn't sit still. He couldn't go anywhere. He couldn't call anyone. What he knew was eating away at his gut like acid. *Or maybe like poison nerve gas.* Heavens above, he'd put the first half of a binary nerve agent into the ice at the Hamilton Arena. He was an accessory to a crime of such magnitude it took his breath away. He'd actually thrown up when he'd finally identified the white powder.

He was a monster. A murderer on an incomprehensible scale.

He didn't know, dammit! They'd made him do it!

And he'd let them. He'd known they had to be up to something terrible. But he'd gone along with it anyway. The right thing to do was to sacrifice his wife and tell the authorities what was going to happen. Oh, God. Emma.

He fell to the floor, kneeling as he wept yet again for her. How could he condemn his own wife to death? He wasn't strong enough. He couldn't do it. Instead, he moved from place to place, staying at fleatraps and truck stops, paying with cash, staying one step ahead of those women from Olympic security.

They'd nearly caught him in his lab. But those guards had kept walking by and he'd finally gotten spooked enough to run. As an undergrad at Syracuse twenty years ago, he'd played Dungeons and Dragons in the steam tunnels. Strange to think that had come in handy all these years later.

He'd gone home to feed Fritz, but he'd gotten spooked there, too. It looked like someone had been in the house. The area rug and the bedspread weren't where he remembered them. The details of that horrible night were still vivid in his mind, and the picture when he'd gone home hadn't matched what he recalled.

Now what? He'd gotten his cell phone charger in that brief stop, and his phone was up and running again. Why hadn't the terrorists—for surely that was what they were—contacted him? Was Emma okay?

He climbed painfully to his feet and began to pace again.

Was Dex making an offer to have a relationship with her? Holy freaking cow! The guy was direct, all right. Now what? Okay, hot shot, she could give as good as got. She took a deep breath. "Yes, I do want a relationship. Very much."

His gaze went white-hot. Incendiary. He leaned closer to her and jumped straight up in the air when his cell phone rang.

"Goddamn it," he snapped under his breath. He jerked out the phone and flipped it open. "What?" he said irritably. He listened for a moment, and said only, "Thanks." Then he stood up briskly. "Let's go. They've spotted your girl."

She jumped up, heading for her coat. "They who? Is she okay?"

"New York state troopers spotted her and Lazlo crossing the line into Essex County. If they go straight back to Lake Placid, they should be at the Olympic village in a half hour. I'm assuming you'd like to speak to the two of them?"

She snorted. "That's a word for it. Am I allowed to do bodily harm to Olympic athletes if they can still compete when I'm done with them?"

He smiled grimly. "Don't ask and I won't tell."

"Deal."

Anya and Lazlo burst into her room, laughing then stopped cold when they caught sight of Isabella and Dex in the armchairs on the far side of the room. Waiting. Dex had been kind enough not to talk to her after they left his apartment. He seemed to understand her need to focus on what she was going to say to her errant charge—and on controlling the fury raging in her gut.

Anya said in a small voice, "Are you mad at me, 'Bella?"

It had taken her most of the ride over here and the twenty minute wait in the room to arrive at the proper frame of mind for answering that question. She said evenly, "It's not my job to be mad at you."

Dex said tightly, "Would you mind telling us where you went?"

Anya answered quickly, "It was amazing. I got to see the Statue of Liberty. I ate a Coney Dog, and stood in Times Square and saw Central Park. There were so many people, and it was so *big*…" She trailed off as the flat, cold menace of Isabella and Dex's expressions registered.

Lord, it was like they were the girl's parents, lowering the boom when she'd missed a curfew. She and Dex made a brutal combination for any teenager to face. Any kids of theirs would be so hosed when it came to messing up— Whoa. Kids of theirs? Uh, no. Not likely. Maybe not *impossible,* but definitely not likely.

Dex stood up. "Young Lazlo and I are going to take a walk and have a little talk about taking care of the people he cares about."

The boy looked scared spitless. Having grown up away from his own father, he might not have a whole lot of experience with parental ass-whupping. But from the look in Dex's eyes, Lazlo was about to get a crash course. Isabella waited in silence until the two men left. Dex had employed the classic divide-and-conquer technique. Together, the two teens might have stood their ground and defended their little excursion. But apart, they didn't stand a chance. It had been a good read of the situation.

She turned her coldest, most menacing look on Anya. "Let us be clear on one thing. If you *ever* pull a stunt like that again, I will let them kill you. Do you understand me? I will give my life to save you from an attack, but I will not die to save you from your own stupidity."

Anya nodded, thoroughly frightened. "I never thought of it that way. I'm sorry, 'Bella. Really." The girl began to cry. Tears piled up in her eyes and spilled over, streaking her cheeks. Her remorse appeared genuine. Probably time to turn her over to her coach. Isabella had faith that Liz was going to rip Anya a new one.

She stood up and moved to where Anya sat on the edge of the bed. She put an arm around the girl and gave her a hug, just like she would have with one of her own little sisters. "I was worried about you, sweetie. I'm glad you're back safe and sound."

Anya nodded against her shoulder and cried all the harder.

Isabella stepped out into the hall. Crisis solved. She headed back to the ops center, absolutely drained. The adrenaline of the past fourteen hours dissipated so abruptly she felt light-headed. Since Dex had given her a ride over here, she would need a ride home. He hadn't come back from his little chat with Lazlo yet, so she went into his office and sat down at his desk. Too exhausted to keep her eyes open, she cradled her head in her arms on his desk and passed out in about three seconds flat.

Abdul sat at the kitchen table with his entire cell. It was rare that he gathered them in one place, but he needed to make a small adjustment to the plan. They were so close now. The end was in sight. Excitement surged restlessly in his heart and he could feel the hand of fate coming closer and closer. Soon, his place in paradise would be assured. But even more important than that, he was on the verge of making his children's future more secure by protecting their way of life from the infidels. While he worried about his own immortal soul, he worried infinitely more about theirs. And that was as it should be.

The last man arrived. Abdul looked around the six faces at the table—his two nephews not in police custody, the three Chechnyans and the sixth man—his secret weapon. He said solemnly, "Gentlemen, there is one more task we must do before the moment of reckoning. So much attention has been drawn to the Khalid whore that she has been given extra security. That means there are many more soldiers and police at the figure skating stadium than we anticipated."

The experienced terrorists in the group—the Chechnyans—scowled at this news. They knew the possible implications of it better than the rest of them.

Abdul continued, "Rather than respond with more force, our strategy will be this— We will use the Khalid whore to our advantage. We will increase the apparent threat to her until all the extra security personnel are concentrated entirely around her. If we do this well, the stadium will be even less defended than it was before she drew so much attention to herself with her lewd display. She will help us teach the West a lesson."

Nods all around, and the Chechnyans looked less tense.

"Here is what we will do…"

It was almost midnight when something touched her shoulder. She woke with a jerk, battle alert. Dex. The first shock of waking faded, leaving her feeling like she'd been run over by a train.

"Hey," she mumbled.

He smiled kindly. "Sorry to wake you. But I thought you might sleep better in your own bed."

She looked around, registering fully that she was in his darkened office with the only light coming in through the open door to the ops center. She'd been asleep in here for a solid four hours. "I'm sorry. I was so tired, I just sort of crashed."

"You're authorized. It's been a rough couple of days. Do you want to come get the midnight briefing with me?"

She blinked. That woke her up. The midnight briefing was a classified recap of all the day's events and any developments that might be of interest to the security group. Only the top-level supervisors attended, and they passed any pertinent information down to their people. "I'd love to go. Any reason why I get to play with the big dogs?"

"The FBI lab told me the initial forensics on the Holt lab and home should be ready tonight. And, Reda Aziz, the guy you nabbed in the alley, was interrogated again this evening. I thought you might want to hear both reports firsthand."

They walked down the long hallway to the IOC Security team's conference room, "Why are you being so nice to me?"

He glanced at her. "I'm not being nice. I'm doing my job."

She rolled her eyes. "Don't B.S. me."

"So, maybe it took me a while to warm up to the idea of women on the teams."

"In other words, you were only temporarily a jerk before and now you're back to your normal self. Gee, and I was so sure the asshole was your regular self and this guy was the exception to the rule."

"I love you too, Torres," he said sarcastically.

She smirked at him. "I dare you to say that like you mean it."

He blinked. Startled. And then it hit her what she'd said. She stopped cold, right there, in the middle of the hall. "I'm *so* sorry. That was out of line. I don't know what I was thinking. Forget I said anything. Really—"

He put up a hand. "Stop. I'm not going to court martial you for sexual harassment. No offense taken." He reached behind her and opened the door to the conference room, which was crowded with senior Olympic officials. As she moved past him, he murmured, "Besides, I may take you up on that dare sometime."

It was her turn to blink, stunned. What in the hell was happening? Well, she *knew* what was happening, but how was it possible? Well, she knew how it was possible, too, but *Dexter Thorpe?* Come on. Surely she had better sense than that! She jumped as he put his hand under her elbow and guided her to a pair of seats near the front of the room. Nope, apparently, she didn't have a lick of sense at all.

The briefing covered a brawl among some spectators at a hockey game. There was discussion over extra manpower that would have to be shifted to the downhill skiing run tomorrow in response to the heavy snowfall that was expected within the next couple hours.

"And now for Major Thorpe and company," Manfred Schmidt said. "Marcy Hammersmith, here, is from the FBI. I hear you have some lab reports for us."

The surprisingly young woman nodded and stood up. "We were given two different sets of samples to analyze. The first was a series of swabs from Dr. Holt's laboratory. Sample number four was a white, powdery substance swabbed from a stainless steel countertop. It turns out this powder is a chemical compound whose name is classified. For the purposes of this briefing, we will call it Agent Alpha. It is one half of a binary compound considered to be one of the deadliest nerve gas toxins in existence."

Oh. My. God. The powder at the ice rink came from Holt's lab.

"This sample of Agent Alpha is identical to the trace amounts of powder that were found on the paper bag of, uh, excrement that was thrown at Ms. Khalid. It will take further testing to verify that the two samples came from the same manufacturing process, but given the rarity of this chemical, we speculate this will be the case."

Manfred Schmidt leaned forward aggressively in his seat

and asked archly, "What other uses does this Agent Alpha have besides being half of a nerve gas poison?"

"None. It is an engineered molecule with no other purpose."

It was severely satisfying to watch the dismay and then horror cross the German's face. The seriousness of what the Medusas were investigating had just hit him.

The briefer moved on. "We also were asked to analyze a number of blood samples from the Holt home. We lifted DNA from two different subjects, one male and one female. The female DNA matches DNA taken from hair samples on Mrs. Holt's pillow and hairbrush. So, we are tentatively identifying the female subject's blood as hers. We will need to get DNA from family members or a known sample of her blood to make a positive ID."

Dex spoke up. "We're not officially investigating a crime at this point, so your tentative ID gives us enough to work on for now. What about the other blood?"

The briefer smiled. "That one was more interesting. The DNA is male and Middle Eastern. We compared it to the list of subjects that Captain Torres gave us as possible persons connected to Mrs. Holt's disappearance. We got an interesting match."

Dex leaned over to her. "What list?"

"The FBI lab called me this afternoon and asked for names of any Middle Easterners who might be involved with Emma Holt so they could check the DNA database for a match faster."

The briefer flashed up a black-and-white picture on the screen behind her. It showed several long, vertical rows of the distinctive stripes of DNA. "We got a partial DNA match between our sample blood here, and this DNA print." She pointed at a second strand. "It belongs to a man named Al Abhoud."

Isabella gaped. "The Muslim cleric who declared the fatwa on Anya?"

The briefer shook her head. "Not exactly. This strand is Ahmed al Abhoud's DNA on file at the FBI. You can see here and here how our sample is not quite an exact match. It's only about a seventy-five percent match, in fact. Our sample DNA came from al Abhoud's son, Abdul al Abhoud."

Isabella stared in shock. A son? And he bled in Emma Holt's bedroom?

The briefer continued. "Our spatter analysis of the photos provided says the blood samples came from a struggle. Mrs. Holt thrashed around after she developed a small, bleeding wound, possibly on her arm or hand. Mr. Abhoud bled from a more stationary position, again probably a small wound that dripped."

Dex asked, "So we're not looking at a murder scene?"

The briefer laughed. "Oh, no. The scene of a struggle, but no more. Much more in keeping with a domestic altercation, and assault, or, say, a kidnapping."

Isabella frowned. Had Emma Holt learned of her husband's work with Agent Alpha? Had they fought about it and Holt had his wife kidnapped to keep her quiet? Was he taking care of her while he was hiding?

It was a logical explanation, but something in it didn't jive. She thought about the photo albums she'd gone through in the Holt home. Harlan and Emma Holt were crazy in love, or they were the best actors she'd seen in a while. Why would Emma squeal on her husband, and why would he attack her and help someone kidnap her? The only possible reason Emma would turn on him would have to be something terrible—like he was planning to use the nerve gas he'd synthesized. But on whom? Nerve gas was an agent of mass death. You didn't target one person. You targeted a whole lot of people. An army or a city.

Oh, she *so* didn't like where *that* line of thinking was taking her. She glanced over at Dex, and from the rippling muscles in his clenched jaw, she'd lay odds his thoughts were running in the same direction.

Into the heavy silence that had fallen over the room,

Isabella said, "What can you tell us about Agent Bravo, or whatever the other half of this compound is called?"

The briefer shuffled her notes and then said, "It's an odorless liquid that's faintly amber in color in large quantities but appears clear in aerosol form or in a small quantity. Agent Alpha, in powdered form, can be stirred directly into it to achieve the release of poisonous gas, or Agent Alpha can be mixed with any nonreactive liquid and added to the liquid Agent Bravo to achieve the same results. Generally, contact is sufficient to create the reaction. Neither agitation—as in shaking it—nor heating are necessary to promote the chemical reaction."

Dex asked grimly, "And exactly how nasty is the gas this stuff produces?"

The briefer's answer was succinct. "One lungful will kill you."

Isabella leaned forward. "What quantities of these agents are needed to knock off a large number of people?"

"That's the good news. Both of these are bulk chemicals. To take out a room this size, you're looking at maybe an ounce of Agent Alpha and around two ounces of Agent Bravo. On a large scale, several hundred pounds of Agent Alpha—which is the catalyst by the way—would be required to activate anywhere from several hundred to several thousand gallons of Agent Bravo."

This stuff sounded like Agent Orange; something that would be sprayed out the back of an airplane to blanket a large area. "Is the gas lighter or heavier than air?"

"It's slightly heavier. But not by much. If there's any significant air movement, it will circulate rapidly throughout a space."

"How does the United States deliver this stuff?" Manfred Schmidt asked.

The briefer was terse. "The United States has *not* developed this weapon and does *not* maintain a stockpile of it. Therefore, we have no delivery method. It has simply been studied because of intelligence received that other nations might be considering developing it as a weapon."

Schmidt's curled lip made it clear he didn't buy the briefer's answer. "Then how would this hypothetical other country deliver it?"

"Probably by airplane. Something along the lines of a crop duster."

Schmidt nodded. "Well, there you have it. Let's ban any sort of crop duster type aircraft over Lake Placid."

One of the other men at the table leaned forward. "It's not that simple. Many planes can be retrofitted with sprayers. We'll need to put flight restrictions on all small aircraft, not only over the town of Lake Placid but all the outdoor venues, as well. We probably ought to put a no-fly zone over this part of the state and let in and out only aircraft on IFR—instrument flight rules—flight plans to the Lake Placid International Airport."

The meeting devolved into a technical discussion about how to define the no-fly zone and Isabella let her thoughts wander. Why would Harlan Holt want to gas the Olympics? He'd never shown any signs of political extremism nor of mental instability. It didn't add up.

Eventually, the meeting moved on. The next briefer to stand up was a grim-looking guy in a black suit. If he put on dark sunglasses, he'd look like he'd stepped off of a movie set. No real person dressed like that! The guy in black cued up a video. Then, he began to speak in a predictably deadpan voice. "We interrogated Reda Aziz earlier this evening. The gentleman seated to the prisoner's right is his attorney, and the man to the left is the interpreter. My associate who conducted the interview and I are fluent in Arabic, but we elected to conduct the interview in English."

Standard procedure for interrogators to understand more than they let on.

The guy continued, "As you know, Mr. Aziz has steadfastly

refused to answer any questions. He continued to refuse tonight. However, that does not mean we learned nothing from him. I want to play you a short video clip and let you draw your own conclusions."

Isabella went into visual analysis mode as the lights dimmed and the still image on the screen jerked into motion. A voice off camera said, "Mr. Aziz, have you ever heard of a group called the Red Jihad?"

The translator repeated the question in Arabic, and the young man jerked like he'd just touched a live wire. His eyes darted around the room, and his skin went visibly pale.

The voice off camera again. "Repeat the question, please."

The translator complied, and the kid shook his head back and forth in quick, tiny negative movements. That was panic if she'd ever seen it. The kid looked about ready to pee his pants. He was definitely considering fleeing the scene, even if that meant jumping through the wall.

The briefer in black stood as the clip ended and the lights came up. "We infer from this young man's reaction that he has, indeed, heard of the Red Jihad."

Duh. Anybody could tell that.

"At Major Thorpe's request, some of our overseas operatives have contacted their informants to inquire about this group. Our only hit was in the Middle East. I cannot reveal the exact location or source, but the Red Jihad was described as a small, relatively wealthy group of highly educated persons with very high-level political and possibly religious connections and activist goals."

Isabella spoke up. "So, in other words, they're a terrorist group?"

The man turned his withering gaze on her. "I am not in the business of speculating. I am merely stating the facts, ma'am."

She'd laugh at the guy if this weren't such a serious matter. "We first heard the name in connection with Chechnya. Is this an international group, then?"

The guy answered dismissively, "Our Chechnyan operative found no evidence of the Red Jihad in that country."

She retorted, "That doesn't mean the Red Jihad isn't there. It only means your guy didn't know about it."

The suit shrugged.

She pressed him again. "Did your Middle Eastern contacts have any names of possible members? Any specifics?"

Black Suit replied, "Negative. Just what I told you already."

Well, it wasn't a lot, but it was better than nothing. So. A kid from Bhoukar was scared silly when Red Jihad was mentioned. Informants in the Middle East called it a small, rich, smart "activist" group. And an old cell of Chechnyan Muslim terrorists was talking about it. Clearly, it was time to find out more about what those Chechnyans were up to and see if Reda Aziz's buddies could be located and brought in, too. She could only pray that Harlan Holt had nothing to do with this Red Jihad that seemed to have converged upon Lake Placid.

The meeting dragged on for a while, but eventually came to an end. Dex gave her a ride home. He stopped the car in front of the sidewalk leading to her place.

"Let me park and I'll walk you up to your apartment," he said.

She met his gaze across the dim interior and said candidly, "I think maybe you'd better not, tonight. I'd be too tempted to invite you in."

It was too dark to see the expression in his eyes, but a long silence followed. His jaw clenched. Unclenched. Finally, he replied, "Yeah, you're probably right. I'd be tempted to accept the invitation." He added, "Another time, though."

She got out and headed for her place as Dex drove toward the other end of the complex. Yeah, another time. Not only was it about meeting the right guy, but it was about doing it at the right time and place, too. She and Dex had a spark, but now was neither the right time nor the right place. She had a sinking feeling that their window of opportunity was going to pass them by. They'd go home after these Olympics, get tied up in their respective jobs, get sent in opposite directions halfway around the world, and a few years from now look back and wonder why they'd never hooked up.

It was the bane of dating military men. Syncing up two busy, travel-filled careers never worked. It had been a nice idea, though. She unlocked her door, dropped the keys in her pocket, and stepped into her dark apartment.

Something big and dark came flying at her. It slammed into her and knocked her to the ground.

Intruder!

She flung up her arms to ward off the fists that flew at her face. A few of the thick, bony blows got through her defenses, though. She tasted blood and registered impacts to her face and head. The guy was sitting on her chest and she could barely breathe.

She was in trouble. A combination of fear, fury and raw adrenaline kicked in as the realization hit her that she could die. She might never get to kiss Dex, to see where their relationship went, to know if he was The One or just the one for now. Desperate to live, she kicked at the back of the guy's head and he swore. But then something heavy grabbed her legs and jumped on top of them.

Another assailant.

Crap. She threw a flurry of elbows and fists, and bucked and squirmed as best she could under the crushing weight of two big, burly men. She'd scream, except she had no freaking air. The guy on top of her must weigh two hundred and fifty pounds or more. Spots were starting to dance in front of her eyes.

The guy on her chest grabbed her left wrist. If he got both of her hands, she'd be defenseless! Desperately, she jabbed up with her right hand, her fingers extended and stiff. She stabbed him in both eyes and he cried out. He let go of her wrist and clutched at his face.

She followed with a punch to his nose. She threw everything she had into it. He howled like she'd broken it as she pulled her fist back and slammed it squarely into the guy's solar plexus. He was heavy enough that his breastbone was padded with fat and muscle, but he still made the horrible gasping sound that went with having his breath knocked violently out of him. Whoever was on her legs must have figured out his buddy was in trouble. He jumped up and moved around the gasping guy to take over pounding on her.

He knelt beside her, his face out of reach. But his crotch wasn't. She faked a swing at his face and got him to lean back away from the wild roundhouse. Then, as fast as she could, she yanked the fist down and jabbed forward, slamming it into his groin with everything she could muster. The guy yelled in pain and fury, swearing in some language she didn't recognize.

She heaved with her body. The guy on top of her lost his balance and she managed to turn on her side. She slipped slightly out from between his legs. He sat down on her again, but he was on her left hip this time. She drew in great gasps of air and twisted back and forth, flailing her fists and screaming at the top of her lungs.

The guy on top of her half fell off of her and rolled away. He panted something to his buddy, who was still on the floor, curled up around his cupped hands. The first thug reached down and dragged the second man to his feet. Still holding his crotch, the second guy half limped, half ran to the door. The two men fled into the night.

Isabella rolled to her hands and knees. Tried to push to her feet. Discovered she couldn't do it. A wave of dizziness and nausea slammed into her. She panted like a dog, her head hanging low between her shoulders. The threat of barfing passed, and she managed to push unsteadily to her feet. She staggered to her door and out into the parking lot. It wasn't like she could take them on again, but maybe she could catch a glimpse of a car or something. An engine revved and she ran clumsily into the parking lot to get a look at it.

She couldn't make out much. It was too far away. Dark,

two door sedan. Vague, generic outline. She turned to head back to her place, and the shivering set in. Her whole body shook, not fine ripples of cold across her skin, but an intense trembling that made walking hard. Nope, definitely not cold. Shock.

She pulled out her cell phone. Its face didn't light up when she flipped it open. Must've been busted in the ruckus. She cursed under her breath and turned toward the far end of the parking lot. Besides the fact that the idea of stepping into her dark apartment alone right now gave her the heebie-jeebies, she needed to report the attack. Could probably use some medical attention, too. She wasn't tasting blood anymore, but there was a ragged spot on the inside of her left cheek that hurt when she probed it with her tongue.

She made the long, cold walk to Dex's apartment. Climbing the stairs to the second floor was a painful exercise she was only able to do one step at a time. Those guys must've gotten in more licks than she'd realized. She knocked on Dex's door.

After a short pause, the lock rattled and the door opened. Dex took one look at her and threw the door wide open. She couldn't help it. She stepped forward, straight into his arms. He didn't hesitate. His arms wrapped tightly around her. God, that felt good. Safe.

"What happened?"

She exhaled slowly, the sound of his heart thumping steadily in her ear. "Two guys were waiting in my apartment. They jumped me just as I entered and knocked me down. I fought them off eventually. They ran and I followed them out into the parking lot. I didn't get a good look at them or their car. They were big. Beefy builds. Strong. Seemed to know their way around a fight."

He let go of her and headed for the phone in the kitchen.

"Facial features?" he asked, his voice strangely tight as he dialed.

"Ski masks," she replied. "They also had on black jackets and black leather gloves. Thin ones. I felt knuckles when they hit me."

He spoke quickly into the phone. "Detective Picconi. I'm glad it's you. Isabella Torres was just attacked in her apartment. The intruders got away and she's okay. If you could send a couple guys over to check out her place, that'd be great. She's pretty rattled. Can she file a report in the morning?" A short pause. "Thanks. Eight o'clock would be great. She'll be there. Oh, and Picconi, she's got permits for any weapons your men find."

He hung up. "Is your door unlocked?"

She smiled crookedly. "I think it's standing wide open."

"Don't worry about it. The cops will button it up when they're done. Now, let's have a look at that bruise on your jaw."

He led her into his bedroom and gestured for her to sit while he rummaged in his field pack for a first aid kit. "You gotta stop taking on gangs by yourself, Torres," he called from inside his closet.

"Hey, they're the ones coming after me," she called back.

He stepped back into the room. Man, he filled the place with his presence. "Any guesses as to who it was this time?"

She sucked in her breath as he pressed an alcohol soaked gauze pad against her scraped jaw. From between clenched teeth, she said, "It wasn't Reda Aziz's buddies, that's for sure. These guys were huge. More like—" she paused as it hit her "—more like Gorabchek and his men."

Dex nodded as he smeared some white cream on her cheek. It numbed the sting of the wound. "We've got a connection between the two, so it would make sense."

"Why does Red Jihad want to beat me up? What have I done to piss them off?"

He knelt in front of her and reached out for her ribs. She jerked back, surprised. He studied her closely. "All they did was hit you? Nothing else?"

He thought they might have sexually assaulted her. She quickly disabused him of that notion. "That's all. You just surprised me. And," she confessed reluctantly, "I'm ticklish."

"For crying out loud, woman. Don't scare me like that." He reached out again and laid his hands on her ribs. "Let me know if anything hurts when I push on it."

"I know the drill. And I've seen guys with busted ribs. You'll know if it hurts."

He grinned. "I've cracked a few myself over the years. They're a bitch. Every time you inhale it's like a knife in your lung. You end up holding your breath a lot."

His hands crept underneath her breasts and she tried really, really hard not to think about it. But when he pressed his palms against her and then swore quietly, it was pretty damned hard to ignore.

"Okay, so I'm attracted to you," he said abruptly. "This is incredibly uncomfortable for me to do, but it has to be done. Better me than some stranger in an emergency room."

She wasn't so sure about that. Suddenly she was having more than a little trouble breathing herself. She was sure he checked her ribs as fast as he could, but it was an eternity until his warm, strong, gentle hands lifted away from her. He rocked back on his heels and stood up. "You'll live," he announced.

She looked up at him and said soberly, "I'm not so sure about that."

"What's wrong?" he asked quickly.

"I'm attracted to you, too."

He stared down at her for a moment and then laughed shortly. "Last time I checked, nobody ever died from that."

"Did you talk to Romeo and Juliet and get their take on it?" she retorted dryly.

He laughed again. "Stay right there. You're shivering again." He strode over to the walk-in closet and came out with a blue ski sweater that had white snowflakes running up the arms and across the shoulders.

She shrugged into the surprisingly light and warm garment. "Angora?" she asked in surprise.

"Yup."

"I suppose you like the feel of it against your skin," she accused.

"As a matter of fact, I do," he retorted. "Is that some kind of crime?"

She shook her head and followed him into his tiny kitchen. "It's no crime. Just surprising. You do like your creature comforts."

He shrugged as he poured milk into a pan and commenced shaving chocolate into it.

"Good lord. Homemade hot chocolate?" she exclaimed. "It's two o'clock in the morning!"

He gave her a slow, sexy smile and his gaze drifted down her body and back up. "Anything worth doing is worth doing right, don't you think?"

She took back her assessment that this man would be a selfish lover. Revised estimate—this guy would be a relentless lover. In his pursuit of excellence in all things, he'd pleasure a woman until she screamed or collapsed or both. Her nether extremities tingled, and the feel of his hands supporting the weight of her breasts sprang to mind. She mumbled something inane and sagged in relief when he turned back to the stove to stir the hot chocolate. In a matter of minutes, he'd served up two steaming mugs.

"Let's go sit in the living room. I've got a fantastic view."

She followed him, watching as he pulled open the drapes. She gasped. In front of her rose a snow-covered mountain, reflecting moonlight off its silvery surface. Big, fat snowflakes fell in lazy silence, a thick curtain of white in the night sky. No wonder Dex's couch was parked awkwardly in the middle of the room facing the window!

They sat down, and he reached under the coffee table to pull out a quilt that he tucked around their legs. Then he handed her one of the mugs. "Be careful not to burn yourself. It's hot."

She murmured back, "It won't be the hot chocolate that burns me."

He took a sip from his mug and stared outside at the mountain for a long time before he said, "I don't get involved with women. Ever."

She waited for more. Besides, what was there to say in response to a line like that?

"And I would never consider getting involved with anyone I work with."

She laughed. "Considering that you've worked with only men for the last decade, I'd have to say that's a good thing."

He grinned reluctantly. "You know what I mean."

She sipped the creamy hot chocolate. God, it slipped down her throat like silk. She moaned her pleasure and took another sip, savoring the richness on her tongue before reluctantly letting it slide down her throat. "You've ruined me for instant hot chocolate forever, you brute!" she groaned.

He chuckled. Another silence fell. The snow was falling more quickly now. Maybe the big snowstorm the forecasters had predicted days ago was finally here.

"So, what am I going to do with you?" Dex asked.

She tore her gaze away from the spectacular view outside and turned it on the spectacular view beside her. He was exasperating. Prone to arrogance. More than a little chauvinistic. Too smart for his own good. A godlike physical specimen. Funny. A great cook. Challenging. Interesting. Honorable to the core. Sexy.

Man, was she in trouble.

Chapter 15

"I don't know what happens next," she finally answered him. Darn it, she was shivering again. This time it wasn't shock or cold. It was something else altogether. And she had *no* intention of putting a name to it.

"Come here." He looped an arm over her shoulders and pulled her close to his side.

Her arm naturally fell across his hard waist and her head landed on his equally powerful shoulder. They sat there like that for a long time. Finally she raised her head and looked up at his lean profile. "How about we just take this one step at a time and see where it leads? In another week you won't be my boss anymore. We'll both go back to Fort Bragg and we can figure it out from there."

He gazed down at her, and his eyes were pools of black shadow. "I can't promise you a wedding ring. I don't know where this will go."

She shrugged. "I can't wear rings in the field anyway. Safety hazard, you know."

His arm tightened around her shoulders.

"No strings, Dex. For either one of us. I just don't want whatever's meant to be between us to pass us by. Life's too short to wait for the next time around."

He grunted. "No kidding. Have you lost any friends in the field yet?"

She leaned forward to knock on the wood coffee table. "Not yet."

He sighed. "You will."

She knew it to be true. She only prayed when the time came it wasn't one of the Medusas—or him. She watched the hell Vanessa went through every time Jack went out on a mission. Viper was quietly a wreck until he got home. Of course, Scat wasn't worth a hill of beans when Vanessa was out in the field either, according to his teammates.

Did she really want to set herself up for that kind of misery? Thing was, she'd seen the way Jack and Vanessa looked at each other when they thought no one was watching. They practically breathed each other in. What they had wasn't love. It was Love. Capital L. She could do with a little misery to get a whole lot of that, she supposed.

She said slowly, "Tonight, when those guys were on top of me, pounding on me, and I thought I might die," he drew her closer against his chest and he seemed to surround her even more completely, "I had a weird thought."

"How weird?" he murmured into her hair.

Oh, my, that felt good. Yup, he'd be an incredible lover. He'd take his time and do it oh so right. She hesitated and then plunged ahead. "I thought I didn't want to die without kissing you first."

Nope, the man was not the slightest bit slow on the uptake. His hands speared into her hair and he shifted until she was lying back against the end cushions.

"I would never deny a dying woman her last wish," he said just before his lips touched hers.

It was better than death. This was the fast train straight to heaven. She arched into him, into the haze of heat and wet and lust that exploded around her. His mouth tore away from hers, almost as if he were startled.

"Again," she demanded.

He came back for more, lifting her to him, sucking lightly at her lower lip, pressing into her until her mouth opened for him and it felt like her heart was going to fly out of her ribs. Okay, this was not lust. This was whatever came beyond lust. Instant obsession, maybe.

She looped her hands around his neck and ran her tongue around the edges of his mouth experimentally.

"Holy cow," he breathed.

She laughed, that is, until he stopped it with his own mouth, drinking in her joy and turning it into fire. His body felt like fresh steel beneath her hands, hot and eager. She tugged at his hair until he lifted his head. She laughed again and leaned forward to kiss the column of his neck. The muscles jumped beneath her tongue. "You taste like whiskey. Single malt. The good stuff, of course," she added.

"Of course," he replied. "Twelve-year-old Glenfiddich Reserve."

"Honey, you're a Glenlivet 1964 Cellar Collection."

He pulled back to stare down at her. "Where did you hear of that? I've only seen it in Dublin. Ran about a thousand bucks a bottle."

She smiled up at him. "I'm a woman of many passions. And I happen to like a fine whiskey."

Keeping eye contact with her, he lowered his mouth to hers once more. This time he sipped at her delicately, licking and plucking at her lips, tantalizing her until she felt on the verge of shattering. His gaze bored into her all the while, raising the level of the kiss from sexy to incendiary. Women were not supposed to have orgasms from kissing. This was nuts. A little voice in the back of her head taunted, *Yeah, but this is Dex.* 'Nuff said. She sighed and let the zinging pleasure tingle through her.

"Armagnac. 1900 Gelas et Fils. That's what you taste like."

She mumbled against his mouth, "I don't know that one."

"When we get home I'll pour you a glass."

"And what does a bottle of this stuff run?"

He laughed against her mouth. "About two thousand dollars a bottle."

The sensation of his stomach contracting against hers with that laugh galvanized her. Oh, yes. She wanted a lot more than a couple of kisses out of this man. But not now. Not when they were working together and had to get up in the morning and make a police report. Not when she had to act professional and call him sir.

As if he'd plucked the very thought out of her brain, he said quietly, "When the Olympics are over, I'm taking you on vacation. Someplace where we'll be alone. My family owns a beach house."

"Where is it?"

"On a private island." He winced and continued, "That we own."

Her eyebrows lifted. "Dang, you really did want to make a difference if you walked away from all that."

He dropped a kiss on the end of her nose and sat up, dragging her with him. "I won't be inheriting a dime of it, so don't get your hopes up. My old man cut me out of his will the day I joined the army."

"Believe me, Dex. I wouldn't put up with you for the money."

"Gee thanks," he growled as he tackled her and tickled her backward once more. Or at least he tried to. She put a nifty thumb lock on him and forced him to twist his whole body into it to keep his thumb from popping out of joint. With a shove of her shoulder he fell over onto his back. She pounced on top of him.

"Uncle," he laughed. He added threateningly, "This time."

She laughed down at him. "This is going to be an interesting relationship."

She savored having this man on his back between her knees, and only reluctantly swung her leg off of him and stood up. "And you may walk me home this time."

He rolled to his feet in a single easy, powerful movement and looked down at her in the dark. "It wasn't like you had any choice in the matter."

She stuck her tongue out at him. "Chauvinist."

"Bra burner," he retorted.

She shook her head in horror. "Not me. Clearly all those feminists in the sixties were A-cuppers who never jogged. I like my bras, thank you very much."

He grinned. "Let me get us coats."

He walked her home in the deep quiet of the snowstorm, and a blanket of white accumulated quickly in their hair and on their eyelashes. There was no wind and the snow fell like petals of cherry blossoms in the spring. Even a simple parking lot was breathtakingly beautiful. A few inches of snow already covered every horizontal surface. Dex took her keys, opened the front door and spun inside in a combat crouch. Even though the police had obviously come and gone, he flipped on the light switches and searched her place from top to bottom. Not a mouse could've escaped his scrutiny.

Finally, he declared, "All clear. When I leave, I want to hear those locks turning."

"Yes, sir," she responded crisply and completely irreverently.

He glared at her. "Get used to it. I care about you."

She glared back at him. "All right. I will."

Their scowls dissolved into grins and Dex said, "I gather you're not going to take well to me ordering you around after we leave New York?"

She patted his cheek as he stepped close to leave. "Bright boy, Thorpe. There's hope for you yet."

He snagged her around the waist and planted a fast, hard kiss on her mouth before turning her loose. "Get some sleep. I'll see you tomorrow."

Nearly a foot of snow was on the ground by the time she got out of the police station the next morning. Detective Picconi was a nice guy in a nerdy sort of way, and he assured her they'd do all they could to apprehend her intruders. She assured him equally sincerely that she had no expectation that they'd catch the guys.

She was on her way back to the Olympic village, driving down a narrow, one-way street that could barely accommodate her subcompact little car when, out of nowhere, a dark sedan came barreling at her head-on. The guy was going the wrong way!

She looked around fast. Nowhere to go. The street was narrow, clogged with vehicles parked down both sides. Quickly, she jammed on the breaks and yanked hard on the steering wheel. The little car squealed its protest and whipped around in a one-eighty J-turn. She stepped on the accelerator. The tires spun, then caught in the snow, and the car leaped forward. It fishtailed wildly and she fought the wheel until she brought the vehicle under control. The sedan turned a corner behind her fast and disappeared.

She pulled into the first available parking space and sat there, breathing hard. That was not an accident. That car had been gunning for her. Not the action of an innocent driver going the wrong way down a one-way street. What the hell was going on? First last night, and now this! Very carefully, she drove the rest of the way to the Olympic complex. She walked into the ops center, and her knees still felt wobbly.

Dex took one look at her and steered her into his office. He shut the door behind him. "Sit," he ordered. She took his desk chair and he perched on the edge of his desk.

She was acutely aware of the window in his door that the men outside could look through. "Someone just tried to ram my car." Quickly, she relayed the details of what happened.

He swore under his breath. "I suppose I can't talk you into locking yourself in a nice, safe, padded vault until this whole thing blows over, can I?"

She smiled up at him. "Sorry. I've got a job to do."

"Who was it?" he asked. "What's your gut saying?"

"Probably the same thing your gut is. It was the guys from last night."

"Why do you think they're coming after you?"

"Because I'm Anya Khalid's bodyguard. And it's a hell of a lot easier to get at me than it is at her. She's tucked away in the Olympic village with all its high-tech security measures."

"Which is where you're about to be, too," he said grimly.

"I beg your pardon?"

"I want you on Anya around the clock from here on out. These people are getting too damned aggressive for my taste."

"For mine, too," she replied dryly.

Startled, he smiled down at her. "You can sleep on the pull-out bed in Anya's room."

"She's not going to like it."

He shrugged. "Tough. It's not her call." He leaned over and stabbed at the intercom on his desk. "Hobo, get all the Medusas who aren't guarding Ms. Khalid in here, will you?"

In a few minutes Aleesha, Misty and Karen walked into the ops center. Aleesha drawled, "What 'choo be needin' mon?"

Dex said tersely, "Two of Lazlo's Chechnyan pals were inside Isabella's apartment when she got home last night and jumped her."

Her teammates looked equal parts appalled and furious.

Dex continued, "And they just tried to run her off the road. I need something on these guys. Follow them. Catch them jay-walking for all I care. But give me a reason to bring them in and hold them."

Misty said regretfully, "First, we're going to have to find them. They've moved out of the house they were staying in."

Dex stared. "When?"

"They left sometime early this morning. All their cars are gone, and their razors aren't sitting in the bathrooms anymore. The FBI crew on watch last night wasn't equipped for the snow and left about 5:30 a.m. They went down to the corner and sat in their car to watch from there. The next shift came on at 8:00 and reported that the Chechnyans had left. We just got back. There's no sign of life at the house."

"How the hell did they get out?"

"Apparently there's a back way. We're guessing it was a lane of some kind that was covered with snow. You'd have to know it was there to find it. And, at the rate it's snowing right now, it got snowed over again before we went looking for it."

Dex was silent for a minute. "Pick up surveillance on Lazlo and see if he leads you to them. Surely he'll get in touch with his family."

The three women left and Isabella looked up at Dex. "Whatever's going to happen is picking up speed. I can feel it."

He nodded grimly. "Me, too."

Isabella spent the next twenty-four hours following Anya from her room to the skating rink, back to her room, to the cafeteria and back to her room. And, for variety, they went to the gym and then back to her room. The girl was meek and obedient. Probably figured the 24/7 Isabella leech was some sort of punishment for her little excursion to New York City. Which was just as well. There was no need to scare the girl with how aggressive her would-be attackers were becoming.

The day of the ladies' short program competition dawned. Thirty girls would skate tonight, and only twelve would advance to the finals in two days. In the late morning, there was a knock on Anya's door, and Isabella opened it to reveal Judy Levinson, the wonder seamstress.

"Is Anya here?" the woman asked. "Her coach said she had time for a fitting."

Isabella frowned. She thought the white costume was finished and delivered yesterday. It should be hanging in Liz's closet right now, hidden under a warm-up suit. She stepped back to let the woman enter.

"Anya, dear," the seamstress said, "I watched a recording of your long program, and I couldn't resist working up a little something for you for the finals. You don't have to wear it, of course, but I thought I'd show it to you."

She unzipped the garment bag and pulled out an absolutely stunning costume. It was a flesh colored bodysuit with long sleeves, long legs, and a high neck, covered in crystals in every shade of yellow, orange, and red. It shimmered like a fiery sunset as the fabric moved in the woman's hands.

Anya drew in a sharp breath. "Oh my gosh. It's gorgeous." She disappeared eagerly into the bathroom and emerged, smiling widely.

The skirt was made of asymmetrical wisps of silk attached at random points all around the hips. Strands of faceted crystal beads were attached among the strips, giving the effect of a belly dancing belt. The crystal flames rose strategically on the chest, covering Anya's breasts, and flickered to an end just below her chin. It hinted at the all-over henna body tattoos of harem women, but with sinuous, flashing movement, twining all over Anya's body.

Judy said to the girl, "It covers all of you from your neck to your wrists to your ankles. The conservatives can't complain about that, right?"

Isabella made a skeptical sound. "She looks like a belly dancer made of fire."

"That's exactly the look I was going for!" Judy exclaimed.

"Well, you achieved it," Isabella said grimly. The costume was beyond sexy. Beyond daring. It was dramatic. Stylized. Avant garde. Shocking. Absolutely stunning. And there wasn't the slightest doubt in her mind that Anya would want to wear it, and furthermore that she *ought* to wear it. It was the exclamation point to her fashion statements so far.

"I'm not even going to try to talk you out of wearing it." Isabella sighed.

Anya laughed. "Oh, Judy. It's spectacular. How can I ever repay you?"

The older woman staggered under the girl's enthusiastic hug. "Never fear. I charged the ISU an arm and a leg for it."

Anya peeled out of the costume carefully. "Now all I have to do is skate well enough tonight so I get a chance to wear it."

Judy made a face. "You're in fifth place. All you have to do is stand up through your program and you'll make the finals. Go out and enjoy yourself and you'll do fine."

As the afternoon progressed, Anya focused more and more tightly on her short program. She walked through it in her room, hopping around in circles and going through arm movements, head turns and poses. She listened to the music, humming along with it, her eyes closed, visualizing the program. And same as before, Liz talked her through every excruciating detail over and over, until even Isabella knew every last nuance.

About fifteen minutes before they were due to leave, there was another knock on Anya's door. This time it was the American figure skater, Ashley Caldwell.

"Hi, Anya. I just stopped by to wish you luck and to see if you'd like me to take your skates to the arena for you. You know. Just in case."

Anya nodded and gave the American a rueful smile. "That would be awesome. You're sure you don't mind?"

Ashley laughed. "Nah. My coach carries my bag for me anyway. He gets to deal with the extra weight."

The two girls chatted for a couple of minutes, then Ashley said, "Well, I'd better get going. My coach will wonder where I am." She took Anya's skates by the blades and carried them out of the room.

"You know, I could protect your skates, too," Isabella commented as the door closed behind the American.

Anya grinned. "I wouldn't want you to have to choose between the two. In a crisis, I'd yell at you to save the skates first."

She probably would at that. Isabella had learned it took about 60 hours of excruciatingly painful skating to break in a new pair of boots, and all skaters guarded their broken-in boots like gold. It would be a nightmare for a skater to have to skate in new boots. They'd be too stiff, too tight, and would rub their feet raw in a matter of minutes.

Liz came in, carrying Anya's glorious white costume in a garment bag. "Let's go get 'em, kiddo."

They rode over to the Hamilton arena in a minivan Karen drove, parking in the official lot beside the stadium. Tall piles of freshly plowed snow lined the edges of the parking lot, which was gritty with little green pellets that looked like kitty litter. It acted like salt to melt the ice and snow but was friendlier to the environment.

A set of metal barricades held back a small crowd of fans waiting near the entrance. A cheer went up as Anya drew near, and voices called out good luck and encouragement. Karen opened the door to the building and something came flying out of the crowd.

Acting purely on reflex, Isabella jumped lightning-fast and knocked Anya to the ground, covering the girl with her body. "Incoming!" she shouted as the projectile flew past and connected squarely with the back of Liz Cartwright's head.

The Aussie dropped to the ground, out cold. Karen jumped over the coach to help protect Anya as chaos erupted in the crowd, with screaming and shouting.

The metal barricade beside Isabella rocked as the crowd surged forward. "We've got to get them out of here!" she called to her teammate.

Karen bent over quickly, grabbed the injured coach under the armpits, and dragged her into the building. Isabella yanked

Anya to her feet and hustled her inside, her arms around Anya's head and her body crowded against the girl. The door closed behind them as the sound of sirens filled the air outside. Isabella dropped to her knees beside Karen who was checking over Anya's coach.

"She got hit in the back of the head. She's unconscious and unresponsive." Louder, Karen said, "Somebody call an ambulance."

A frantic voice from nearby said they'd do it.

"Pupils?" Isabella asked.

"Dilated and fixed."

Not good. This wasn't a faint. The woman was out cold. Isabella reached down for Liz's boot and pulled it off the woman's limp foot. She tore off Liz's sock and ran her fingernail up the length of the woman's foot. There was the faintest of jerks. Isabella took an Olympic pin off her jacket and used the pointed tip to poke Liz's ankle. A slight jerk. She poked Liz's hands and her other leg. All four limbs responded. Thank God.

"She's got reflexes and movement," she announced. Karen traded relieved looks with her over Liz's still form.

"What does that mean?" Anya demanded.

"It means the blow to her head didn't paralyze her," Isabella replied as she stripped off her coat and took off her sweater. She wadded it up on one side of Liz's head while Karen did the same with her sweater on the other side.

"Now what are you two doing?" Anya asked. The girl sounded scared stiff.

"Immobilizing her neck and head. It's just a precaution," Isabella explained.

The paramedics were fast getting there. Two, maybe three minutes. They took over quickly, immobilizing the still unconscious coach's head and neck with a backboard and foam neck brace. As the team of two men and a woman prepared to transport her to the hospital, Karen and Isabella stood back.

"Python, did you see what hit her?"

"It looked like a snowball."

"A snowball wouldn't do that kind of damage."

Python looked down at the floor inside the door. "It would if it had a rock in it."

Isabella looked down at where her teammate was staring. There lay a round rock almost the size of her fist with a puddle of water around it. She swore under her breath. "Python, tell ops what happened. I've got to get Anya down to the locker room. She's still got to skate if she can pull herself together."

"Take care of our girl," Karen muttered.

Isabella nodded grimly. She hurried to the crowd of people surrounding Anya. All the fussing probably wasn't helping her. She looked pale and shaken. Isabella waded through the crowd to the girl's side. "Let's go, sweetie."

Anya nodded numbly and followed her to the relative quiet of the dressing room.

Isabella led the girl to a bench and sat down beside her, taking the skater's hands in hers. "Liz is going to be okay. She got hit in the back of the head by a snowball and it knocked her out. All that stuff we did upstairs was purely precautionary. She'll be calling you on her cell phone and nagging you with last-minute instructions in no time. Okay?"

"You're not just saying that? You're telling me the truth?"

It was only part of the truth and completely glossed over the potential seriousness of Liz's injury, but Isabella looked the girl squarely in the eye and lied through her teeth. "I'm telling you the God's honest truth. Liz will be fine. Now, do you feel up to skating?"

Anya took a deep breath. "I have to be up to it. Liz will kill me if I don't."

Isabella laughed. "She will at that. For a little thing, she's pretty tough."

"Did you know she was an Olympic pairs skater? Her brother is the head American coach."

"Peter What's-his-name?"

Anya nodded, mustering up a weak little smile.

Isabella looked at her watch and tried to remember what Liz had done with Anya before the qualifying round of competition. "It's about time for you to get dressed."

She stayed with Anya, hooking the neck of her white costume for her. "Do you need help with your hair?" she asked.

Anya eyed her askance. "Liz usually does the hot rollers for me. Are you sure you won't mess it up?"

Isabella laughed. "I have three little sisters. I used to do their hair all the time." It was another bald-faced lie, but she wasn't about to rattle Anya any more than she already was. If the girl needed her hair set, then by God, her hair was going to get set. The rolling part went well. Isabella remembered how Liz had done it before and managed to get all the rollers lined up pretty much the same way the coach had. But when the rollers came out and Anya's head exploded into a mass of uncontrolled curls, Isabella looked at it in minor panic.

"Can I help?" one of the Russian coaches said from the next makeup table over.

Isabella threw the woman a look of abject gratitude and stepped back. In minutes, Anya's hair was pulled up and back into a rhinestone clasp and fell in graceful waves to her shoulders. The Russian finished it off with several extra bobby pins she said were for luck, and then she lacquered the living heck out of it with hairspray.

Thankfully, Anya did her own makeup, and in a few minutes had drawn out the shape of her eyes with eyeliner into exotic points. Her high cheekbones looked smashing, and her mouth shone with just the right amount of gloss.

"Where'd you learn to do that?" Isabella asked. She rarely used makeup herself.

Anya smiled, and for a moment returned from exotic creature back to bubbly nineteen-year-old kid. "My cousin is a makeup artist for the Sydney Opera Company."

Ashley Caldwell, already in her skates, clumped over to

Anya. "Here are your skates. We have thirty minutes until the warm-up."

Anya laced up her boots then went to the well-heated room lined with mirrors and waist-high ballet bars. While she stretched, she listened to her music on a portable radio and headphones. Isabella tried to remember what came next. Last time, Liz had talked through the program with Anya.

The girl finished loosening up her muscles and Isabella said, "Okay. Now how does that go again? Two ballet hops, three-turn, four back crossovers into a glide. Waltz jump, big step, camel spin…"

Anya nodded and walked a dry run of the program as Isabella recited what she'd heard Liz going over all afternoon. After the second run through, Isabella said, "Again?"

Anya shook her head. "Now's the part where you leave me alone for a few minutes to gather my thoughts. Although what really happens is we all stand around trying to psych each other out by pretending to be totally absorbed in our own programs."

"Right. How long does that part last?"

"Until the last skater before my warm-up session steps onto the ice. Then we head out to the ice."

Isabella nodded. "Got it. Are you okay? You feel steady? Breathing calmly and deeply?"

"Yeah, I'm fine.

"Besides," came a German voice from behind Isabella, "today we're not going to psych each other out. She's had a scare, and we're going to talk about happy things until it's time to skate."

Isabella turned around in surprise. The skater currently in first place, Karis Neidermeier, stood there, along with the Takamura sisters, Alyssa Walcheka, and Sara Dormonkova.

"Is there any word yet on her coach?" asked Sara in a surprisingly slight Ukranian accent.

"Not yet," Isabella answered. "But she'll be fine. She just got hit by a snowball and it knocked her out temporarily."

"You're lucky it didn't hit you," one of the other skaters said to Anya.

Isabella looked at her charge quickly. Her eyes clouded over with awareness of that fact, but determination rapidly replaced the look and not fear. Good girl.

An ISU official came in to announce, "Five minutes, ladies."

The girls went their separate ways at that point, and Anya talked through her program one more time with Isabella. Then it was time to go. Anya stepped out onto the ice with the other five women who comprised the top six placed skaters. They would skate in reverse order of their current placement, which meant Anya would skate second after the warm-up.

Isabella stood on the rail with the other coaches and watched Anya zip around the ice. She didn't have the faintest idea what to say to her by way of coaching. She would just have to hope Anya knew what to do from here on out. The girls started jumping, and Anya threw her troublesome triple salchow. She fell, landing on her bottom.

She got up and skated over to the rail in front of Isabella. "I need a tissue," the girl said.

The American coach, Peter Something, leaned over and said to Anya, "You're gliding too long going into that jump. Pull your arms in harder and start the rotation earlier. Then you'll have time to finish it before you land."

Anya looked startled, but went back out and tried the jump again. She landed it flawlessly.

Isabella looked over at the American, who said merely, "She's my sister's student. Of course, I'm going to help her."

"Thanks."

He nodded. "Just before she goes on the ice to perform, tell her to focus and go out and do what she knows how to do. Then tell her she's beautiful."

"Is that what Liz tells her?"

He shrugged. "I have no idea. But it's roughly what all the coaches say to their skaters when they put them on the ice."

Isabella nodded. "I'll remember that."

The warm-up period ended and Anya dried off her rear end with a blow dryer. She did a couple of stretches and jumped up and down a few times, and then an ISU official was in the door. "We need you by the gate, Ms. Khalid."

Isabella and Anya's gazes met.

Isabella said, "Are you okay?"

Anya nodded. "This one isn't for me. It's for Liz. And for all the women who wish they could do this but can't, either because of culture or lack of opportunity. How can I mess up if all of them are out there with me in their hearts, supporting me and cheering me on?"

Isabella blinked. Anya had done a lot of growing up in the past week. She would, indeed, be just fine. They walked down the tunnel. The sixth-place skater, the elder Takamura girl, came off the ice and headed for the kiss-and-cry area.

Isabella took Anya's skate guards and said, "Focus. Go out and do what you know how to do."

Anya recited along with her, "And you look beautiful. I know, I know."

Isabella added with quiet sincerity, "You do look beautiful. You're amazing. Now go show all of them that."

Anya met her gaze warmly and nodded. "For Liz," she murmured, and then she was off, sailing on one foot out toward the middle of the ice. An appreciative "ahh" went up from the audience as they got their first look at her swanlike costume.

One good thing about that snowball. Isabella had the sense that lightning had already struck. Nothing bad would happen inside the arena now that today's attack was over with. It was completely illogical, of course. Anya was still in danger out there all alone on the ice. But there wasn't a blessed thing anyone could do about it now, so she might as well not worry and enjoy Anya's skate.

The music started, its graceful, waltzing strains carrying Anya lightly around the ice. It built in speed and power, and she soared around the rink effortlessly, nailing all of her required elements. Then it was time for the triple salchow. It was the hardest jump for Anya except the triple axel. But, it earned big points, especially when performed at the end of a program like this when the skater was getting tired.

The music crashed to a mighty crescendo, and Anya leaped into the air. Whether she glided less or pulled her arms in faster and sooner, Isabella had no idea. But Anya went up, up, up, twirling almost too fast to see. And then down she came, landing cleanly, her free leg checking out perfectly, stopping the rotation and leading her glide out of the jump.

Isabella started as the American coach beside her said, "Yes!" and pumped a fist. She knew the feeling. The music ended with Anya bent over from the hips, her arms extended out and back behind her shoulders, slender and graceful, evocative of a swan finally at rest after a glorious flight of fancy.

Yet again, the crowd went wild. Resigned to the necessity of a lengthy ovation, Isabella looked around the giant arena. The place was nearly full, with only the seats up in the rafters unoccupied. She'd put the crowd at a solid twenty-five thousand. They all were screaming for Anya. How must that feel? She had only to look at her charge to know. The girl glowed from the inside out.

Finally, the ice was cleared of flowers and stuffed toys, most of which would be donated to hospitals around the state.

Anya stepped off the ice and flung herself at Isabella in an exuberant hug. "Come sit with me."

"Who me?" Isabella squeaked. "I don't want to be on TV."

Anya threw her a soulful, puppy dog look. "I don't want to sit there all alone, and Liz isn't here. Pleeeease?"

"Oh, all right. But Manfred Schmidt is going to have my head for this."

"Who's he?"

"Nobody you need to worry about," Isabella replied.

The bright camera lights turned on the two of them, and

she could hear the commentary from the broadcasting booth above. The commentators were still transported by ecstasy from Anya's skating, describing it in superlative terms. Here's hoping the judges felt the same way.

The scores came up, and Anya squealed with delight. Isabella didn't have the foggiest idea if the numbers were good or bad, but given her charge's reaction, she probably ought to act pleased. "Way to go!" she congratulated Anya.

They stepped out of the glare of the stage lights and were waylaid immediately by a smaller, but no less intense, set of lights from a shoulder held TV camera. "May I have an interview, Anya?" a well-known skating journalist called out.

"Sure!" the girl answered.

"About twenty feet farther back into the tunnel, you can have it," Isabella said. It was high time to get her girl out of the line of fire.

The reporter and her cameraman moved, and Anya was her usual charming self as she described how great it had felt to be out there and how she was just glad she'd done her best. Interview over, they headed back into the waiting area, which was outfitted with monitors showing the action on the ice.

But instead of watching her competitors, Anya turned on Isabella as soon as they entered the room. "How come Liz hasn't called me yet?"

Isabella laughed lightly. "Are you kidding? She's probably got tubes up her nose and down her throat. You know how hospitals are. How 'bout I make a quick call and get an update for you?"

"That would be great, mate."

Isabella pulled out her new cell phone and dialed in the ops center number. Sleepy McCoy answered the phone. "Hey, it's Adder. Any word on Anya's coach yet?"

"Lemme check." He came back in a moment. "Still unconscious. They just finished an MRI. There's some swelling at the base of her brain, and that's probably what's keeping her knocked out. They're going to give her anti-inflammatories and see if that brings her around." He left unsaid the part about how, if the drugs didn't work, the Australian woman could be in serious trouble.

"Good thing it wasn't your girl who got hit," McCoy commented. "Nice tackle, by the way. We saw it on tape."

"I heard there was a rock in that snowball. What asshole would do that?"

She had a sneaking feeling she knew exactly which assholes would do something like that. They were called the Red Jihad.

Chapter 16

Anya pulled up to fourth place in the overall standings, but to first place in the frenzy of the press pit. Everybody wanted to interview the competition's Cinderella. An ISU official finally led Anya to a podium and set up an informal press conference where the journalists could take turns asking her questions rather than all screaming at her at once. Isabella knew the podium was bulletproof, so she stood back, out of camera range and watched the crowd for threats.

Of course, they all asked if Liz was okay. Isabella stepped forward and whispered in Anya's ear, "Tell them they'll have to ask the hospital, but you've been assured that she'll be fine."

Anya repeated the answer. The reporters asked her the usual questions about her family, her hometown, how she got started in skating. And then they moved on to more difficult issues. "Anya, how do you feel about the fatwa that's been issued against you?"

The girl replied, "I find it hard to believe that a single

young girl's pursuit of a dream is the stuff of death sentences. I hope at some point Mufti al Abhoud will reconsider. Perhaps he will watch me skate and feel my love for the beauty and grace of this sport."

Not bad for an unrehearsed answer.

"What about your costumes?" a woman reporter called out.

"What about them?" Anya replied. "Didn't Judy Levinson do a spectacular job on such short notice?"

Nice of her to put in a plug for the seamstress.

"What do you have to say about the controversy surrounding them?"

Anya shrugged. "You know, as costumes go, this one is pretty conservative. If any other skater in this competition were wearing it, you wouldn't be asking that question. So the real question is, why should I be any different than the other skaters? If one woman wants to wear the *abeya* and veil and another wants to wear a beautiful and tasteful figure skating costume, they should both have the right to do so without having to justify their choice, don't you think?"

Ah. Excellent answer. Respectful. To the point. When had she thought that one up? Wasn't little Anya just showing all sorts of newfound maturity today?

"How do you respond to statements that what you're doing is obscene and blasphemous?"

Anya took a long time before she answered that one. An expectant silence fell over the press core. "I think it is obscene that young people are blowing themselves up to express their frustration with their lives. I think it is obscene that armies are fighting each other around the world. I think it is obscene that airplanes get flown into buildings and children get killed by car bombs and women are forced to live in servitude and fear. These things are obscene. What I do—sharing my love of dance and music and creative expression with other people who enjoy the same—is not obscene. We need more of this in the world."

Okay, give the girl an A+ for that one. It was the perfect

note on which to end the press conference. Isabella stepped forward and murmured in Anya's ear, "That's enough questions. Thank them and let's get out of here."

Anya smiled pleasantly and said, "If you'll excuse me, it's undoubtedly time for you to speak to my friend Karis Neidermeier who just stepped into the room. She is the current leader and real story of the competition."

The German girl waved at Anya, who smiled and waved back. As the reporters turned around to look at the German girl, Isabella took the opportunity to whisk Anya off the dais and out into the covered loading area. She should have made special arrangements to bring Anya in this way earlier. Liz wouldn't be lying in a hospital right now if she had. Isabella berated herself. She was tired. Distracted by too many things. It was time for her to focus on her game just like Anya did when she skated.

She leaned forward to Karen and said, "How about we swing by the hospital?"

When they got there Liz was showing signs of rousing. The anti-inflammatories were working, but it was taking some time for the swelling to go down. Anya spent a couple minutes with her coach, and then the doctors suggested that the short visit had been enough stimulation for their patient.

It was time to be unpredictable. To go places the Red Jihad wouldn't expect Anya to go. To keep the bastards off balance. Instead of parking in the usual lot behind the Olympic village, Isabella had Karen drop them off in front of the facility. It was more exposed this way, but they'd never done it before. Great piles of snow lined the sidewalks from last night's storm. More snow was falling now, but accumulations were forecast to be no more than an inch. It was just enough to keep everything sparkling white.

While Anya had a celebratory late dinner with several of her skating friends under Karen's watchful eye, Isabella headed to the ops center. Vanessa was there, talking with Dex when Isabella walked in.

"Hey, Viper. Any luck finding the Chechnyans?"

"Not yet. But Lazlo's been acting plenty weird. I was just telling Major Thorpe how he bought an armload of women's clothing this afternoon."

He hadn't been at the rink watching Anya? That was interesting. "Buying gifts for his family?" Isabella suggested.

Vanessa shrugged. "We're not talking souvenir clothes here. We're talking shoes and skirts and panty hose. And wigs."

That *was* weird. Sounded like disguises. If they were for his mother and sisters, why would they need such things?

"And he rented a van this morning. Had a little trouble doing it because he's not old enough, but he used the whole, 'I'm an Olympic athlete. I'm really responsible' argument and talked the clerk into it."

"What sort of van?" Isabella asked.

"Utility type. Two seats in front and cargo space in the back with no windows."

The sort that might come in handy for hauling hundreds of pounds of dangerous chemicals. "Have we tagged it yet?" she asked.

Dex replied, "The FBI is bringing over a satellite transmitter as we speak. Viper's here waiting to pick it up so the Medusas can attach it to the van and track it."

Lord, just the sound of his voice sent shivers down her spine. It was a struggle, but she managed not to make goo-goo eyes at him in front of Vanessa.

"Where's Lazlo now?" she asked.

Vanessa exhaled hard. That sounded like frustration. "No idea. He parked the van in a lot a couple blocks from here and walked back to the village. He went into the men's locker room attached to the workout facilities and hasn't been seen since. We sent in one of Dex's guys to have a look and he's not in the locker room anymore."

That was damned annoying.

"We're staking out the van right now, but that's all we've got."

Isabella frowned. "We might have a little more than that. What do you want to bet Anya has his cell phone number?"

"Think she'd help us?" Vanessa asked.

Isabella nodded. "If I asked her, she'd do it."

A few minutes later, Isabella stood beside the table full of laughing girls. The village was crowded and loose as the Games neared their conclusion since the majority of athletes were done with their events.

Casually, she said, "Hey, Anya. Why don't you give Lazlo a ring and see where he is? Maybe he'd like to join the fun."

Anya blinked up at her, surprised.

C'mon, c'mon. Don't think about it. Just pull out your phone.

Anya said, "Why, 'Bella. That's a great idea!"

Out came the cell phone. Speed dial number seven. She'd get her hands on that phone later and lift Lazlo's number.

"Hey. It's me. I'm fine. Thanks, I'm really excited, too. Not much. Just sitting around with a few friends. We were thinking about catching the concert on the veranda tonight. Some awesome bands are coming in to jam. Where are you? I was wondering if you'd like to come." A pause. "Oh. That's too bad. I can't tomorrow. It's the night before the finals and Liz will want me to go to bed early. Thanks. You too."

Anya disconnected the call.

"Can't make it? Where is he?" Isabella asked casually.

"He's down in Olympic Square. Said he's meeting some people there."

"Need me to head down there and beat him up for you?" Isabella replied.

Anya smiled. "He said it's some guys. No girls."

Isabella shrugged. "Well, I'll leave you ladies to your fun. Enjoy the concert." She nodded at Karen and wandered off. As soon as she was out of visual range of the girls, she pulled out her cell phone.

"Viper, it's Adder. He says he's at Olympic Square to meet some guys. He may be lying, but it's worth a try."

Isabella met Vanessa at their minivan. They called Kat, Misty and Aleesha, who were watching Lazlo's mysterious van, now rigged with the satellite tracking device, and told the women to meet them in Olympic Square. The five of them arrived nearly simultaneously and fanned out. The noise was deafening, the party raucous. Isabella adopted relaxed body language, worming her way through the dancing crowd in search of their man. The Medusas worked a standard grid search, each taking a chunk of the square and methodically searching every face within their sector.

Aleesha piped up over the radios. "Got him. Northwest corner. Almost to the sidewalk by the big barricade that blocks off Main Street. Instructions, Viper?"

Vanessa replied, "Let's keep the net loose. Cobra, Sidewinder, the two of you head up Main Street. Get around to his other side. Adder, Mamba and I will box him in from this side. Mamba, take the south position. Adder, you take the east. I'll take the southeast corner. No rush. Let's all just slide into position."

Isabella made her way to the north side of the square and then eased west, keeping an eye out for their man. "Contact," she murmured when she finally spotted him. One by one, the others reported contact as well. "He looks about ready to puke."

Aleesha commented, "Fear, if I ever saw it. The kid's no actor."

They didn't have to wait long. About three minutes later, a man in a ski jacket and knit cap emerged from the crowd and stepped up to Lazlo. Where had *he* come from? "Slick move," Adder muttered.

"Isn't that Lazlo's father?" Kat asked.

Vanessa came up. "Anyone else in position to see this guy's face?"

"Gimme a sec," Aleesha replied. "Yup, that's the father."

"Any sign of the rest of the family?" Isabella asked. Silence followed. To save radio clutter, when a question was asked, standard procedure was to indicate a negative answer by saying nothing. Only if someone had seen Lazlo's mother or sisters would they speak up.

"They're on the move," Aleesha reported. "They're coming right for you, Cobra."

"Got 'em," Kat replied. She gave a running report on their status for about thirty seconds while Vanessa and Isabella left the square and sprinted down a side street that paralleled Main Street. Isabella heard Kat murmur, "Coming at you, Sidewinder. I'm falling in behind them."

"Got 'em," Misty replied.

"We're almost in position," Vanessa said.

Isabella cut left with Vanessa. If they'd been fast enough, they would come out ahead of Lazlo and his father on Main Street. They slowed down, split apart, and each emerged onto the crowded street. They both turned right, which would keep them moving ahead of their targets in the same direction.

Aleesha murmured, "Got you two in sight. You're about a hundred yards in front of our boys. Pick up the pace a bit."

Isabella did as directed.

Kat said, "They just cut into a building. Gift shop. Local art. I'm going in."

"Cutting down an alley about two hundred feet east of the store," Karen said. "Dunno what's back here. Will look for a rear exit."

Vanessa and Isabella both reversed direction and took off running again. Isabella panted, "I can't go in. Lazlo knows me."

Misty replied, "I'm almost there. I'll go in."

"They're going up a set of stairs," Kat reported. "Marked Employees Only. Clerk saw them go. Isn't following."

Isabella stopped in the street and looked up at the building. "Looks private above the shop. Curtains on the third floor but none on the second. Maybe storage on the middle floor and an apartment on the top floor."

Misty muttered, "I'll try to distract the clerk. You head upstairs, Kat."

Isabella grinned. Misty was beautiful and built like a comic book sex goddess. The clerk would be distracted, all right.

Karen reported, "I'm in the alley behind the shop. Definitely living space on the top floor. Can't tell about the second floor."

Silence fell on the radios while Kat no doubt waited for Misty to get the clerk's undivided attention so she could slip upstairs. Then Kat murmured, "Open storage space on the second floor. No joy."

"No joy" meant no contact with the target.

Another murmur from Kat. "Locked door at the top of the stairs to floor three. Can you get up here with your toys, Adder?"

As the team's communications expert, she was the designated keeper of bugs, microphones, and other listening devices. "I don't have my vest on, so I've only got a partial stash. We might be able to place a device on the floor or on a heating duct, though."

Vanessa hand signaled Isabella to head into the store. It was a tight space crammed with T-shirts and candles and carved wooden clocks. She moved into the store, pretending to browse. Over there. An unobtrusive opening leading to a staircase.

Vanessa asked, "Has Misty still got the clerk's attention?"

"Mmm-hmm," Isabella breathed. The guy was drooling as Misty chatted him up.

She eased over to the T-shirt rack by the stairs, thumbed through it until Misty moved left, leaning her elbows on the counter and giving the poor clerk a blatant look down her shirt. Isabella eased into the stairwell and out of sight. "I'm coming up now," she murmured to warn Kat. It was never a good thing to sneak up on a Medusa. They had a tendency to break people who did.

The second floor was cluttered, part storeroom and part break room. A desk with an ancient computer and a refrigerator sat in one corner. Kat was in the middle of the room, perched precariously on the very top of a decrepit ladder, her ear pressed against a galvanized aluminum heating duct near the ceiling.

"Hearing anything?" Isabella asked quietly off mike.

"No." Kat climbed down quickly while Isabella steadied the ladder.

Isabella transmitted, "Any suggestions, Python, as to where we try to listen?"

"Yeah. Try the southwest corner. Looks like a kitchen window over there."

Kat and Isabella moved the ladder to the corner of the room. Quickly, they shifted a few boxes of T-shirts out of the way. Kat climbed the ladder again, but couldn't reach the ceiling. Isabella, who was several inches taller, tried it, but over here there was only the wood of the ceiling and not the downward protrusion of the ducts. The two women stared at the ceiling.

Kat murmured, "Were you ever a cheerleader in high school?"

"My parents wouldn't let me wear skirts that short. Why?"

"I think if I sit on your shoulders and then you climb the ladder, I could reach the bottom of the floor."

Sounded dicey. But Lord knew, they'd done worse before. Aloud, Isabella said, "It worked on the assault course at Fort Bragg. Let's give it a try."

In short order, Isabella shouldered Kat's slight weight, and then climbed the ladder, step by careful step. Kat reached up and pressed Isabella's stethoscope against the ceiling, or rather floor of the space above.

"I've got voices," she whispered down.

Isabella concentrated on keeping her balance and breathing.

"It's Lazlo. And a female voice. They're speaking Russian, though. We need Misty up here."

Isabella inched her hand across Kat's thigh and freed up a finger to press her throat mike. "Only way Misty's coming up

here is hanging all over the clerk. Let's get a mike and transmitter in place and then get her outside to listen to it."

Vanessa replied, "Makes sense. Wire it up, Adder."

Kat's hand appeared in front of Isabella's face, indicating
that they should go down. Carefully, Isabella descended the
ladder and then squatted so Kat could climb down. The two
women stared up at the ceiling again.

Isabella said, "I need to get up high enough to work with
my hands." They looked around the space. Although lots of
boxes sat around, none of them looked sturdy enough to
climb. And the ladder wasn't tall enough.

Kat said, "How about we bring the desk over here and put
the ladder on top of it?"

That would work. "Misty, can you hold the clerk's attention for another ten minutes or so?"

"Mmm-hmm."

Isabella and Kat worked fast. They moved the computer
onto the floor and each grabbed a corner of the desk. It was
the old-fashioned kind, solid wood with six drawers. It was a
bitch to pick up and move without dragging it across the floor
noisily. Isabella was panting hard by the time they set it into
position. Kat lifted the ladder onto the desk and then jumped
up beside it to steady it. Isabella wasted no time. Three
minutes of the ten she'd asked for were already gone.

She had one transmitting microphone on her, and she pulled
it out quickly. It wasn't made to work through a heavy wood
subfloor and whatever covering was on top of it. She'd have
to enhance it, somehow. She unfolded the collapsible parabolic
dish that went around her long-range microphone. It was
twelve inches across and the preferred tool of paparazzi
because of its concealability and rapid deployment capability.

Quickly, she tore out the long-range mike and taped the
remote-transmitting mike in its place. Next, she tore off half
a dozen strips of duct tape and applied them lightly to her
sleeve. Then, it was up the ladder. Damn, this thing was

tottery. She activated the microphone and taped it and the parabolic dish against the ceiling. That should do it.

"Karen, switch to the receiver frequency and see if you can hear anything."

A pause. "Nope. It's garbled."

Damn! "Ideas anyone? I've got my parabolic dish around the mike right now."

Karen said, "How about we put the mike against a window instead?"

"How do we get to it?" Vanessa asked.

Karen replied, "Fire escape. I'll climb up to the roof. Drop a rope down. Adder can climb up to the window and plant the mike."

Vanessa's response was immediate. "Do it. Time's a-wasting here."

Isabella and Kat carried the behemoth of a desk back to its original position and put the computer and its jumbled wires back into place while Karen got into position on the roof. Two minutes left in the ten.

It took a razor blade around the window sill to loosen it from the last time it had been painted shut, and it took both Kat and Isabella shoving at it to finally get it to move. It gave a terrible squeak and both of them stopped pushing abruptly. *Crap.*

"Hide," came the terse order from Misty. "I lost him. He's coming up to see what that was."

There wasn't a chance in hell they were getting that window back down without at least as much noise. A cold breeze was coming in, too.

"Quick," Isabella hissed. "Help me block it with some boxes."

She and Kat threw half a dozen boxes of T-shirts into a stack in front of the window and then ducked for cover. The floor squeaked as someone stepped into the room. A moment of tense silence.

"Everything okay up there?" Misty's voice drifted up the stairs.

"Yeah, I guess so," the guy called back.

A pause, and the floor squeaked again. He was gone. God, that had been close.

Quickly, Isabella squeezed through the narrow window opening. They dared not try to move the window any further. A rope slithered down in front of her nose.

"Tied off?" she asked Karen.

"Go for it," Karen replied from above. "I tied in a foot loop a few feet below window height for you."

Thank God. She wasn't the strongest in her upper body, and she hadn't been relishing trying to hang on to the rope and place a microphone simultaneously. She wrapped her left foot around the rope and stepped on it with her right foot where it crossed the top of her left foot. A big reach up. Pull. Reposition her feet. Again.

The foot loop hit her knee. Hanging on hard with both hands, she let go with her feet and fished around blindly until her right foot slipped into the loop. She stepped down. Her shoulders burned like fire. She reached into her pocket and pulled out the microphone. A piece of duct tape across the back of it, and then she carefully taped the mike against the corner of the glass. She looked up. Karen peered down over the edge. Isabella tapped her ear and pointed at Karen.

"Just a sec," her teammate transmitted. Karen disappeared to fiddle with her radio frequency. "Loud and clear," Karen reported.

Time to get out of here. Isabella shimmied down the rope, swinging her feet in through the narrow second-floor window. Hands grabbed her legs, pulling her in. She nodded her thanks to Kat and glimpsed the rope sailing upward as Karen reeled it in.

"Misty, we're heading down. One more minute of distraction and you're off the hook. Make a noise if that's a problem."

Silence. *God bless bodacious blondes.*

She and Kat slipped downstairs quickly. Kat paused only

long enough to stick a small periscope around the corner. She signaled an all-clear over Isabella's shoulder. The small woman disappeared and, trusting her, Isabella followed blind. The guy's back was turned while Misty modeled a T-shirt for him that was at least two sizes too small. Braless. The sacrifices they made in the name of duty.

Isabella said, "We're clear, Sidewinder. You can put your clothes back on."

"Say again?" Vanessa bit out sharply.

Isabella explained quickly, "She's trying on T-shirts for the clerk."

"Oh, good Lord," Vanessa retorted.

Aleesha came up, laughing. "Them ta-ta's of hers ought to be registered Double-D lethal weapons."

Isabella chuckled as Vanessa ordered her and Kat to take up positions in opposite directions from each other a ways down the street. It took Misty another few minutes to buy a T-shirt and disengage from the drooling clerk without making him suspicious. Isabella spotted her leaving the store with a last wave over her shoulder.

As soon as Misty was outside, her demeanor changed completely and she headed quickly down the street toward the alley and Karen, who had the radio receiver.

In another two minutes, Misty's voice came up over the radio. "They're arguing. Lazlo wants to do it now. The father is insisting that Lazlo skate."

Do what?

"Lazlo says it's dangerous to wait. Papa says it's more dangerous not to wait. One of the women is talking. Sounds like a young one. Says this is crazy. Is berating Lazlo for running from his responsibility."

There was a long pause while Misty presumably listened some more. Then she came up and said, "She's pissed off that Ilya paid for all of Lazlo's training and now Lazlo's backing out on the deal. Lazlo said he was a child when he was sent to the U.S. and he had no idea what he was agreeing to. The sister says he's lying. Said he was as committed to the cause as the rest of them. Lazlo says, 'Well, now our land is free. So why do I still have to be a sleeper for the rebels?'"

Yowza. A *sleeper?* As in a terrorist put in place for a long time, living undercover and staying dormant, sleeping as it were. Waiting to be activated?

Misty continued. "He says if they're abandoning the cause, why the hell shouldn't he? He's accusing the sister of wanting to sacrifice him to pay for their freedom."

Ouch. Little bit of familial discord, there.

"The mother's intervening. Telling them both to stop. Says the nature of the rebels has changed. They no longer fight for their country. Now they fight for power and love of blood, even if they say it's for their religion. If they were truly faithful, they would not fight. God does not love violence."

Amen.

"The father is suggesting they get back to the plan. They'll go to Lazlo's competition tomorrow night. They need a way to get away from Ilya and get outside before Ilya's plan kicks off. The women can wear the new clothes Lazlo got them under their robes and head for a bathroom. Once he—the father—distracts Ilya, the women can head outside. Lazlo is worried about how his father will get away. Is accusing Papa of planning to sacrifice himself to get the others out. Says they're *all* getting out."

Aleesha interrupted tersely, "Somebody's coming. A woman. She just ducked into the store and headed upstairs."

Vanessa commented quietly, "Maybe the apartment's owner."

"Lazlo says once they get to the van," Misty continued, "they'll drive down to New York City. He knows the way."

Ya think? After his little road trip with Anya, he damn well should.

"They'll go to the State Department and ask for visas. If that's a no-go, they'll go to the FBI and trade what they know for asylum. The father says that's a last resort, though. They don't want Ilya to come after them, and he will for sure if they do that."

These people were defecting? Because of Gorabchek? Had to be. Because Chechnya was a free nation. They could apply for regular immigration status to the U.S., no problem.

"New voice. Must be Aleesha's lady. Says they've been here long enough. It's time to go. Says she's got sandwiches for them so they can actually eat supper like they're supposed to be doing. Mom's griping that it's hamburgers. Doesn't like them."

Beggars can't be choosers. So, they'd ditched Ilya to have this little planning session, eh? What the hell was Ilya's grand scheme, then? If Lazlo was a sleeper, he'd clearly been activated.

But to do what?

Chapter 17

They followed Lazlo uneventfully back to the Olympic village and talked over their options. It was less than forty-eight hours until the ladies' figure skating finals and whatever Gorabchek had planned. Vanessa went back to the ops center to report on what the Medusas had learned, and Isabella refrained from begging to go with her. Dex was a busy man, and she needed a decent night's sleep. But she missed him as she crawled into bed, and she fell asleep wishing he were with her.

Isabella spent all of the next morning going from interview to interview with Anya, and came away knowing more about television studios than she'd ever cared to. They'd declined all interviews with any potentially hostile news agencies. Anya didn't need the stress of being attacked, and Isabella didn't need the security risk.

Liz Cartwright was awake, and Anya went to visit her after lunch. Liz's brother, Peter, was also at the hospital, and at

Liz's request, agreed to step in for his injured sister and coach Anya for the next couple days.

To that end, he met Anya at one of the practice rinks late in the afternoon. Dex had arranged with the ISU for the session to be closed to the public, and the space echoed with the slicing sounds of blades digging into the ice. Anya ran through her long program and then the American coach worked with her on her jumps. It was a light workout that looked designed more to build Anya's confidence than anything else.

Peter skated off the ice with Anya. "You're ready. Go home, have a good dinner, and go over to the athletes' spa for a rub down. Then get a good night's sleep and we'll see if you can't snag a medal tomorrow. You've got the point value in your program to do it."

Anya nodded in determination. The girl already had her game face on. Usually Isabella didn't see it until three or four hours before the competition. Anya was tucked into her room for the night by eight o'clock, with Misty babysitting her.

Isabella didn't quite know what to do with herself. She wasn't used to being done this early. She wandered over to the ops center to see if there'd been any new developments. Nada. She sat down at one of the empty desks and laid out the entire folder of case notes on Anya. Maybe there was something in here they'd missed. Some clue as to what the Red Jihad and Gorabchek had planned.

It was nearly midnight when she spotted it. She rocked her chair forward abruptly and read the last paragraph again. It was an inventory listing all the equipment in Harlan Holt's lab. She picked up the phone in front of her and dialed Dex's cell phone.

He sounded falsely alert, like she'd woken him up and he was still in that thirty-second window of jolted awareness before his body's protest at being dragged from sleep slammed into him. "Thorpe here."

"Hey, Dex, it's me."

"Hi, sweetheart. Are you coming over to help me get back to sleep?"

"I wish. I just found something in Anya's file. I should've seen it earlier."

"What did you find?"

"I don't think Harlan Holt's lab is adequately equipped to manufacture Agent Alpha."

Dex sounded wide-awake now. "Talk to me."

"I was looking at a list of the equipment in his lab. When I was in college, I took some chemistry classes, and I recognize most of this stuff. It's really basic. I don't think any of it is high-tech enough to engineer complex chemicals."

"I'll be right there."

While she was waiting for Dex to arrive, Isabella looked up the phone number of the FBI briefer who'd told them about Agent Alpha two nights before. She called the woman at home. "This is Isabella Torres from the Olympic Security Group. I was at your briefing night before last."

The agent gave a cautious acknowledgement of remembering her.

"Since this is not a secure line, I'm going to read off a list of laboratory equipment, then I'd like a yes or no answer out of you. Would this equipment be sufficient to manufacture what you briefed us on?" Isabella read off the list.

At the end of it, the agent gave a succinct, "No."

"Thank you," Isabella replied. "You've been immensely helpful."

"Do you need any help with your…research?"

"We may. We'll call if we do."

"You do that."

Cryptic phone conversation over, Isabella hung up. She leaned back in her chair. If Holt didn't make Agent Alpha in his lab, what was it doing there? Their assumption that he was part of the Red Jihad's conspiracy might be premature. But he and his wife were still missing, and he *did* have Agent

Alpha in his possession. Her gut rumbled in foreboding. The guy had access to Agent Alpha and to the figure skating rink. Was he trying to kill Anya?

She picked up the phone. Called the FBI scientist again. "Hey, it's Isabella Torres again. One more question. Can our research product be packaged in individual servings?"

A long pause. "I suppose. Why?"

"Just asking."

"I'll be right there," the FBI agent announced.

The line went dead in Isabella's ear.

An hour later, all the Medusas minus Misty sat in the ops center's conference room with Dex, Hobo, the FBI scientist, and a couple other unidentified men Dex vouched for but did not introduce. Spooks, then. Spies. Or guys with jobs so classified they weren't really sitting here and didn't legally exist.

The Khalid folder lay open on the table, and Vanessa stood at the big whiteboard. A green line ran vertically down the center of the board—a timeline of the threats and attempts on Anya's life. Then, off to each side were two arcing lines that started at the top of the green line and ended at the bottom. The whole thing resembled a giant football standing on end.

The left curving line listed the events surrounding Lazlo, his family and Ilya Gorabchek. The right curving line listed the events apparently connected directly to the Red Jihad and its Middle Eastern operatives. Drawn like that, it made Anya appear as more of a catalyst than an end target.

And all three lines led to a box at the bottom of the board labeled, Ladies' Finals. Vanessa finished her drawing with a flourish and turned around to face the room. "We have more than a simple security problem, ladies and gentlemen. We have a bona fide terrorist threat on our hands. I don't think Anya Khalid is the target. I think the ladies' figure skating final and its thirty thousand spectators are."

Isabella nodded her agreement. "Put in this context, the attacks on me start to make sense, too. I was jumped in the alley by guys from the Red Jihad timeline. But, I'm convinced I was attacked in my apartment by guys from the Gorabchek timeline. Why me? I'm a measly bodyguard. Yeah, I symbolize Anya Khalid and I've been easier to get to than she is. But what if the attacks were a distraction? What if both groups are coming after Anya and me to draw attention away from themselves?"

Nods around the table. Dex commented, "That feels right."

Isabella stood up and went to the board. "There's somebody invisible up here." She pointed to the top of the timeline. "Somebody out of sight. He or she wants to blow up the figure skating venue when it's crammed to the rafters with people. So, he makes a stink about Anya and launches this highly visible chain of events down the middle. Then, he secretly sends out not one, but two terrorist cells to attack the end target. That way if one fails or gets caught, he's still got a backup team in place. After all, an opportunity like this only comes along every four years—or every thirty years if you want to make the attack at an Olympics on U.S. soil."

The line of reasoning felt spot on to Isabella. "These cells know about each other. Maybe they even met once or twice. But for the most part, they operate independently. They don't know that both groups attacked Anya and me a few times, not with any intent to kill either one of us. Because let's face it. If these guys wanted us dead, they'd have come at us with a hell of a lot more than bags of doggie doo-doo and snowballs."

A grim chuckle sounded around the table.

"I think both groups wanted us to concentrate our manpower around Anya. The fatwa itself may have been a feint to hide the real target."

The FBI scientist leaned forward. "So we're looking for elements outside that diagram. People and events that can give us some clue as to how they plan to take out the Hamilton Arena—or at least all the people in it."

Vanessa took over writing on the board as the group brainstormed possibilities:

—Harlan Holt
—Lazlo Petrovich
—the Agent Alpha powder
—Agent Bravo?
—Emma Holt's disappearance
—the Petrovich family's apparent attempt to defect

They all stared at the list for several minutes in silence. It was a Special Forces technique to let everyone sit and percolate during these sorts of sessions. As folks started to get fidgety, Dex asked, "Anyone come up with anything?"

The FBI scientist dived in. "We need to search the figure skating venue from top to bottom for any sign of the two halves of that nerve gas. To target a place that size, you're talking about a couple hundred pounds of Agent Alpha and several hundred gallons of Agent Bravo if you want to actually kill everyone."

Dex wrote a note. "Anyone else?"

Isabella leaned forward. "We approach Lazlo and make him talk. He may be a sleeper, but he's not a hardened terrorist. He'll crack if we put him under pressure."

Dex looked over at Vanessa. "Can I put the Medusas in charge of that since you know him better than the rest of us?"

Isabella snorted. "After you chewed his butt over the road trip, he won't want to talk to you any time soon."

Dex rolled his eyes. "He deserved it."

Isabella shot back, "He deserved worse."

Vanessa nodded. "We've got it covered. We'll figure out the best way to approach him and take care of it in the morning." She added, "And in the meantime, you all can move heaven and earth to find Harlan—and Emma—Holt."

An APB was put out on the Holts in addition to the FBI

launching a good, old-fashioned manhunt. Television and radio stations would be blitzed with the Holts' pictures, and agents all over the country would be put on high alert. Informants would be squeezed and snitches shaken down. Wherever the two Holts were hidden, their lives were about to get really damned difficult.

Next, the biohazard guys were dragged out of bed and sent over to the figure skating venue with a team of FBI agents to search the place. Even using forty agents, it would take several hours to clear a building that size.

There wasn't much more the Medusas could do until morning. Lazlo Petrovich was an Olympic athlete scheduled to compete in the men's singles finals. Without concrete evidence of his participation in a criminal conspiracy, there were some lines even the OSG dared not cross.

Too wired to sleep, Isabella went over to the Hamilton Arena to watch the FBI search. It was an impressive thing. Forensics experts crawled all over the venue with high-tech gadgets, spraying, swabbing, scraping and generally poking and prodding everything. And in spite of it all, they didn't turn up any white powder or barrels of suspicious liquid.

The biohazard guys were equally anal. Although they had somewhat more interesting results. They kept picking up shadow readings of Agent Alpha—traces too faint to be definite hits, but enough to trigger the sensors in their equipment. This time the machines were saying the Agent Alpha was airborne. Except when small air samples from different parts of the building were specifically run through the sensors, they came up empty. The chemical warfare experts were like bulldogs smelling an enemy no longer present, but the lingering scent of it still agitated them.

About 4:00 a.m., Isabella packed it in. Her eyes were gritty and she finally felt like she could sleep. She made her way back to the Olympic village and slipped quietly into Anya's room. Misty nodded and left to get some sleep herself.

Isabella had made Dex promise to call her if there were any developments overnight. So, with her cell phone set to vibrate under her pillow, she crashed on the sofa bed.

Anya's alarm clock went off at nine o'clock. Isabella leaped out of bed, wide-awake. The two of them had established a routine over the past few days. Isabella got up, took a shower and did the morning bathroom thing while Anya rolled over and caught an extra half hour of sleep. With a nudge to Anya at nine-thirty, Isabella answered the door and let in Kat, who was on guard duty next.

Time to go put the squeeze on young Lazlo. First, she headed for the ops center to get approval for her plan and to get wired for sound. With Dex's permission still vibrating in her ears and Vanessa manning the receiver at the other end of the microphone taped to Isabella's stomach, she headed for Lazlo's room to offer the boy a deal.

Abdul finished his midmorning prayers and rolled up his prayer rug, stowing it in the closet. Distastefully, he reached for Western clothes. It was necessary to blend in with the infidels on this day, this greatest of all days when he would earn his place in paradise forever. Ironic that he should have to lower himself like this, to mingle with the unbelievers as one of them, to accomplish such a sublime goal.

The van his nephews had used for the Holt woman's abduction was still parked behind the house. He went outside into the miserable cold, despising the wet mess of it all. What possessed anyone to live in a climate like this? It chilled a man right to the bones and could kill in a matter of hours. It might get hot in Bhoukar, but at least a soul had a day or two in the desert to find water before he perished outright.

He got into the generic, white van and backed out of the driveway. He pointed the vehicle south and west toward his target, which was in an even more remote and isolated house than this one. He wound down the half-mile long driveway.

His boys had spent yesterday afternoon riding up and down it on snowmobiles, packing the new snowfall until it was passable once more by car—or van. He'd had a moment of panic that the plan, so many years in the making, might be foiled by a simple snowstorm. But he'd prayed all night as the storm raged, and his prayers had been answered by the cessation of new snow yesterday morning.

It would take him a couple hours to reach his destination. Although he only needed a few minutes to tie up the woman and put her into the van, he would also need to sanitize the house she'd been kept in for fingerprints or other evidence. No reason to make it easy for the FBI to identify them. After all, the idea was not to die here. The idea was to accomplish the mission and go home. As heroes. As the chosen of Allah.

Isabella knocked on Lazlo's door.

He threw it open, clearly not expecting her, and whatever he was going to say died on his lips as he recognized her.

"May I come in?" she asked with a certain amount of insistence.

"Uh, I guess so." He stepped back to allow her into his messy room. A clumsy attempt to pack fast was in progress. Lazlo unobtrusively pushed two suitcases off the bed as he passed by it. Preparing to flee with his family to New York. Of course, she wasn't supposed to know that.

"Lazlo, I know you have to skate tonight and don't need any distractions, so I'm going to get right to the point. I'm here to offer you a deal."

He looked startled. "What sort of deal?"

She stated it baldly for maximum shock value. "A few of my colleagues and I will help you and your family escape from Ilya Gorabchek and his cronies if, in return, you will tell me exactly what Gorabchek is up to and what he's got planned for the ladies' figure skating finals."

Lazlo stared. Collapsed into the chair behind him. Stared

some more. Swore long and hard. Finally managed to splutter, "How in the bloody hell do you know about that?"

Whether he was referring to his family's upcoming escape attempt or Gorabchek's conspiracy, she couldn't tell. Probably, he meant both. At any rate, she could capitalize on his shock.

She shrugged. "The Olympic Security Group is the best-trained, best-equipped security force in the world. Did you honestly think the messes you're embroiled in would escape our notice? You're an amateur, Lazlo. You're in way over your head."

She shut up to let him stew. Sometimes silence was a more powerful argument than any words.

It took a few minutes, but finally he spoke. "You'd have to guarantee political asylum for my family."

"They'll have to agree to tell us everything they know about Gorabchek, Red Jihad—" that got a big lurch out of him, but she pressed on "—and any other illegal activities they're aware of."

"How…" Poor kid was too stunned to even form a sentence.

"I told you. We know everything that's going on in this town. Your family—and you—agree to spill the beans, and yes, I'll guarantee all of you asylum in the United States. If you don't take this deal, all of you can expect to be prosecuted to the full extent of the law for collaboration with the Red Jihad and as coconspirators in the plan they've got cooked up for tonight. Oh, and did I mention there's a death penalty for certain terrorism convictions in this country?"

Lazlo went pale.

The screws were now sufficiently applied to his thumbs. She leaned against the door, telegraphing that there was no escaping her. It didn't take long. Under a minute. He nodded slowly. His shoulders slumped in defeat, and then rose as if a great weight had been lifted off of them.

"You're making the right decision," she said gently. "You had no choice. No choice at all. Now, here's what we're going to do tonight…"

* * *

Harlan Holt slouched on the end of the bed, staring at his face on the TV. And now they thought he was a terrorist? Would this nightmare never end? Despair squeezed his heart until it felt empty. If he couldn't show his face in Lake Placid, how was he supposed to retrieve Emma? They said they'd bring her to him. She'd be left at the figure skating rink after the…event. That's what they'd called it. *An event.* Tens of thousands of people murdered was an *event.* And he thought they would let his Emma live?

They would. They would! They had to. He'd tell if they didn't. And they'd get caught. *Harlan Holt, the biggest dolt. Believes anything you tell him…* The memory of a child's voice taunted him. His own childish voice. He'd always been the gullible kid. The brilliant nerd who couldn't even tell when someone was pulling his leg. He'd cried over kittens that were never killed, raged over injustices that were never committed, and he'd never learned. Nope. Never learned.

A feverish hallucination of Emma's dead body being handed into his arms made him scramble backward on the bed, scrubbing at his arms in horror.

No! They *would* hold up their end of the bargain. He'd kept quiet. And they would let Emma live. *Harlan Holt, the biggest dolt. Believes anything you tell him…*

The rhyme went around and around in his head, getting louder and louder until it was so insistent he clapped his hands over his ears. Finally he collapsed on the bed and yanked the pillow down over his head. Still the voices sang.

Then another voice intruded. A strong, determined male voice. "…anyone with information regarding the whereabouts of Dr. Holt or his wife is urged to contact the authorities immediately. This is a matter of national security."

National security? *Did they know about the terrorists' plans?* They must!

If they knew already, then he wasn't breaking the deal with

those bastards. He could talk to the police! Tell them about Emma without putting her in more danger. Ask for help. Sure, the FBI had a manhunt going on for Emma. But they'd never find her without his help. But he could do that now!

His hands shook as he fumbled with the phone. He picked up the receiver and stared at the archaic dial. Who should he call? Who knew the truth? Those suits on TV wouldn't know the whole story. They'd want to debrief him and verify his story and waste too much time filling out paperwork. He needed to talk to those women who'd been chasing him. That dark-haired one in particular. The one who'd been the girl figure skater's bodyguard.

He dialed the operator. "Connect me to Lake Placid. To whoever's in charge of security for the Olympics." He waited impatiently.

"How does the Olympic Security Group sound, sir?"

"Fine, fine. Just put me through." Even if it wasn't the right people, maybe they'd be able to forward his call to the perceptive brunette.

"Breckenridge here. Go ahead."

Harlan blinked. This guy sounded like another one of those suits on TV. "Uh, I need to speak to a woman. She's got dark hair. Dark eyes. Pretty. She's the bodyguard for that Arab skater girl."

"Isabella Torres."

"Uh, yeah. Her."

"May I tell her who's calling?"

"Tell her it's about that guy on television that everyone's looking for."

"Harlan Holt. If you have information about him, I'll forward you to the FBI field office—"

"No! I want Ms. Torres!" He broke off. His voice was rising hysterically that probably wasn't the way to get connected to her. He calmed his voice down, but it still shook. "Please. It's urgent."

The suit named Breckenridge sounded skeptical. "Lemme see if she's available."

"C'mon, c'mon," he muttered under his breath. "Be there."

A cautious voice spoke in his ear. "This is Isabella Torres. May I help you?"

Thank God. His bladder threatened to empty down his leg, his relief was so intense. He crossed his legs tightly. "I… my name…this is Harlan Holt. Thank God you figured out what's going on. They've got my wife and that's why I didn't call you sooner. They say they'll give her back to me after tonight, but I don't believe them. I mean, I wanted to believe them, but this song kept going through the back of my head, and I finally figured out it was trying to tell me something."

"Who's they?" the woman asked.

"The terrorists, of course," he replied, alarmed. "You do know what they're doing, don't you?"

"Uh, of course," she replied. "The ladies figure skating final."

"Right. Killing everyone."

"Right. With a binary nerve agent."

He nodded vigorously. "Nasty stuff."

"What else do you know about their plan, Dr. Holt?"

"I don't know how they'll get the second half of the agent onto the ice, if that's what you mean. But now that you know the plan you can get Emma back."

"So, they did kidnap your wife?" the woman exclaimed.

"Yes, I already told you," he replied impatiently. "That's why I didn't come to you sooner. But when I saw on TV that you'd figured out their plan, then it was okay for me to call you. They told me they'll give her back to me alive after the event. But I don't believe them. I think they'll kill her after it's all over. I need you to follow them and find my Emma. You're a woman. You'll understand. She's all alone with them. She has to be terrified. And I—" his voice cracked "—I wasn't strong enough to save her from them. I…need your help."

"I'll help you, Dr. Holt. But I need you to help me, too. What can you tell me about the terrorists' plans?"

"They didn't tell me anything! They just made me put their powder in the rink and told me to disappear until tonight was over. Said they'd contact me after they succeeded and arrange for Emma's return. But, I figured out what that stuff was. Obviously, they're planning to gas the crowd." Panic gripped him. Had he misread what that suit on TV had said? "I thought you knew everything!

"That's why I called you—" He slammed down the receiver. They'd probably traced the call, too. Had he just ended Emma's life?

He grabbed his backpack and his coat and rushed out of the room, tossing the key on the bed. He wouldn't be coming back here, that was for sure. Sick to his stomach, he stumbled to his car, climbed in and drove out of the parking lot.

Isabella glanced around the ops center. Pretty much everyone in the joint was gaping at her. Hobo broke the silence. "Well? What'd he say?"

"He said terrorists kidnapped his wife and forced him to put Agent Alpha in the rink. He doesn't know how they're planning to get the Agent Bravo into the arena, but they said they'd give him his wife back after they succeeded at tonight's figure skating finals."

"It's a lie!" Hobo blurted. "We went over that arena with a fine-toothed comb, and there's no Agent Alpha there."

She frowned. "It's a hell of an elaborate story. The evidence we found at his home is consistent with a forced entry and abduction. And we know he couldn't have made the Agent Alpha at his lab. He said he analyzed the powder and figured out what it was. That *would* explain how the chemical made its way into his lab."

"You believe this guy?" Hobo asked just as Dex came

striding into the ops center. From the look on his face, someone had already told him who'd just called her.

She made eye contact with Dex as she answered, "My intuition says Dr. Holt is telling the truth. He sounded scared to death, somewhat disoriented, impatient, not quite rational. Just like a man whose wife has been kidnapped and who's terrified of the consequences of what he's been forced to do."

Dex replied quietly, "He could also be a brilliant scientist who has pieced together what we've got on him from the television reports and has cooked up a wild story to explain it all."

She nodded in candor. "He could indeed. But he's not. The man I just talked to is the real deal. He was a mess."

Dex studied her for a moment. And then nodded. "I concur."

Her relief that he'd agreed with her was tempered by the tiniest niggle of fear that he'd done it because he was about to be her boyfriend. Note to self: never, *ever* work with Dex again.

"Now what?" Hobo asked.

She looked down at the guy. "Now, I go take my girl to a skating competition. And hope like hell we can spot the mechanisms by which these two nerve agents are going to be delivered and stop them before thirty thousand people die."

Chapter 18

Isabella held the door of the armored SUV as Anya climbed out into the secure parking garage under the Hamilton Arena. The skater had her game face on tonight. She had a distant look in her eyes and wasn't speaking to anyone. She hadn't since the American skating coach had shown up at her door to lead her through the usual verbal run-throughs of her program.

He'd had her jump a bit in the middle of her room, too, to practice something she needed to remember about her arms. It had been impressive to see the girl fly up into the air from a standing start, twirl around three times and land on one foot. It was easy to forget just how extraordinary an athlete Anya was. Only a handful of the greatest ballet dancers in the world could jump and twirl like that, and they weren't landing on a knife edge going upwards of thirty miles an hour.

Anya ignored the arena's security measures as Isabella led her through them tonight, so focused was she on the performance to come. Judy Levinson was going to meet them at the rink with the fire dancer costume, and Ashley Caldwell, who'd brought Anya's skates the last time, had volunteered to do it again. Isabella let the American skater do it, more because Anya was being superstitious today, wanting everything to be exactly identical to her preparations for her last two skates, than because Anya's skates were in danger.

Isabella was pleased to see the tension surrounding the entry checkpoints. Word had clearly gotten out to the building security team that something bad might be planned. This was the premier event of the entire Winter Olympic Games. Tonight, both the men's and ladies' singles finals would be skated. Many times, international competitions paired ice dancing with ladies' singles. But because of the global nature of this event, the ISU had decided to do both competitions on this Saturday evening to maximize the worldwide audience. The men would go first. They were slated to begin in an hour, in fact.

Anya and Isabella made it through the last checkpoint and headed for the ladies' dressing room. Isabella put the girl's hair up in rollers while Anya applied her makeup.

It was almost time to take Anya's hair down and Isabella was starting to sweat it because the Russian coach wasn't here to bail her out when a voice made Isabella turn around.

It was Lily Gustavson, the ISU official. "Ms. Khalid. You have a visitor."

Liz stepped out from behind the taller woman. Anya squealed and launched herself at her coach, but checked herself and only gave her coach a gentle hug. Which was probably a good call given how pale and drawn the Aussie looked. Liz said sternly, "You didn't think I'd let you skate in the finals of the Olympics without me, did you?"

Anya smiled from ear to ear.

"Okay, young lady. Let's get your hair out of those rollers while you go over your program for me."

Isabella sagged in relief at escaping further hair duty. She stepped close enough to murmur to the coach, "My colleagues are just outside the dressing room. A brigade of bad guys couldn't get in here right now. I'm going to go out and have a look around."

Liz nodded, absorbed in gathering Anya's hair into a long clip.

The plan was for Isabella to leave Anya in the locker room while she helped the Medusas pull out Lazlo's family. Now that Liz was back, Isabella felt a whole lot better about doing so. As soon as she stepped out of the locker room, she murmured into her collar mike, "I'm out."

Vanessa replied, "The fourth skater in this group is skating now. You have about fifteen minutes to get in place."

"Sorry I cut it so close. Liz is here, though. Looks like hell but isn't about to miss her girl skating."

"That's great!" Vanessa replied.

Isabella hurried to the concourse level. Kat, Misty and Aleesha should already be inside the women's restroom she'd just passed. Karen would be hiding in a stall of the men's room nearby. All of them had worn the distinctive black wool coats of Olympic officials tonight, along with hats and scarves. If Vanessa wasn't already out front in the SUV on loan from the FBI, she would be soon.

Isabella found the entrance into the right section of seats and had a look below. The arena was crammed to the rafters. It was a sea of bright color, and dozens of huge halogen lights washed the ice in brilliant light. Television backdrops dominated a full quarter of the arena down at ice level, and lights bathed those as well. The atmosphere was electric. This was the holy grail of figure skating, and the worshipers were out in force to pay homage to the quadrennial event.

Isabella leaned against the steel railing to one side of the tunnel, trying to look like she was merely standing at her post. She scanned the arena and spotted several security men, unobtrusively strolling around the very top of the arena behind the nosebleed seats. She'd lay odds they were snipers carrying concealed rifles. Dozens of other security types were here, combing the place for any sign of the two nerve agents, but she didn't spot any of the teams.

The last skater in this group of men took the ice. Four-and-a-half minutes until the intermission. Until the Petrovich family would excuse itself from its seats and head for the bathrooms. Her job was to spot whether or not Ilya or his men were following the family. The Medusas had a plan for it either way, but one was considerably more violent and dangerous than the other.

There would be a fifteen-minute break while the Zamboni resurfaced the ice and a six-minute warm-up period for the last group of men. After that, the sixth through first place men would skate their programs in reverse order. Lazlo was in sixth place going into this evening's competition, so he would skate first.

His mother and sisters were in the stands all wearing long robes and full burkas, ostensibly in protest over Anya's upcoming performance. In reality, however, the coverings would play a pivotal role in the family's escape from Gorabchek.

Soon, now. Adrenaline started pumping into her system, revving her up to full combat speed.

The last skater fell twice in the last minute of his program, and took a disappointed bow as his music ended. No lengthy ovations for him. A few flowers sailed onto the ice and were picked up, and then the Zamboni drove out. A crowd of people rushed the tunnel, heading for the snack stands and restrooms. She held her position against the flood, all the while keeping a close eye out for Lazlo's family.

There they were, coming up the steps toward her. The black robes and veils were hard to miss. Interestingly enough, they weren't the only women here tonight so attired. She had to wonder if the women under those veils truly objected to Anya's skating. But then, maybe she was just cynical.

She kept an eagle eye peeled for Gorabchek or his associates, but saw no sign of their bulky forms in the crowd anywhere near the Petrovich family. "They're clear," she said. "Heading your way."

The family had been warned to expect to stand in long lines to get into the restroom and the Medusas had counseled them to be patient and wait their turns like everyone else so as not to draw attention to themselves. Isabella turned and headed for the concourse, trailing the family at a distance. No sign of any tails from here. She loitered nearby, getting two drinks from the drinking fountain and even standing in the bathroom line herself for a while to mask her continued presence in the area.

"Papa Bear just went inside. Mama Bear and the cubs are about two minutes from inside," she reported.

A few seconds later, Karen came up. "Got him. Man, did some folks squawk when that end door suddenly turned out to be unlocked. Starting the switcheroo."

Karen and Papa Petrovich would exchange clothes. She would put on his red jacket and ski cap and he'd don her sober Olympic security coat. At six feet tall, Karen was almost exactly the same height as the elder Petrovich. A spray-on tanner had matched her naturally fair skin tones to his darker ones. With her hair up in a cap, she could pass for the man at a distance. Well, maybe if the viewer was drunk and squinted very hard. Fortunately, all Karen had to do was pass for the guy at a glance.

"We have contact on our targets," Kat announced. "They're coming into the stall with us now." The three Medusas had claimed one of the oversized handicapped-access stalls in which to make their clothing changes with the Petrovich women.

Karen replied, "We're done. Call us when you're ready to roll."

"Roger," came Kat's muffled reply. Sounded like her head was in a sweater.

Vanessa piped up. "FYI, I'm ready to roll out here as well."

In no more than a minute, Kat spoke again. "Visibility

sucks in this burka. No wonder women can't drive in these getups. They can't *see* anything!"

Isabella grinned. "I gather then, that you're ready to roll?"

"Yup, they're all dressed up as Olympic officials and we Medusas look like Black Moving Objects."

Isabella took one last look around the concourse. "All clear out here. Let's do it."

All four Medusas, now wearing the Petrovichs' distinctive clothing, emerged from the bathrooms and met in front of the drinking fountain. Without making eye contact with Isabella, they headed purposefully back toward their seats to watch "their son" skate.

Meanwhile, a somewhat motley group of "Olympic officials" made its way down the concourse and toward the nearest exit. Isabella trailed just behind them, covering their six and making sure none of them freaked out or did anything stupid.

"Coming at you, Viper," she muttered as the family passed through the exit doors.

"In sight," her boss replied tersely.

Isabella stepped outside and looked left and right. All clear. Papa Petrovich opened the back door and helped his family into the vehicle. Then, after a long look over his shoulder, he climbed into the front seat and pulled the door shut. For a second there, she hadn't been entirely sure he'd get in the car. He'd been violently opposed to fleeing before his son skated. But his true reluctance was precisely why the plan would work. Gorabchek wouldn't expect them to run before Lazlo skated.

"The vehicle is pulling out now," Isabella advised her teammates inside the arena. She doubled back quickly to the tunnel to keep an eye on her teammates who were still in the aisle, slowly making their way to the Petrovichs' seats. "Remove the robes now and get to safety."

Karen bit out, "I just spotted Gorabchek. He's sitting in the stands."

"Did he see us?" That was Misty sounding a bit tense.

"No," Karen answered. "There's Lazlo coming onto the ice to skate. Ilya and friends just turned to look at the kid. Robes off, now."

"Where are the tangos?" Isabella asked. "I'll cover your retreat if you guys can back out of that area now."

"Twenty rows up from the ice, left of the aisle by about ten seats. All three side-by-side. Four empty seats in front of them."

"Got it," Isabella replied. "They're looking around now. Starting to act concerned now that he's seen the seats are empty. Aw, crap. They're getting out of their seats. Get out of there, ladies. Scatter!"

Each of the four Medusas headed in a different direction. Kat went down toward the ice, passing Ilya and friends at a range of about twelve inches. Karen moved left at the intersecting horizontal aisle, Misty headed right. And Aleesha came straight up the stairs at Isabella. Mamba passed her by, making eye contact and giving a fractional smile. Isabella held her ground and continued to lean against the steel railing. "Ilya and friends have split up."

Isabella pulled out her cell phone and hit the speed dial for the security team. "A little help in section 106. Three subjects have just left their seats. Male. Black leather jackets. All three are probable hostiles. I repeat, probable hostiles."

A flurry of voices responded to that as FBI agents and OSG security forces converged to pick up pursuit of Gorabchek and his men.

Dex came across the frequency. "If one of those guys takes a piss, I want you there to help him. These guys do nothing and go nowhere without eyes on them. Everyone got that?"

A murmur of affirmatives.

Dex ordered, "Backup Channel 1 will be devoted to Gorabchek. Channel 2 to the taller of his two buddies, Channel 3 to the short one…"

Isabella tuned out as he divvied out surveillance teams to watch the three men. If the terrorists tried to approach a hidden cache of nerve agents, they'd have so many people on top of them they wouldn't know what hit them.

She headed back down toward the locker room and Anya. She monitored the surveillance of the three Chechnyans on her radio, but based on their movements, it sounded like the three men were merely searching the arena for Lazlo's family. She'd leave them to the teams upstairs. She had a skater to look out for.

Isabella tried to stay out of sight and out of mind as Anya completed her final preparations for the skate of her life. Sixteen years of daily practice, sore feet, missed fun, and hard work all boiled down to this moment.

The first six women were called to the ice. The ladies' final would run in the same fashion as the men's with a break after the first six skaters to resurface the ice followed by the final six skaters. Including Anya.

Too restless to stand in the warm-up area any longer watching Anya stretch and listen to music, Isabella headed for the ice. If Red Jihad was going to do anything tonight, it would have to be soon. This group would take a little less than an hour to skate and be judged. Then, fifteen minutes for the Zamboni, another hour of skating, and it would all be over.

As she emerged from the long tunnel leading to the ice, she looked around the arena. If possible, the atmosphere was even more charged than it had been for the men. She wondered idly how Lazlo had finished. She hadn't paid the slightest bit of attention. He probably hadn't pulled up into a medal position from sixth place, but he'd still had a great showing for the representative of a tiny country at its first Olympics.

What was the Red Jihad planning? She could almost feel the violence of it in the air. The anticipation was so thick she could slice it. Of course, maybe it was just her own nerves about Anya's upcoming skate. If the girl really hit her program, she might even pull out a medal. And how big a statement would *that* be to the world?

Isabella fretted through the first group of skaters. But she saw nothing. During the fourth skater's performance, all three surveillance teams reported that the three Chechnyans had left the arena. Completely, as in outside. Bye-bye. What was up with that? A rolling surveillance team followed them to see where they headed.

Please, God, let this whole threat to the skating venue not be a giant feint to disguise some other target! All of the OSG's security resources were concentrated here!

The Medusas reported in now and then. None of them had spotted anything suspicious. The last skater in the first group flew past Isabella on the other side of the boards, nearing the end of her program. From this angle, the ice looked like unnaturally white glass, despite six long programs having just been skated on it. Holt's super ice held up well to hard usage. It glistened with an almost magical quality. Some ice-skating rink this was.

Wait a minute. Ice-skating rink. Harlan Holt said he'd put the powder in the *rink*. Not in the arena. In the rink specifically! He was a scientist, not a skating expert. He wouldn't necessarily have used the proper terminology to distinguish between the ice surface and the facility which held it. Lots of people called the ice itself a rink.

Holy shit.

Could it be that the Agent Alpha was right there in front of all of them? In the rink itself? In the *ice?*

The current skater, Alexandria Marweshandra of India, finished her program and commenced taking her bows.

Isabella thought furiously. It was all there, right in front of her. Harlan Holt inexplicably insisting that the ice be torn up and resurfaced right about the same time his wife disappeared. The hit from the chemical detectors on the paper bag of poop—*that had lain on the ice!* The anomalous readings when this place was searched last night. A trace of vapor rose from the ice when it got cold in here, like late at night. A tiny amount of the Agent Alpha was evaporating into the air—*from the ice!* Even Holt's distraught remark last night that he'd put the powder in the rink made sense. He'd told her exactly where the Agent Alpha was. He'd mixed it into the ice!

Marweshandra headed off to the kiss-and-cry area. Meanwhile, a gate opened at the other end of the arena where the Zamboni would enter as soon as the girl's scores were posted.

Her brain leaped to the next step. How would the Agent Bravo come into contact with the Agent Alpha? *Think, 'Bella, think!* It was liquid. There'd need to be a whole lot of it. Hundreds of gallons. It would have to come into direct contact with the ice.

A rumbling engine coughed to life at the far end of the ice. *Oh shit.*

The Zamboni!

She yanked out her phone, hit the speed dial, and screamed into it, "Stop the Zamboni! It's the Agent Bravo! The Alpha agent has been frozen into the ice and the Zamboni is about to spray the Bravo agent right on top of it!"

She looked around wildly at the coaches and skaters milling along the boards. What had that scientist said? The nerve gas was slightly heavier than air. It would sink. But she'd said that if it was stirred up, it would mix with the air in an enclosed space!

"Get back!" she shouted at the top of her lungs. "Everyone, get back from the ice! Head down the tunnel!"

Dammit, they weren't moving. They were all staring at her in uncomprehending shock. Like she'd lost her mind.

"Poison gas," she shouted desperately. "From the Zamboni! Terrorist attack!" She was about to yell "Fire!" if they didn't get moving soon. She grabbed the arms of the people nearest to her and shoved them toward the tunnel.

Over her shoulder, she heard the Zamboni rumble out onto the ice. Holy crap. Thirty thousand people were about to get nerve gassed.

Into her phone she shouted, "Somebody stop the Zamboni! Make an announcement over the P.A. system for everyone from the bottom rows of the building to move up higher as fast as they can. Evacuate the place, dammit!"

Chaos erupted over the radios.

A few people around her began to pick up on her panic and moved in alarm toward the tunnel.

But that damned Zamboni kept rumbling closer, spraying its heated load of Agent Bravo in a glistening sheet of liquid death.

An agitated male voice came over the building's loud speaker. "We need everyone in the lower rows of the stadium to move to higher parts of the building immediately. A hazardous fumes sensor indicates that the Zamboni machine may be emitting a dangerous gas at the level of the ice. Please move as quickly as you can."

She noted dimly that the guy didn't suggest they do it in an orderly fashion.

"Move!" she screamed yet again to the crowd of people around her. In combination with the general announcement, they finally got the lead out and headed for the tunnel en masse. A traffic jam resulted, but with her shouting behind everyone like a bulldog nipping at their heels, the mob shoved forward and kept moving.

The Zamboni rounded the corner at the end of the ice and drew parallel to her position. She looked back over her shoulder in horror. The Zamboni driver was swarthy. Bulky in build. And looked like a carbon copy of Ilya Gorabchek. *Brothers, maybe.*

But what really captured her attention was the maniacal gleam in his eyes as he looked over at her. And smiled. That was the smile of a man anticipating meeting his Maker in Paradise. The bastard knew what he was about. He was committing suicide. She yanked out her pistol and took off running from the tunnel entrance toward the Zamboni and its cargo of doom.

She ran out onto the ice, slipping and sliding wildly. She

ran after the machine, which was moving at a fairly stiff clip. When she was as close she could get to the guy, she fired every last one of her rubber dum-dum bullets at his head. He tilted over and the Zamboni swerved wildly.

"Snipers, take him out!" she screamed.

And then she dared not say any more. The scientist's warning about a single lungful of the poison gas killing a person was vivid in her mind. A faint mist was rising from the ice, swirling around her legs. She held her breath and ran off the ice clumsily, praying not to fall down. For to do so would mean death.

At least the report of her pistol had put the fear of God into the spectators who, until that point had been making their way in fairly leisurely fashion up the stairs and milling around on the concourse level walkways.

"Everyone out of the building!" a voice bellowed over the loudspeakers.

The reports of several rifles firing simultaneously rang out deafeningly.

Screams erupted, and she caught a glimpse of pandemonium above as people fought their way to the exits, now appropriately hysterical.

As she stumbled off the ice, she glanced back and saw a black lump lying on the obscenely white surface, a bright red stain spreading under it. The Zamboni weaved wildly down the middle of the ice, driverless, slipping almost sideways as it careened out of control, still spraying its load of death.

She used what little oxygen she had left to herd the last few remaining people near the ice toward the tunnel. The four men and two women of a pair of camera crews ran with her down the tunnel. Her lungs were on fire, her chest about to burst. Stars danced in front of her eyes. She was going to have to breathe soon.

The group fled past the big steel blast doors, and she nodded at the frightened men manning them, signaling with her hands for them to close the doors. She stopped and took a gasping breath. And prayed it was clean air.

"Everyone out of the building," she shouted down the tunnel. Her voice echoed impressively, and the people running ahead of her picked up the pace even more. They went through the parking garage and outside into the cold, dark night. It had never felt so good to draw in bracing, fresh air to her lungs.

People poured out of the building from every exit, screaming and yelling and running in search of loved ones. She herself looked around wildly, trying to spot Anya and Liz to make sure they got out.

"Report," Vanessa's voice yelled in her ear.

Isabella waited her turn in the standard order they used, and after Kat, she came up and said, "I'm outside." Aleesha reported in, and Isabella sagged in relief. They'd all made it out.

Vanessa said, "I've dropped off the Petrovich family at the safe house and am on my way back. I'm almost there. I'll meet all of you in three minutes. Head for the north entrance and rendezvous there."

That was on the other side of the giant building. Isabella took off running. She wove in and out between hundreds of other running, panicked souls, many of them screaming names as they went. Total chaos reigned. Fire trucks and police cars were pulling up, but they didn't stand a chance of imposing order on this mess.

Firemen in full oxygen suits ran for the entrances. Although it wasn't as if victims of the gas would need assistance, if the descriptions of its lethality were accurate. Hopefully, they'd cleared the place before the Agent Bravo created a deep enough cloud to reach—and kill—too many people.

The emergency radio frequency that came across her headset in addition to the discrete Medusa channel crackled with people shouting instructions and calling for help. And then one voice in particular caught Isabella's attention as she ran across the parking lot full of people dodging between cars.

"Tally ho on hostile target. I have Harlan Holt in my sights. Requesting instructions."

That was one of the snipers. Asking for permission to shoot Holt.

She came up on the frequency urgently. "Negative on taking down Holt. Say location of target!"

"West side of the arena. Moving toward the building, approximately sixteen rows of cars out."

She wasn't far from there. They needed to apprehend Holt alive. Find out what had really happened with him and his wife. If he had been helping the terrorists, he'd be put to death later for treason. She veered to her left, away from the arena. A man moving toward the building shouldn't be too hard to spot in this melee. Everyone else was running away from the rink and its cloud of death.

Ten…eleven…she counted the rows of cars as she ran past. She looked left and right, visualizing his features. Tall. Lean. Dark-haired. Glasses.

Over there. She took off to her right, circling back to get between Holt and the arena. Running in a crouch, she dived in and out among the vehicles full of terrified people.

She ducked left and stood up. If she'd calculated correctly, he should be coming right at her. *There he was.* Two cars over. She sprinted at the guy, approaching him from the side. She left the ground in a running leap and tackled Holt around the waist in a blow an NFL lineman would have been proud of.

Holt fought like a wild man. She hung on, rolling with the guy and gradually working her way into a better grip until she was able to give one last heave, flip him on his back, and sit on top of his chest.

"Gotchya," she panted.

His eyes were frantic. Unseeing. And then they finally focused on her face and a strange thing happened. He went still. "You," he gasped. "Thank God."

She blinked in surprise.

"You've got to help me find Emma."

"Come again?" she asked.

"She's here somewhere. They brought her in a van. Said I could have her back if everything went well inside. But it didn't go well, did it? All these people got out! They'll kill her for sure unless we get to her first!"

"What van?" Isabella bit out.

"I don't know. They only said a van. They said they'd drive it up to the north entrance and I could meet them there after... well, after."

Isabella transmitted into her radio, "Harlan Holt's wife is in the parking lot somewhere in a van, possibly on the north side of the arena. The terrorists who kidnapped her will kill her if they get to her first. Medusas, start checking vans. Look for a bound and probably gagged woman inside."

She climbed to her feet and dragged the scientist to his feet as well. "If you're lying to me, I'll kill you myself."

The guy nodded.

"You and I are going to take off running again and check inside every van we come across. No stunts. I'll call in a sniper shot and you'll be dead before you know what hits you. Got it?"

He nodded vigorously. "Yes. Now please, let's go!"

The two of them took off, weaving through the parking lot from van to van, peering inside the windows frantically. She transmitted as she ran, "I'm on the west side of the arena, working my way north. They said they'd bring the van to the north entrance, so let's assume it's parked where they can see that door."

"Roger," came the brief reply from her teammates. They all sounded like they were running around out here, too.

"I'm just pulling in," Vanessa reported. "Everyone meet me at the north door and we'll fan out from there. Plus, I've got weapons."

Of course. The Medusas had put loaded guns in the getaway vehicle in case Gorabchek and his pals decided to play rough.

"This way, Harlan," Isabella called. "Follow me."

"Where are we going?" he called back as they sprinted around the arena.

"To even up the odds." There was the SUV. Vanessa was at the back door, pulling out the canvas bags that held their guns and ammunition. Misty and Kat were already arming themselves.

Isabella screeched to a halt beside the vehicle. Vanessa shoved an MP-5 submachine gun into her hands along with two spare clips of ammo. "We'll divide the north parking lot up in wedges," her boss said. "Go to the back of the lot and work your way toward the arena. Odds are they parked well away from the building. Take the center section. I'll be on your immediate right and Mamba will be on your immediate left. Go!"

Isabella and Holt took off running. It took them several minutes to reach the back end of the giant parking lot. They turned around and began crisscrossing their portion of the asphalt as they ran from van to van, looking in the windows. As they ran, she panted, "How many men are there, Harlan?"

He replied in a half sob, "Four came into our bedroom to kidnap her. I've only seen three at a time since then."

"What do they look like?" Isabella demanded.

"Young. Early twenties. Dark complexions and hair. Western clothes. One of them looked older, more like late thirties or early forties. He was the leader."

Isabella relayed the descriptions to her teammates. It wasn't much to go on, but it was better than nothing. The good news was that in their panic, frantic spectators had completely gridlocked the parking lots. Nobody was going anywhere soon.

They'd worked their way about halfway through the lot when Vanessa radioed, "Adder, do you have that gray van in your nine o'clock, or do you need me to get it? I'm on the far side of my sector."

"We'll check it," Isabella replied, spotting the vehicle in question. Light gray utility van. No windows in its sides or back doors. A group of maybe twenty people was just passing by it. She ran around the minor mob to have a look in the passenger side window. It was dark in the back of the vehicle. No seats, just storage space. She might've run on by when there were no obvious signs of a person lying on the floor, but her gut said to have another look. She darted around to the driver's side window, yanking out a flashlight as she went. She shined it in the window.

The first thing she saw was a small cardboard box lying on top of some wires. Then she saw a heavy canvas drop cloth stained with paint. And then she saw the foot sticking out from under one corner of it.

"I've got her!" Isabella called over her radio. "Medusas to me!"

"Get down!" Vanessa shouted. "Incoming!"

Months and months of round-the-clock training kicked in, and acting on reflex, Isabella dived for the ground in response to her boss's command. She grabbed Harlan Holt's arm on the way down and knocked the poor guy off his feet as well.

"What in the world—" he started.

Isabella rolled, simultaneously pulling her MP-5 out from under her coat. A sharp metallic ping sounded just above her head.

Son of bitch. Somebody had just fired a bullet at her!

Chapter 19

Isabella looked around frantically. The car beside her was too low to crawl under. The van was tall enough, but if she and Holt took cover under it, they'd draw gunfire to the van itself and put Emma Holt, whom that foot presumably belonged to, at grave risk. The metal skin of the van would hardly slow down a bullet, let alone stop it.

The ring of paint chipped off around the hole above her head was slightly wider on the left side. It was all she had to go on. She pointed to her right. "Crawl that way," she ordered Holt. "And stay the hell down."

She belly-crawled after him, dragging herself along by the elbows while Vanessa shouted for fire support. Whether or not anyone heard her in the jumble of voices on the emergency radio frequency was anybody's guess.

Viper's voice came across perfectly clearly on the private Medusa channel, though. "Anyone got visual on the shooter?"

Silence answered that question.

Dammit. No one had seen anyone.

"It looked like maybe the shot came from my left, which would put the shooter in the direction of the arena."

Vanessa ordered, "Bust open a door and get Mrs. Holt out. We'll cover you."

Isabella nodded. She pointed at an SUV in the next row of cars. "Get under that, Harlan. *Move.*"

He made to stand up, but she snapped, "Stay low if you don't want your head shot off." That dropped him back to his belly instantaneously.

She crawled to the back door and reached for the silver handles, and her gut screamed a warning. What was it? Her hand hesitated on the latch. Vaguely she heard her boss say in her ear, "What's the hold up, Adder? Get her out of there!"

She closed her eyes, picturing the interior of the van. That box. Sitting on the wires. *Oh, shit.* A bomb! "Vehicle's booby-trapped." That explained the lone gunshot. Whoever'd taken that pot shot at her had only wanted to keep her from peering in the windows, he'd wanted to give her a sense of blind urgency so she'd throw open the van door to rescue Mrs. Holt.

"How?" Viper demanded.

"Bomb. In the back with Emma."

Her boss cursed. "I'll move in to defend the right side of the van. Adder, you take the back for now. Transition to the driver's side when I get into place. The rest of you, circle around it and see if you can spot our tangos."

Isabella peered beneath the van and the car directly behind her and saw feet running in every direction. How were they going to spot the terrorists in this zoo? She waited, her back against the bumper of the car behind her, looking straight ahead at the back of the van. Her peripheral vision caught movements on either side of her, and every few seconds she jerked her weapon to one side or the other as something or someone would move.

How long she waited there, exposed and vulnerable, she

had no idea. It felt like a week. It was probably more like three minutes. Then something hot touched her ear, and the van door pinged again. She hit the deck and rolled fast, wedging herself in as best she could under the front end of the car parked behind the van. Damn, that was close! That bullet had creased her ear on the way past. She didn't bother to reach up and check for blood. Nothing she could do about it right now.

Kat's voice came up on radio, as tense as she'd ever heard the sniper. "I've got visual on our shooter."

Vanessa was succinct. "Kill him."

"No shot," Kat retorted. "He's crouching behind a big group of people. I'll have to work my way around them."

"Do it," her boss ordered.

Another bullet pinged somewhere nearby. And another. Was the same guy doing all this shooting? If so, his targets were wildly divergent. She peered up at the marks on the side of the van. No way had those come from the same spot. One of the holes looked bigger than the other one. Different caliber rounds!

"We've got at least two shooters out here," she transmitted.

Karen piped up. "I think I've got one of them over here. I just saw somebody pop up from behind a car and then duck back down. I didn't see a weapon, though."

"Check it out," Vanessa replied.

"Roger," the Marine responded tersely. Then, "He's running! Toward the van."

Suddenly, all the Medusas were talking at once, stepping over each other on the frequency as three men matching the general descriptions of the hostiles took off running from various locations around the parking lot toward the van.

Here she was, lying at ground zero. Right where all their guns were pointed. But she dared not move. Somebody had to defend the van and keep anyone from triggering the bomb. As close as she was to it, if that bomb blew, she was toast.

Vanessa shouted over the general emergency frequency, "Request permission to open fire on terrorist suspects!"

Either nobody heard her or nobody who did had the author-ity to give her permission. Finally, she came up on the Medusas' frequency and said, "To hell with it. Fire at will. If you have a shot at our suspects, take it."

Several shots rang out around Isabella. Kat reported a hit but not a take-down. The guy she'd shot was still ambulatory, and now he was mad. The three terrorists erased any doubts about their identity by firing back.

Karen said, "Sidewinder, adjust your field of fire to the right so I can move in and get a better shot." A couple more terse transmissions were traded as the Medusas managed their fields of fire. They had to stay positioned in such a way that they wouldn't shoot at each other as they converged on the van and the three men.

Isabella felt stupid, helpless, lying here on the ground. She stared up at the silver freckles on the side of the van where the tangos had shot at her. And something dawned on her. They weren't shooting at her! They were shooting at that cardboard box located just behind the driver's seat. The bastards were trying to detonate their bomb!

Maybe that meant they didn't know she was here.

Karen swore as she hit one of the tangos for the second time and still he didn't go down. Desperation did that to a man.

Isabella had heard stories of soldiers taking a dozen bullets and continuing to fight. By rolling flat on her stomach, she was able to wedge herself all the way under the car at her back. Using her hands and toes, she slid completely under the vehicle, her MP-5 held awkwardly in front of her.

"They're coming at you, Adder," Vanessa reported. "Take cover, for God's sake."

"I'm there," Adder murmured as a pair of feet ran around the front end of the van and stopped by the driver's side. She dared not transmit any more or he'd hear her. And she wasn't exactly in the best position to defend herself here.

A second pair of feet came from behind her. One of the pairs of feet moved to about where the van's door should be. Crap. If the doors were wired, all that guy would have to do was open it to send them all sky-high.

A barrage of gunfire slammed into the side of the van, high. That sounded like an MP-5 on automatic fire. And the Medusas would aim for the top of the vehicle to avoid hitting the hostage inside. *For the love of God, Emma, stay down in there.*

Then a third pair of feet ran up to the others. The three owners of the feet crouched and she could make out knees and rear ends. They were reloading their weapons. They stood up in unison and gunfire erupted. The distinctive popping noise was punctuated by brass casings striking the ground as one of the guys emptied a revolver and reloaded fast.

Kat transmitted, frustrated, "They have to be wearing body armor. I've hit all of them in the chest and they're not going down!"

And then Vanessa shouted, "Get out of there, Adder! They're going to open the door!"

She rolled, scraping the hell out of her shoulder on the undercarriage of the car. She popped out, lying on her back, her MP-5 extended beyond her head. Frantically, she looked back and up, sighting her targets, and pulled the trigger.

In slow motion, they raised their weapons toward her, the expressions on their faces infinitely surprised.

She held her trigger down, pointing her weapon at their heads and unleashing a barrage of lead at a range of approximately ten feet. The guy by the door dropped. One of the others staggered backward, a hand over his bloody face. The third one spun and fell across the hood of a car. Slowly, he slid off the sloping surface and collapsed to the ground.

Isabella leaped to her feet, MP-5 in front of her. A single shot rang out.

Kat announced in satisfaction, "That one got him between the eyes. Target down."

Something came in fast from behind her. She spun and dropped into a firing crouch. *Holt,* who was reaching for the back door handle.

"No!" She dived forward, knocking the man away from the latch. Into the struggling scientist's ear she ground out, "There's a bomb in there. It's booby-trapped. We'll have to bring in the bomb squad to get her out."

Holt subsided beneath her, sobbing and swearing.

She stood up and helped the man to his feet for the second time. Another person moved toward her quickly, but this time she recognized the long stride and fluid grace of Dexter Thorpe. He kept right on coming until his arms were around her, holding her against him like he'd crush the life out of her.

"Are you okay?"

"I'm standing, aren't I?" she replied. "Do you know if Anya's okay?"

"She and her coach both made it out. I found them around the other side of the building when I went looking for you."

Her arms tightened around his lean waist. He'd been worried enough about her to come looking for her, had he?

Dex muttered against her temple, "Don't get in any shoot-outs again, okay?"

"Sorry. It's in the job description. We get to blow shit up and shoot at stuff."

He laughed reluctantly. "Okay, I'll rephrase. Don't get into any shootouts in front of me where I'm helpless to do anything."

"You saw it go down?" she asked, surprised.

"I couldn't see a lot, running as fast as I was, but I saw enough. Nice move coming out from under that car like that. You must have shocked the hell out of them."

She shrugged within the vice of his grip. "They looked surprised, yes."

Finally, he let go of her, although he kept one arm looped around her shoulder.

"Uh, Dex. Isn't this a PDA?" Public displays of affection were a big-time no-no among uniformed military members while on duty.

"We're not in uniform."

"Same difference," she replied. "My team is eyeing you like you've grown horns and a third eye."

He grinned. "Too bad. Life's too short to hold back on some things. When I saw them start shooting at the van with you right beside it, I swear your life flashed before my eyes."

"My life?"

He amended, "Well, our future life. I saw everything we weren't going to get to do together if those bastards killed you."

"Oh yeah?" She looked up at him with interest. "Like what?"

He scowled down at her. "I'll tell you later. When we're alone. Somewhere private where we can do something about some of those things."

She smiled up at him, letting her feelings all hang out. He was right. Life was too short. So what if her teammates did tease her from now till eternity about the way he'd come charging in after her or about the way she'd made goo-goo eyes at him?

Aleesha had moved in front of the van and was peering through the window using a high-powered flashlight. To Holt, Dex said, "If you'll step away with us, we need to let the experts do their thing."

The scientist nodded reluctantly. They moved back, threading between cars.

"I make it a policy not to embrace armed women. How 'bout if I carry that thing for you?"

Isabella grinned and relinquished the weapon so he wouldn't let go of her. Dex held the MP-5 down at his side where the already panicky crowd in the area wouldn't freak out about the weapon.

Why she looked off to her left just then, she had no idea. But she did. Something about the way a man was walking purposefully toward them caught her eye. And that was why she saw him open his long coat and reach inside.

To pull out a sawed-off shotgun.

She dived across Dex, snatching the MP-5 out of his hands, rolling across the hood of the car in front of her, and firing her weapon all in one motion. She fell onto her feet in a crouch, MP-5 at the ready. The incoming man lay motionless on the ground. Dex grabbed the MP-5 back from her and took off running, approaching the downed man with extreme caution. She watched, her heart in her throat, as Dex flipped the guy with his foot. Then he straightened. Dex pointed at the center of his forehead and then down at the corpse.

He leaned down and rummaged in the dead man's pockets. He stood up, taking the shotgun as well. He strode back to her.

Her knees started to shake. Great, knee-knocking shivers that made it nearly impossible for her to stand. She'd coolly killed three men at point-blank range, and now a fourth without a hint of a reaction. But watching Dex put himself even mildly in harm's way had about done her in. Go figure.

"Says here his name is Abdul al Abhoud," Dex announced as he walked up to her.

Holt looked at the driver's license picture and said, "That's the leader of the gang that took Emma. And he's the one who talked to me on the phone."

Dex said quietly, "He's not going to be talking to you ever again." He glanced over at Isabella. "Nice shot."

It was a lucky shot, but hey. She was willing to take credit for it being intentional if it impressed Dex. And besides, maybe it wasn't all luck. Sometime during the past year, it appeared she'd turned into a hell of a shooter.

Over the next two hours, a bomb squad arrived and carefully gained access to the bomb inside the van using a nifty, remote-controlled robot. They were able to get the driver's side door open, and then, after the robot threw a protective blanket over Emma Holt, a man entered the vehicle and manually finished disarming the device.

Mrs. Holt was hungry, tired and traumatized as hell, but basically unhurt. She and her husband enjoyed a tearful reunion while everyone looked on. And Dex's arm stole around Isabella's shoulders again, this time in front of most of his own Delta team, who'd come over to offer assistance.

Beau pounded his boss affectionately on the shoulder and threw Isabella an apologetic smile. "'Bout damn time you caught on there, Dex. I had to practically throw myself at her to get you to admit how you felt."

Slowly, the police and National Guard troops gained control of the situation around the ice-skating arena. Less than a dozen people were killed by the lethal gas. Although a number of spectators claimed to be suffering from respiratory distress as a result of exposure to the gas, the truth was that their own fear and breathing difficulties were the culprit. Had they actually ingested the gas, they, too, would have been dead.

It was well after midnight when Dex finally ordered the OSG troops to go home. They were only adding clutter to the scene, and other agencies had the crisis in hand. Besides, news crews hovered in the area looking for interviews, which most of the OSG members could seriously do without.

Isabella walked into the ops center conference room three days later for the final debrief of these Olympic Games. It seemed like only yesterday that Dex had demanded she bring him a cup of coffee. He wasn't here yet. The room was mostly full, though, and all the seats were taken. She spotted the other Medusas in their usual place up front, standing along the side wall.

The end of the Olympics had been anticlimactic after the excitement of the terrorist attack. The remaining six female figure skaters had quietly performed their long programs at a municipal skating rink in nearby Elizabethtown on Sunday afternoon, just hours before the closing ceremonies. The IOC had gone ahead with the closing celebration, albeit in a subdued fashion, and a short memorial was added in honor of the nine spectators and two cameramen who had died in the terrorist attack. Sara Dormonkova of the Ukraine overtook the German skater, Karis Neidermeier, to capture the gold medal, and the American, Ashley Caldwell, had captured the bronze.

Anya finished fourth. Funny how sometimes the greatest triumphs weren't marked by gold medals, or any kind of medal for that matter. Anya had done something much more important, much more courageous than win. She'd stepped out onto the ice and *skated*. And that was truly a triumph of historic proportions.

A stir in the back of the conference room marked Dex's entrance. Isabella didn't need the flurry of greetings to know he was here, though. She could feel his presence as clearly as if he'd reached out and touched her. Their relationship was no secret to anyone in this room, but nonetheless, she schooled her face to a professional expression of polite disinterest as she glanced up at him.

He was headed straight at her, and that glint in his eye did not bode well.

He stopped in front of her. Held out his hand. A white object was grasped in his fist. He was offering it to her. She frowned. Looked down.

And burst out laughing as she took the cup of coffee from him. "Do I dare drink this?" she asked drolly.

"I swear. No spit and no snot. Nothing in there but coffee and a little sugar."

Just the way she liked it. Everyone in the room was grinning as Dex turned and made his way to the podium. Someone called out, "You gonna make an honest woman out of her, or are we gonna have to kick your ass, Thorpe?"

Dex leaned against the podium and drawled, "I don't think the good captain will need your help. If my ass needs kicking, she and the Medusas are perfectly capable of doing the job themselves."

My, my, my. The boy certainly had come a long way in two weeks. They all had.

Dexter whipped through the debriefing. The federal prosecutor's office had decided not to press charges against Harlan Holt for his role in the gas attack, as he'd been under duress and extreme coersion at the time. Emma Holt was fine. The terrorists had not harmed her. Manfred Schmidt had tendered his resignation from the International Olympic Committee. The Petrovichs were singing like birds and had been granted political asylum in the United States.

Dex rattled off the names of a dozen men who'd been detailed to stay behind and help with the breakdown of the ops center's electronic equipment.

Then he adjourned the meeting.

It was almost over. She had just one more job to do and she needed to hurry if she was going to make it. She stepped outside into the raw wind that was sending low, gray clouds scudding across the sky. It looked like snow was on the way.

"Need a lift?"

She turned at the sound of Dex's voice. "I'd love one."

He held the door to the white, Olympic SUV for her. In another few days, this car would get regular license plates and enter a rental car fleet somewhere. She climbed inside, shivering until the heater finally conquered the frigid chill. The traffic wasn't bad as they headed out to the airport, southeast of town.

She rushed into the terminal, looking around. Had she missed them? Her heart jumped into her throat. But then a white minivan pulled up outside and Isabella saw Karen hop out of the driver's side and head around to the back of the van. All the other Medusas climbed out, followed by Liz Cartwright and Anya.

Isabella smiled. She'd always think of the skater as a little sister. She stepped outside and the two of them embraced. She pressed a business card into Anya's hand. "That's my cell phone number. If you ever need anything, anything at all, you call me. Okay?"

Anya grinned. "Okay, 'Bella, my mother hen. I promise."

"On the back side of it is an address. Any mail you send there will find its way to Lazlo. It was the best I could do. He's in protective custody for a while at a secret location."

Anya smiled her gratitude and hugged her again. Sometimes words weren't necessary. Anya resumed her enthusiastic chatter as she and Liz checked in and headed for the gate. Boarding for their flight, first to Los Angeles and then on to Brisbane, was called. A pair of tall, fit-looking men stepped up to the women.

Isabella made the introductions. "Anya, these gentlemen come from the Australian equivalent of the Secret Service. They're going to act as your bodyguards for a while."

The happiness in Anya's eyes dimmed for a moment. "I wish I didn't have to live this way."

Isabella shrugged. "You could always put on the veil."

Anya glared. "I'm not going to hide or take the easy way out. I've come this far. I'm not going to back out now. Did you know a bunch of people want me to give speeches about being a modern Muslim woman?"

Isabella grinned. "You'll make a great spokesperson for your peers."

"You're one of them," Anya accused. "Why don't you make some speeches?"

Isabella grimaced. "My job's all about staying out of the spotlight. And you'll do just fine on your own. I'm proud to have you represent me."

The final boarding call came, and Anya flung herself at Isabella in one last hug.

"Take care of yourself." Isabella squeezed the words past her tight throat.

She watched as the girl walked down the jetway, her body-guards in exactly the right position to cover her from an attack. Anya was in good hands. That fatwa wouldn't go away, but perhaps with time, it would fade into insignificance and the girl could resume a normal life. In the meantime, Anya planned to keep skating. Her theory was that the world would get used to her eventually and that something more important would come along to take the heat off of her. She was probably right.

"Ready to go?" Dex murmured.

"Go where?" she asked.

"I took the liberty of asking your teammates to bring your gear to the airport."

Isabella glanced over his shoulder. Aw, crap. The Medusas were all grinning like they had something evil up their sleeves. "What have you done?" she asked them direly.

Vanessa shoved a ticket jacket into her hands. "Here are your baggage claim stubs. Your bags are already checked."

"Checked for where?" she demanded, looking back and forth between her team and Dex.

"She's all yours," Vanessa murmured.

Dex grinned and grabbed Isabella's hand. "C'mon. We have a flight to catch."

"Where to?" she protested as he dragged her down the concourse toward another flight that had just started boarding.

"Does it matter?" he asked.

She smiled. Nope, it didn't. She'd go anywhere with him.

"Let's go see what the future has to offer us," he said softly. "Are you up for the challenge?"

She laughed. "One thing you should know about me up front, Dexter G. Thorpe the Fourth. I never could turn down a dare."

"Me, neither."

Arm-in-arm, the two of them headed down the jet bridge together into whatever the future held.

MILLS & BOON®

Classic novels by bestselling authors for you to enjoy!

PASSIONATE PARTNERS

Featuring
The Heart Beneath
by Lindsay McKenna

&

Ride the Thunder
by Lindsay McKenna

0507/064a

On sale 18th May 2007

THE MATCHMAKERS' DADDY
by Judy Duarte

Zack Henderson was starting over. But he hadn't
planned on falling for Diana Lynch. He knew she and
her two adorable matchmakers were better off without
a man like him…

UNDER THE WESTERN SKY
by Laurie Paige

When compassionate midwife Julianne Martin was
accused of stealing Native American artefacts, investigator
Tony Aquilon was sure he had the wrong woman…

DETECTIVE DADDY
by Jane Toombs

Fay Merriweather was in labour when a storm stranded
her on the doorstep of detective Dan Sorensen's cabin.
He gave Fay and her baby the care they needed, but he
never intended to fall for this instant family…

From No. 1 *New York Times* bestselling author Nora Roberts

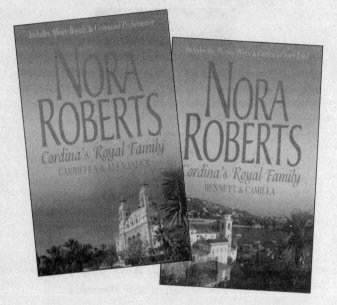

Romance and intrigue are woven together in these classic stories about Cordina's royal family

Gabriella & Alexander
Available 2nd February 2007

Bennett & Camilla
Available 4th May 2007

"When the bullets finally ceased, the bodies lay in a coiled embrace on the lifeboat."

The sinking of a cargo ship and the slaughter
of its crew seemed a senseless act of violence.
But Clea Rice knows the truth and is determined
to expose the culprits.

When Jordan Tavistock is asked to steal the indiscreet
letters of a friend, he reluctantly obliges, only to be caught
red-handed—by another burglar. The burglar is Clea, who is
looking for something else entirely.

Only together can Jordan and Clea find the answers to
the sinister questions surrounding the sinking of
the ship. Answers that some are prepared to
kill for to keep buried.

20th April 2007

FREE

4 BOOKS AND A SURPRISE GIFT!

We would like to take this opportunity to thank you for reading this Mills & Boon® book by offering you the chance to take FOUR more specially selected titles from the Intrigue™ series absolutely FREE! We're also making this offer to introduce you to the benefits of the Mills & Boon® Reader Service™—

- ★ FREE home delivery
- ★ FREE gifts and competitions
- ★ FREE monthly Newsletter
- ★ Books available before they're in the shops
- ★ Exclusive Reader Service offers

Accepting these FREE books and gift places you under no obligation to buy; you may cancel at any time, even after receiving your free shipment. Simply complete your details below and return the entire page to the address below. You don't even need a stamp!

YES! Please send me 4 free Intrigue books and a surprise gift. I understand that unless you hear from me, I will receive 6 superb new titles every month for just £3.10 each, postage and packing free. I am under no obligation to purchase any books and may cancel my subscription at any time. The free books and gift will be mine to keep in any case.

I7ZEE

Ms/Mrs/Miss/Mr..Initials ....
BLOCK CAPITALS PLEASE

Surname ....

Address ....

....

....Postcode ....

Send this whole page to:
The Reader Service, FREEPOST CN81, Croydon, CR9 3WZ